CAST NOT
THE DAY

PAUL WATERS

CAST NOT THE DAY

MACMILLAN

First published 2009 by Macmillan
an imprint of Pan Macmillan Ltd
Pan Macmillan, 20 New Wharf Road, London N1 9RR
Basingstoke and Oxford
Associated companies throughout the world
www.panmacmillan.com

ISBN 978-0-230-53032-4 HB
ISBN 978-0-230-71147-1 TPB

Map designed by Raymond Turvey

1 3 5 7 9 8 6 4 2

A CIP catalogue record for this book is available from
the British Library.

Typeset by Set Systems Ltd, Saffron Walden, Essex
Printed and bound in Great Britain by
CPI Mackays, Chatham ME5 8TD

Visit **www.panmacmillan.com** to read more about all our books
and to buy them. You will also find features, author interviews and
news of any author events, and you can sign up for e-newsletters
so that you're always first to hear about our new releases.

For K.W.

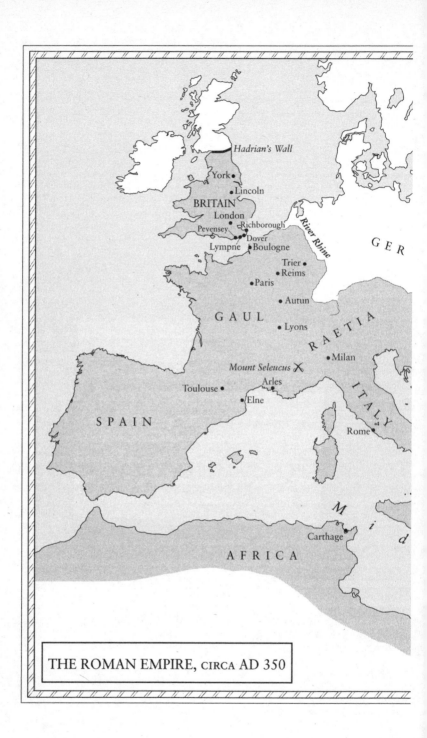

Hadrian's Wall

York
Lincoln

BRITAIN
London
Pevensey   Richborough
Lympne   Dover
Boulogne

River Rhine

GER

Trier
Reims
Paris
Autun

GAUL
Lyons

RAETIA

Milan

Mount Seleucus ✗

ITALY

Arles
Toulouse
Elne

SPAIN

Rome

M

i

d

Carthage

AFRICA

THE ROMAN EMPIRE, CIRCA AD 350

For thy kingdom is past not away,
Nor thy power from the place thereof hurled;
Out of heaven they shall cast not the day,
They shall cast not out song from the world.

Algernon Charles Swinburne, 'The Last Oracle'

ONE

WHEN I WAS A BOY, and wanted to be alone, I would climb the ancient apple tree at the back of our house, up onto the roof above the kitchens. From there, propped against the gable over the portico, where it was highest, I used to gaze out across the barley fields at the ships on the distant estuary, and dream of adventure and escape.

High summer was best, when the sea-lanes were busy and my tutor was in no mood for teaching. Then I would spend warm afternoons dozing naked in the sun, watching the merchantmen as they rode the tide upriver to London, or out seawards on their way to Gaul or Spain or the Middle Sea.

I was a solitary child, though I may say at the outset that this was not my own choice. I was lonely and yearned for friendship. But my father forbade me to play with the farm-hands, saying they had their own work to do, and I had mine. He was rearing a Roman gentleman, not a country peasant. And though I disobeyed him often enough, I remembered that, but for me, my mother would still be alive, and I had already brought him enough trouble. For she had died in childbirth when I was born.

He kept a picture of her in his study, a small image painted on wood. I suppose he must have missed her, though he never spoke of it. He was private, stern and remote. Indeed, in most ways he was a stranger to me. But I knew well enough that he believed in decorum and firm discipline, for which, it seemed, I was ill suited. He used to say, before he beat me, that character is wrought with the rod, like a sword beneath the hammer.

My only real companion in those days was Sericus, my tutor. He said he preferred books to boys, and had a strict air. But I believe he loved me all the same, and the strictness was just to please my father. He used to let me wander. But when he thought I had been away too long, he would come looking, and from my rooftop eyrie I would hear his voice in the courtyard, asking the slaves where I had gone. Then with a sigh I would pull myself up, pad across the sun-warm tiles, dust my tunic at the foot of the tree, and make my way to the front to find him.

Sericus was an old man even then. He had come into our family years before as my mother's tutor, when she was still a girl at her father's house in Gallic Autun. Sericus had known her longest of all, longer even than my father, and it was he who brought her back to life for me, telling me about her smile, and how she threw back her long dark hair when she laughed, and how she had loved me even when she was carrying me in her belly.

I never tired of these stories, which I must have asked him to repeat a thousand times. I used to think that if only I could see her clearly enough in my dreams, some magic would bring her back to me.

But of course she never came; for there is no magic that brings the dead back to the living, whatever the Christians say.

That year, near midsummer, I began to see something new on the water of the estuary: dark bulbous troopships, heavy and sluggish as they made their way in convoy downriver towards the sea, bearing our men away to Gaul.

I asked Sericus who would protect us from the Saxons, with the army gone. But he answered sharply and told me to speak to my father. I frowned at this, and bent my head to my wax-board and my exercises. One did not go to my father without being summoned, as Sericus well knew.

For as long as I could remember, high-ranking visitors had come to our villa, Father having been the emperor's deputy in Britain, and so an important man. We received a steady stream of counts and tribunes, fat finance officers, wealthy landowners, and decurions from the cities, with their soldier escorts and smart carriages. The steward would meet them at the door and usher them inside, and I would run to the courtyard and talk to the waiting soldiers as they brushed down their horses, or lounged beside the fountain.

They were rough men who smelled of sweat and leather; they joked and spat and tousled my hair, feeling the childish muscles in my arms and asking, while the great

men conducted their business inside, when I was coming
to join them in the army. They would tell me stories
of battles and exotic places far away, sometimes rummag-
ing in their satchels to find some trinket for me – a fragment of broken lamp, a rough clay votive figure, or a shard
of polished glass – saying it had come all the way from
Spain or wild Thrace, or sun-baked Egypt, older than time.

I daresay, in truth, these mementoes had travelled no
further than the nearest tavern or barrack-house. But for
me they were full of mystery and promise, and I ranged
them on the sill of my bedroom, where I would gaze at
them and dream of heroes.

We had our own jetty on the water's edge, by a hamlet
fortified against raiders from the sea. From there, each
harvest time, we loaded barges with grain destined for
London. For the rest of the year traffic seldom stopped
there; but late one afternoon at the end of summer, when
I was basking on the roof, I spotted a naval cutter veer
suddenly from midstream and put in. I watched, and
presently two men on horses appeared on the track. They
paused, like dogs seeking a scent, then struck out through
the barley fields, spurring their horses and throwing up a
plume of dust behind, riding at a gallop under the avenue
of limes that led to our house, and clattering into the
courtyard – two men in uniform, with the straight-backed
poise of officers. But when they were close I saw they had
removed the marks of rank from their tunics.

They shouted for the groom, ordering him to wait:
they would not be long. Then they strode up the steps
under the porch.

The groom was still at the fountain with the reins in

his hand when they returned. They mounted, wheeled their horses, and urged them away under the gateway. And as they turned, one of the men glanced up and caught sight of me looking down at him. For a moment he paused, grim-faced, and shook his head. Then he looked away and was gone.

I waited, feeling the first cold fingers of fear creep in my hair. A stillness had descended on the house, and I was just about to return inside when hurried footfalls sounded on the ground below.

I craned my head over the cornice to see, and found myself looking straight into the face of Sericus.

'Come down this instant, Drusus,' he cried, 'and be quick; your father is waiting.'

He was standing in front of the tall windows of his study when the slave admitted me, half turned away, staring out across the barley fields. Though he must have heard me enter he gave no sign; and so I waited, standing formally with my hands at my sides as I had been taught, feeling the cold of the marble floor beneath my feet and remembering that, in my haste, I had forgotten to fetch my sandals from my room. He would have something to say about that, and my dusty tunic too. He always remarked on such things.

The pause lengthened. I shifted uneasily on my feet. Eventually, when still he did not move or acknowledge me, I said, 'Father, I am here.'

I heard him draw in his breath, and then with a sudden movement he turned. His face was in shadow, dark against the sunlight; and, as if seized by some sudden purpose, he strode across the floor, so swiftly that I almost thought he intended to strike me. But I knew that was not his way. When he reached me he suddenly dropped down on one knee and gripped my shoulders, and touched my hair and brow like a man deranged. I stared down at the white inlaid marble, confused and afraid. For never in my life had I known him show such feeling, either of joy or anger; not even when he beat me, when he was always calm and precise, like a man who breaks horses.

He made to speak, and his voice was so strange and broken that I looked up and stared. His eyes were shimmering, and there was water on his cheek. I think I even gasped out loud, for it shocked me beyond all reason to see my father crying.

Whatever he saw in my face caused him to master himself. He took a long breath, and after a pause released me from his grip and stood to his full height. When he spoke again it was in his usual voice, measured and businesslike.

'You are too young,' he said, 'for what I have to tell you. But it cannot wait, and I want you to listen carefully. Today I had two visitors, men bound by bonds of old friendship. They brought me a warning. Our new emperor, it seems, is no longer content merely to remove me from office. I am summoned to Gaul, to the court at Trier, to answer certain . . . questions.'

He paused, and his face twisted in irony at this final word.

In my innocence I asked, 'When will you be back, sir?'

I had not yet come to know the language of the court, where every horror bore a pretty name.

He looked from me, casting his eyes over the stacked books of his library, and the little faded picture of my mother on the shelf.

'I cannot say . . . I expect to be a long time. There are certain arrangements that must be made. I shall send you to your great-uncle in London, Lucius Balbus; he is of your mother's bloodline, and he will take care of you.'

I had never heard of this man Balbus, and did not want to be sent away. 'But, sir!' I cried, 'Sericus and the slaves can look after me.'

He shook his head. 'You cannot stay. I have instructed Sericus to accompany you, for your studies. Do not neglect your education. Such things are of no great concern to Balbus, by all accounts; but there is no freedom without it. How old are you now?'

'Fourteen.' It was something he never remembered.

'Well, I believe Balbus has a son about that age, who will be a friend to you. Now stop staring like a fool, and attend to what I say. I suspect, in the future, you will encounter difficulties: a man like me has enemies as well as friends, and only at times such as this does one discover which is which. You will have to face them as best you can; and through it all, Drusus, I hope you will remember you are my son, and bear yourself accordingly. It is in your own hands now to make yourself a gentleman, and to learn what that means. Now prepare yourself. You leave today, before nightfall.'

I stood in silence, while he talked on, details I cannot

recall. But then, seeing my eyes on him, he broke off and drew a long breath.

'Listen then,' he said, 'and hear the truth, though by the gods I would spare you this. Someone at court, some intriguer, has brought a charge against me, and I must go to answer it. Such are my enemies: small men, who dare not show their faces, who have worked in the shadows to bring me down. In the meantime you will be safer elsewhere. Is that clear?'

'But, Father,' I cried, 'what have you done?'

'Done?' He gave a bitter laugh. 'I have done my duty and served the emperor. And now that he is dead, his sons squabble over their inheritance, like dogs fighting for a bone. My loyalty has been my undoing, for loyalty to one is treason to the other—'

He ceased, and with an impatient motion of his hand turned away, and stood with his back to me, beside the great onyx desk.

'Now go; the slaves are already packing your things, and Sericus is waiting.'

So ended my childhood. I never saw him again.

TWO

WE CAME TO LONDON through the open suburb of farmsteads and villas to the south, halting at the watering-place by the bridge, where the carters and litter-bearers gather.

The house of Balbus lay in the heart of the merchants' quarter, off the Street of the Carpenters, close by the Grove of Isis. Everywhere was crowded. The hot air smelled of dust and unwashed bodies. Behind the street the workshops sounded with the noise of hammers and saws and engravers' chisels.

An old house-slave admitted us. He asked after our things, which we had left with the wagon, and said they would be fetched. Then he took Sericus off, leaving me with a sullen-looking servant-girl. She led me past rooms hung with bright silk draperies, and cluttered with fussy, gilded furniture. But my room was elsewhere, on the uppermost floor below the rafters, bare and low and whitewashed.

'The Mistress says you must sleep here,' mumbled the girl, avoiding my eye and stepping past me to open the shutters. I glanced about. There was a narrow bed with a grey coverlet, and, in the corner, below a festoon of cobwebs, a washstand. But otherwise it might have been some old attic store. It was not the kind of room my father would have offered to a guest, however humble.

Just then the girl let out a small, smothered cry. The breeze had snatched the shutter from her hand, sending it banging against the outer wall. It was a small enough thing; but she glanced back at the door, biting her lip.

'It's just the wind,' I said, smiling to put her at her ease. 'Here, I'll help you.' I leant out and secured the rusted catch, saying, 'See, it is done.'

She nodded, then turned to the washstand and busied herself with the few things there, brushing off the dust.

I asked brightly if my aunt was at home, and at this she stiffened and paused. She was as timid as a snared bird. The Mistress, she said, staring down at the floor, was resting in her private rooms, and must not be disturbed.

'And my cousin?' I asked, frowning. 'What of him?'

'Albinus is out, sir. He is at the bishop's.'

Her voice was so low that it took me a moment to realize what she had said. 'But what,' I asked, staring, 'has he to do with such a man?' I had heard my father talk of Christians to his political friends. They were meddlesome zealots, he said, always stirring up trouble. And I knew the farm-hands drove them off with sticks, whenever their whey-faced wandering preachers came onto our land.

The girl looked quickly at me, then looked away, her mouth setting firm, as if I had lured her into saying more than she ought.

'You must ask him yourself,' she answered. Then, before I could speak again, she hurried off.

I listened to her footfalls recede along the boards of the passageway, and sat staring down at my dusty boots. I rubbed my eyes. I was tired; I felt it now.

The night before, we had put in at a wretched off-road inn, and lain on filthy beds full of fleas. I had asked Sericus if the emperor's family were really so terrible that we must travel thus, dressed as backwoodsmen and hiding like thieves. But he had told me crossly to hush; my father had good reason, and we were doing as he had ordered.

After that I had left him be. I could see he was unhappy enough already.

The flea-bites were sore. I pulled off my boots, and scratched at my heel. The city noise was carrying in, and with it the stench of rancid cooking, charcoal mixed with goose fat. I got up and padded to the window, and looked out.

Below me, two floors down, a sickly damson tree was growing in a grim, paved court, straining for the light; and as I looked the old house-slave passed under the colonnade, hurrying with his old-man's gait towards the kitchens and servants' quarters at the back.

He had said, when he admitted us, that my uncle Balbus was out at the docks, attending to business there. I thought of how my father had spoken slightingly of Balbus, saying he was some sort of trader, whose business was ships, and buying and selling. But then, I reflected with a shrug, my father had little good to say of me either. So perhaps, after all, my uncle and I should like one another.

A slave brought water in an earthen jar. I stripped, and washed my body at the basin; and presently the girl came tapping at the door, and told me my uncle had returned and would see me now.

I had wanted to dress in something fine, to show I was not just nobody. But my clothes-chest had not yet come, so in the end, telling myself that clothes do not make a man, I pulled on my grimy homespun tunic once more, and made the best of it.

In my imaginings on the road I had thought to see in my uncle Balbus some reminder of my mother, since he was of the bloodline; and it was true his eyes were brown like hers, and mine, but they were sunken in a face gone jowly and fat.

He looked up from a mess of open scrolls and writing-tablets as I entered. He put me in mind of a great indolent bull, stirring from its bed of grass. But as his eyes fixed upon me I remembered the formalities and said, 'I am Drusus, son of Appius. My father sends his greetings, sir.'

'Does he? Well, come here, boy, and let me see you.'

He remained seated. My father would have stood.

I stepped forward. Light shafted in from a small high window. In the corner a cluster of hanging lamps, suspended on little chains from a bronze standard, illuminated the wide stone slab of his desk.

12

He sat back and cast an appraising eye over me, clicking his tongue like a farmer inspecting a goat at market.

'I see you have picked up your father's frown,' he said eventually. 'But you have your mother's black curling hair and fine looks, at least.'

'She died when I was born, sir. I did not know her.'

'No, of course; but I remember her, though it is long ago now, when we still lived in Gaul, before the barbarian Franks robbed us of our lands and we were forced to scatter. Did your father not tell you? . . . No, I suppose not. He was always the great man, and what were we to him? Still, the headstrong horse does not always win the race, eh? And now the wheel has turned and you are here.'

It was clear to me this man and my father would have had little in common, but remembering I was his guest I said, 'I am sure, sir, that my father always regarded you with honour.'

At this his eyes widened. He slapped his hand on his thigh and gave a great laugh. 'Well, you have his diplomat skill at least . . . How old are you, boy?' And when I told him he went on, 'Fourteen is old enough to make yourself useful. Now you are here, you can learn something of trade. That will please Appius.'

He scratched himself and chuckled, and reaching forward took up a wax-tablet and pushed it towards me. 'See here, I have a shipment just in from Gaul, a fine consignment of Rhineland glass. How is your reading?'

I peered down at the inscribed words. It was a list, and I read out loud, 'Ten-inch platters – three hundred;

wine-jars – one hundred and fifty; engraved pitchers – fifty; drinking cups – one hundred . . .' and on through the manifest. And, as I read, my uncle Balbus craned his head over the desk and described to me each piece, and what price it would fetch, and where it would best be sold.

In the midst of this I did not hear the door-latch sound behind me. Suddenly he broke off; and then I turned.

A woman had entered, attended by the old male house-slave who had first admitted us. She was much younger than my uncle; but there was nothing soft or girlish in the stare she gave me. I felt it like a blast of cold air.

My uncle, suddenly meek, said, 'Ah, Lucretia, here is the boy . . . I was just telling him about our new shipment from the Rhine—'

But she cut him off before he could finish. 'The child has brought his slave. Why was I not told?' And then, to me, 'Well, you are unexpected. And I thought we were beneath Appius's notice . . . how quickly fortunes change.' Her lips moved in a thin smile. But her eyes were lifeless, like lamp-wicks in daytime.

I looked at her. I could not understand her dislike, to one she did not even know. I understand it now. I am older, and I have seen more of humanity.

She was wearing a long silk robe, so thin her legs showed through; and around her neck a chain with one large inlaid stone of amber. The colour made her look pallid, like straw beside gold. Her black hair was pinned up, in a way that just then was the fashion, and from her ears clusters of earrings hung like grapes.

'Madam,' I said, 'he is not a slave. He is my tutor, and a freeman. His name is Sericus. But if he is not welcome here, then I too shall go, for he is old, and I will not leave him all alone.'

It was of course the wrong thing to say. I expect she had had no intention of casting Sericus out into the street: she merely wanted to complain and have her say, like a dog that marks its ground. But now, as I stood straight-backed and looked her in the eye, I saw I had confirmed and branded on her mind every prejudice that she had ever held.

She glared, and I glared back.

'Look at him,' she said, talking over me. 'Can he dress in nothing better?'

I drew my breath to answer, to tell her I had other clothes in my clothes-chest, and that my father had ordered me to travel thus. But she must have guessed that for herself. And I knew I had said enough.

Black desolation seized me, and for the first time I felt the full meaning of my loss. I wished with all my heart to be back among familiar things: the house-slaves who knew me; the dogs in the yard who lounged beside the stable; my own room, with its childish treasures, and my bed of oiled beechwood. I knew at that moment that if I was to live as a guest here, it was in the teeth of her opposition, and she wanted me to know it. It was a hard thing to bear, after so much else.

The draught from the open door had caught the hanging-lamps. The fine smoke pricked my eyes and I looked away, not wanting her to think it was she that caused me to blink away the tears.

15

Meanwhile Balbus was talking on, consoling, concili-
ating, like a man calling for peace when the battlefield is
already strewn with corpses. I believe he was actually
embarrassed for my sake, and I liked him for it.

'All this,' he was saying with an air of cheer, 'can
be dealt with in time, and anyway, let us not worry the
boy today, so soon after he has arrived. Appius has
provided a significant sum for his keep, and no doubt
matters will resolve themselves . . . Do you not think so,
Drusus?'

I looked him in the face and answered that I hoped so.
'And I thank you for your hospitality, sir, while my father
is away. But I am keeping you from your business, and I
should like to go and see my tutor.'

I had wanted to sound like a man, like my father when
he spoke to his political friends; but my young voice
broke and betrayed me. I pressed my lips together, feeling
foolish.

I heard Lucretia's earrings jangle. I did not look at her.
But Balbus laughed and said, 'Yes, yes, of course you
would.' He snapped his fingers at the door, where the
slave was waiting. 'Patricus, give the boy something to
eat, and take him to his tutor as he asks.'

And so I left them. If I had known how long I was to
stay in that house, and what misery I was to endure, I
daresay I should have pushed past him, run to my room
and leapt from the window. It is not for nothing that the
gods deny us foreknowledge.

And besides, I had Sericus to think of.

*

I found him in a room off a passageway behind the kitchen, sitting on the bed with his hands in his white hair, like a man in despair.

He sat up quickly when I walked in. 'Ah, Drusus, I was just coming to find you.'

I looked about, appalled. The room reeked of damp, and the walls were stained with green and black growths. In the corner his casket stood open with his few things still unpacked. I think he had realized there was no other place for them.

'What is this?' I cried, gesturing at the filthy walls. 'Do they take you for a dog?' My father would not have accommodated the lowest creature in such squalor, let alone a man, slave or freeborn.

But Sericus said, 'Hush, and let it be. It will be better when it is aired, and I imagine they are pressed for space. Come now, the courtyard at least is pleasant. Let us go and enjoy the last of the light.'

So we went outside, to the little square garden I had seen from my window, with its patch of grass and its solitary damson tree. The breeze had died. Smoke from the kitchen ovens hung in the air.

'What news?' he said, when we had sat down on the stone bench. 'Have you met your uncle yet?'

'Yes, and his wife too. Her name is Lucretia. She hates me.'

He let out a sigh. 'Really, Drusus, what talk! How can you possibly suppose it? She does not even know you.'

I snatched at a tall weed growing at the foot of the bench and was about to cry out that I knew I had judged this woman Lucretia well enough. But then I thought of the fetid dark room he had been consigned to, the indignity and insult of it, and how the stable life within our family was all he had ever known. I think, then, I first felt in my heart what it was to be powerless in a hostile world.

And so I said instead what he wished to hear. 'Yes, Sericus, perhaps you are right. It will seem better tomorrow.'

'Good boy.' He patted my knee. 'Remember, we must give them no cause to complain.'

No, I thought, we have nowhere else to go. But I said nothing, and for a moment we sat in silence, considering the ruin of our lives.

A pigeon fluttered down and settled on the damson bough in front of me. It clawed the wood and shifted, and gazed at me with its head cocked. Then, in a flurry of angry movement, it was gone. Already the sun had passed behind the high surrounding wall, leaving us in shadow.

'Have you met your cousin yet?' asked Sericus.

'He is out.' And, looking him in the face, I said, 'He has gone to see a *bishop*.'

'Ah, yes.'

'You knew?'

'I heard it from the cook while you were with your uncle. It seems the people here are Christians.'

I stared at him. It was worse than I feared. 'But Sericus, why would Father send us to such a place? The Christians drink human blood and kiss bones – I know; the boys at the farm told me. And they cast spells to make corpses walk, rising from their tombs!'

'Really, Drusus! Why do you heed such foolish nonsense? The farm-hands make up these stories to scare you.'

'But my cousin—'

'Calm yourself, and let me finish. The bishop is their high priest, after all, and I daresay they pay their respects from time to time. Now come, I know a little of Christians, and you have nothing to fear from them. Remember only that they do not take kindly to talk of the gods, or offerings, which they consider insulting to their own particular god. So better to be discreet in what you say, out of courtesy; for do not forget we are guests, and must honour their ways.'

I did not see Albinus that day. But next morning, while I was dressing, I heard a harsh, impatient voice bark out my name from the courtyard below. I had slept fitfully, disturbed by the unfamiliar city noises – a woman's sudden scream from the road outside the house; a dog's constant barking; and later, near dawn, the draymen calling to one another as they brought market traffic through the streets. But the chest of my belongings had finally arrived, and I had dressed in my smart maroon tunic, with its border of ivy leaves.

'Where have you been, slow-belly?' Albinus cried when I appeared. 'Didn't you hear me calling?' It was the only greeting he gave me. Then he turned and yelled down the passageway at the slave, 'Get a move on, Patricus! I am still waiting, and I shall be late.'

He had the same pinch-lipped face and yellow complexion as his mother; but where hers was touched with carmine and kohl and lip-paint, his was plain and puffy with sleep. His hair was lank and unwashed, and though he was taller than I, he stood badly, with the posture of one who has never been taught how to hold himself.

The old slave came hurrying from the back of the house. 'Carry my bag!' ordered Albinus, snapping his fingers at a satchel of brown leather lying on the flagstone. Then, turning to me, 'Father says I must take you to his offices, though I cannot think why you want to go *there*. And now I shall be late for the bishop again, and it will be your fault.'

We set out, with the old slave walking ahead.

'Well?' Albinus said, stalking along beside me, 'How long are you staying?'

'Not long.'

'Is that so? If your father has upset the emperor it may be longer than you think. That's what Mother says.' He gave a quick high-pitched laugh, like a fox's bark.

'Let her say what she likes. She does not know my father.'

'What of it? Everyone knows what happens to people who displease the emperor.'

This brought back all the fears and misery I had spent the waking hours of the night wrestling with. 'My father will send for me soon; you'll see.' I kicked hard at a stone, sending it skittering over the cobbles. Albinus regarded it with amusement as it hopped along and rattled into the gutter, but he said no more, and for a while we walked in an uneasy silence.

Then, a new idea coming to him, he said, 'Guess what? The bishop says I shall soon be made a Reader.'

I shrugged. 'Well I can read already.'

'So can I, you fool. A *Reader* is something else. It means I shall one day be a priest . . . Mother wants that very much.'

I thought of the stories the farm-boys had told me, and remembered I must be careful.

With a wary look I asked him why he wanted to be a priest.

'Why? Why? What sort of question is that?' He snorted in derision. But then a vacant look settled on his face, and he brought his long bony finger up to his mouth and began chewing the nail, sucking and crunching at it. 'Anyway, I shall be excused civic duties if I am a priest, and the family will be exempt from tax, and that will make us richer.'

I considered this. 'Then it's a good thing everyone is not a priest, or there would be no one to govern the cities, or fight off the barbarians.'

He sniffed and said, 'Fool.' But I perceived he had no other answer, and was pleased to see I had silenced him for a while.

He walked on sulkily, with his ungainly stride. It was a humid, cloudless morning, early still, and in the street the traders were opening their shops and setting up their brightly coloured awnings.

'Anyway,' said Albinus, 'what will *you* do when you are a man? I bet you don't even know. You had better think of something, now you are on your own.'

His barb had found its mark. I drew down my brow and looked ahead, wondering what to say.

The slave Patricus had halted beside a water trough,

21

waiting for us to catch up. Beyond him, on the street-corner, a young legionary was standing outside a cob-bler's shop. He had taken off his boot, which was broken, and was leaning on the doorpost, with his broad sun-tanned foot resting on the stone step, while the shoemaker worked at the boot. He glanced round, and catching me looking gave me a white-toothed smile.

I smiled back. Against the busy people around him, rushing to and fro, intent on their dreary business, he looked strong and free and beautiful, like a sleek horse in a field of donkeys.

But Albinus had seen he had vexed me, and was not going to let his question drop. 'So?' he demanded. 'You don't know, do you?'

'Yes I do,' I flared back at him. 'I shall be a soldier.'

'A soldier?' He broke into a mocking laugh and rolled his eyes. 'How ridiculous! What sort of man chooses to be a soldier? Anyway, don't you know it is sinful to fight for the empire? Do you know nothing at all?'

I ignored him. His words made no sense. Meanwhile the legionary had turned away. I saw him hand the cobbler a coin and take his boot. Then he crouched down at the kerb and tied it on, his fingers moving swiftly over the hide laces in quick familiar movements.

Albinus jabbed his finger in my ribs. 'Hey, didn't you hear me?'

'I heard,' I said, slapping his hand away.

'Well I pity you. That's all.'

'I don't want your pity, Albinus, and I don't care what your bishop says. I shall be a soldier and a warrior, and do something fine and good.'

This set him off again, and he was still chuckling to himself when we reached his father's offices.

We found Balbus among a group of attentive-looking clerks, reviewing a shipping list. He dismissed them when we entered, and greeted me in his loud bluff voice. He seemed genuinely pleased to see me. His shipment of glass, he said, was being unloaded that morning, and we would go to the docks together to see. I saw him cast a questioning glance at Albinus.

'No, Father, you know the bishop is waiting, and I am already late. I only came to bring him here.'

'Yes, of course; the bishop.' And for a moment a cloud of resignation crossed his heavy face.

Albinus shrugged and turned. 'Goodbye, little warrior,' he said with a snide smile. Then he left. I could hear him laughing to himself all the way through the anteroom.

I set out with Balbus.

As we made our way along the route, he pointed out the shops and trades of the men he knew, greeting them with loud good-natured friendliness and pausing for a word; Lampadius the ship's chandler, Maltius the cooper, Arminus and Phason the sailmakers, and Gabinius the coppersmith, who had a wide yard behind the street, full of men working.

From the alleyway that led to the docks there came wafting up on the damp air the smell of caulking and rope, fish and stale wine. But instead of turning that way we continued to the city wall, and out through the eastern gate, to an open place of wagons and mule-carts. Here a driver, one of my uncle's men, was lounging beside a gig. He leapt up when he saw us, but Balbus waved him aside, saying he would drive himself today.

'See those ships?' he said as we set off.

I looked out across the grassy flatland. Some distance away, at a looping bend in the river, a line of merchant-men lay berthed.

'Yes, sir. But why do they not come to the city dock?'

'They cannot – not the biggest freighters. Their keels are too deep. So they put in there. It is where I have my warehouse.'

At the wharf, a line of bare-chested stevedores were unloading a ship, passing crates from hand to hand, chanting a Keltic worksong, and from high up on the poop a shaven-headed foreman stood barking instructions – 'Careful with that, you ditch-born whore . . . You! Yes, you! Pick up that crate, don't stare at it.'

'What of my cargo?' called Balbus.

'One crate broken, sir, and one in the river. I sent the bastards in after it.'

My uncle glared at the water. 'Careless fools. The wealth of Croesus must lie in this mud. One day someone will dredge it all up and make his fortune.'

In the warehouse, men were unpacking crates of glass-ware, separating each delicate piece from its straw lagging and setting it down on a long bench, where a clerk was busy marking each item off against the manifest. Balbus picked up a flask of cherry-coloured glass and turned it in the light, nodding to himself and making satisfied grunts.

'Good, good,' he said, showing me. 'Fine work; no

blemishes. One can never be sure nowadays, with the barbarians marauding over Gaul, and all the good craftsmen leaving. There is always a market for quality pieces like this.'

He set it down and moved on to inspect the rest: embossed dishes and wine-cups; a wide-brimmed fruit-bowl of clear crystal; a pair of fine worked lamps of yellow glass, decorated with garlands. When at last he was satisfied we walked on into the body of the warehouse, between the aisles, and he pointed out bales of wool from Spain, dusty slabs of veined Tuscan marble, tall red-earth amphoras filled with wine from Italy or Sicily, or fish sauce shipped around the coast from Cadiz.

I stared, and touched, and asked him what he would do with it all.

'Most,' he explained happily, 'I shall sell to my contacts in the province. I have agents in York, Lincoln, Colchester and in the cities in the west.' He tapped his nose and smiled. 'But the best I keep for my own shop in the forum.'

He seemed pleased at my interest, and taking up a stick he sketched a map in the dust. 'We are here,' he said, indicating the western corner by my foot, 'and here is the Middle Sea. That is Rome, and over there – yes there! that's right – is Arabia.' Mostly, he explained, he imported from Gaul or Spain or Italy. 'But if I can bring a spice cargo from the East, it will be worth more than all the rest put together.'

I crouched down, staring in wonder, and asked how long it took to sail so far.

'Twenty days, with fair weather.'

He traced the route with the stick: Alexandria in Egypt, through the Middle Sea by Africa or Sicily, past the Pillars of Hercules and then up along the treacherous coast of Spain and Gaul.

'Soon,' he said, 'I shall have funds for such a trip, and it will make me rich.' His eyes flashed as he imagined it.

As for me, I gazed at the whorls and sandy curves at my knee, seeing oceans and painted ships and magnificent cities. Here was something I could dream of. I asked him how often he went to these places.

'Go to them?' He looked surprised. 'Why, not at all, why should I? I am much too busy for that.' He knew only Britain, he said, and Gaul, and that was more than enough for him.

Back outside, a wide-girthed troopship had come up with the tide, high in the water, unladen. The crew were furling the great sail and preparing to throw the lines.

The shaven-headed foreman stepped up. 'How many more?' he said, eyeing the ship with a frown. 'The Saxons know an unguarded house is easiest robbed, even if the emperor has forgotten.'

But Balbus looked sharply at him. 'Watch your tongue, Gaius. Do you want to scare the boy with your foolish dockyard talk? Take no notice, Drusus. There have been no Saxons for three years, nothing but a few stray ships, and the garrison commander himself has promised we have nothing to fear.'

'But I'm not afraid,' I said.

There was a pause. The foreman grinned at me, showing his black teeth.

'No one is afraid,' said my uncle crossly. 'We gave the

Saxons a gift of gold last time, and they promised not to return. Have you no work to do, Gaius? I don't pay you to stand about gossiping. Come along, Drusus.'

Glancing back for a last look I saw the foreman shrug his shoulders, hawk loudly, and spit into the water. Then he turned and launched a volley of abuse at the dust-caked stevedores, who were calling out and joking with the men on the troopship.

Summer drew on. In the fields beyond the city walls the farmers brought in the harvest, and I adjusted to my exile, like a man who grows used to lameness, because he must.

I spent each afternoon helping my uncle, at his offices, or down at the docks, or at his fashionable shop of perfumes and fine wares under the forum colonnade.

He knew that better-born men looked down on him; but did not care, so long as he grew rich. He had no time for learning, other than what he perceived he could use, and made jokes about my early-morning lessons with Sericus, saying he saw no point in them: I could count, and read a manifest; what need more?

He assigned me tasks, saying I would learn by doing. At first I had thought, if I found myself at a loss, the clerks at his office would help me. But that was before I understood them.

From the outside, they appeared obedient and dull and timid, like a field of sheep. But now I was among them I discovered their lives were riven with feuds, bitter jealousies, and complicated intrigues. When I needed help, they were suddenly too busy, or, worse, they would affect to explain, only to confuse me. It did not take long for me to realize, as I saw them smirking and making eyes at their colleagues, that this game amused them and they wanted me to fail.

All except one. The others, out of spite, gave him the nickname Ambitus, because he worked hard, and because he laughed at their backbiting. But he wore the name with pride, saying that if they wanted to mock him for trying to make something of himself, then that was the least of his concerns.

He was a small-boned youth with a clever monkey-like face and close-cropped black hair. His example held up a mirror to the others' laziness and stupidity, and they hated him for it. He did not care. He had his own plans, which did not include them.

When he saw me struggling, Ambitus came to me and said that I must ask him if ever I needed help. And so it was that he became my first friend in London.

Some mornings, every small matter – a tiny error in an inventory, a mislaid scroll or tablet, a late delivery – would send my uncle into a fury, making him bang his fist on the long clerks' table, and rage and curse.

When I asked Ambitus what was wrong he said, 'You ought to know more than anyone.'

'Is it me?'

'No, not you. He likes you. It is *her*. Nothing he does is enough. She has him like this.' And with his small brown thumb he made a motion of squashing an insect on the bench.

But Balbus's outbursts were like summer squalls. One

waited, and kept one's head down, and they quickly passed. He was not choleric by nature, and, in his way, he was big-hearted. The same, however, was not true of my aunt.

She perceived slights everywhere, and brooded on them till she had worked herself into a frenzy of incandescent rage. She accused the house-slaves of trying to thwart her, and of laughing behind her back. The Christians claim they are all one another's brothers and sisters: rich and poor, freeman and slave – even the wild Saxons, who delight in slaughter, and would kill us all. Yet I have never seen one person treat another with such habitual lack of humanity as Lucretia treated those who served her. She did it because she could, because she had power over them; and they, since they had no choice, swallowed her abuse and took her blows meekly.

But they gained their revenge in other ways, making it look like an accident: they overheated the water for her bath, and I would hear her hoarse, enraged voice screaming through the house with impotent fury; they spoiled the food when she wished to impress her friends with a lavish dinner; they spilt water on the charcoal of her pretty ornamental brazier, so that it filled the room with acrid smoke.

Her friends, over whom she lorded it in the most shameless way, she suspected of falseness, and of liking her only for her money. But that year, as Ambitus dryly explained, her main complaint was the house. Balbus dishonoured her, she said, because he was content to live on the eastern side of the city, though he knew very well that she hated it. It was not fashionable; all her friends – Volumnia, Placentia, Maria – lived better, and did he not see how they made her feel it, with their polite comments and tolerant smiles and pitying faces? Volumnia had even commented on the smell, one day when the wind was blowing up the river. How could Balbus cause her to suffer so? The humiliation was making her ill.

In most matters, Balbus accommodated her whims. But in this one thing he was adamant: he liked the house and the suburb; he wished to be close to the city docks, among his friends and fellow merchants, who would not look down their noses at him. He would not move.

At first, when I went out each day with him, Lucretia had been glad to see me go, thinking the lowly work must be a misery and humiliation to me; for she had formed the opinion, without justification and without evidence, that I was a spoiled, pampered brat.

She was less happy when she realized I did not care about the dull work, and even enjoyed the diversion. After that, scarcely a day passed when she did not summon me to her private sitting-room, with its silk hangings and plush cushions and clutter of gilded furniture, to complain of my wickedness. Why had I scrubbed the walls of Sericus's room without her permission – did I suppose I now owned the house? Why had I spoken disrespectfully to Albinus of the bishop, who was a dear friend of the family? What had I been muttering about to Claritas the housemaid in the courtyard? What had the cook been saying about her?

If I said nothing to these outbursts, she accused me of

being sullen and recalcitrant. If I answered her, she complained that I was insolent.

One afternoon, when I was sitting with Sericus in the damson courtyard, I wondered bitterly what my uncle could find to like in such a woman.

Sericus glanced up from the scroll that lay spread across his lap and mine and said, 'He is losing his hair and going fat. And she is young.'

This was tart for Sericus, but we had been reading Terence that day, which always put him in a good mood.

'It seems a poor trade then,' I said. 'I had rather have no wife at all than one like that.'

'Yes, well; his choice is not yours. There are some men for whom the bloom of youth is everything.'

He said no more, and we bent our heads back to the scroll.

But presently, when he thought I was not looking, I saw a private smile pass across his old lined face.

It is in the nature of youth to hope. During those first months, whenever I heard a knock on the door, or a carriage in the street, my ears pricked up, listening for the messenger with the summons from my father to return home. But the weeks passed, and no messenger came, and as autumn advanced I ceased to say to myself each morning, 'Maybe today.'

One day, when the first winter storms had closed the sea-lanes and Balbus was at home more than he cared for, I swallowed my pride and asked if he had heard news of my father.

He shook his head and ruffled my hair. 'Perhaps soon, my boy; perhaps soon. I expect we shall have something of him in the spring.'

But though he had spoken kindly, I noticed he did not meet my eye.

He had told me, soon after I arrived, that more than one hundred thousand people lived in London. It seemed an almost impossible number to be gathered all together. The best place to live was westwards, on higher ground across the stream called the Walbrook. It was this fine suburb that Lucretia coveted, with its large mansions, high walls, and hidden gardens. And it was the old dock quarter, whose noises could be heard even from the house, that she detested most of all – a warren of steep shadowy alleyways, climbing the hill between tenements, taverns, brothels, and cheap eating-houses.

After dark, the torchlit streets seethed with ship-workers and river bargemen, and anyone who preferred to make their purchases, or their sales, under cover of night. And when they had filled their bellies with drink, they emptied their purses at the gambling dens and whorehouses, where companions were to be had at any price, and of either sex.

As for my uncle Balbus, his interest was solely the business at the docks, not the entertainment in the streets behind – as he told me himself, many times, and at some length. But one morning, as we were walking down the narrow stepped street to the river to see off a barge of

Samian ware, a coarse-featured girl leered from a window and enquired when he was coming to visit her again.

'The foolish blind trollop,' he cried, hurrying away, 'she mistakes me for someone else, of course. I expect she is drunk. Has she no shame?'

I agreed, and looked away smiling.

When, later that morning, we made our way back, I noticed he was careful to go by a different route.

If Albinus wanted something from me, he would demand my immediate attention; otherwise he ignored me. Although his mother doted on him, there were times when they would quarrel, and then he would enlist me as his ally against her, telling me in vehement tones that he hated her.

At first, being lonely, I was quick to trust, and mistook these advances for friendship. But as soon as their squabble was made up, he would once again turn against me; and if I had been foolish enough during that time to confide in him, I found he had stored away this knowledge as a squirrel stores acorns, to use against me when it suited his purpose.

His slyness he got from his mother; but whereas her every waking moment was driven by ambition and resentment, he cared for nothing. He was lazy and slovenly; he would lie in bed until midday unless she sent a slave to rouse him; he washed himself only when told, and never exercised his body. Just the sight of such dissipation was a kind of discipline to me.

Lucretia's life-work was the promotion of Albinus in the Church, and this task she pursued with unfailing single-mindedness.

She would make secret, expensive gifts to the bishop; and when my uncle found out, I would hear them in his study, him remonstrating and pleading, and her yapping back at him.

She always won these bouts, for after hours or days of her silences and sulks he would grumpily declare, 'Oh, let the bishop keep the silver casket' or, 'Curses on it, take those silks to him if you must' or, 'Yes, I shall send the amphora of Moselle, have Patricus see to it.' Afterwards, all would be calm and honeyed smiles, until the next time.

Never have I met a cleverer politician. She knew when to grant her favours, and when to withhold them. Ambitus was right. She spun him like a top.

I took little notice, not realizing that I was soon to become a tool in her great scheme. But that winter, one early grey morning, she summoned me to her rooms.

'I have a small errand for you,' she said, setting down a dish of sweets she was eating. 'I wish you to go with Albinus.'

I had arranged, that morning, to go with Balbus to his shop in the forum, to meet his agent from Colchester, who was at that time visiting.

'He no longer needs you,' she answered briskly, when I reminded her of this. She began plucking at the beads of her bracelet, and did not meet my eye. 'Now do not stand disputing with me. My hairdresser is waiting, and Volumnia and Maria are coming for dinner.'

Albinus, when I found him already dressed in his boots and winter cloak, was equally tight-lipped. 'Come along, then you'll see for yourself,' was all he would say. He even attempted a smile. I should have guessed then that he was up to something.

'Are you coming or not?' he demanded.

'Yes, I'm coming.'

We set out west through the city, taking the street past the stone-gated entrance to the forum, then over the Walbrook and into the old quarter of shabby houses built on rising ground around the fort. The place had once been fashionable, before the wealthy citizens had moved out to the more spacious suburbs. Now the houses were run-down and subdivided.

'This way,' said Albinus, striding ahead.

We passed a group of women washing clothes at a fountain-house, conversing at the top of their voices in a pidgin mix of British and barrack Latin. Children stared from open doorways. Ahead, over the roofs, I could see the old towers and walls of the fort, with tufts of stone-crop growing in the crumbling mortar.

I wondered again what business Lucretia could have here, and what part I had to play in it. I was about to call out to Albinus when we rounded a corner at the top of the hill and emerged into a wide, open square, planted with linden trees.

I glanced about. I could see the square had once been fine. The northern side was dominated by a half-ruined temple. Gimcrack timber houses spread around its stone base. Some of the lindens had been felled, leaving gaps like broken teeth.

'What is that place?' I asked, calling to Albinus.

He tossed his head. Sneering he said, 'Diana's temple, what's left of it. But it will soon be gone, and good riddance when it is.' He spat, to show his disgust.

But I walked off across the precinct and climbed the ancient steps. The tall doors under the columned porch were gone, and in the grey light I could see the inner walls had been stripped of their facing marble, leaving bare red brick.

'Come away from there!' cried Albinus, who had held back.

He was standing beside a doorway built into a high wall. The door stood ajar. As I crossed to him, I saw that within there was a paved forecourt, and a low sprawling building behind. The walls were rough and undecorated. Pieces of sculpted marble, pillaged from the ruined temple, had been crudely mortared in between the brickwork.

'This way,' he said, beckoning. 'There is someone who wants to meet you.'

I eyed him suspiciously. 'Meet me? Who wants to meet me?'

'Oh, it's only the bishop.'

I stared at him, then looked again at the squat, ugly building behind.

'The bishop?' I cried. 'Are you mad, Albinus? What business do I have with *him*?'

I pulled back; but he caught me by the sleeve.

'You can't go now! He's expecting you. What shall I tell him – that you were afraid, and ran off like a girl?'

He was right: I was afraid. In my mind I was imagining

every sort of horror. But before I could answer, or pull away, a door across the forecourt opened and a gaunt black-cloaked figure stepped out.

'Who's that?' I said, staring. Already the man had seen us. He was approaching, treading across the flags with odd tiptoe steps, like someone picking his way across a muddy field. 'Is that him?'

'No, of course not. That's Faustus. He's the deacon. Now come along, little soldier-boy, or are you going to run away and let him think you're nothing but a coward? He only wants to speak to you. Are you scared even of words?'

The Bishop of London rose from his upholstered couch. 'My dear Drusus, greetings. How pleased I am. I have been looking forward to this opportunity to chat for some time.'

He was a short, fat man, with hair done in the ecclesiastical manner. An air of sweet Asiatic scent hung about him. He motioned with his small, plump hand at the seat opposite and asked me to sit. His fingers, I saw, were festooned with rings – thick bands of silver and gold, set with huge, glittering gemstones. He put me in mind of an expensive merchant.

I sat, uneasily, on the edge of the seat. He was looking at me with a pleasant smile. But I saw, under his thin black brows, that his pinprick eyes were appraising me.

Albinus had gone to stand apart, by a sideboard of carved ebony. I glanced angrily at him, but he ignored me. Then the bishop snapped his fingers and a manservant appeared from behind an embroidered hanging, bearing a silver tray.

He poured two cups of honey-coloured wine, from a flask of cut glass, and set them on the low table that stood between us. He offered nothing, I noticed, to Albinus, nor to the strange deacon called Faustus, who was waiting by the door.

The bishop drank, then took up a silk napkin and dabbed his lips. 'For some time,' he said, 'ever since dear Lucretia mentioned your stay in London, I have been hoping you would come to visit me. Your poor father Appius has been much on my mind.'

'You know my father?' I said, staring.

'Why naturally. You seem surprised. Yet it is only to be expected that men of significance should know one another. Did he not speak of me? – No? Well, perhaps not. But we were acquainted nevertheless, and often had cause to discuss questions of importance.'

I narrowed my eyes at him, disliking his unctuous manner, his quick smiles that died on his lips, and the smooth self-conscious movements of his bejewelled hands.

He paused, then sat forward. 'And now,' he said, beaming, 'your father is in difficulty; it is most unfortunate. In a way, that is what I wished to speak of. But what is it? You have gone quite pale. Here, drink your wine. You are not thirsty? No matter; the kitchen-slaves will help themselves to what is left, no doubt.'

He smiled, and once more drank, taking his time, touching the little napkin to his mouth afterwards.

'The Church,' he continued, 'has great influence. After

all, the emperor Constans is one of our own, and heeds our guidance, as do all good servants of the One God. Many things are possible. A word here, a letter there. The bishop in Trier might be persuaded to speak up for your father. You see, Drusus, I am a man who is listened to, and I have many friends.'

He sat back into the heavy cushions and looked at me, forming his fingers into an arch. His tunic was of some fine close-woven cloth, the kind of thing my uncle imported from the East; and on his feet were bright red-dyed doe-skin slippers, clasped with Keltic silverwork in the shape of twisting serpents, with gaping mouths and bulging eyes. What was this man saying? I asked myself. That he could bring my father back? That I could soon go home again? He must have seen the confusion in my face; but, whatever it was he was leading up to, he seemed in no hurry.

'Lucretia has told me so much,' he went on. 'I feel already that we are friends. How old are you now – fourteen, isn't it?'

'Fifteen.' I had turned fifteen during the autumn.

'Well, you are almost a man . . . and a handsome one too, wouldn't you say, Albinus?'

Albinus grunted. The bishop smiled and then drew down his thin black brows, giving the appearance of considering what to say next, though I had the sense that he had long ago thought out this conversation.

'You know, perhaps there is something you might do for me. A favour for a favour, you could say.' He eased himself forward from the couch and stood. 'But come, let us walk, and discuss what may be done.'

Across the room Albinus and the deacon moved to follow, but with a snap of his finger the bishop gestured at them to stay. Then he placed his hand on my shoulder and guided me under the hangings, out through a door into a cloistered courtyard. He talked as he walked, I do not recall of what – commonplaces, something to do with the Church, the city, and his own importance. I was feeling uneasy. I did not like the feel of his hand on the back of my neck, nor the rich, sickly scent that filled the air around him.

But he had said he could help my father; and so, remembering this, I steeled myself.

He halted at a door and slipped the latch. 'Let us go this way,' he said, easing me ahead of him into the narrow vestibule beyond, into what seemed at first to be total darkness.

I stood blinking and realized, as my eyes adjusted, that we were in a long chamber. At the far end, a weak glimmer of light penetrated from a high aperture. The air smelled of incense, and old earth, and unwashed humanity.

'This,' whispered the bishop, 'is our place of worship.'

I stared into the gloom. Thick squat pillars receded into the blackness, like tree trunks in a night-time forest. Within the body of the room there was a stone-topped table like an altar. I shivered, remembering the stories, expecting at any moment grasping hands to lunge at me from the shadows. Where else, I asked myself, did these Christians obtain their blood to drink, if not from living victims? I wondered what kind of god could be pleased with such a lightless, ill-smelling place.

Beside me the bishop's voice sounded, smooth and amused. 'Are you afraid?' he asked.

'No,' I said loudly, and my voice echoed in the silence. I took a step forward, to show I meant it.

'This was a bathhouse once,' he said. 'What could be less fitting? But soon I shall clear it all away, and in its place build a proper monument, something to the glory of God that men will tremble at. In the meantime this serves for our followers – poor townsfolk and slaves for the most part, know-nothings looking for food and salvation.' He gave a quick sardonic laugh. 'They count for little, but they are useful foot-soldiers; infantry in a war they do not understand.'

I heard the shuffle of his slippers on the stone, and felt his damp fingers on the nape of my neck. I turned sharply. He took his hand away.

'What do you want from me?' I demanded.

He let out a sigh.

'Be calm, young man; there is no need to raise your voice. We have many followers: but that is not enough. We need high-born friends – notables, men who carry weight in the province, who can persuade other simpler folk. We are resisted, you see. We need men of authority . . .' He paused, then added in a tone I was not intended to miss, '. . . or their sons.'

Like a rising sickness, understanding dawned within me. 'But sir,' I answered slowly, 'it is not the religion of my ancestors.'

He laughed – a careful, calculated laugh, devoid of humour – and when he spoke again there was a new edge to his voice. 'Nor was it the religion of the great emperor

Constantine, who was raised an unbeliever, as everyone knows. Yet he saw the truth and followed it, by God's grace. If he could, so can you. Besides, there is much to be gained, and' – with a significant pause – 'much to be lost. No, no, do not discomfit yourself, I am not asking for an answer now. Still, I think we understand each other, and I can see you are no fool. Take account of your situation . . . But do not delay too long, for your father's sake.'

I found Sericus in his room, seated on the edge of his bed, reading a book and trying to ignore the noise from the kitchens. When I told him what had happened, he stared at me and said, 'You cannot put your trust in such a man. It is out of the question.'

'But Sericus, he says he can help us!'

'So he says, but a decent man does not invite a poor guest to dinner and then ask him to pay for it after. Let us say you agree to what he asks, what will come then? What will be his next demand? How indeed do you know he will do anything at all for you? And by then you will have made a public commitment – for that is how he wishes to use you – and you will not be able to retract without disgrace.' He shook his head. 'No, there is an ill smell about the whole business; your father would tell you never to deal with a man who promised a kindness upon such a condition. No gentleman would behave thus.'

'Then do you forbid it?' I asked.

He began to answer, but then he hesitated, frowning

at the mildew-speckled wall. 'No, Drusus,' he said eventually, 'I cannot forbid it, for I cannot know the secret places of this bishop's mind. I am old, and you will soon be a man. This is a question you must decide for yourself.'

THREE

THAT NIGHT I LAY IN BED, staring at the black rafters and wrestling with my thoughts.

When, earlier that day, I had at last left the bishop's residence, for the first time I had been truly angry with Albinus.

'You deceived me!' I shouted at him.

But he had merely given me a look of blank wonder, as if such things were normal and I was making much out of little. When I went on and pressed him, he shrugged, saying, 'Mother wanted it, and the bishop told me to bring you. What are you so angry for? You would not have come otherwise.'

After that I gave up, not trusting myself to speak to him further.

I knew Sericus was right. It would be disgraceful to submit to such a man as the bishop. His promises of assistance had been vague, his tone and expression almost mocking. I had no assurance that he intended to do even what he said, or whether his influence, which he seemed to think so much of, counted for anything at the court of Constans.

I considered going to Balbus, and laying the whole matter before him. But he was not the kind of man to understand such intrigue, and instinct told me he would go straight to my aunt, and she to the bishop. Everything could be denied; anything I said against the bishop could be dismissed as the frustrated imaginings of a resentful boy, the son of a traitor.

Thus my thoughts turned, and my mouth felt dry and bitter, as if I had eaten rotten fruit. And behind it all, the prospect of home beckoned, like the glimmer of bright morning beyond a closed door.

So I was at a loss, and did not know where to turn. But it happened, next day, that I fell to talking with Ambitus, my friend at Balbus's office.

I had gone with him to the city dock, to see to the loading of a cargo of olive oil bound for Lincoln. We were making our way back up the narrow alleyways when from ahead there came the sound of men shouting. All along the street, people were craning their heads from the windows to see what the fuss was. Then, rounding the corner, we walked into a large crowd blocking our way.

At first I could not believe what I saw. I had expected, I suppose, some sort of tavern brawl. But instead I saw the crowd had with one mind set upon a building, a small antique temple with fine delicate columns and steps at the front, which I had often passed on my errands to the city dock. It was, I knew, a shrine to Mercury, of the sort one saw all about this part of town, Mercury being the god of traders and merchants.

We pushed our way forward. The crowd broke out in a sudden cheer as a great slab of marble facing came crashing down from the side of the temple and shattered on the flagstones.

'But why are they doing this?' I cried, shouting into Ambitus's ear over the din.

He gave me a grim look. 'It is nothing new. Every few weeks there is an attack like this. They will not stop till every temple is gone. But see, even now they are afraid. They stand back, and dare not venture inside.'

He was right. For all the mob's noise and cheering, not one of them dared mount the steps under the porch, where in the dark interior the image of the god waited in his shrine. They were like men setting upon some noble captive beast, darting forward to strike and wound, but too timid to make the kill.

I stared in disgust. Only then did I think to ask, 'But who are these people?'

He turned to me. 'Do you really not know? Why, they are Christians of course. Who else?'

I remembered then how Albinus had held back when I had ventured into Diana's temple. For all his ridiculing of the gods, he too was afraid of what he mocked.

Just then the crowd broke into a cheer. We craned our heads to look. A gaunt-faced youth had stepped out and was advancing with a rope, prancing to and fro, swinging the rope about his head and smirking at the bystanders, who were egging him on with cries of encouragement and motions of their arms. After making a show of this for some little time he suddenly darted up the steps at the front of the temple, hurriedly laced a noose around one of the fluted columns, and tossed the rope-end to the crowd.

There were cries of exertion; the rope jerked taut – but nothing happened.

Others ran forward to help. A shout went up and they heaved again. The rope – a mooring line taken, I suppose, from the nearby docks – strained and creaked. The temple stood firm. But then, just as I thought they might give up, mortar dust began to rain down onto the steps. With a grinding crack the column shifted on its base, then broke at the point where the noose was wrapped around it, and toppled forward like a stack of packing-crates.

All around us, the mob let out a howl of joy. They surged forward, and set about beating and kicking the broken cylinders as if they had some life in them. An old woman was standing in front of us, screaming and jigging about and waving her fist in the air. Suddenly, as if she had been struck, she swung round and glared at me with red, wild eyes.

I gazed back at her, transfixed. Her features were flushed, her black-toothed mouth was flecked with spittle. It was like the look of the Gorgon.

Suddenly Ambitus thrust himself forward. 'What is it, old woman?' he shouted.

She jabbed a filthy hand at him. 'Why do you hold back? Why aren't you cheering and praising like the rest?' She began casting her eyes about and calling.

'Come on,' said Ambitus, shouting in my ear over the din, 'before she brings her friends.'

We hurried away, pushing through the wild crowd. Behind, I heard the woman screeching insults and curses.

'Anyway,' said Ambitus, when we were clear of the worst of the mob, and could talk without shouting, 'why are you so shocked? I thought you were one of them.'

'Not I!' I cried indignantly.

'No?' He shrugged. 'Well, it's none of my concern.'

'But why on earth, Ambitus, should you suppose it?'

'Everyone in your house is Christian. Or haven't you noticed?'

'Yes, of course I've noticed. But they don't go about breaking up temples, do they?'

'No, they don't. They leave that to the mob. Come, Drusus! The mob do not act alone. They never do. They are guided and instructed and encouraged by others, who never get their hands dirty and never show their faces.'

'In any case,' I said, 'I am not a Christian.'

He frowned and tossed his head. 'It doesn't matter. As I said, it's none of my concern.'

We walked on. Presently I said crossly, 'And you, Ambitus? What about you? You have never told me. Are you not a Christian too, then?'

'I?' He laughed. He reached to his tunic and took out a coin, and held it up between his thumb and forefinger. 'See this?' he said, fixing my eye, 'this is what I trust in.'

'A coin? What are you talking about?'

'Money. The great all-powerful god. It is what makes me free.' He placed the silver piece carefully back into his purse. 'As for the rest, what do I care if they tear down Mercury's temple? Let them do it. What has Mercury done for me?'

48

He strode on, glaring at the dirty pavement.

'Do you know how I came to learn this trade? My father was a dockhand. He was a drunk and a good-for-nothing, and gambled away everything he earned. When he was incapable, which was most of the time, he sent me here to do his work for him. Then, when I was eleven, the plague took him. One day he was his usual drunken self, the next he was gone, just like that.' He held up his open palm and blew, as a man might blow off a feather.

'I'm sorry,' I said.

'Don't be. I hated him. He left us with nothing, of course, like the wastrel that he was. My mother would have starved, but for what I brought in, and I was forced to turn my hand to what I could find – and some of it would make you blush, Drusus, if I told you of it, which I won't. So let the Christians play their games, as long as they leave me alone. Needs must . . . or have you not learned that yet?'

He jerked his head and spat in the gutter. But then he paused, and tapped my arm gently with his small brown fist.

'I am sorry, Drusus. That was unfair of me.'

I looked into his face. 'So you know, then, about my father?'

He nodded. 'Everyone knows. Albinus made sure of it. What do you think those gossiping fools talk of in the office when you're not there?'

I shook my head. I could feel the colour rising in my face. I considered for a moment. Then I said, 'Ambitus, I need some advice.'

'Only ask.'

And so I told him about the bishop.

He heard me out in silence. When I had finished he whistled slowly through his teeth and pulling me into a doorway said, 'Listen to me, Drusus. I don't usually give advice to people, but your tutor is right: you cannot trust that man. He would be a laughing stock in this town if he weren't so dangerous. There is nothing he will not do to get what he wants.'

He nodded back down the street. 'Who do you suppose was behind *that*? It happens every month or so. The Council complains to the bishop; the bishop says he had nothing to do with it, and for a while things are quiet. Then something else happens. And it is not only buildings that are harmed: people have died. You saw that old woman. She would have torn us apart with her bare hands if she could, just because we were not screaming like the rest. Understand this: the bishop wants power, and he stops at nothing to get his way.'

'But Ambitus, why does he want *me*? Why do I matter so much to him?'

He gave a bitter laugh. 'Think as he thinks, Drusus – if you can bring yourself so low. You are the son of an aristocrat, and so you are useful. Well-born fathers keep their sons away from him – and their daughters too, for they also have their uses. And until the men with real influence – the Notables and the Illustrious and the rest – take him seriously, he must make do with the city rabble who count for nothing. Everyone else thinks he is a joke.'

I frowned, and stared down the sloping street. The nook where we were standing led to the back yard of a tavern. The air smelled rancid; someone had pissed in the doorway.

'I believe everything you tell me, Ambitus,' I said eventually. 'I've met him, and I do not trust him. But if I refuse and my father dies, what then?' I paused, biting my lip. It was this thought that I had returned to, again and again, during the long night.

He let out a sigh. I felt his hand close about my arm and I turned to him.

'You had better hear this from me, since your uncle will not tell you. If the emperor intended to execute your father, he will already be dead. If not, then nothing that fat fool the bishop does will make any difference. He thinks he is important, and because no one dares stand up to him, his friends can break temples and bully good citizens. But in truth he is no more than a cock preening himself on a midden. Take it from me, Drusus: forget him, and forget your father too.'

He looked round. From an upper window across the street a raddled crone was calling out to us, enquiring if we were in the market for a girl, or maybe one each, or perhaps a boy. Ambitus threw her a fluent gesture and she withdrew, clucking.

'Let's get away from here,' he said. And when we were walking once more, 'Have you told Balbus any of this?'

'No.' I told him why.

'Quite right; he would go running straight to her, like a dog to its master. He's good at his trade, but hopeless otherwise. I don't suppose you know this, but Lucretia is the daughter of a shipwright, and a miserable second-rate one at that. Balbus found her serving in some dockside tavern, and if he hadn't taken a fancy to her she'd still be there now. I'll tell you this too: if *she* is involved, then she will be trying to promote her own advantage, either by enriching herself – if there's money behind it – or by obtaining favours for that brat of hers. I imagine the bishop has promised a great deal, if she reels you in. No, friend, don't let them use you. You'll be sorry otherwise.'

We said no more. After what I had seen that morning, and what I had heard from Ambitus, it seemed to me that ugliness and cruelty was the true heart of life, and all else nothing but empty dreams. I felt sick with the world, and with all humanity.

We parted at the streetside colonnade of Balbus's offices. I thanked Ambitus for his advice, and told him I was going to walk for a while, and consider what to do.

At first I had no clear purpose, but as I went I conceived the notion that I needed to be free of the noise of men. Coming to the eastern gate I passed through, taking the open track into the marsh scrub on the north side of the river.

A sharp wind had picked up, snapping at the tall grass and urging flat, turbid cloud inland from the east. At a low rise, beside a tangle of gorse, I sat, and pulled my cloak around me, and looked out over the mud-flats. The tide had peaked. It was turning now, starting to ebb. In the distance a coaster was making its way upriver, its lines taut, its buff square sail straining in the wind.

I looked down, and pulled idly at the long grass. I felt a great coldness in my heart; but now, at last, I saw what I must do. I would submit to the bishop, and let him use me as he chose. The trade he offered was shameful; yet nothing else was possible. If I refused him for the sake of my pride and honour, the knowledge that I had left my father to his death would dwell with me forever. The bishop had seen that, and sprung his clever trap. He had used my weakness.

I filled my lungs with the chill air and let out a bitter laugh. What anyway was honour to me, with all else lost? It was just another empty dream. Easier by far to live like Ambitus, seeking for self, worshipping coin, and trusting no one. And though I told myself I did not care, yet I felt something precious, like a spark of light, flee protesting from my soul.

The sound of far-off shouting pierced my thoughts. I glanced up. On the deck of the coaster the pilot was waving his arms and calling towards the shore, words I could not make out. I scanned the water without much interest, thinking perhaps a man had fallen in; but there was no one in the river, no panicked flailing of arms or splashing on the surface.

Suddenly the vessel veered shorewards, making for the deep-water dock where Balbus kept his warehouse. Something was wrong. The pilot was signalling to the men on the wharf. I could see them in the distance, cupping their ears to show they could not hear.

I stirred myself and, being in no hurry to return home, decided to investigate. I set off at a jog, taking the riverside path. By the time I arrived the ship was alongside, its bow hitched clumsily to a bollard, its stern swinging out with the current, untethered and forgotten.

The pilot and crew were on the quay, talking urgently

to a gathering crowd. I pushed in to listen. Even before I heard the dread word being passed back from man to man I had guessed. I had seen the look on the men's faces. For no one grows up on Britain's shores ignorant of the wild raiders who come from the sea, the death-bringing Saxons.

I pushed in closer. Someone said, 'How many ships?' Another, turning impatiently, cried, 'What matter how many? Let the man finish.' But by now others had arrived who had not heard. The pilot drew his breath and in a torrent of words began again.

He had been sailing round the coast from Richborough – a voyage he made many times each year. Joining the estuary, he had spied hidden in the marsh inlets a flotilla of Saxon longships, lying in wait among the tall rushes. They must have been foraging inland, or raiding, for they had not followed him. Even so, his crew, he said, had been for beaching the ship on the opposite shore and running for their lives. But he had kept his head and sailed on.

Already word was spreading along the wharf, and I could hear the fear in the men's voices, catching from one to the other, like flame in tinder. Already some were running back to the city. Discarded crates and baskets lay abandoned on the quayside.

The group around me began to scatter. Someone, in his haste to escape, shoved me aside. I stumbled. Suddenly an iron hand clapped onto my shoulder. I cried out and turned. It was my uncle's black-toothed foreman, Gaius.

'What are you doing here?' he cried over the din. 'Where is Balbus?'

I said I was alone.

'Then come at once, and hurry, before the gates are closed against us.'

It is said that rumour travels faster than a running man. By the time I reached Balbus's house the news had preceded me, and had amplified with the telling, so that one might have supposed an army of Saxons were already within the walls, sacking the city.

The house-slaves were running about; and at the sound of the door, Lucretia came clattering down the passage, wailing and crying, dressed in her silk dressing-robe and little gold-strapped house-slippers, with her elaborate hair falling about her face, and her eyes smeared with kohl.

Seeing me, she ran and snatched me by the shoulders. 'Where is he?' she cried, shaking me so hard that my sleeve tore.

'Who?' I asked, staring.

'Albinus! My own darling Albinus! Is he not with you? Where then? Have you not heard? The Saxons are here!'

I told her I had not seen Albinus all day, and tried to calm her. There were no Saxons; only a rumour of boats in the estuary. But she would not listen. She kept on shaking me, demanding to know where her precious Albinus was, her voice rising louder and louder as she lost all control.

It was only when thickset, shaven-headed Gaius stepped up and said, in the hard voice he used on the stevedores, 'He was alone, madam, as he has already told you,' that she finally released me. For a moment she glared at him. Then she flung herself round and went flailing and sobbing down the corridor, calling for her maids.

I looked at Gaius; and he looked back at me. Then, across the dark atrium, I caught sight of Balbus, standing solemn-faced in his study doorway.

'You had better come here, Drusus my boy.'

I thought, 'What now?'

But as he closed the study door, he said gravely, 'I have received news of your father. I think you should sit down.'

He tried to spare me, in his heavy-handed way. The details I got long after.

The emperor Constans, when my father had arrived at the imperial palace at Trier, had refused even to admit him to his presence. Eventually there was a trial. Even before it began, everyone knew the outcome.

'I never thought it would come to this,' Balbus kept saying, his voice wavering. 'He died with dignity. I am sure he died with dignity.' In the end, releasing us both, he said, 'Well, I expect you want to be alone.'

I nodded and walked away. But at the door I turned.

'Was it from the bishop that you heard this?' I asked.

'The bishop? Why no. It was my friend Ambrosius the cloth-merchant; he has an agent in Trier, and can be trusted.' He paused and frowned. 'But why the bishop? What has he to do with this?'

'He said he could save my father.'

'He did?' Balbus's eyes widened. 'Who told you this?'

'He told me himself.'

He began to speak, but thought better of it. Then he said, 'Still, it is odd that you should mention him now.'

'Why is that, sir?'

He scratched his head and looked uneasy. 'I daresay it is nothing, it is just that your aunt Lucretia tells me . . . But now is not the time.'

'Uncle, please. What is it?'

He gave a reluctant sigh. 'It is just talk, and perhaps she is mistaken. But it seems the emperor has granted your father's property to the Church.'

My hand had been on the door-latch. I released it and turned to face him. There was a ringing in my head. Time turned slowly. Somewhere outside, I could hear Lucretia railing at the maid.

'What?' I whispered. 'But how?'

He spread his hands. 'I cannot say. I ought not to have mentioned it, not now, not today. It is said the bishop has friends at court . . . or perhaps, after all, your father decided in his will—' He broke off and shook his head. 'But no, not that. To tell the truth, I do not believe your father had much time for Bishop Pulcher.'

I did not weep. I felt hard and unmoved. I surveyed the wreck of my life, and some part of me blamed my father for it. But Sericus wept; it was the first time I had ever seen him do so.

Even this did not move me. I stood silently beside him, my hand on his trembling shoulder, remembering that my family had been everything to him. He had tutored my mother when she was a girl, and had come to my father's house when they married. Now both were dead, and he was too old to begin afresh.

Eventually he eased me from him and said, 'Perhaps we shall find a way to return, even so.'

I shook my head. There was no use in hope. 'No, Sericus,' I said, and told him how our property had been confiscated, and who had gained by it.

I had seen him angry before, or thought I had. His tears ceased. His red-rimmed eyes flashed. In a slow voice taut with fury he said, 'Then your father has been robbed, and so have you. I do not know who lies behind this injustice: but look who gains, and you cannot be far from the mark.' He looked sharply into my face, then said, 'Tell me, did you go to the bishop? Did you give him what he asked?'

I shook my head and said, 'No.'

'Good then, for he would have said your father had willed it, and you were the proof. He has taken what is yours because you cannot fight to keep it. Remember that.'

I nodded and said, 'I will remember.'

When, soon after, Lucretia summoned me to her private room and asked how, in the absence of an allowance from my father, she was expected to keep me, I answered that her friend the bishop had lately grown rich at the cost of one she knew, and perhaps I should go to him for alms.

For all her goading I had never spoken to her thus. She caught her breath, and clutching at the beads around her neck cried that I was a wicked, evil boy. But when she complained to Balbus he said, 'Calm yourself, my dear. We shall easily find for him. He has been useful, and we cannot abandon him now.'

Sericus's cure was study, and he worked me at my lessons: grammar and arithmetic, the poets, prosody and history.

A grim determination had settled upon him. I should not let trivia fill my life; it was time, he said, that I worked on my mind, before I became stale and humdrum.

'Balbus sees no point in it,' I said.

'I do not care what Balbus sees. You are your father's son, not Balbus's. Do you know what a gentleman is, Drusus?'

'A rich man,' I said.

He told me sharply not to talk nonsense, saying, 'That is what the vulgar may tell you, because they know no better.'

'What then?' I asked.

'A gentleman prefers what is true to what is easy. He is not content with small things. He knows what he is, and what he can be. Do you understand?'

'Not really, Sericus.'

'Then all the more reason for you to learn. It is a lifetime's work, and time is short.'

He obtained books from somewhere – from a friend he had made in the teaching quarter, he said – and in the pages of those scrolls and tomes he stretched and challenged and exercised my mind. We read of old battles, old generals, old virtues – but never of what was happening across the water in Gaul: there were no books to tell me that – for no one dared write one.

But what the historians would not tell, I heard from Sericus. The old emperor Constantine, having seized the empire by force, had divided it upon his deathbed among his three sons, like a barbarian chieftain carving up the spoils of war. To one son – also named Constantine – he had given the provinces of Britain, Gaul and Spain; to another – Constans, my father's murderer – he gave Italy and Illyricum; and to the third, Constantius, went Thrace and all the rich provinces of the East.

But, not content with what had been allotted to them, they had quarrelled. There had been civil war; and in the end only two sons remained, Constans in the West and Constantius in the East, ruling the empire between them.

'That,' said Sericus when he told me, 'is where our troops went. They were summoned to go and fight in this needless war. And now, though the war is over, I doubt they will return.'

Constans had purged the Western court at Trier, exiling or beheading the most able of his conquered brother's generals and advisers.

As for my father, he had never cared for court intrigue. He had served under the old emperor Constantine, and had retained his position under his successor. When Constans had taken over in the West, he had offered to resign, or stay, as the new emperor required.

But even this had been taken as a sign of disloyalty. At Trier, the sycophants and schemers had whispered day and night into Constans's ear: yes, my father claimed he was loyal – but loyal to whom? Gaul, having been ravaged by years of barbarian incursions, was weak. But the British province was prosperous, well garrisoned, and had a history of independent action. Who could say, they insinuated, with so many troops at their disposal, what the leading men of Britain might do? Was the emperor prepared to take such a risk?

Constans, when it was put to him in such a way, decided he was not. So he had summoned my father, who had been foremost among those leading men; and, one day in winter, when the clouds hung low over the bleak imperial residence at Trier, he had signed the order for his execution.

Balbus announced he had business in York. He would be gone for the winter, visiting his contacts and clients, and asked me to see to a few matters at the office while he was away.

It was a kindness of sorts. He had no power in the house, where Lucretia ruled; but the office was his own domain. I saw him off, walking with him to the northern gate, where his carriage was waiting. The journey would have been easier by sea; but like everyone else that year, he was avoiding the coastal route, in case of Saxons.

Next morning, Lucretia's attack began. I was in my room, dressing, when there was a tap on my door. It was Claritas the housemaid, to say the Mistress wished to see me, and was waiting in her private sitting-room.

I finished dressing – without hurrying, I confess – and went downstairs.

I found her pacing in front of her new turquoise couch – a recent gift from Balbus, an expensive item imported from Italy, with fine worked ends inlaid with ivory, and dainty silver stag's feet at the base.

'Ah yes, Drusus,' she said, not meeting my eye. 'I saw Bishop Pulcher yesterday. He wishes you to call on him.'

I looked at her in disbelief.

'Please tell him, madam, that I have more important business to attend to.'

She ceased her pacing and spun round. Her beads and bracelets jangled.

'Important business? Listen to you, boy! Do you set yourself above me now? You will do as I ask.'

'He wanted me to join his cult. I will not.'

Her face stiffened. I had spoken sharply back at her, without the fawning she took for proper deference. Even so, no one had told me the Christians disdain the word *cult*, which they reserve for followers of other gods than theirs – of Mithras or Isis or the Great Mother.

'You may have gulled your uncle,' she snapped, 'with your melancholy air, and your fine aristocratic manners, but I am not such a fool. The bishop is a friend of mine and a great help to our family; I will not have him treated with disrespect.'

'He asked me to make a choice. I have made it. That is all.'

'And who are you,' she said in a low, venomous tone, 'to set yourself against the Church?'

It was a question I should never forget, and on which I spent many years brooding and formulating an answer.

But then I merely said, 'I am not his slave, madam, nor anyone else's.'

'We are all slaves before God,' she retorted. But the force had gone from her voice. I saw her long neck redden, and knew that in our war this battle was mine.

'I trust,' she continued, turning from my gaze and fingering the ivory rosette on the couch-end, 'you will reflect on your position here, and reconsider. Now leave me. I will not be treated with contempt in my own home. You may be sure my husband will hear of this, when he returns.'

And so I left her.

She may have been a slave before her god, but she was mistress of the house, and made sure the servants felt it.

The cook, a burly Spaniard, was her constant enemy and the only one of the staff who dared speak back to her. She would have dismissed him, but she knew good cooks were hard to come by, and liked to impress her friends with the elaborate dinners he prepared. He knew it too.

'What is for dinner?' she would demand.

'Roast kid with figs, lady, and woodcock and goose eggs.'

'I don't want that.'

'Then you will have to make do with a dish of beans and dripping.'

'We will have the roast kid.'

And so, between them, there was an uneasy bristling truce.

The slave Patricus, who was so infirm he should have been laid up with a nursemaid of his own, she sent out on the smallest whim in any weather – to take a note to a friend; to inspect a newly arrived shipment of linen at the forum and return with samples; or to run petty errands for Albinus. To her maids she was sharp and violent and bullying. At the least slip she would scream abuse, slap them, and send them sobbing to their bedchambers at the back of the house beside the woodstore.

I was spared the worst of this. I believe, behind her disdain and hatred, she actually feared me.

On appointed days each month, and on certain holy days, she attended gatherings with other Christians, and sometimes afterwards I would glimpse her mumbling invocations to herself, kneading between her fingers a string of little black beads. But I never saw a sign of the fearsome rituals the farm-lads had scared me with – dismembered human victims, blood-drinking, or the kissing of dead men's bones; and, in time, I came to suppose these must after all be the inventions of ignorant minds, as Sericus had told me.

One day, when she had called me to her rooms on some matter, I noticed a thing that had not caught my eye before. Half-hidden in an alcove behind the silk hangings there was the faded fresco of a youth, his delicate hands outspread, his dark eyes looking calmly across the crowded opulence. Though it was striking, I wondered she had not had the image painted over, for it was old naive work, almost jarring to the eye after the fashionable clutter. There was something about this solemn figure with his sad eyes and knowing smile that stayed in my mind, and later I asked Claritas the house-maid about it.

My question seemed to amuse her and she even smiled. She knew at once what I was speaking of. He was, she said, the chief hero of their religion, and for my aunt to paint over him would be thought an impiety.

By such small things did I come to understand Lucretia.

There were certain virtues which she set much store by. One of these she called *humility*, a strange word to make a virtue out of, reminiscent of lying in the dirt, but which the Christians had taken for their own. This particular virtue was something, she told me, that I lacked; and, after I had refused to obey her and see the bishop, she took it upon herself to teach me. She gave instructions that I was to eat my meals alone, so that I could reflect upon my selfishness; and she ordered the cook to serve me slops.

Suffering is a great teacher, she informed me. But I did not go hungry. The cook tossed the slops to the dogs, and instead served me with choice portions of meat or spiced fish, intended for Lucretia's table. And the house-slaves, seeing we shared a common enemy, became my friends and allies.

So much for my instruction in humility. But chief among my aunt's virtues was what she called purity, or chastity. The purest act of all, it seemed, was to renounce marriage and live alone in some wild place, or in self-chosen exile shut up with other Christians. I heard this first from Albinus and, amazed, I asked, 'But who will give the farmers sons, or breed soldiers for the army?'

'Salvation lies in the death of the body,' he primly answered.

I gave him a sidelong look, to show I knew he was lying. He was always trying to deceive me with such absurd stories. I knew him better by now than to let him make a fool of me.

Soon, however, I was to hear more about chastity.

I was woken one morning by a scream of rage coming from Lucretia's rooms. I bolted upright in my bed; the noise came again, ringing through the house, followed by Albinus's wheedling voice, strained and high-pitched.

They were quarrelling. I went down to find my friend the cook, who would be sure to know what had happened. But before I reached him, there was a hiss from behind a storeroom door.

'Hello Albinus,' I said smiling. 'You are up early. Couldn't you sleep?'

'Shut up,' he snapped, pulling me by the elbow. 'Come with me, I want to speak to you.'

He led me with many a backward look through the rear courtyard and out by the servants' door at the back, into the narrow alleyway behind. Then he turned to face me.

'What have you told her?' he demanded.

I said I did not know what he was talking about.

He eyed my face suspiciously, then cried, 'So it *was* that gossiping bitch Volumnia, after all. I knew it!'

I had seen Volumnia often at the house; she was one of Lucretia's most frequent visitors, a bony middle-aged woman who wore wigs of straw-coloured hair shorn from German slave-women. She and Lucretia talked together of the Church, when they were not reviewing in hushed, glowing-eyed whispers the wrongdoings of their friends.

'What has she done?' I asked. But he just ignored me, and stood frowning, with his finger in his mouth, biting his nail.

A fine drizzle had started to fall and I did not have my cloak. It was cold, and I was in no mood for his riddles. I turned to go inside.

'All right, I'll tell you,' he cried.

So I turned back, cocked my head, and stood leaning against the brick wall with my arms folded. By the time I had heard him out the drizzle had turned to rain and my tunic was wet through. But it was worth it, for what I heard.

Albinus had been seen in one of the notorious gambling dens of the city, the ones behind the theatre, in the close company of a street-trull. Before the night was out, word had got back to Lucretia, and when he came slinking back before dawn, she had been waiting.

All this took him some time to relate, because every few words he would break off the tale and launch into a volley of self-righteous curses, stamping his boot on the cobbles. He cursed Volumnia particularly, calling her a slack-tongued vixen, a sour-faced traitorous bitch, and other such things.

'Do something right,' he said, 'and she never notices; but just put one foot out of step and her hawk-eyes are on you. I don't know what business it is of hers anyway. She has spies everywhere. And now half of London will know.'

I said, trying to look serious, 'But I didn't think you

spent time with whores, Albinus.' Actually this was not quite true. Over the past months he had not been able to resist confiding to me his drab fantasies. That he should have done something about it came as no surprise. In the end, as men say, a hammer needs an anvil.

'She's not a whore,' he answered with a sniff. 'She was short of money, that's all. She had left her purse at home and so I gave her something, and bought a flask of wine because she was thirsty. But she's a nice girl. And it's not true that she stole my purse, as Mother thinks. She picked it up because it looked like hers; anyone could make such a mistake.'

'She stole your purse as well?'

'No! Not stole! Why don't you listen? Anyway I got it back; but Mother doesn't see it that way . . . What's the matter? It's *not* funny, Drusus! It won't take long for the bishop to find out – I expect Volumnia will pay him a special visit, curse her! She ought to keep her beak out of other people's business.'

One of the kitchen cats came sidling up, a balding black and white creature. Albinus gave it a vicious kick, sending it scrambling over the wall with a resentful squeal.

'Will you see her again?' I asked.

He pulled himself up and gave me an arch look. 'Maybe, if I choose to; anyway, that's *my* secret, she's my girl and you needn't think you can—' He suddenly broke off and leapt almost as high as the poor kitchen cat. The door had snapped open. Lucretia's head appeared in the gap.

In a low, dangerous voice she said, 'Get inside, Albinus, now!' Then she vanished, leaving the door ajar. She hated to be seen in the street without a retinue or a litter, in case she was taken for a slave, or one of the dockyard women.

Albinus gaped at me. 'Do you think she was listening?'

Seeing his face, I could contain myself no longer. I coughed and spluttered into my fist. 'I cannot tell. But she's waiting. You'd better go and find her.'

Lucretia sent the bishop a flask of Egyptian oil in a delicate fluted bottle of Phoenician glass, stoppered with a cap of white silver; the bishop, after consideration and prayer, decided the scandal could be forgotten and, shortly after, at the time of a Christian holy day, amid much celebration in the household from which I was excluded, Albinus was made a Reader.

Uncle Balbus was still away in the north, and so heard none of it. Each morning I attended his office, and most afternoons I went walking with Sericus, out across the bridge, to the open smallholdings and plantations to the south and east.

Now that our past lives were lost to us, we both missed the open spaces – the silent paths, and woodlands, and towering skies. Although, in London, I was surrounded by noise and people and activity, yet I perceived for the first time that there is no worse solitude than the company of strangers.

Whatever Sericus felt, he did not speak of it. Since the news of my father's death he no longer talked of the past; and when we walked together he spoke only of small, seemingly insignificant things – the birds and animals, the farmsteads and hamlets along the way – like a man who treads carefully on the surface of a frozen lake, lest the ice should crack and the chill waters engulf him.

But one day soon after, in the midst of winter, our minds were wrenched from these concerns.

We were making our way back to the city, following a farm track, when up ahead, where the track joined the high road, we saw a crowd gathering – carters, men with mules, foot-travellers.

'Run ahead and see what it is,' said Sericus. 'If there is trouble, we will go by another way.'

I sprinted off. The men had gathered at the crossroads, beside an old shrine. There was a stone watering trough, and leaning beside it a lone soldier, holding forth to the rest. His body and scarlet cloak were mud-spattered; clearly he had travelled far, through bad terrain.

He stooped to splash his face and neck at the trough. A young farm-lad stood beside him, holding his helmet for him while he washed, looking grave and full of moment. I knew the boy by sight – he belonged to the nearby villa – and seeing me he gave a grim nod of acknowledgement.

'What news?' I asked, stepping up.

He answered in British, the language of the land.

'The Saxons is what. They have landed at Richborough. The man here says the fort has fallen.'

Others were pressing round, coming along the path from the hamlet beside the villa. A red-faced man in a farrier's apron cried, 'That cannot be! Who ever heard of

Saxons coming in winter, or taking fortresses? They are no more than raiders and cattle-thieves.'

'Believe what you want, friend,' said the soldier. 'I know only what I saw, and what I got from the men on the road, retreating from Richborough. I was on my way there myself, for a tour of duty.' He gave a bleak laugh, adding, 'No need for that now.'

The farrier laughed, and with a mocking look asked, 'Did they bring siege-engines in their longboats then?'

'You think I am here to joke with you? If you want to find out how the fortress was taken, go and ask the men who should have been guarding it – the ones who decided to spend the day fishing in the river instead. Even fortresses fall, when no one is minded to defend them. It seems our men caught a bigger fish than they expected.'

Sericus, who had come up beside me, asked if word had reached the city yet. The soldier said the others of his troop had gone ahead to inform the Council. 'As for me, I'm going the other way . . . My father has a farm on the Medway, and no one else will think to warn him. Word is that raiders have landed all along the coast, even as far as Dover.'

'It is no more than hearsay,' shouted the farrier, who all this time had been grumbling and murmuring at the back. 'There have been rumours of Saxons all year. This will come to nothing, like all the others.'

The soldier looked at him. 'You know a lot, for a stay-at-home. Well I hope you're right, because if you're not, then there is nothing between the coast and here to stop them.'

Men started to glance around, thinking, no doubt, of their private concerns: their families, their farms, their savings stashed at home under some kitchen pot. Already, across the flat land in the middle distance, where the roads meet at the southern approaches to the bridge, the traffic was building – and it was heading only one way: northwards, to the safety of the city walls.

The crowd began to fragment and scatter.

'Let us go back,' I said to Sericus, 'here, rest your weight on me.'

He had grown less easy on his feet of late.

In the days that followed, a stream of citizens arrived, each carrying what he could in wagons, or on his back. The Saxons had descended on the coast at a time when the seas were normally quiet. Richborough fort had fallen; Dover was cut off, and the raiders were swarming over all the land between, torching farmsteads and putting to the sword, or carrying off into servitude, those too foolish or too slow to flee inland.

Just as the soldier had said, the roads to the coast were unguarded. No one knew how far the barbarians had advanced, or how many there were.

But there was worse to come; and it was my uncle Balbus, returning at last from York, who brought the news. The great northern frontier wall had been breached all along its length, and the fearsome painted Picts had come sweeping south. The troops at the undermanned border forts, seeing themselves about to be surrounded, had lost their nerve and fled. The enemy had been left to plunder at will.

Balbus, abandoning his own slow carriage, had been forced to part with a fortune to secure a swift light gig from a York merchant with an eye to the main chance, who knew a terrified rich man when he saw one. He arrived filthy from the road, to a house that was already like an upturned ant-nest. Lucretia sobbed, and went to the cellar to bury her jewels. Balbus retired to his study, and sat with his head in his hands, staring at the wall. Amid the chaos and panic, only the slaves seemed to retain any composure.

Terror did more damage even than the Saxons. The country-folk flocked to the city, abandoning their homes and crops. A few brave souls stood fast, intent on staying until there was sure news of the enemy's approach. Of these, some managed to bring in the harvest and turn a good profit on it, if their slaves and farm-hands had not fled to the hills. Nor did we begrudge them what they made, for if they were caught, the Saxons showed no mercy.

They killed, it seemed, for the very joy of killing. They burned what they could have possessed for themselves. It was as if they hated the very idea of civilization.

In London, the Council convened. The magistrates voted to send a fast messenger by the long western route where the barbarians had not yet penetrated, to beg Constans for help. We went about our business out of habit, and because there was nothing else to do. Then, one blustery dawn near midwinter, they arrived.

I had just walked into my uncle's offices and was talking to Ambitus when shouts of alarm echoed along the street. We broke off and looked at each other, knowing what it meant, then ran out and joined the rush to the walls, and gazed out from the ragstone crenels with all the rest.

The Saxons had penetrated as far as London: never in men's memories had such a thing happened. They came not as a fearsome army, as I had imagined in my mind's eye; but as scattered bands of dishevelled men, wandering without order, tall and flaxen-haired under their pillaged Roman helmets, clad in damp half-cured fur, unwashed from the day they were born.

A great silence fell over the city. The gates were closed; the ramparts, though old and crumbled and neglected, would keep the Saxons out. But we were hemmed within, unarmed citizens without an army, like men stranded on an island in the midst of a dangerous sea. We watched smoke pluming from the outlying farmhouses; then, when they were done with that, they burned the fine suburban villas on the south side of the river, which lay beyond the walls.

Next day, one of their black longships appeared on the river. We watched as it put in at the deep-water dock and carried off from the warehouses what they could bear away, setting fire to the rest. The flames were fuelled by oil from the jars they smashed; there must have been a few sacks of spices among them. All that day, wafting over the city with the smoke, came the exotic scent of coriander and roasted cinnamon.

One of the Roman ships, a large merchantman, had

not managed to get away, its captain being too fearful to run the Saxon gauntlet to the open sea. Nor could he move upriver to the safer waters of the city dock, where the walls would protect him, for the keel of his vessel was too deep. He stood with the rest of us and watched grim-faced as the barbarians, their sport at the warehouses done, turned their attention to his ship. It was, he said, his own property, a lifetime's investment. Now he waited to see the first flames lick the rigging.

But no flames came. Then someone, one of his deckhands, cried, 'Look, she's casting off!'

We stared out. A band of Saxons had swarmed on deck. They cut the ship's moorings, and slowly the vessel parted from the quayside, drawn by the tidal current.

The Saxons began jumping about, waving their swords in the air, howling and barking out threats in their uncouth tongue. (There had been a large store of wine in the warehouses.) The captain of the merchantman cried, 'What fools are they? They are bringing her up to the city. Can they not see there is not the depth?'

At this, a shiver of fear spread along the crowd on the wall. The city was weakest from its river side.

But the Saxons had put out before they had mastered the rigging or the steering oar. As the distance from the quayside grew, the current strengthened. Their wild cries died in their mouths. They ran to the starboard rail, scrambled around, then cast out the lanyard to their friends on the shore.

Yet already they were too far out. The lanyard fell short, dropping limply into the water. Slowly the ship yawed out into midstream, gathering way as it was seized by the full force of the current. For a moment they gaped – at the water, at one another, at their barbarian friends gesturing wildly from the shore. Then one leapt, and in quick succession the others followed, dropping into the swirling water like stones, still clad in their heavy furs and sword belts.

Some made it to the far bank; but most we did not see again. Like many seafarers, Saxons are poor swimmers. And then it was our turn to howl and whoop and cheer.

The Council took charge, distributing food from the municipal granaries, organizing work-gangs to pull down derelict buildings for their bricks, which were used to patch up the neglected city wall.

Word was that an old aristocrat by the name of Quintus Aquinus had been recalled from retirement, and Balbus told me it was owing to this one man that the city continued to function at all, for the rest of the Council, the ruling magistrates and the decurions were, he said, incompetent.

I listened to all this with half an ear, not knowing that this man Aquinus would later bring so many changes to my life. At the time I merely reflected that, although Balbus had no good word for the city government, yet he himself had contrived not to serve; and Lucretia had plotted that Albinus, when he came of age and was made a priest, would not have to serve either – Christian priests being exempt from public service by order of the emperor. Little wonder the government was incompetent, I thought, if all men did as he.

Balbus was not a man who was able to cope with leisure. There was no trade, there were no ships, the market was empty, and the gates were closed. He went from the house to the office, and from the office to the house, like a man trying to escape his own shadow.

Lucretia snapped at him, or squabbled with the servants, or went off to pray; and I, to get away from them both, took to spending my time at the baths and the gymnasium.

On one such day, returning by way of the forum, I saw a crowd gathered on the steps of the basilica, waiting under the columns by the high bronze double-doors of the Council chamber. As I approached someone called my name. It was Ambitus.

'What news?' I asked, crossing to him.

'They're talking still. They're going to send another envoy to plead with the emperor.'

'Another? But what of the first? Did the Saxons get him then?'

'Oh, he reached the court safe enough,' he said, giving me a dry look, 'but Constans told him he could spare no men.'

I stared at him. 'Then what does the emperor expect us to do?'

'He says the cities must look to their own defence.'

I cast my eyes over the crowd of frightened citizens – urban poor, merchants, artisans, bureaucrats – and shook my head. These people were no match for the blind, unreasoning violence that the Saxons brought.

We were standing beside one of the great columns. A man near us who had overheard – an old country farmer in a homespun smock – cried, 'Then why are we bled white for taxes, if the emperor will not protect us?'

There were shouts of agreement, and he went on, 'Better to keep our money and raise an army of our own, one that the emperor can't call away whenever it suits him. That's what I say.'

'And who's going to fight in your army, old man?' cried a youth dressed in the drab garment of a minor official. 'Will you?'

'Go on and laugh!' the farmer shouted back, waving his stick. 'I lost everything – my house, my slaves, and all my livestock. You'll be laughing on the other side of your face when you go hungry.'

At this, everyone began arguing.

'Come on, let's go,' said Ambitus.

We descended the steps, and drew away across the great rectangular open space of the forum, with its surrounding colonnade of shops and offices. In the street we paused at a wine-stall. Ambitus ordered two cups of watered wine.

'If you ask me,' I said, leaning on the stone counter beside him, 'that old farmer's right. The Saxons would not be here if Constans had not called the garrison troops away.'

'Perhaps so. But it's not something the emperor cares to hear, and I'm not going to be the one to tell him.' He took a gulp from the cup, spat the wine back out of his mouth, and scowled down into the opaque liquid. 'What's this?' he cried at the stallholder. 'Vinegar?'

The man gave an indifferent shrug. 'The beer's better. You should have asked for that instead. Haven't you heard? There's a siege on.'

Ambitus tossed the contents of the cup on the ground, and, without asking, took a raisin-cake from an earthenware dish on the counter and bit into it.

'What's the matter with Balbus?' I said. 'Have you noticed?'

'Yes, I've noticed. York shook him badly. He thinks death, and Saxons, are something that happen to other people, not him.'

'He said the Saxons would not come.'

'He says what he wants to believe. But now they are here.'

'Do you suppose he is afraid?'

'Come Drusus, aren't you? You'd be a fool if you weren't. You know, I've stopped going onto the walls these last days, because every time I see one of those grinning savages I don't sleep at night. Have you any idea what they would do to us if ever they broke in?' He paused and chewed. 'Well, you've heard the stories; every man has . . . and every woman too.'

He turned and looked towards the great open square of the forum, absently regarding the marble statues that lined the basilica roof.

'Still,' he said, 'we have something to thank the Saxons for.'

'Oh? And what's that?'

He lifted his little black simian brows and gave me one of his ironic looks. 'Haven't you noticed? The Christians are nowhere to be seen. The townsfolk are saying the disaster is a sign of the gods' anger.'

I too had heard this rumour. The old gods had protected Rome. What could we expect, people said, when time-honoured observances were thrown over and ancient shrines desecrated? I thought of the little temple of Isis, in the walled garden near my uncle's house. It had long been the haunt of pigeons and vagrants; but lately, if I rose early and went out before first light, I caught the glimmer of a candle or a lamp in the shadows, and sometimes a morsel of food – an apple or a flat-cake – placed on the threshold as an offering.

With a laugh I said, 'Well, I did not expect I'd find a reason to praise the Saxons.'

But Ambitus looked serious. 'A drowning man will cling to anything, if he thinks it will save him.' He blew down his nose and looked disdainfully at the forlorn crowd, milling about on the basilica steps. 'Look at them; they wait like sheep at feeding time, for someone to tell them they have nothing to fear. Why should the gods listen now? They have never listened before.'

Later I found Balbus sitting alone in his office, by the light of a single lamp. His eyes were puffy and red.

I told him what I had heard at the forum, and he listened in silence, staring into the lamp-flame with such a look of anguish that I wished I had kept the news to myself.

When I had finished he said with a sigh, 'Let the Council send another envoy. And if Constans still will not listen, send another after.' He planted his heavy chin in the ball of his palm and gazed down at the desk. For once it was tidy. I do not know what he had been doing all day. Then, looking up, he said with sudden vehemence, 'But these Saxons are like flies: swat them away and an instant later they are back. We gave them gold. What more do they want?'

There was a scratch at the door; a nervous office-boy edged in, carrying a tray of refreshments. He must have been no more than ten years old. He set the tray down on a side-table, a pretty olive-wood import from Spain with delicate fluted legs, which my uncle had kept for himself.

'Good lad,' said Balbus absently, as the boy withdrew.

I saw the child smile at the acknowledgement and leave happy. In spite of the collapse in trade he had dismissed no one, knowing they had nothing else and would go hungry. It was a secret we kept from my aunt. Reflecting on this, and seeing his bleak face staring at the empty desk, I was filled with a sudden pity for him. He was like a ship becalmed, waiting for a change in an element he could not control.

I went to the side-table, filled a cup from the pitcher and took it to him.

'All this—' he began, gesturing behind him at the racks of stored tablets and scrolls, records of suppliers and transactions and stocks. But he shook his head and did not go on, and stared down into his cup. 'I am truly sorry about your father,' he said, after a long pause. 'We were not close; I suppose you have guessed that for yourself. But he was a decent, honourable man, and you are a credit to him. I know you have not been happy, and I am sorry for it.'

He sighed and looked up. 'You are a young man now. Have you considered what you will do? I may as well tell you, I had hoped you might join me; by God you are more help than that good-for-nothing son of mine, and more deserving.' He shook his head. 'But what is the use of all this effort, unless a man can defend what is his from those who would rather take it than build something for themselves?'

I had been doing some thinking of my own that year, and now I answered, 'We shall drive the Saxons off, Uncle, for we are better men. But only so long as we are willing to fight them. That is why I will be a soldier, if I can find a way.'

He looked at me surprised. But then he slowly nodded.

'You are right. We have lost the will; and soon we shall lose the knowledge too, like the masons who can no longer build as our forefathers did, and know only how to patch and mend. We have grown soft, and entrusted our safety to others, while we sit like women, trembling and helpless behind our walls.'

He gave a long sigh. 'Well, we have brought it upon ourselves. Look at me: I am fat and old before my time, and what use now are the gold coins buried in my cellar? They will not buy me life, or self-respect. Every year the barbarians return, and every year there are more of them. One day they will drive us from the land and burn our cities, and we shall be blown away like lamp smoke in a gale.'

He ceased, and I stared at him. The bleakness of his vision chilled me. I said, 'But Uncle, it need not be so. The Saxons are only men, and so are we.'

He gazed at me like a condemned man peering from the window of his cell. 'The voice of brave youth,' he said. 'Yet sometimes youth can teach old age wisdom.'

He shoved pointlessly at the few papers on his desk. 'Take no notice of me, lad; I am being foolish. Go and become a soldier. I honour you for your choice, whatever others may say. And perhaps, with God's grace, you may do some good.'

Four

HARD WINTER CAME ON. Gales scythed up the river from the east, stripping the last dead leaves from the trees, whipping them in swirling eddies against the white- and ochre-painted walls of the houses. Then the wind swung westwards, bringing low cloud and a steady, fine rain, which sat on one's hair, and crept through winter cloaks and tunics.

Beyond the walls, the Saxons were discovering it was easier to break than to build. They ranged around the treeless flatlands outside the city, wet and hungry; everything that might have sustained them, they had already destroyed.

Then one morning we woke to blue skies and sunlight and deserted fields. All that day the citizens looked out from the walls, not daring to venture outside, suspecting a trap.

The Council convened. It was said that the Saxons,

being unable to take the city by force, had resorted to trickery, withdrawing only to lure us out. The magistrates deliberated and came up with a plan, calling for volunteers. They would lead out a train of carts piled with food and wine-jars from the city store: if the Saxons were lying in wait, these easy pickings would surely bring them out, like meat thrown to starving wolves.

Next day, we watched from the walls as the mule-carts set out into open country, led by a band of nervous men armed – uselessly – with forks and pikes. Everyone scanned the horizon. But nothing stirred in the oak woods on the rising ground to the north; no one emerged from the concealing walls of the ruined farms. The south was clear, all the way to where the hills began to rise and the land was lost from view.

We asked ourselves where the Saxons had gone, and why. Then, on the following morning, came our answer, emerging out of the dawn mist from the east: rank upon rank of armoured men, marching beneath banners of purple and black and gold, with the low winter sun glancing off their burnished helmets and gilded standards – Roman standards, Roman eagles. It was the imperial army.

A great cheer echoed along the ramparts. As news spread, it was picked up by those in the streets, until it seemed the whole city was cheering.

The army halted on the south side of the river, among the burnt-out villas. A troop of horsemen separated from the rest and took the road to the bridge: straight-backed men in plumed helmets and scarlet cloaks; and in their midst, upon a horse of purest white, a man resplendent in a gold cuirass and helmet, trailing a cloak of purple from his shoulders.

I was on the walls with Ambitus. Down the line a voice asked, 'What general is that?'

Someone else cried, 'It's no general, look again! It's the emperor himself, come to save us!'

The man who had spoken began dancing a clumsy jig. Everywhere there was merriment and laughing.

The city gates were thrown open; the magistrates hastily assembled. From across the bridge the emperor approached, accompanied by the officials of the imperial household: the grand chamberlain in a fur-collared cloak bordered with bullion; the under-chamberlains, the Marshal of the Court, the Tribune of the Stable, the Master of Offices, the Count of the Imperial Purse, and, following behind them, in strict hieratic order, their liveried clerks and notaries and quaestors.

The emperor sat rigid like a statue, not looking left or right, his features fixed into a look of sublime arrogance; Constans, youngest son of Constantine, of the house of Constantine, a man less than thirty, with the power of a god.

'Today,' said Ambitus dryly, 'it seems everyone is the emperor's friend.'

I nodded and said nothing, for that was not the place to express what was in my mind. I was glad, in all that noise and wild joy, to have Ambitus's sardonic presence beside me. I felt a strange solitude. I was in no mood to cheer and laugh. Constans may have driven off the Saxon pirates, but all I could think was that below me in the road, riding on his fine white horse, was the man who had decreed my father's death.

'A crossing in winter!' came Balbus's voice, echoing from his study. 'Can anyone remember such a thing?'

'Not I,' said Ambrosius the cloth-merchant, and others spoke up in agreement. Lucretia and Albinus were there, with a crowd of his business friends.

'Ah, there you are, Drusus!' he cried, seeing me at the door. 'Did I not tell you we had nothing to fear? I intend to charter a fleet, and bring in wine and spiced sauces, and glassware and Iberian plate. With the army present, there will be demand for luxuries; and gold to pay for them.'

He laughed with pleasure and beamed at his companions. From the corner Lucretia muttered, 'Praise be to God!' and fluttered her fingers at me in a gesture of dismissal. I left them talking business and money, and went off to find Sericus.

Constans had made landfall on the flat sands near Richborough. The Saxons, having sacked the town and fort there, had moved on, leaving their black longships where they beached them. Our army, advancing inland, had cornered the main horde in the farm country between Dover and London.

What had followed could hardly be called a battle: the Saxons, faced with a wall of locked shields and trained men, had turned and fled. They were scavengers at heart, and thieves; they were content to rape and murder and burn, but they lacked the discipline to organize themselves into a fighting force. They scattered like barn-rats before a pack of terriers, heedless of the safety of their comrades, and as they fled they ran into Constans's second column, advancing from beyond the ridge.

The few that escaped reached the coast only to find their ships burned, and our men waiting.

Constans was no strategist and had sense enough to know it. He brought with him his most accomplished general – his name was Gratian – and placed him in command of the campaign. While Gratian was busy fighting, Constans attended church in London, and the bishop attended Constans, fussing and clucking about him like a mother-in-law at a wedding.

But elsewhere, away from the sycophancy and adulation, people quietly said the old gods had heeded the prayers of the people. They reminded one another that the stormy winter sea had stayed calm while Constans crossed with his bulky troop-carriers, and the sun shone during Gratian's campaign.

The Christians condemned such talk, calling it superstition and devilry. They had a new champion – the emperor himself – who was one of them. And yet, for all the emperor's show of public piety, it was whispered (I heard it from Ambitus) that when it came to deciding upon war or peace, or considering the propitious time for a sea-crossing, it was the astrologers and diviners he turned to, not the Christian priests. These ancient seers would study the motions of the planets, and inspect the dissected livers of beasts, and see in them the answers that he sought.

Gratian soon finished his campaign, then Constans toured the province to receive the praise of the grateful citizens. The coastal fort at Richborough was repaired, and he ordered new ones to be built, in an impregnable line all along the eastern coast known as the Saxon Shore. In future the Saxons would have to take the forts before they could move inland; and the forts, it was said, could not be taken.

The Council commissioned a statue of Constans to stand in London's forum, upon a plinth of polished red granite, in a place of honour outside the basilica, with an inscription proclaiming that he had saved the province. I should not mention this statue – they are common enough, after all – except that it never arrived. It was carved in Gaul, from finest Carrara marble. But the vessel appointed to ship it to Britain was caught in a storm and sank, a detail – or an omen – his advisers prudently kept from the superstitious emperor.

Meanwhile, at the home of Balbus, there was prosperity: he had negotiated a supply contract for the army. Lucretia bought herself a new dress – a cerise gossamer robe embroidered with bees and flowers – and invited her friends to a banquet.

One day during this time, returning with Ambitus from my uncle's shop in the forum, we caught sight of the bishop, passing grandly along the far colonnade with his train of pale-faced acolytes. Lately he was everywhere, publicly calling himself a friend of the emperor.

'See there,' said Ambitus, following him with his eyes, 'just like a fat goose with her chicks . . . you know where *he* was during the siege, don't you?'

'In hiding,' I replied. 'Everyone knows it.'

'That's not what he says now. He says he was praying night and day for the salvation of the city, and it is thanks to him and his god that the Saxons are gone.'

I laughed. 'And who believes *that*?'

'Constans, for one. Have you been to that side of town lately? He's pulling down what's left of the temple of Diana. You'd better take a last look; it'll be gone before month's end.'

'So he's got his cathedral at last.'

'Well, so far he's got a wasteland and a few broken columns; but all the Christians are crowing about it. I'm surprised your cousin didn't tell you . . . isn't that him there, behind the bishop?'

I glanced round. I had not noticed Albinus before, for he was dressed in coarse homespun, like a pauper, and his hood was pulled up. But I should have known his gangling walk anywhere.

We watched him pass along the colonnade, distaste showing on both our faces. Lately Albinus had become even harder to stomach than usual. While the Saxons had sat outside the walls, fear had cowed him. Now all his old traits had returned, made worse by his promotion in the bishop's staff.

Ambitus turned to me. With sudden vehemence he cried, 'I tell you, Drusus, I have had enough of this place! I want to find somewhere without Saxons, and there I shall become a rich man.'

I laughed. He was always so sure. With a grin I said, 'Well, the Saxons are gone for good, so Balbus says.'

At this he threw up his eyes. 'Oh, Balbus! He always

thinks endless summer has come – until the next winter takes him by surprise. But the barbarians are like wolves around the camp fire, waiting in the shadows till the flame burns weak, and the guard nods off. Will he never see it?'

In late January the fine weather that had lasted all winter finally came to an end. The wind swung round to the north-east, and brought with it a biting cold.

With the destruction wrought by the Saxons, and the requisitions of Constans's army, the supply of charcoal became scarce, for there is little woodland around the city. Balbus was better supplied than most; but even we went short, and what there was my aunt Lucretia kept for the house furnace, and the little embossed brazier in her room, which she always kept as warm as summer. Sericus caught a chill; a small matter, he said, and nothing to fuss over.

During February it went to his chest. By the time the first flower buds appeared on the damson tree outside my window, and the crocuses showed like a snowfall in the fields, he had taken to his bed.

I was asleep when he died. Claritas the housemaid shook me awake and led me by lamplight to where he lay, quiet at last. A learned man, he had spent his last years among people who despised him, and treated him like a common slave.

He was sixty-four.

With Sericus's death my final link with home was broken. A terrible emptiness came over me. When I was not working, I idled away my time watching the game players under the arches by the theatre, or wandering among the market stalls and expensive shops in the forum colonnade. I went to the hippodrome to watch the chariot races, or walked out alone beyond the city walls.

I was like a man who has lost his path, but keeps on walking. The drunks, the gamblers, the street pedlars and old retired courtesans who hung about the taverns by the theatre started to know my face, and when I came they greeted me as one of their own. They were hard folk who found a living where they could, who could fall no further, except into death, if that was worse. They were a comfort to me.

At home I grew closed and taciturn, and for the first time there was justice in Lucretia's words when she called me sullen and aggressive. I fell into street-fights. I came home scratched and bruised. Yet there was a yearning in my soul, for what I could not tell.

What preserved me – though I did not see it at the time – were the habits I had been bred to, which little by little had become part of my nature. I rose at cocklight still, and I exercised my body. I pored over Sericus's old books; I clung to life.

Constans sailed away in triumph, conferring the title of count upon Gratian and leaving him behind to order the province.

With peace restored, people dug up the special places in their cellars, or lifted secret flagstones beneath the kitchen pots, or opened bricked-up niches in their walls, and took out the caskets and urns where they had hidden their savings. The smart shops in the forum grew busy;

tools sounded from the workshops; the taverns and wine-shops filled, and the whores around the dock bought themselves bright dresses for the summer.

One day Ambitus, emerging from an interview with Balbus, drew me aside and said with a grin, 'Wish me well. I am away, at last.'

Gratian, he explained, had engaged my uncle to send one of his trading ships to Carthage, to collect the personal effects he had left at his house there. Ambitus was being sent as agent, to supervise this lucrative commission.

I congratulated him. It was what he had worked for.

When, a few days later, I arrived at the dock to see him off, I saw a shrunken old woman clutching at his hand. He pulled away embarrassed; but in a voice invested with more tenderness than I had ever heard from him he said, 'Drusus, this is my mother.'

I greeted her civilly. She was shy and soft-spoken, full of emotion at the departure of her son, and reluctant to look at me, lest I see the moisture in her eyes. She was wearing a pretty new dress, with a necklace of coloured glass. The clothes did not suit her, being made for a younger figure; but I could tell she delighted in them.

Soon the pilot shouted orders to cast off. I stood with her on the quayside, waving to Ambitus.

I missed him when he was gone, though I scarcely admitted it, having persuaded myself I had no need of friends. So I busied myself with my own desultory affairs, and revelled in my solitude.

All about the city were unknown faces: soldiers from the new garrison; pompous imperial clerks in their col-oured liveries; architects and surveyors from Italy and southern Gaul; officials of the civil service; staff of Count Gratian; and the slaves and retinue of all of these.

Gangs of the city poor were put to work clearing the moss and rampant ivy from the neglected walls; masons repointed the crumbling mortar; and Gratian added a new wing to the long-empty governor's palace, where he had taken up residence.

One early morning, a few weeks after Ambitus had sailed, I made my way up to the great precinct in front of the temple of Diana, and watched with a few others – Christians, judging from their cheers – as the last of the mighty granite columns were torn down. The cheers were ugly; the columns had been built to last, and cost the demolishers some effort. Somehow, I was glad of that.

Already, all about the precinct, work had begun on the foundations of the bishop's new cathedral. It would stand, so the triumphant Christians put about, for a thousand years.

Though she disapproved of the baths and the gymnasium, calling them sinful, Lucretia had allowed me to visit them so long as I took Sericus as chaperon. Now that he was dead I went alone, full of anger, defying her to forbid me.

We used to go to the fashionable bath-complex behind the forum, with its high vaulted ceilings and inlaid floors and long ornamental walkways. It was close to home, and considered respectable.

But, during my solitary wanderings, I had discovered another place, in the old part of the city, in the poor neighbourhood between the bishop's residence and the fort, small and run-down, set back from the street under a squat red-painted porch.

It was a place that suited my grim mood. The only patrons were old men who had gone there since they were young, when the neighbourhood had been better. Now they went through habit, and to be with their friends. They sat in twos and threes in the old portico behind, or in the warm room where the heat was gentle, taking no notice of me.

As everyone knows, a youth at the baths can be the object of attention, much of it unwelcome; but here I could exercise in the quiet sand-court beneath the plane trees, undisturbed by anyone.

Until, that is, one afternoon in late spring.

I had arrived at my usual time. I paid the old attendant who sat in his cubby-hole in the vestibule. I stripped, and made my way barefoot over the tiles through to the sand-court at the back.

The old men were in their usual corner under the portico, their stools pulled up, bending over a game of dice. I greeted them, and they muttered back. Then, from behind, I heard the sound of cries and laughter.

I turned to look, and saw what I had come to regard as my private domain occupied by a group of young men, stripped down for exercise, wrestling and tumbling one another, darting and running between the trees of the surrounding gardens.

I glanced back at the old men.

'From the fort,' said one, raising his eyes with a look that said, 'Something else to disturb our peace.'

Frowning I took up my hand-weights and went off

to a sandy corner beside the wall, and soon, going through my movements, I had ceased to think of the strangers. It was a day of sun and passing showers. As I was finishing the rain came on. I was just about to go inside and clean off when I sensed movement behind me, and caught the rank smell of sweat in my nostrils. I swung round, and found myself staring into a gap-toothed ugly, grinning face. He must have crept up at me through the gardens.

The man turned to his friends with a harsh laugh, amused that he had startled me. He was thickset, like a wrestler. His chest and legs were shaggy with black sand-caked hair.

I glanced to the portico, but the dice-players had gone. Looking at him I said slowly, 'You're standing in my light.'

At this the grin dropped from his face. He took a deliberate step forward, blocking me.

'Is that better?' His Latin had the broad accent of Spain.

I ought to have left then. I was no weakling, but I was no match for such a brute. He was broad as an ox. His arms and thighs were knit with great coils of ugly muscle.

But my anger had risen. And so, instead, I locked my eyes on his and said, 'Were you born stupid, my friend, or did the wet-nurse drop you on your head?'

I do not know where I got this from; I daresay I had picked it up from the drunks around the theatre. Somewhere behind I heard his friends slapping their thighs and guffawing. But the Spaniard did not laugh. He flinched as if he had been struck. His black eyes bulged and he jutted his jaw into my face. 'Hey, pretty boy, didn't your mother warn you not to come alone to places like this?'

'Who said I'm alone?' I answered. It was a cheap trick, but maybe he would believe me. I was starting to realize – too late – what I was getting into.

Up above, a sudden breeze shook the branches, scattering drops of cold water. My sweat was drying on me and I shivered. I thought: 'Well Drusus, you have brought this on yourself, will you run now like a coward, or will you take a beating?' Yet even as I thought, already I knew the answer, and there was a kind of rage and self-destructiveness in it.

I would not let this brute trample on my pride, whatever it cost me.

I took a step forward. Immediately his hand sprang out, barring my way. With the other he seized my bare shoulder and hauled me round to face him.

I shoved back, resisting; but I might as well have tried to shift the tree-trunk behind me. I watched him, searching his body with my eyes, waiting for the telltale pull of his muscles that would show he was about to strike.

He was strong, and could hurt me badly; I had not doubted it. But now it came to me that, though he was built like a plough-ox, he was as slow as one too.

With a wrestler's move he flicked me round, trapping my head in an elbow-grip. I could feel his other hand snatching at my waist, trying to gain a hold around my midriff. I struggled and fought, and as I twisted, his seeking hand caught on the strap of my loincloth. He heaved, trying to lift me, but instead there was a tearing sound and my loincloth came away.

He hesitated, confused, staring at the piece of fabric as if some part of my body had been ripped off. Seeing my chance I squirmed and twisted, freed myself from his grip, and landed a heavy kick behind his knee. He yelled out and stumbled. Then, before he could regain his balance, I charged at him. He staggered, paused, tripped over his own thick calves, and with a cry of anger fell heavily backwards into a puddle of rainwater.

Once more his friends were whooping and laughing. But my eyes were on the Spaniard. He lay on the ground, propped on his elbows, glaring up at me. Fear had cleared my head. I thought to myself, 'Time to run, before he breaks my back.' But then he relaxed and fell back with a splash; and lying in the puddle like a vast hairy she-pig he let out a great hoarse laugh.

By now the others were around me, prancing about, slapping me on the back and shoulders, taking my hand and shaking it.

One of them, a sturdy youth with close-cropped hair and blue eyes, called through his laughter to the Spaniard, 'Looks like you've met your match, Tascus. Now leave him be, you great oaf, and pick on men your own size.' He turned to me with a smile and handed me my loin-cloth. 'Take no notice of Tascus: he means no harm; he's been cooped up too long in winter quarters.'

I took the cloth from him. It was rain-sodden and the strap was broken. I wrung it out and began trying to untwist it; then, feeling foolish, I shrugged and left it. 'Are you soldiers?' I asked.

'Is it so obvious?' Then, seeing me look uncertain, he

said, 'Yes, we are; my name's Durano.' He extended his hand, and after a moment I took it. His grip was strong and confident.

The others began walking off towards the portico. He gestured and said, 'Are you coming to clean off?'

I glanced dubiously at the Spaniard. He was strutting up and down, fooling around and shadow-boxing.

'Oh, don't mind him. He wouldn't have hurt you.' He grinned, showing fine white teeth. 'Anyway, you floored him, so I reckon you can look after yourself.'

'I can,' I said, giving him a serious nod. But then he caught my eye and smiled, and I could not help smiling back.

Later, sitting on the stone bench in the hot-room, he asked where my friends were. I told him that, in truth, I had come alone, adding, 'I prefer it that way.'

'Is that so?'

He nodded and frowned into the steam.

Across the room, opaque to my vision, the others were splashing water at one another. With a laugh Durano said, 'They're always like that – games and dares and playing the fool.'

'But not you?'

'Sometimes. I have my moments.'

He dabbed the water with his foot and lapsed into silence. I could almost have supposed he was shy.

After a pause, for something to say, I asked when he had arrived in London, and he told me they had sailed with Constans from Gaul, having been called against all expectation from winter quarters. He had joined the army as a common soldier, he said, but his centurion had thought well of him, and now he had a company of his own.

Once again he fell silent; yet he kept taking glances at me and seemed eager to talk, so gesturing across the steam-haze I asked, 'Are they your men?'

'Them?' He shook his head. 'I know them from before, from my time as an infantryman. But now I head a band of raw recruits. It is better so: this lot know me too well. It's not good to lead the same men you have served with in the ranks, especially when there's discipline to be done.'

I nodded, as if I understood such things.

Later, when we were dressing, Tascus came up and slapped me hard on the back, and asked who it was had taught me how to fight.

'No one,' I said. 'I learned it in the street.' I said the trick I had used to trip him was the only one I knew. This amused him, and he shouted it out to the others, word for word, like the details of some comic story.

From across the room Durano, who was towelling his fuzz of hair, said, 'Then come back tomorrow, and I'll show you a few more tricks.' He finished with the towel, screwed it into a ball, and tossed it into the wicker basket by the door.

'Save your breath, Durano,' said Tascus. 'He's too young for the likes of you. He's afraid. He won't come back.'

'Afraid of what?' I cried. I screwed up my own towel into a ball, and, taking careful aim, threw it into the basket on top of Durano's. 'I'll be here tomorrow; be sure of it. And then I can throw you again.'

100

There was an open-mouthed pause. And then, as I had hoped, they all burst out laughing.

'The bishop promises I shall soon be made a subdeacon.'

Albinus had found me at the table in the servants' kitchen, chewing on some bread.

'That's good,' I said, uninterested.

'Mother will be pleased.'

I carried on eating.

'Anyway,' he said crossly, 'where were you today? I was looking for you.'

'Here and there,' I said, regarding him with suspicious eyes as I chewed.

'At the baths again, I suppose. Your hair's all wet.'

'It's raining.'

'You know what the bishop says about the baths?'

'I know. You've already told me.'

'Baths promote lust.'

I sighed and rolled my eyes. I had heard this many times from him. It was true that the baths, as well as being a meeting place for civilized men, are a market for every kind of vice. The Christian way was to avoid them; and I believe they would have closed them down altogether if they could.

How they felt they honoured their god by staying unwashed I could not understand. As for the rest, that was a man's own choice, and he could not blame the baths for what he chose.

Fixing his eye to make sure he got my meaning, I said, 'Best keep away then, if you cannot trust yourself.'

He huffed, and told me not to be disgusting, and went strutting off.

I had taken my time coming back from the gymnasium. The violence with Tascus, for all it had ended harmlessly, had drained me. But though my muscles hurt, I felt, too, an undertow of excitement and promise. I had already decided I liked Durano, with his fine looks, honest smile, and shining blue eyes; and as I wandered home through the rain I knew I should go back, come what may.

I asked myself what Sericus would have said, or my father. Sericus, no doubt, would have warned me off. As for my father, I had never known him well enough and could not tell. But now, I reflected, kicking my way slowly through the wet streets, both were gone, and my choices were my own.

So next afternoon I returned to the old bathhouse and gymnasium, and found Durano and the others in the sand-court under the plane trees. When they saw me they called out as if I were some long-missed friend, and the old men under the portico shook their heads and shrugged, and returned grumbling to their dice game.

'I thought you would not come,' said Durano.

'Well I am here,' I answered, standing tall.

Tascus came lumbering up beside him. 'Ready for more, young one?' He grinned and caught at my neck.

Durano gave him a good-natured cuff saying, 'Leave him be.' And then, turning to me, 'Come on, I'll show you some moves. It's easy to outwit a brute like Tascus, once you know how. And later, if you want, I'll teach you how to fight off a man with a dagger, and maybe show you some swordwork too.'

And thus it was, in that run-down back-street bath-house, that my training began.

He taught me headlocks and bodylocks, blocks and feints and avoiding moves. I learned throws that could floor a man by using his own strength against him; and ways out of holds that seemed impossible to escape. It was rough work, and though Durano took care not to cause me any serious harm, he was never soft. During those first days I was constantly spitting sand from my mouth, and went home bruised and scratched and aching.

There were days when he had to show me the same thing again and again, and it seemed I should never learn. But then, just as I was beginning to think I had reached my limit and could go no further, I perceived with surprise that I had become stronger and quicker and better, and I was once more fired with the will to press on. If I became angry, or fell hard and cried out in pain or frustration, he would tell me we were not a pair of girls at some harvest-time dance, and if I was serious in wanting to be a soldier – as I had confided to him – I had better attend, for my life might hang on it.

And so, seeing the truth of his words, I would swallow my anger and climb to my feet, ready for another beating.

I was reaching the age where it was clear to me I should never be tall. Albinus, who was taller, goaded me with it, and though I told him I did not care, privately I determined that what I lacked in height I should make up for in strength and wit and sheer ferocity.

103

By the time the planes in the gymnasium court were thick with summer leaves and we were glad of their shade, I was holding my own in my contests with Durano. Then, one day, he arrived with two wooden practice-swords and a pair of wicker shields. He used them to train his new recruits: and now, he said with a grin, it was my turn.

I laughed and took up the toy weapon, and swung it about. I had long been eager for sword-training, which seemed to me the real skill of a fighting man. Always up to now he had held back, saying a man must know how to fight with his hands, and how to move, before he began to hide behind a sword. Good swordsmanship, he said, was not just hacking and thrusting, as many men thought; indeed the real skill lay not in the weapon but in the movements, which is why he had taught me those first.

In Durano's circle there was Tascus the Spaniard, and two others: Romulus, from the remote hills of southern Gaul, and Equitius, tall, fair-skinned, and placid, whose family lived in the wild mountain country that divides Gaul from Raetia.

I soon came to understand that Durano, though he was the youngest, was the quickest-witted, and they deferred to him in most things, trusting his judgement, which seemed sure. Though they were much given to loud horse-play and practical joking, they were straightforward and honest with it, and accepted me with open, artless warmth. They were always shoving and hugging one another, and I, never having known it, at first found their physicality off-putting.

But, like a creature that is made tame by kindness, as the weeks passed I grew used to their touching and feeling and hair-ruffling, and allowed myself, slowly and by careful degrees, to be drawn into their rough male closeness.

Even Tascus, whom for a long time I was wary of, I grew to like, and realized that Durano had been right: he would never have harmed me, for under his harsh exterior he was like a child eager to please.

My new friends took me for what I was. In doing so, they allowed me to become a man I had not been. For the first time since I had come to London, I began to feel happy.

With the daily exercise my muscles filled out and my body grew lean and hard. But the changes were not only outward ones. I grew in confidence, and began to be guided by my own true lights. Nor was it only fighting skill I learned from them. I left Albinus shocked and staring when, after one of his sly digs, I threw out some barrack-room crudity in reply. He broke off from what he was saying and gaped.

'You'd better not let Mother hear you speak like that,' he haughtily declared.

I shrugged. 'Let her hear what she likes.'

But that, I knew, was empty bravado, for all I felt better for saying it. My way of escape was not yet open: I was sixteen; still too young to enlist in the army.

Meanwhile, an uneasy truce had settled between me and Lucretia. She complained to her friends that I was a violent, wicked heathen; but, whatever she had said to Balbus, she had not succeeded in having me cast into the street. I had refused to let her co-opt me into her schemes;

but in spite of this Albinus's career in the Church was progressing. So she kept her distance, and was content to let me know I was despised.

Summer came on. When the weather grew hot we broke from training and, taking me to a spot he knew upstream, Durano taught me how to swim.

This I hated more than anything, and told him so, saying men were no more intended to swim than fly. But he just laughed and said most soldiers never troubled to teach themselves, and when their troopships foundered, or they fell off a pontoon, or slipped fording a river, they drowned for want of a skill easily learned.

I asked him why, this being so, he was any different.

He paused at this, and I saw his face darken.

'Because,' he said, 'of my father.'

His home had stood beside a quick-flowing river prone to flood, and his father had forced him to swim as soon as he could walk; not, he told me, by gentle easy lessons as he was doing, but by tossing him headlong into the icy torrent, then sending the slave to fish him out before he drowned.

I shuddered at the thought, and said his father sounded a harsh man.

'So he was. But I learned fast, and knowledge of swimming has saved me more than once. I suppose you could say I have him to thank, though I should choke on the words before I told him.'

We were together on the grassy bank, drying off in the sun. The hot air smelled of river mud and the faint animal scent of Durano's body lying beside me.

'Where is he now?' I asked.

'At home in Gaul, for all I know.'

'You don't see him?'

'No.'

And then, as if this had been too abrupt, he said, 'I never pleased him; it's easier not to go. Anyway, he has a new, young wife. She doesn't care for me.' He glanced up, and the sun caught his blue eyes. 'Or maybe,' he added with a wry laugh, 'she cares too much.'

He fell silent and frowned out at the flat wooded islet in the middle of the river. We had spent the afternoon swimming out to it and back. Absently, he reached out and touched my side, and traced the contours of my ribs with his finger. He was always doing such things.

'What of your own father?' he said presently. 'Was he a good man?'

At first I did not answer. Instead, I drew back my arm and skimmed a pebble at the water, and watched it hop away. I had told him this and that about myself, when he had asked; but I was uneasy speaking of the past. There was too much pain in it.

'So it is said,' I answered with a shrug. 'But I hardly knew him.'

He nodded and frowned. Before he could speak again I stood and with a wide swing threw another stone – too hard, so that it did not skim, but sliced under the surface and vanished.

For a moment I watched the place where it had gone.

'It's warm,' I said. 'I'm going back in the water.' And I went splashing off through the shallows.

I did not look back.

But I knew his eyes were watching me.

The time of Midsummer festival came.

The Christians, who are patient in their schemes, have tried to usurp it, as they have with all the old high days, knowing the people will continue to celebrate it no matter what they say.

My aunt and uncle and Albinus went off to some banquet of the bishop's. Most citizens, though, were out under the warm evening sky, garlanding the streets with sprays of lilac and broom and honeysuckle, and laying up bonfires in preparation for nightfall.

I waited till the house was empty, then slipped off to see my friends.

We had arranged to meet at a tavern in the old quarter. When I arrived, Tascus, Romulus and Equitius were already there, boisterous and loud from wine. Durano came soon after, dressed in a tunic of dark red, with a flower-garland on his head. I had never seen him look so fine.

He shoved the others along the bench and sat beside me. All around us people were talking and laughing. A great charcoal fire glowed in an open grate, and above it a pig was turning on a spit, filling the air with the smell of roasting meat.

Durano filled my cup, and then his own, and raising it said, 'To you! You too should celebrate tonight.'

Laughing I asked him why.

'Because if you were one of my recruits you'd be ready to pass out, that's why. There's not much more I can teach you; the rest you'll get by yourself – from practice, and from being in battle. So drink and be happy. You deserve it.'

I threw my arm over his shoulder. 'Then we should both be celebrating, you and I, for I have learned only what you taught me.'

'To happiness then!' he cried. We crashed our bronze wine-cups together and drained them, and refilled them from the jar, and drank again.

Tascus, Romulus and Equitius, meanwhile, were discussing at the top of their voices where to go next. Tascus favoured old Phason's place, up by the theatre; Equitius was for taking a turn by the river before the crowds gathered, to decide on a vantage place to watch the bonfires. So we argued, and drank, and laughed, and drank again. Even in that crowded rowdy tavern we were the loudest, shouting out to one another, banging down our cups when they were empty, and bawling out for the serving-boy.

Romulus had heard there was music and dancing in the forum, and so, in the end, we decided to go there. By then Hesperus was risen, shining like a beacon low in the pale dusk sky, and when we reached the forum the torches were flaring high in their cressets along the wall of the long colonnade. There were pipes and flutes and tambourines. Someone pulled me into the throng of dancing people, and for a while, reeling and leaping, I lost sight of the others. But then I felt a hand on my shoulder, gently urging me away.

I turned. 'Come,' said Durano, his face lit by wine and firelight, 'let's walk awhile.'

We edged out of the press, our arms slung around one another, and at length came to the city wall. Then we climbed the foot-worn ragstone steps to the high walkway. From the top Durano pointed, saying, 'See there.'

I looked out. I had forgotten the bonfires. They had been kindled in the age-old tradition, and were blazing up into the star-flecked sky, yellow flame and rising red-glowing embers, dotted across the dark land, with tiny hopping figures dancing around them.

'A fine sight,' said Durano, drawing me close.

I agreed, and for a while gazed out in silence.

Perhaps it was no more than an effect of the wine – for I had drunk a good deal – but, as I stood looking out from the walls, a surge of joy ran through me, clear and pure, like a note of music. I felt my soul straining against the tether of my body, like something shining and entire. Wishing in some manner to share what I felt, I leaned to Durano and kissed his cheek. He smiled; and after a short pause he returned it.

We stayed for some time, alone in the warm night, until eventually a crowd of drunken revellers came stumbling and shouting along the walkway, and the perfect thread was broken.

'Come on,' said Durano, frowning at their noise, 'let's go and look for the others.'

We found them in the thick of the dancing still, reeling and stumbling and laughing – and very drunk. Seeing us they pulled us in. I do not know how long we remained, leaping about and falling; but by the time we moved on, my head was spinning and everything was warm and hazy and amusing.

Burly, ugly Tascus led us on, pressing ahead through the crowded streets towards the quarter behind the theatre, shouting out that the time had come for better things than dancing.

I knew from my own private investigations this warren of alleyways and courtyards – and its reputation too. To be sure, there are taverns in abundance. But it is not for drinking that the area is known.

We pushed and stumbled our way along the street. For some reason Durano was reluctant: but we all urged him on with the usual lewd jokes, and soon we came to a garlanded two-storey house, painted with curling vine-stalks, and lit outside with flaring torches.

'Oh, by the Mother, not Phason's,' cried Durano.

'Come on!' yelled Tascus and I together, pulling him in.

We entered a low smoky crowded room. There were tables, each with its own little lamp, shaded with a cover of fretted earthenware – the kind of thing one sees in eating-houses, when they want to give themselves an air of something special.

I had never been inside Phason's before, but Tascus and Romulus were clearly well known, and as we pushed in among the tables they shouted greetings to friends, and slapped shoulders, and grabbed proffered hands. Some of the patrons were busy at dice or knucklebones; but for most it was the girls that were the attraction.

Phason himself came bustling from the back. He was a large Syrian with a black bush of beard and jangling bracelets. With a good deal of elaborate greeting he conducted us to a free table, and clapped his fat hands for the serving-slave. The wine came quickly, and with it the girls, wearing low-cut dresses of see-through orange silk, open at the sides. One squeezed in between Tascus and Romulus. The other pushed Durano along the bench, then edged in next to me.

'Hello,' she said, reaching across me to fill her wine-cup and mine. 'My name's Brica. What's yours?'

I told her. She was emaciated and grey-skinned, with red-painted lips, and cheeks smudged with carmine. She looked as if she were sickening with a fever.

As she wriggled in beside me, her tiny dress rode up. I noticed she had a large yellow bruise on her thigh, high up near the groin. She reached out and began toying with Durano's close-cut fuzz of hair, plucking and smoothing the little soft tufts, saying it was like a puppy's. Durano flinched. He seemed not to like this; after a moment, when she did not cease, he removed her hand.

Then, pouting, she turned back to me.

'That's a nice name,' she said, making eyes at someone across the room. From her hot body came the odour of cheap perfume, and female sweat.

I made some answer and drank. Across from me, Romulus was laughing like a man possessed, though no one had said anything funny; and Tascus's thick face was a mask of concentration as the girl beside him jabbered some nonsense about her earrings. His thick, hairy hand, I noticed, had slipped beneath the table, and was moving slowly in her lap.

I rubbed my eyes. My head was spinning from the wine. Now that I had sat down, I could feel a vague rising sickness in the pit of my stomach. I asked myself why I could see nothing beautiful in these women, when the other men clearly saw so much.

The girl had hooked her calf around mine. I could feel her sharp toenails scratch my skin. She kept giggling and pulling faces at her friend opposite. I glanced at Durano, wishing he would talk to me. But his head was down and he was looking glumly into his wine-cup.

Over the weeks I had known them, along with all the other jokes, there had been the usual banter about women. Tascus and Romulus were the worst. Durano, at such times, said little, though once I heard him say, when Tascus was holding forth, that he was all talk and no action. As for me, I had my own reasons for silence, never having mentioned – not even to Durano, with whom I was closest – that I had never been with a woman.

It was not that I had not thought about such matters. Once I had even ventured alone to one of the city's many whorehouses, to test myself against what was to be found there. But, after a cup of rancid wine, Albinus's prurient fantasies had come swimming into my head, and even before the girls came to join me I had got up and walked out, tossing a coin onto the table as I left.

Afterwards I told myself I had other things to think about than women; and this was true, or partly true.

The girl Brica kept filling my cup and urging me to drink. And I drank, for it took the edge off my uneasiness. I cannot recall how I ended up upstairs. I remember seeing Tascus, lolling drunkenly in the dim-lit passage-way, with a girl on each arm; I remember the smoky corridor, hot and noisy and crowded. And then I was in a lightless room.

113

I looked around, blinking. In the corner a tiny lamp glowed under a shade of blue glass. The air was heavy with the smell of sweet incense. I shook my head to stop it spinning, and as I turned I saw a movement. A slender figure had stopped in front of the lamp; I realized I was not alone.

I shivered, though it was not cold. I think I spoke out; but the touch of a hand in mine silenced me, and drew me down to a shadowy, tousled bed.

I reached out and felt an arm and naked shoulder. A mouth came up to mine, and a little darting tongue forced itself between my lips. Then a hand rested on my thigh, and began gently, expertly pushing up under my tunic. I closed my eyes, and felt my reeling senses start to respond.

I do not know how long it was before I opened my eyes again. Only a few moments. I saw the blue lamp and a three-legged bedside table; and then, slumped in the corner, its dead painted face staring up at me, a child's doll. It came into my clouded consciousness that the girl had offspring. Well, I thought, no surprise there. Yet it troubled me all the same, and I pushed the thought from my mind.

The girl shifted, touching my body, pulling herself up, intending, I think, to position herself on my lap.

The shock of realization, when it came, hit me so hard I gasped out loud. It was all I could do not to strike her away; but forcing myself to be gentle I eased her off me and stared. Between my strong hands she was trembling, like a small bird when you cup it in your palms.

'What is wrong?' she said, the first words she had spoken.

Then I knew.

Pointing to the corner I managed to say, 'Whose is that?'

'Oh,' she said brightly, 'that's Poppaea. She's mine. Do you like her?'

'*Yours?*' My voice was shaking.

She returned her hand to my groin, grasping and impatient, eager to complete what she had started. I leapt back as if scalded.

'What is it?' she cried, and there was a new harshness to her voice, 'am I not pleasing?'

I stared, straining to see her in the gloom. 'How old are you? Tell me how old.'

'Why, ten next birthday,' she answered. 'Mother says I may have a sister for Poppaea if I'm good.'

'You're *nine*,' I whispered. I reviewed in my mind the moments that had passed, as a man might consider the bites he has taken from an apple, before he found the worm lurking in its core. 'But where is your mother?'

The child gestured at the wall behind. In the silence I could hear, through the partition, a rapidly creaking bed, and a man grunting, and a female's bored encouragements.

A wave of nausea and grief swept over me. I brought my hand up to my eyes, as if to block out what my mind saw.

'What is it?' she said, pawing me. 'What is wrong?'

'Don't touch me. I have to go.' I pushed her away and stood. She grabbed my arm, but I shook her off. In a little plaintive voice she called behind me, 'Don't say I didn't please you. Please don't say; or they will beat me.'

I halted then, and punched the tears from my eyes with the flat of my palms.

'Never fear, little one,' I said. And then, remembering what she was at, I reached in my belt for a fistful of coins.

'Here!' I said. 'Take this. Take it and show them, and tell them that you pleased me.'

In the passage outside I paused, gathering my wits, such as were left to me.

The air was rank with lamp-smoke and stale incense. From downstairs I could hear raucous laughter, suddenly devoid of merriment or joy.

I could not bring myself to face the others. I stepped the other way, along the dimly lit corridor, looking for an exit at the back. As I went, a crone emerged from an alcove and jabbed out an obstructing arm. She must have been waiting there.

'You were quick,' she said, eyeing me suspiciously. 'Was she no good? Or,' she added, leering and showing black teeth, 'was she too good?'

I felt my fists tighten. It is a wonder I did not strike her. She looked at me, and opened her mouth to speak; but whatever she saw in my face made her blanch. Then, before she could utter another word, I had shoved past her. By the time I heard her angry, crow-like voice I was halfway down the back stairs to the street.

Outside I paused, leaning forward, resting my hands on my knees. My eyes were burning, not with tears, but with fury.

Presently I stood up straight and looked around. I was in a narrow alley behind the tavern. There were piles of rubbish. The air stank of rotting food and urine. On this side of the building there were no welcoming torches burning, but I was used to darkness now, and I hurried away before anyone came looking.

I cannot recall what path I took. Soon I came to a quiet square of old shuttered houses, with a tall ancient oak growing in the middle.

There was a stone bench beside it, and I sat. My hands had started shaking. I could taste the child's tongue in my mouth and saw, if I closed my eyes, the grimacing painted face of the hideous doll. I spat, then wondered why.

After some while, when I had regained a little self-command, I got to my feet and walked on; and when I passed a tavern I went in and downed a cup of wine, and then another, and then a third.

But what I was feeling was not to be cured by wine. Eventually I stumbled out, my head spinning, and threw up at the nearest corner.

FIVE

THAT SUMMER, BALBUS'S SHIPS began to arrive. From Spain they brought olive oil and preserved sauces; from Sicily wine in tall pitch-sealed amphoras; from Italy marble, and little straw-packed boxes of Etrurian jewellery.

His greatest pleasure, however, came on a sleek trader from Egypt. It was the smallest ship of all those he had chartered, but it bore the richest cargo: Arabian frankincense; Indian saffron; essence of violets and hyacinth and cedar; unguents in alabaster, precious lotions, and finely blended oils, all prepared to the closely guarded recipes of the perfumeries of Alexandria.

In that one summer, even without his other business interests, his fortune was made.

Ambitus too returned, on the ship bringing Count Gratian's furniture from Africa. I went down to the wharfside to greet him, and to hear his news.

Gratian, though he came of rough Pannonian peasant-stock – or perhaps, as Ambitus said, because of it – had a passion for fine furniture and precious artworks. He collected them like a jackdaw. He had purchased crystal goblets and jewel-encrusted caskets from Asia, paintings from Athens and Constantinople, antique wine-kraters from old Corinth; and, from wherever he found them, gilded tripods, mahogany chests, and fine marquetry cabinets. He had acquired, in short, beautiful objects from across the empire, treasures indeed that an emperor would have been pleased to own – which is why he kept them at a discreet distance from the court.

Gratian had begun life, I learned, as a common soldier in the ranks, and it is doubtful he would have risen so high, except that as a young man he possessed a particular skill in wrestling.

It was this that got him noticed. One day, during a bout, a senior officer partial to wrestlers was watching; and thereafter Gratian was singled out and promoted. He was found to be able; he had risen fast.

Now, in grizzle-haired middle age, with a distinguished army career behind him, he preferred to forget his rude beginnings, and adopted the outward trappings of a gentleman.

News of the upturn in my uncle's fortunes spread around the city, even without Lucretia's careful sowing. Suddenly the house was full of well-wishers and old friends, who felt it was time to renew their acquaintance.

Lucretia gloried; Balbus was civil, thanked them for putting themselves out, said he was pleased to see them again after so long, and told them he hoped they would excuse him, but he had work to do.

That summer a new obsession had seized my aunt. She

had conceived, from her friends, that a family of quality must possess a country villa. She nagged and wheedled, reminding Balbus that trade in land was slow and prices still depressed after the terror of the Saxons. There were excellent bargains to be had, which in a year would cost half as much again.

She was shrewd as a stoat. She knew the right bait to bring in her quarry. She had heard, she said, that there was a perfect villa for sale, out west, in pleasant rolling country. Balbus could return to London easily by river whenever he chose; meanwhile she would take up residence, and decorate, and entertain. What could suit him better? But he must hurry and make up his mind: already she had heard from Volumnia that there were others interested, and such a bargain would soon be snapped up.

She got her house, of course. Then Volumnia reminded her she needed furniture, and it all began again.

All this I shared with Ambitus, amid much laughter. But I did not tell him about Durano and the others, and when he eyed my muscled arms and broad shoulders and asked what I had been doing, I said I had exercised a little, and quickly changed the subject.

Since Midsummer Eve I had stayed away from the little back-street gymnasium with its red-painted porch. Like many a self-deceiver, I scarcely acknowledged what I was doing, even to myself. I persuaded myself that it was only this or that petty chore that held me back, and I should return tomorrow, or perhaps the day after. But, as the old wives say, tomorrow never comes, and each day away made returning harder.

I felt shame, and self-disgust; and, with it, some unclear notion that my friends had contrived to make a fool of me. I was, I told myself, no better than Albinus, for all my wishing otherwise. Night after night I lay awake in my bed, stifling in the summer heat, trying to remember and dissect every detail of how I ended up in the child's room. Surely I did not go there of my own accord, knowing what lay within. But the more I tried to recall what had happened, the harder it became, like a man who reaches into a pool, trying to touch his own reflection. I reminded myself, truthfully and with relief, that little had taken place, and I had fled as soon as I knew. But I started to have bad dreams.

They began with some pleasing image, of a pretty girl or – worse still – of my mother; but they always ended the same, with the staring doll and the child in the room, pawing and pleading, trying to thrust her squirming body upon me.

I would cry out, and jolt awake wet with sweat, and find the sheets coiled around me, or in a heap upon the floor. Then, lest the dream return, I forced myself to lie awake, staring up at the roof-beams, fearing sleep.

I remembered the tales of the snake-haired Furies, daughters of Night, older even than the old gods, who pursue men for crimes too terrible to mention and drive them into madness. Could it be that I had awakened them? Was I guilty, deep within my secret soul? I was like a man who in an unexplored cellar of his house finds a door that leads far below, to a fearful pit he had not conceived of. I saw that door in my mind's eye, and stared at it transfixed. But I dared not open it.

Such thoughts haunted me, filling my nights. By day a semblance of perspective returned, and I knew I missed my friends, Durano most of all.

I reminded myself that, out of all of us, it was he who had resisted going to the tavern; and how I had joined with Tascus, Equitius and Romulus in urging him on against his will. I asked myself what kind of man I was, that I should blame him, when it was I who was at fault?

And so finally, one afternoon, goaded by remorse, and recalling some sense of the justice I owed to others, I made my way to the baths to find him.

Nothing was changed. The sour-faced attendant was still in his cubby-hole at the entrance. The old men were still at their dice-games beneath the colonnade.

But Durano was not there.

I went next day, and the day after, and each day for a week. Finally, on the last day, I ran into tall, placid Equitius in the changing-room.

'Where have you been?' I cried. 'Where are the others?'

He frowned at my shouting. Out of all of them, Equitius was the one I had conversed with least. Indeed, he had so little to say that I had even thought him rather simple. But I learned, this day, that I had been wrong.

'Well where were you?' he answered shortly.

I told him some nonsense about having been busy; and when I saw in his face he did not believe me, I resented it.

'Durano is not here,' he said, returning to strapping

on his sandal, 'nor are the others. The army is transferring out. He left with the advance party. He would have come to tell you, if he knew where you lived.'

'He could have found me,' I said, sulking.

'And you could have found him.'

I shrugged. I think, in my heart, I already knew the truth of it, for which I had no words.

'Ah well,' I said, affecting indifference and turning for the door. 'I expect I'll see him here sometime.'

'I doubt it. He left half a month ago, and so did the others. I'm the last, and I'm about to ship out.'

At this my foolish attempt at nonchalance collapsed. I turned and gaped. I felt as though someone had slammed a punch at me, and I suppose my feelings were written on my face.

'Why don't you wait?' he said, less harshly. 'I'm almost finished. I'll walk with you.'

So I waited, awkward and shuffling at the door, while he tied his sandal and buckled his belt, and mussed his fleecy blond beard in the old mirror of polished bronze.

He did not speak until we were outside in the street. Then he said, 'You are angry. Why?' And when I shook my head he said, 'By the Bull's blood, Drusus, I may be a mountain peasant, but I know what I see. It's not my business, but did Durano do something to offend you?'

I shrugged. 'No.'

He let out a long patient breath.

'It was you who disappeared. You must have known how he would take it.'

I replied that I did not know what he meant; and at

this he cried, 'Come, Drusus, you are young, but not that young. I never saw Durano so taken with anyone, boy or girl, as he was with you. Are you telling me you had no idea?'

I felt my face redden to the ears. I hardly knew where to look. So I stared at the cobbles in the road.

'I suppose I wondered,' I said eventually. Then, after a pause, 'Did he say anything?'

'He's not one to talk of such things. But he was miserable; that much was clear. That night he thought you'd found a girl – we all did – and what harm is there in that? But I suppose he was hoping for something else, and when you didn't come back, day after day, he took it badly . . . It must have been quite a girl, to keep you away for so long.'

I shook my head. 'No,' I said. 'It wasn't that.'

'Then what?'

'Something happened. I don't remember, Equitius . . . or only parts. I can't speak of it. I was drunk.'

'Who was not?' – and, when I said nothing – 'Tascus, that great wit, told him you had tasted better wine than his. He always manages to say the wrong thing. After that, when I told Durano to go and look for you, he said he was not your keeper. But I think he was afraid of what he might find.'

'I wish he had come looking.'

He gave me a long, considering frown. 'You are a hard one to fathom, young Drusus. I would have sworn . . . but never mind. Durano is not the kind who snatches food from another's table. He might have been fond of you, but he has his pride.'

124

He drew his breath to say more; but instead he glanced up frowning. I followed his gaze. We had rounded the corner. Ahead, at the bottom of the street, there was some sort of commotion, and as we approached, a group of soldiers came stumbling out of a tavern and began shouting ribald abuse at the innkeeper. I could hear him from somewhere inside, yapping angrily back at them.

'They will be in for it,' said Equitius, 'drunk when they're supposed to be packing.'

'When are you leaving?'

'In the morning, with the tide.'

'So soon?' I said wretchedly. I looked up into his face, which cost me some effort. But there would be no other chance, and so I said, 'It is my fault. I did not know my own mind.'

He reached out and rubbed my shoulder, and gave me a smile.

'Do not trouble yourself overmuch. What's done is done. After all, it is in some men's natures and not in others'. Durano should have guessed. He will get over it.'

I nodded at this. But in truth his words had fallen wide of the mark. It was not my nature that had held me back, I saw it now. It was something else: a weakness, a shyness, a fear of showing my naked, barren soul to another.

He had been right: though I was young, I was not so young I did not have some sense of what Durano was about. If I had minded, I could have withdrawn; yet I had remained by my own choice, bathing in his attention, learning from him, filling my days with his company. And, during it all, whatever he may have hoped for in his heart, he never demanded anything from me in return.

125

What right had I, I asked myself, to feel aggrieved? Though I knew my spelling and grammar and numbers, to my own heart I was a stranger. I had learned to fight, and liked to think myself brave. Yet, through it all, I had not the courage to face myself. I shook my head. Durano had not asked, and I had not given. Was I really so blind?

We were drawing close to the rabble from the tavern. One of them, falling-drunk, called out to Equitius because he knew him.

Equitius cursed under his breath. 'Listen,' he said, stopping in the street, 'you don't want to get caught up with this lot.' He looked at me. 'Shall I say anything to Durano?'

One of the soldiers cat-called; and when I looked, made a lewd unmistakeable gesture. I suppose he thought I was some clinging bath-boy Equitius had picked up and could not shake off. My face burned. It filled me with shame to be taken for such a creature.

'No,' I said. 'Leave it.'

'As you wish. Well, I must go.'

He hesitated. Then, leaning forward he kissed me on the cheek; and outside the tavern the drunken soldiers cheered, and whistled through their fingers.

Three days passed. I could not settle to anything.

Equitius, in his straightforward way, had shown me what I could not, or would not, face. I felt the absence of my friends. I realized, now that it was too late, that I had assumed Durano would be waiting when I was ready to return. I grieved – for time wasted, and words left unsaid.

But then Balbus received the deeds to his new villa, and announced he had hired a pleasure-barge to take us upriver.

'Leave me in London, sir,' I said.

But he cried, 'No, no; come and enjoy yourself, my boy; you have been looking peaked these past days; the change will do you good.'

The barge was my aunt's idea. She summoned her friends to see her off, and they stood on the quay beside the dock-workers, vying to outshine one another in their fine jewels. Volumnia was at the front, in a low-cut dress and an array of rubies set in Keltic silver, wearing one of her blonde German wigs. She cast a pinch-faced glance at me, and snapped her head away when I looked. I was loathed by all Lucretia's friends.

The oarsmen pushed out. Lucretia took her place under the garlanded canopy, and I went to sit at the front beside the anchor, away from her ceaseless chatter.

At another time, I daresay an escape from the city would have pleased me. But I was in no mood for Lucretia and Albinus. As for the villa, I took little interest, not knowing then what it would bring for me. It was a pretty enough place, run-down, with rain-stained, pink-washed walls, set within an old orchard. It lay down a dusty track, about a mile from the river. A small tributary brook flowed on the eastern side, shaded by a thick line of rowan and willow.

We passed under the gateway, into a walled inner

court thick with unkempt bushes of yellow honeysuckle. The stables and outhouses, which filled one side of the courtyard, stood abandoned and broken; but the agent, on my uncle's orders, had travelled ahead to tidy the main house. Hearing our approach he came hurrying from within – a dapper, fast-talking city man – just as Lucretia was stepping down from the curtained carriage.

She scowled at the stained and flaking walls, and the ruined outhouses dense with brambles and nettle. 'What are all these plants?' she enquired, fluttering a hand at the chaos and decay.

'An aspect of farming, madam,' answered the agent quickly. 'It can soon be cut back if the lady requires it, and of course the house can be repainted . . . But we were advised' – with a nod at Balbus – 'that you may wish to make changes, to modernize and decorate, and with a new mistress such as yourself, who is known in London for fashion and refinement, I did not think it my place to impose my own tastes upon the property without consulting you.'

Her aggressive expression softened. The agent, seeing she was taken in by this patter, continued talking, at the same time conducting her to the porch, where the servants were waiting in an obedient line. I left them and wandered off to explore. Albinus came following grumpily behind.

He had sulked all the way from London, and bickered with his mother. He hated the country; why had she forced him to come, when he had things to do in the city? The motion of the barge made him feel sick. He was too hot. He was hungry. He was bored. Eventually Lucretia, reclining on a pile of silk cushions under the canopy, while she picked languidly at a bowl of sweets, snapped at him that he was spoiling her special day, which she had looked forward to all year, and if he was hot he had better put his hat on. At this he threw the hat in the bilge and came up to the bow to sit with me, and grumbled under his breath about her.

So today he was my friend. Now, seeing me wander off, he came trailing after me, with many a backward resentful glance at his mother.

'Wait, can't you!' he cried as I stepped out beyond the courtyard.

I waited, kicking at the grassy pathway while he snatched, cursing, at his sandal strap, trying to free a stone.

To the east, following the edge of the grounds, the brook looped round a low, wooded hill and disappeared northwards between fields and woodland towards the river. Nearer the house, in what must once have been gardens, there were overgrown remains of terraces and crumbled trelliswork. The whole place had an air of lush desolation, and I half expected, if I dug through the rampant shrubs, to find forgotten dried-up fountains and the marble plinths of statues.

'Where are you going?' demanded Albinus. He glanced back at the house. Through the courtyard archway, the servants were unloading Lucretia's baggage. I could see his mind working in his sulky face: she liked to know where he was. He was considering whether to tell her, or punish her for being sharp with him. After a moment he sniffed and hurried on after me, slapping irritably at the overhanging branches as they caught his hair. Just then the desire to irk her was uppermost.

The path narrowed and steepened. We came to steps cut into the rock, old and foot-worn and soft with moss. On one side, down a slope of rowans and fern, I could see the brook glittering in diffused shafts of sunlight. Someone had built a dam of boulders and branches, and a pool of clear water had formed behind, a perfect place to swim.

'You swim if you want to,' muttered Albinus. 'I'm not going in there.'

He hated water like a cat.

We went the other way, climbing the steps. At the top of the hill the path opened into a clearing dominated at its centre by an ancient brown-barked yew, surrounded by oaks and twisting hazel. I paused and looked about. There was a pleasing balance to the place, like the precinct of a temple.

Albinus, meanwhile, had gone wandering off, and after some moments I heard him call out, in a voice tinged with disgust, 'Come here! Look at this!'

He was standing on the far side of the yew, beside a great block of rectangular stone, frowning down at it. The sides were rough and lichen-covered; but the surface, I saw, had been carefully smoothed, and at the edge there was a shallow channel.

'It's an altar,' he said, twisting his face with distaste. He traced his chewed finger-end along the line of the groove. 'See? This catches the blood, and over there is the run-off. Filthy pagans! I hate it here. Why did Mother choose this place?'

Lucretia, in her haste to acquire a country villa, had not thought it necessary to come and view; and Balbus, who was not interested, had left everything to the agent.

I picked at the pale-green lichen. As I turned, something caught my eye. On the ground lay a garland of forget-me-not, bound with a sprig of straw. The flowers had scarcely begun to wilt.

Deciding it would be best to keep this find to myself, with a tap of my foot I eased the little garland out of sight, into a thicket of tall grass at the base of the stone. But Albinus had an eye for the surreptitious. 'What's that?' he cried, snatching it up. He peered at it; then cast it to the ground and trampled it with his heel.

'Why do that?' I shouted at him.

'It's horrible! It's an offering, no doubt from one of those miserable house-slaves. I thought there was something sly about them. Wait till Mother hears; she will turn them out before nightfall.' It was an aspect of Lucretia's religion not to have any servant in the house who did not believe, or profess to believe, what she did. At the house in London, only the Spanish cook seemed to have escaped this rule.

Albinus now became suddenly animated. He began pacing up and down, peering about in the sun-dappled clearing in case there was something else to find. The sun had scorched his nose during the journey, leaving a red blotch between his brows. His thin lips were pressed closed with indignation – an expression he got from his

131

PAUL WATERS

mother – and as he strutted about he prodded clumsily at
the undergrowth with his foot. He looked, I thought, like
some light-hating creature, dragged out unwillingly in
daytime from its lair.

I said, 'You don't have to tell her, you know. It was
just a garland, just flowers. Anyone could have left it.'
Then, deciding to employ a little of his deviousness, I
picked up the trodden flowers and added, 'If we wait a
few days we may discover who left this, for surely they
will return, and then you will catch them.'

He narrowed his eyes at me. After a moment his
mouth formed into a smile.

'Yes, a trap,' he said. 'You shall keep watch and report
what you see. Do you understand? And then I'll decide
whether to tell Mother.'

'Just as you say, Albinus.'

I walked off. After a moment, with a cry for me to
wait, he followed.

We arrived back at the villa to a great commotion. The
servants were rushing about, looking fearful and bewildered; from within I could hear Lucretia's scythe-like
voice, lashing out, and the agent in between, attempting
to reason with her.

I thought at first it was something the servants had
done; but as I entered through the atrium I heard Lucretia
shout, 'I don't care if it is fine work or not, get rid of it. I
shall have no sleep till it is gone. I cannot rest with it
here.'

She must have heard us. She rushed from one of the inner rooms, followed by the pale-looking agent and Balbus.

'Where have you been?' she cried at Albinus. 'Did you not hear me calling?' This was mere ritual complaining; her heart was not in it. Albinus started to answer, but she pushed past him through the doorway behind, into the dining-room. 'See this obscenity!' she cried pointing, her voice rising in pitch as her anger possessed her, 'I cannot bear it! I will not live in a house that is not decent.'

Full of curiosity, we followed her in through the high doorway with its pilasters of red marble.

The dining-room was spacious and light-filled, part square, part oval, with a large curving bay facing west-wards and bathed in afternoon sun. There were couches and a table – for the dining furniture had come with the house. Where the dust-sheets had been removed, I could see the decorated cushions of rich dark-red damask, with a pattern of ivy-twined urns picked out in green and gold.

But Lucretia was not concerned with the furniture. Her staring eyes were fixed on the space behind where, half in shadow, a trompe-l'oeil fresco filled the wall. Within a cascading border of creeper-twined columns and garlanded lyres, it showed an outdoor dining scene of couches and tables, set among shading cypress trees. The diners, having finished their banquet, had turned their attention from the overladen tables to one another. A man sat entwined with two adoring girls on one couch; two youths lay on another, with an older woman laugh-ing in between, all semi-clad in falling silks and festive wreaths, while from the shadows on one side naked Bacchus looked on from a vast wine-krater, goat-legged and smiling.

It was a lush, sensuous scene, vivid and over-ripe; but there was nothing gross, nothing that was not human; and the work was, as the agent had protested, finely done.

But Lucretia would have none of it. 'You told me the house was decorated with taste, but everywhere I look is an invitation to sin and debauchery. Why was I not warned?'

The agent made a helpless gesture. Clearly he saw nothing wrong.

'I will tell the decorator to touch it up,' he said.

'Touch it up?' she cried. 'Touch it up? I want it chiselled off, all of it, chiselled off and buried. Every room is an offence.'

Balbus caught my eye and looked away. Albinus said, 'What debauchery?'

'Don't start!' she snapped, rounding on him. 'Why didn't you come when I called you? Anyway, the bedroom is far worse.'

She was right. In the main bedroom, opposite a large heavy bed-frame, another fresco had been painted in the same style, but this time instead of revellers there was Pan – hairy, horned, point-eared and priapic, pursuing an epicene youth.

'Is that a girl or a boy he is chasing?'

'Don't be prurient, Albinus!' She turned to the agent. 'You see? Already my child is corrupted. It must be removed at once, all of it, cut away, filled in, plastered and painted over. I wonder that you recommended such a house – what kind of woman do you suppose I am? What kind of family lived in such a place?'

'I believe the owner lived alone, madam.'

'I am not surprised. See to the work, and get out of my sight.'

But in the days that followed, while the house was full of the sound of masons' tools and the reek of paint, the previous owner seemed to prey on Lucretia's mind. She cross-examined the servants; but they were slow, rural folk, made halting and inarticulate by her hostile questioning – or so they affected in her presence. The old Master, they said, had been a kindly man. He had removed to Italy, to somewhere near Naples, where the weather would suit him better. He had liked to entertain when he was younger; no, they could not recall a wife; certainly no wife had lived with him at the house, though there were many friends who came and went. He was often away, for he liked to travel. They could not comment on his religion, and her questions on this subject seemed to bewilder them.

'But my dear, what does it matter?' Balbus said to her eventually.

'It matters to me,' she retorted.

Balbus, who knew how to read the danger signs, said no more.

But Lucretia's fantasy of country life had been shattered. From that day, everything was wrong. Each painted urn and ornamental border, each dancing figure or scene of woodland calm, carried for her some hidden hateful meaning which she strained to discover; and soon the meandering patterns, and dryads, and river vistas were lost under a veil of bland whitewash, or, if they were mosaics, of damp-smelling raw plaster.

Next she discovered a colony of ants in the atrium; then she complained of the silence, which unsettled her. The slaves, she said, were slow and stubborn, and she had already quarrelled with the housekeeper, who was, she declared, a stupid, vicious woman.

It was Albinus, with unusual insight, who revealed what lay behind her ill temper.

'There is one thing,' he said to me, 'she did not think to bring.'

'What's that?'

'An audience. Maria and Placentia and that old bitch Volumnia are not here for her to impress, and what pleasure is there without it?'

I laughed. He even laughed too, with his odd, braying fox-bark noise. No one could say he did not know his mother.

Lucretia's irritation was increased by Balbus. He had not wanted to be parted from his work, but now he seemed to be enjoying himself. He made light of her complaints; and then, one day, he announced that he intended to go hunting, like a country gentleman.

'Hunting? Whatever for? Can't you send one of the slaves? I shall not go.'

'No, my dear, of course not. You stay and see to the decorating. The house is looking much better; I told you not to fret.'

And so, one morning at dawn, he assembled a team of footmen and set out on an aged stubborn hack, which the agent had sold to him. I watched from the top of

'Why, the nymph whose pool this is. She comes and goes, but perhaps she has not yet shown herself to you.'

I had had enough of these ramblings. Clearly she was some wandering madwoman. With an angry gesture I made to stand and get my clothes. But as I moved she placed a restraining hand on my arm.

'No? Then you have not looked, or perhaps she is hiding from you. That would not surprise me, when I see how full of rage and movement you are. Will you not be still, and learn to listen and to see? The place is sacred, or have you not sensed that yet?'

She peered into my face, and after a moment nodded, adding, 'But I see you have.'

She was right, and her insight tempered my anger. Now that she had spoken the words, I knew what it was that drew me to this hillside and this pool. Some ancient presence hung all about, like the scent of the soil and the old leaves.

'Yes,' she said, 'you understand.'

I settled once more, forgetting my nakedness.

'Was it you,' I said, 'who put the flowers on the stone?'

'Was it you,' she echoed back, 'who broke them?' She smiled, then said, 'But no; it was not you. It was your friend who lives at the house, the Christian one . . . But you are not Christian.'

'No,' I said, though she had not spoken the words as a question.

In London, Ambitus, who believed in nothing but the coin in his hand, had once said, when I asked him, that there were no gods but man's invention: foolish night-charms to ward off simple people's terrors. I had thought these words clever and true at the time. Now they seemed somehow callow, incomplete, a statement of more than I knew.

'I am sorry about the flowers,' I said.

She touched my hand. Her old fingers were soft, like a girl's. 'I have seen the darkness you hide from; your guardian spirit, your *daimon*, has brought you here . . . Ha! No need to give me that city-boy look, as if the world had no surprises for you. You have much to learn.'

'I do not believe such things,' I said.

'Believe?' She blew through her nose. 'Now you talk like a Christian. What does the lamp-flame care if the moth does not believe; or the mountain if no man ever climbs?' Suddenly she took her stick and stood, supporting herself on my shoulder as she pulled herself up. 'Your daimon is waiting. It is woven into your destiny. Think on it, and come later to the hilltop.' She fixed my eye and added, 'But come tonight, or do not come at all. There will be no second chance.' And with that she turned and scrambled off up the ridge, like some woodland creature.

Afterwards I sat still, glancing about at the deepening shadows, feeling myself observed. But I saw no one, and heard only birdsong, and the bubbling of the stream.

Eventually I padded down to the pool-edge and pulled on my tunic, then set off back to the house.

As I went, I tried to recall the crone; but somehow it was only her green eyes I could remember.

I woke with a start to light shining on my face. I was on my bed, fully clothed.

I blinked. For a moment I thought it was dawn; but what had woken me was the beam of the rising moon, shafting through the open window. I sat up and rubbed my face. It was time to go.

The window of my room let out onto a yard behind the ramshackle stables. I climbed onto the sill and eased myself down, then stepped along the gully between the house and stable wall.

The main gate had been locked for the night. There would be a watchman there. But I had already planned my route, and turning off the path I climbed onto an upturned cart that lay abandoned in the long grass beside the outer wall. From here it was easy to hoist myself onto the ledge and let myself down into the darkness on the other side.

I had known from the start that I should go. I had reasoned with myself, saying it was an ambush, that the harmless-seeming crone was a lure for bandits hiding somewhere in the woods, who planned to kidnap me for ransom, or sell me to the Hibernians, or merely kill me for the joy of it.

So I reasoned. But all the time I knew these arguments counted for nothing against the deeper undertow of mystery and promise.

Her words kept coming back to me, that she had seen the darkness in my soul. How did she know? It was the place I dared not look, the place beyond the hidden door. Yet she, a stranger, had seen. It was that which drew me on, like the moth she had spoken of, drawn to the flame.

A cloud crossed the disc of the moon. I hesitated, listening. The breeze stirred the undergrowth. Somewhere far off an owl called. I went on, moving silently, following the familiar track.

When I came to the clearing on the hilltop, where the mighty yew was, and the stone altar, I paused in the moon-shadow, scanning the open ground. No one was waiting.

I shook my head, thinking, 'She is not here; did you suppose otherwise? You have come out to no purpose, searching after a madwoman.'

And yet I remained. The air was heavy with summer scent – clover and wild thyme and moist tree bark. I drew a breath and stepped out into the exposed open of the clearing. If, as I half supposed, I was to be set upon, then this would be the time.

But nothing stirred. Beyond the yew the altar-stone shone like blue crystal in the moonlight. The wind had picked up. It moved in the high branches, sighing and shifting. Then, somewhere behind me, a voice said, 'So you have come, young satyr.'

I swung round startled. 'Where are you?' I called, staring about at the shadows. 'Show yourself.'

For a moment there was nothing. Then, from the deep darkness between the tree-trunks, a figure stepped out. But it was not the old woman; it was a girl. She wore a long white tunic as bright as the altar-stone. It shimmered in the light as she moved; and below it her feet showed pale and bare. She was, I guessed, about my age. She was handsome in the way of the Britons, with a round open face, and long black hair that cascaded over her shoulders.

She smiled; but after all my nervousness I was in no mood to be toyed with.

'What is this?' I cried, grabbing her arm. 'Where is the crone? Do you take me for a fool?'

She did not struggle from my grip; she merely looked down with disdain at my strong hand locked around her wrist.

'How like a man you are,' she said softly, 'angry and afraid at what you do not comprehend. Are you going to hurt me?'

I released her, ashamed.

'No.'

'Then come; the moon is waiting.'

She skirted the spreading yew, sometimes reaching out and touching with her fingers the overhanging pin-like leaves and scaly bark, as if the tree were something that must be mollified and soothed.

I followed, keeping my eyes warily upon her, until, at the side of the altar, she halted. I turned and glanced at the great flat stone. Then I started back with a cry. Lying on the slab, surrounded by a dark shimmering pool of blood, a cock-bird lay dead, its throat cut.

I drew an angry breath. The sight of the dead creature had shaken me, bringing out all my pent-up fears of the night. But before I could speak she reached out and touched a finger to my lips, silencing me.

'Understand,' she said, 'there are times when the gods demand a death, the loss of some precious thing. Put your fear aside, satyr of the woods. It is as it has always been.'

She took a step forward, gesturing for me to approach,

and as she moved the moonlight touched her face. Only then did I notice her eyes.

They were luminous green. Like moss.

I gathered my wits, telling myself it was nothing. There was no mystery – how could there be? She was the crone's granddaughter, that was all; or some other of the blood-line, part of some peasant country priesthood handed down through the ages.

I swallowed, suppressing a shudder, determined to hide my fear. Then I stepped up to the blood-spattered altar, as she wanted.

She reached out and ran her hand over my nose and along the line of my mouth, parting my lips until her fingers touched my teeth. 'You shake,' she whispered. She reached then into a small leather purse at her waist, and from her closed hand scattered barley and tiny yellow flower petals over the stone. Above me, the yew branches creaked in the breeze. She looked to the sky. 'It is almost time. Take off your clothes; go to the pool and wash, and then return.' And, seeing my face, she added in a voice of infinite tenderness, 'Dispel your fear. It is what you came for, though you did not know it.'

Silently, without comment or protest, I obeyed her command. When I returned, naked and dripping, her hands were outstretched and, as I drew closer, I heard she was intoning a charm or a prayer, speaking in some lilting melodic tongue, part British, part something else, far older, which I could not follow.

She fell silent, then said, 'The god has chosen. She has been waiting for you.'

I stared at her. Water was running from my wet hair

and into my eyes. I wiped it away with the back of my hand.

'Who?' I whispered. 'What god?'

She raised her eyes and gazed up between the branches, to where the brilliant moon shone down.

'She goes by many names. Luna or Selene or Diana; sister to the Sun and to Dawn, daughter of ancient Hyperion, last of the Titans. You have sought the Mother, and she has found you.' She dipped her finger in the black blood, and reaching out traced a line from my throat, slowly down my chest and stomach to my groin.

Suddenly then I caught my breath. Fire surged through my innards. My thoughts ceased and it seemed I cried out loud. My being was nowhere, or everywhere, fleeing with the moon-shadows. I closed my eyes, and felt the touch of lips on mine. I rose to meet her, my body like a light-filled vessel, caught in a place outside time.

The moon had shifted when next I spoke. I was lying on the grass, looking up at the night sky between the treetops.

'Are you the water-nymph?' I whispered, touching her face. 'Are you my daimon come to find me?'

She leant over me and shook her head, and her long hair fell over my chest, soft on my skin.

'Not I,' she said, smiling. 'But your daimon is with you now, and you will hear her, if you listen. She comes in dreams, or speaks through signs, or shows herself in mortal men. For each it is different, but you will learn the ways to bring her close.'

Eventually, though I did not wish it, I must have slept. I woke to birdsong, and the half-light of dawn. I called for the girl, and my voice sounded raw and strange, like some other man's. But she was gone, and no answer came. After a while I walked back to the altar, expecting to see the dead cock-bird there. But the slab was clean as when I had first seen it.

Then, as I turned, something caught my eye and I looked down.

At my feet, bright among the crushed grass, yellow petals lay scattered like specks of gold. And on my naked chest, with the contour of my muscle, there was a dark dry line of blood.

The hot, close weather broke in a night of wind and thunder. Each day I went up to the hill and the altar, or waited by the pool; but I encountered no one.

I questioned the servants, asking if there was a settlement nearby. There was not; only their own simple huts behind the house, and those of the neighbouring landowner some way off. Nor had they seen anyone of the description I gave.

Then, a quarter-month later, after I had run out of ideas and ceased to look, I walked out under the gateway and saw in the distance on the path an old woman. She was dressed in a hooded cloak, and stood gazing out across the overgrown fields, leaning on a rough-wood stick.

I ran, and though she must have heard my footfalls

she did not turn. But when I was close she said in a soft, amused voice, 'Greetings, young satyr.'

'Where have you been?' I cried. 'Where is the girl?'

With no warning her hand darted out from beneath her cloak and locked with a grip like iron around my wrist.

'What is it you seek, boy? An end to mystery? Have you learned nothing at all?'

She paused, studying my face from under the dark shadow of her pulled-up cloak. Then, with a grunt, she released my arm. 'What you had, you had. Think on it. Forget the girl; she is gone.' Then she made a luck sign over me, and with a laugh she turned and hurried off.

I stood rubbing my wrist, watching until she had disappeared into the dark forest beyond the fields.

I say no more. The old woman had her hood up, and though she seemed to know me, I cannot claim that it was even the crone. As for the rest, she said think on it, and that is what I have done, many times. And if I have an answer, it lies in what I have done, which is to tell it as it was, no more or less.

Balbus, restless and bored, returned to London, pleading unexpected business that could not wait. Leisure did not suit him, just as absence from her prattling circle of friends did not suit Lucretia.

She discovered from the servants that the neighbouring villa, which lay about three miles off, was the country residence of the aristocrat Quintus Aquinus, the man who had stepped into the government of the city during the Saxon siege. At once she despatched one of the footmen with a message announcing her presence, and waited for an invitation. When none came she quizzed the servant. Was the senator not at home? Was he ill or infirm? To whom had he delivered her note?

I was in the courtyard outside the window. From within I heard Albinus let out a harsh laugh and say, 'Perhaps he does not wish to see you.'

There was a pause. I stopped by the herb-bed to listen. 'Leave us!' Lucretia cried at the servant. Then, turning on Albinus, she demanded to know how he could be so cruel, and could he not see that she was at the end of her tether, and what had come over him since they had come to this horrible house in the country, for he had been nothing but captious and insolent, even though she had sacrificed everything for him.

The footman, emerging moments later into the court-yard, caught me smiling. 'Tell me, Fabius,' I said, 'what do you know of this Quintus Aquinus?'

He glanced up at the window, where they were still loudly bickering. 'I cannot tell you much, master Drusus,' he said in a low voice. 'It is a great old house – my niece works there, and she is treated well. The land is well tended, and lacks for nothing, because old Aquinus has made it so. He has lived there all his life, and his ancestors before him, time out of mind.'

'Have you met him?' I asked.

'I have seen him, but only from afar. They say he is a good man' – his eyes darted significantly to the noise behind – 'a good, decent man, and I wish there were more of his kind hereabouts.'

I was curious. I decided to go and see for myself. Perhaps, after all, the girl, or the crone, had something to do with this house.

The night on the hilltop had filled me with a yearning; it had touched places in my soul where desire lay, and need, and dark questions that demanded satisfaction. It was as though, just beyond my grasp, there lay the special thing my soul burned for. I felt it; yet I did not know what it was, or how I should recognize it. It drew me on. And so, two days later, on a clear, fresh morning, I took apples and cheese and a loaf from the kitchen and set out across the brook, over the stepping-stones and through the wooded strip of rowan and willows. From there, I followed a cattle track, up over the low ridge and through fields of yellow barley, pausing at the top to get my bearings.

The track led south, skirting the fields until it vanished in a deep swathe of forest. Beyond, in the distance over the treetops, I could see more fields, and sheep enclosures in undulating land. The house, I supposed, must be in one of the valleys, out of sight. I walked on.

From the ridge the forest had seemed easy to traverse; but once I passed between the oaks and high beeches the bright day was reduced almost to twilight, and the track began to twist and turn between dense undergrowth and the contours of the land. Still I followed, supposing it must lead to the other side; but after some time it ended at a great barrier of twined bramble.

I ought perhaps to have turned back then and retraced my steps. But I could see the way ahead was easier – mature beeches, their massive trunks soaring like columns up to the high canopy, with leaf-strewn open ground between – and so I pressed on.

I found I was thinking of something the girl had said: how the gods and spirits come in dreams, or speak through signs, or show themselves in mortal men. I felt like a man who finds the ground beneath him, which he had taken to be solid and immobile, suddenly shifting. What signs did she mean anyway, and how did one know?

I took an apple from my bag, and ate. In the corner of my eye I sensed movement. A rust-coloured squirrel was crouched at the foot of an oak, scratching at the forest floor. He paused and considered me with his head cocked; then, deciding I was no threat, he carried on at his work. Presently I came to another track, recently trodden. But the marks in the churned-up earth were boar, not man. I followed it even so, seeing nothing better. The way narrowed into a defile of hazel and prickly ilex; then, just as I thought the track would peter out, it opened into a grass clearing lit by shafts of slanting sunlight. At the far side, so grown-over with ivy and creeping shrubs that it looked at first glance no more than a rocky outcrop, was a small circular temple.

I stepped forward. The building looked derelict and forgotten. The facing on the walls was crumbling, showing red brickwork beneath. One of the columns had collapsed outwards; it lay like a fallen tree-trunk on the ground. I came to a high double-door, of old weathered wood studded with copper turned the colour of verdigris. The door stood half open, fixed ajar, its hinges rotted away. It would not shift when I pushed, but there was space enough to squeeze through.

Within were ochre columns and frescoes of woodland scenes, creating the illusion of openness. But what held my attention was the cult-statue, which stood in front of me, set back in a recess. It was old Keltic work, of a maiden holding in one hand the crescent of the moon, and in the other a spear. At her feet lay a fallen stag, its head rearing up to regard her. Traces of offerings lay about: burnt-out candles, a clay lamp, shrivelled fruits and old flowers.

I paused in the silence. I had plucked a sprig of white-flowering bryony outside; it seemed fitting now to lay it at her feet. But as I knelt I looked up and caught sight of the statue's eyes.

I froze, and caught my breath; and stared. The eyes were green agate, luminous green, the colour of moss. I remained a long time still, assembling my thoughts, wondering what motions of chance or fate had brought me here.

When at length I returned outside, the sun was obscured by cloud and the clearing was in shadow. I paused on the stone porch-step, looking about me, considering what path to take. I had lost all sense of my direction. Suddenly the silence was broken by a rapid stirring in the undergrowth. I remained motionless, listening, remembering the boar tracks. But I heard nothing more. Keeping my back to the wall, staying under the narrow encircling colonnade, I stepped over a fallen branch and edged around to where I could get a better view. There was a sudden beating in the branches above. I jerked my head up, startled; but it was only a bird, rising in a flurry of wings through the canopy. I let out my breath. Then I heard a crack behind me – the sound of dried wood splintering underfoot. I swung round, realizing what it was. But I was too late. A spear-blade pressed into my ribs, and a voice said, 'Keep still, or I will kill you.'

The cold steel pressed through my tunic, sharp against my skin. It was skilfully held, keeping me pinned against the wall; but not enough to cut me, unless I moved.

My mind turned fast. He had spoken in good well-cadenced Latin; it was not the voice of some country bandit trying his luck. I recalled a lesson Durano had drummed into me: think, decide, then act fast and certain. I said, 'If you kill me it will be the worse for you,' and even as I spoke I was gauging the distance ahead and to my side. In one sudden curling movement, while my words still hung in the air, I leapt away from the blade, grabbing at the javelin-shaft and twisting it.

I had caught him off his guard. He had loosed his grip. The twisting motion forced the javelin from his hands and I seized it. I span it round and turned it on him, and forced him back at the tip of the blade. Only then did I look at his face. He was handsome and sturdy, with clear grey eyes and heavy bronze hair turned gold by the sun. He was staring at the spear-point with a deep frown which showed the fine lines on each side of his mouth. The palms of his hands were open, and below his tunic I could see the muscles in his legs were taut, ready to spring.

But I was not going to let him use my own trick. I jabbed at him, forcing him back against the column.

His eyes moved from the blade to my face.

'Who are you?' he demanded. 'This is my land.'

I could tell he was angry with himself for having let me catch him so easily. I scanned his body for weapons. He was dressed in a leather hunting jerkin with a wide brown belt. I could see no sign of a hidden dagger.

I grinned. 'Now we are even,' I said.

Keeping my eyes on him I tossed the javelin away behind me. It clattered on the stone. He relaxed a little after that, and his eyes studied my face.

'What are you doing here?'

'I was lost.'

'You were in the temple. I saw you.'

'What of it? I wanted to see inside.' I spread my hands, to show I had no knife. 'You can fight me if you want. It is an even contest now.'

He paused, furrowing his brow, and once again his face moved in a frown. He shook his head. 'No. I don't want to fight you.'

For a moment we stood looking at one another, both of us wary. Then he took a tentative step forward and offered me his hand.

I took it. It was broad and strong.

'All this is my grandfather's land,' he said, gesturing over his shoulder, 'but I live here too.' He smiled, adding, 'My name is Marcellus.'

I told him mine, and where I had come from, standing straight, filling my lungs and feeling pleased with myself for having bested him. But then, as I took half a step back, my foot caught on the discarded spear-shaft and I tripped. He grabbed my arm before I fell, catching my weight in his grip. I clutched onto him. I had to, or I should have fallen sprawling on my back. It dispelled all my cock-pride in an instant.

'Well, Drusus,' he said, 'it looks like my spear was some use after all, don't you think?' He heaved me up and I dusted myself off, trying to regain my dignity. When I next looked up he was grinning.

'What?' I said crossly. But it was no good, and after a moment I was smiling back at him. 'Here,' I said, taking up the javelin and handing it to him. 'You'd better take it, before I really hurt myself.'

As I looked at him, something in me, which had long slept, stirred to life. I think I knew, even then, that whatever it took, I wanted this beautiful youth as my friend.

He said, 'I hear Lucius Balbus the merchant has that house. Are you his son then?'

'Oh no!' I cried, appalled that he should think so.

'Then why are you there? Are you visiting?'

I explained, and as I spoke he looked into my face, not insolently, but with genuine concern.

'I heard what happened to your father,' he said, when I had finished. 'Grandfather told me. I am sorry; it is a hard thing to bear.' He paused, then asked, 'Do you still grieve?'

I shrugged. It seemed a long time since anyone had

cared what I thought, and I found the words did not come easily.

'He was wronged,' I said eventually. 'I think about that sometimes . . . Where is your own father? Is he at the house too?'

'He died when I was young. I don't remember him.'

'Then I am sorry too.'

'He died of a fever. It was with the gods, I suppose. What happened to yours is worse. It is the injustice of men.' He looked into my eyes. 'Come, I'll show you where the house is.'

We stepped out. Suddenly, as we began to move, there came from behind me in the undergrowth a violent scrambling, the same noise I had heard before. I leapt round startled, shouting out.

But Marcellus laughed, saying, 'Don't worry, it's only Ufa,' and from the cover of the bracken a shaggy grey wolfhound came bounding out. It strode up to me, wagging its tail and snuffling, and pushing its nose into my hand.

'See, he likes you. He's a good judge.'

I petted the creature's head and let it sniff me. 'But he wasn't there when you were in trouble,' I said with a grin.

'No.' He drew down his brows. 'Well he's not much of a guard-dog really. I suppose he thinks I can look after myself. I can, usually. Where did you learn a trick like that?'

As we walked, with Ufa strutting beside us, inspecting the undergrowth, I told him something of how I had learned to wrestle and fight. I was halting and unsure at first – it made me aware of how long it was since I had

had a proper conversation with anyone. But before I knew it, I was telling him about Albinus and my aunt, and my life in London.

He listened, commenting now and then. He was about my age – sixteen – and, as I had already noticed, he was taller than I, though only by a little. Where I was dark, he was fair. His forearms and the backs of his hands were brushed with a fine golden down, and the sun had tanned his skin the colour of burnished bronze. As we walked he absently swung the javelin to and fro, swishing it at the bracken beside the path. He moved well, I thought, with the powerful grace of a young male deer.

Presently we emerged from the trees, and I realized I had not stopped talking since the temple. I broke off and looked at him. I had never told so much about myself to anyone before.

I thought, 'He is walking with me out of good manners, and to see me off his land, no more than that, though he is too well-bred to say so.' I was about to excuse myself and tell him he need not trouble himself further, but he stopped me with a touch on the shoulder and resting his hand there pointed across the fields.

'See that far ridge, where the tall trees are? The house is below it, in the valley. It's quite a way still, but you can make out the roof between the trees. Stand closer. There, that's better. Now you can see.'

I looked, shading my eyes with my hand. Over the rolling barley-fields and sheep-dotted meadowland there was a line of black poplar and spreading elm, and in their midst, half-obscured, the red-tiled roof of a house. Even from this distance I could make out high pediments and soaring arches, and towers and long walls.

'Is that *yours*?' I asked, impressed. It looked as big as the governor's palace in London.

He gave a quick, shy laugh. 'Well it's Grandfather's . . . But yes, it's mine too; it's my home. The house has belonged in our family for generations, since our ancestors built it in the time of the emperor Marcus, and brought all the land under cultivation. As a house it's too much really, just for Grandfather and me and my mother. But it's where we belong, I suppose.'

'Your mother is alive, then?'

He looked at me and laughed. 'How not? Losing one parent is enough—' But then he stopped himself. 'What, did the emperor take her too?'

I shook my head, and tapped and dabbed at a tuft of grass with my toe. 'No, it wasn't that. She died in childbirth, when I was born. I never knew her.'

The dog came up and nuzzled at my hand, demanding attention. I knelt down and ruffled his ears; he rolled over and smiled up at me, pawing the air.

I heard Marcellus set down the javelin. He crouched beside me, pushing his hand into the dog's fur. Our fingers touched, and then I looked up. I knew my face was reddening; I felt I had stirred old embers of a fire long dead, and found them glowing still.

'But she was beautiful,' I said. 'I know. My father had a picture.'

'I'm sure she was, if you are her son. I can see it. It's a shame we didn't find a better way to meet.'

157

I do not know what possessed me then – some god, perhaps, or some noble spirit, the sort that draws from us the right word at the right time, and makes cowards brave and weak men strong, and discovers for us our potential in the unseen corners of our souls. But I answered saying, 'Any way is better than none.'

For a moment he looked surprised. And then he smiled. 'Yes, I think so too . . . I suppose I feared, after we almost fought each other—' He broke off with a shrug. For a moment I even thought he was blushing. But no doubt it was just a trick of the light, for by then the sun was sinking into a towering sunset of vermilion cloud.

'Well,' I said, standing, 'I ought to get back.'

'Yes.' He hesitated. 'I'll walk with you; I've nothing else to do.'

'It's out of your way.'

'I don't mind – unless you'd rather not?'

'No,' I said quickly. 'I'd like it.'

And so we walked, this time skirting the woods and taking a dusty trail beside the fields, talking all the while.

When at length we reached the brook with its barrier of rowans and lime-leaved willows, I said, 'So, here we are,' and immediately felt foolish.

'Yes. Goodbye then, Drusus.'

'Goodbye.'

But we paused, looking at each other. Then we both said at once, 'But when—?' And then we laughed.

'Tomorrow?' I said. 'I'll come to the house, now I know the way.'

'Yes, tomorrow. Good . . . Until tomorrow then?'

For a moment he looked at me, as if there were

something else. But then, suddenly self-conscious, he gave a quick nod, turned on his heels and strode off.

I watched him as he receded along the path, with the slanting sun on his back, and the wolfhound prancing happily behind him, until in the end he passed over the ridge and was lost from view.

SIX

THE SUN WAS SINKING over the honeysuckle courtyard by the time I returned. Albinus must have been
waiting; even before I had mounted the last of the steps
he came rushing out.

'Where have you been?' he demanded. 'Mother has
been looking all over.'

I pushed past him. If I had been attending more
carefully, I should have realized he already had an audience. He had a particular way of speaking when his
mother was in earshot.

She was waiting just within the door, in the dark of
the atrium, with her arms folded tense across her chest,
and a face like death in triumph.

'Do not ignore Albinus when he speaks to you!' she
cried. Her voice was shaking with anger. I had seen her
like this before. She had worked herself to such a peak of
rage that she could scarcely control herself. 'He saw you
with that youth,' she went on, 'so do not deny it. You

160

have been to the house of Quintus Aquinus. Who summoned you there? What business have *you* with him?'

So that was it, I thought. She supposed I had been invited when she had not.

I answered with the truth, saying I had not met Quintus Aquinus, nor had I been summoned by anyone. I had met his grandson – the boy Albinus saw me with – only by chance.

But she was beyond listening. The sinews in her face were moving, waiting for me to finish.

'You lie!' she cried. I stared at her, at a loss for what more to say. Suddenly her folded arms sprang open and lunging forward she struck me a powerful blow on the side of my face. The clap of it echoed in the high empty chamber.

I reached up to my cheek. When I took it away there was blood on my fingers, where the bezel of her ring had caught under my ear. I bear the mark still.

Albinus gaped at her. 'Mother!' he cried.

'Leave him! He has brought it upon himself. Let him remember he is our guest; I will not have—'

She broke off, for I had stepped up to her.

The wall was behind her. She could not back away. I had broadened and thickened out. I was a boy no longer. Reaching out I took hold of her wrist, locking my fingers hard around it and pulling her resisting arm down from the amber necklet she was clutching.

Her blue-painted eyes met mine. I heard her breath catch.

Slowly I said, 'You will never do that to me again.'

I dreamt that night of my mother, smiling and laughing

and taking me in her arms, and woke with a start to a grey dawn and a sinking feeling of recollection.

I had lain awake till long after midnight, brooding. Even in my great anger I had been careful not to hurt Lucretia; there would have been nothing fine in returning her violence. But a barrier had been crossed all the same. I knew that now I should be cast out. Better to leave before that happened and save my pride.

I heard a scratching on my door. It must have been that which had woken me. I called out, thinking it was one of the slaves; but it was Albinus who entered, looking shamefaced.

'Here,' he said, holding out a platter of cake and raisins. I had been given no food the night before. He set it down, then paused.

'What do you want?' I said, eyeing him warily from the bed.

'Drusus, I don't think she meant it.'

I pulled the cover from me and stepped naked across the stone floor, poured water from the pitcher, and splashed it on my face. Sullenly he watched me.

'She was angry,' he said.

'Then she had no cause. I did not lie to her.'

He sighed. We both knew it was not my truth or lies that had enraged her so.

'Anyway,' he said, 'you must make yourself ready; we are leaving. Already the slaves are loading the carriage.'

But at the door he paused, scraping his foot on the floor. I turned from the basin, my towel in my hand.

'What is it, Albinus?'

'She went too far, that is all.'

162

Then he hurried off.

I stood, looking at the open door. It was the nearest I had ever heard to an apology from him.

By the time we reached the river and the waiting barge the low pewter sky had turned to rain, carried in on a damp west wind. Lucretia arranged herself under the awning at the stern, her face pursed and bitter under a scarf and hat, muttering curses whenever water came dripping through the canvas.

All that morning, during the slow wagon-ride from the house, she had not spoken one word to me. Perhaps she was waiting for me to come grovelling to her. If so, I told myself as I stared down into the dull slack water, she would wait in vain. I would find a way of leaving, whatever hardship it brought me.

When I was not brooding on this I was thinking of Marcellus. I imagined him waiting for me, the realization dawning on him with a fading of any liking he had for me that I was not coming.

That he should think ill of me oppressed me terribly. I hoped he had not waited long. Already, as I sat miserable in the bow, feeling cold rivulets of rain meander down my neck and back, it seemed to me he inhabited a world of light, a perfect world which fate and the natural order of things had set forever beyond my reach. Just as well, I told myself, casting a glance at my aunt huddled with Albinus under the shelter of the awning, that the friendship I had hoped for had died before it began, before he should see the base life I led and despise me for it.

Eventually the grey ragstone walls of London showed through the rain ahead. My aunt's first task, I knew, would be to embellish a tale to Balbus that would have me cast out onto the street. I tried to consider what I should do.

It was not until the following morning that old Patricus the house-slave came to me and said, 'The Master wishes to see you in his workroom.'

I had been expecting it. I went with my head held high.

'Ah Drusus,' he said, looking up from the desk scattered with scrolls and tablets. 'How did you like the country?'

I gave him a careful look – he was not one for small talk – and answered that I had liked it well enough.

'You did?' He prodded at his papers for a moment, then went on, 'Even so, I have to say it wasn't all I had hoped. And your aunt disliked it too. Tell me, how old are you now?'

'Sixteen, uncle. Seventeen in the autumn.'

'So it is. Then you are a young man now, and I daresay you have been wondering what the future holds for you.'

I fixed my eyes on his heavy bull's head, thinking, 'So this is it; well I shall bear it like a man.' Lucretia had been working on him the night before; that much I knew.

Without looking up he went on, 'I saw Count Gratian while you were away. He has asked me to attend him at the governor's palace tomorrow, and now that you are back, I should like you to accompany me.' He paused,

164

then glanced up, adding, 'I may as well tell you now: he has asked after you.'

'Me?' I said, shocked out of my sullenness. 'Count Gratian – but who am I to him?'

'You forget; we are an important family in the city. Besides, it seems he once met your father.'

'But what does he want with me, sir?'

'He has not told me, and it is not my place to question him. I expect we shall find out tomorrow.' He narrowed his eyes at me. 'What happened to your face?'

'I cut it, sir.'

'You should take care. It will leave a mark.' He returned his attention to his papers. 'Anyway, we shall make an early start in the morning, so remind the slave to wake you. And now, Drusus, you can take this manifest and go down to the dock. There is a coaster in this morning, with a cargo of Gallic wool for me.'

Next morning I dressed in my one good tunic – white edged with red meanders – and put on my blue-wool mantle, and set out with Balbus for the governor's palace.

The oldest part of the palace is a marble-faced building with a high pedimented porch, built on three sides of a fountain court. It is as old as the province itself. But the imperial bureaucracy, growing year upon year like a city midden, had found the need for extra space, and the palace had spread over what once had been gardens, into a warren of extensions and annexes, linked by narrow alleyways, covered passages and unexpected doors.

Balbus showed his pass to the sentry at the gate and we were admitted to the inner court. Here a self-important chamberlain received us. He escorted us through vaulted painted rooms of state, and up a marble staircase to an anteroom. He told us to wait, and glided off.

'I thought he was expecting you,' I said.

'Hush, Drusus. He is a busy man.' He sat uneasily, fidgeting and glancing about. It was as though the grandeur of the place, and the ridiculous pomp of the chamberlain, had cowed him.

At last the chamberlain returned and said Count Gratian would see us now. He led us across the polished floor and through high gilded double-doors.

'Ah, Balbus, there you are!'

A tall man with a soldier's lean build and close-cropped grey hair came striding across the chequered floor, leaving a group of uniformed officers. He wore a military tunic and boots, unadorned. But when you were close you could see they were of a fine cut and quality. He took Balbus by the elbow and leading him in said, 'Now, I have an assignment for you.'

His voice was loud and assured. His Latin had the accent of Pannonia. After the airs of the chamberlain, one might have taken him for some common soldier, as indeed he once was. But I had seen his eyes: they were shrewd and alert.

While Balbus answered with an overlong fawning reply, I glanced about. Loitering at a map-table there were young men in uniform, and a few liveried clerks. Elsewhere I recognized the set of three couches Balbus had shipped from Africa, upholstered in zigzag patterns

166

of honey-yellow, green and blue; and in the corner stood a gilded statue of Hercules, stolid and muscle-bound like a boxer, with a lion's pelt draped over his shoulder.

I glanced back at Gratian. He was at that time about fifty, older indeed than my uncle, though one would not have thought it. He was lean and hard as a nut. Beside him Balbus looked old and fat and bumbling.

'Good, that will take care of it then,' said Gratian, finishing off. 'The clerk will give you the details, and arrange payment. See him later.' He spoke like a man used to being obeyed. Then, as if I had been at the back of his mind the whole time, he swung round and looked directly at me.

Though my eyes had been busy, I was still standing straight and respectful (Albinus would have been chewing his nails by now) and had kept my attention on him. I was glad of it: I had the sense, as his sharp eye caught me, that he cared about such things.

'So this is Appius's son,' he said. 'Yes, I see the likeness, though the boy will not grow as tall.' He was a man who dealt in fact, not feeling.

At his side, my uncle began saying something about how he had been taking care of me. Gratian listened for a moment, then silenced him.

'Yes, yes; all this you have told me already. But what are you going to do with him?'

'Why sir, I had considered he might become a merchant perhaps, especially with business so good—'

'A *merchant*?' he cried, as if Balbus had proposed making me a slave in a tanning-yard. 'Is that the extent of his ambition?'

'I believe not, sir. But sometimes necessity—'

Cutting him short, Gratian looked at me and said, 'And what do you want, young man?'

Without a second thought I replied, 'I should like to join the army, sir.'

His black eyes widened. Beside him Balbus chuckled nervously.

'Is that so? Well, you know your own mind, which is a good sign.'

'Yes, sir, I do.'

Just then the chamberlain returned and moved to Gratian's side.

'Yes, Fadius, what now?'

'Your next appointment, sir.' He leant forward, raised a shielding hand, and whispered a name.

Gratian nodded, then turned back to me. 'I think, son of Appius, we can find you something better than merchanting, don't you? But today it seems everyone in the province wishes to see me, and tomorrow I leave for Gaul. Come back when I return, and we will talk some more. Fadius will arrange it. Goodbye.'

Two months later I returned. A mild autumn had turned suddenly to a winter of bitter cold, the coldest the old men at the docks could remember. Ice had locked the barges in their mooring places; cattle perished in the fields; and in the vineyards the vines froze and withered.

Gratian was in conference with a group of tribunes. They stood gathered around the map-table, smart in their red cloaks and military boots. He finished his business, dismissed them, then came to where I was waiting, saying, 'Come, son of Appius, let us eat and talk.'

He led me to what I guessed was one of his private rooms, where a table had been laid with food. The room was hung with tapestries and silks, and filled with too many possessions. But the food was simple soldiers' fare – olives, cheese, sausage and barley loaves. He launched himself at it like a hungry dog, gracelessly, beckoning while he chewed for the steward to fill the wine-cups. But presently he sat back and regarded me.

'All my life,' he said through his food, 'I have been a soldier. My parents were poor peasants on poor land, and their parents and grandparents before them.' He nodded over his shoulder at the rich furnishings – a polished inlaid table decorated with garlands and harps; a pair of precious thin-necked serpentine vases; a gilt wrought standing-lamp – and continued, 'The army saved me from that fate, and I have made something of myself. If you're ambitious, you can get on.' He washed down his food with a gulp of wine. His next question took me by surprise, for suddenly he asked, 'Are you a Christian?'

My mind turned quickly. I asked myself what answer he was seeking. Everyone knew the emperor was a fervent Christian. Had someone told Gratian, I wondered, about me and the bishop?

Inwardly I frowned. I had seen no Christian symbols among the hangings and objects of art; but that was equally true of Lucretia's rooms, except for the fresco of the sad-faced youth with the knowing eyes. So in the end I answered with the truth. It seemed the only thing to do.

'No, sir,' I said, 'I am not.'

'So sure?'

'It is a fact. I know it.'

He considered me for a moment, his face giving nothing away. I wondered if he was waiting for me to retract my words. Then he said, 'I don't much care for them myself, not in the army anyway – though my son thinks differently.'

I allowed myself to breathe again, while he talked about his son. The boy had been reared as a Christian, he told me, at the insistence of his wife, the child's mother, who would have her way in such matters. 'That is women. You can't fight them.' He laughed, then asked, 'Yet Balbus is a Christian, is he not?'

'Yes, sir, he is.'

'But not you . . . Are you happy there?'

'Sometimes I miss my home, sir.'

'I expect you do; no boy should be without his father.' He smeared a wad of cheese onto the last of the loaf and pushed it into his mouth, then dabbed at his lips with a napkin. One might have supposed, after the way he had eaten, that he would merely have wiped his face with the back of his grizzled forearm.

'Still,' he said, tossing the napkin aside, 'what's done is done; a man must make the best of it. As it happens, I am looking for young men of promise to join my staff. I warn you though, the life is not all banquets and parades and entertaining the town trollops, as it is under some generals I could name. I expect discipline, and the life is hard. But if you think you can submit to it, there is a vacancy for you in the corps of Protectors.'

I drew my breath to speak, but he raised his hand.

'No, I do not want your answer now. Go away and consider, for it will mean many changes. For a start you will have to leave your uncle's house, and when you think about it you may decide you cannot do without such comforts. You will receive no special favours, let me warn you; and I make no promises about your future. So go away and think, and when you are ready come back and give Fadius your answer.'

And so I left him. On my way out I passed on the stairway an erect bearded white-haired man. I daresay I should not have noticed him at all, so full was my mind with my own thoughts. But the chamberlain was fussing over him, and as I passed I heard him say with crisp impatience, 'No, leave it; I can manage.' The chamberlain had a well-developed sense of his place among men. Those he considered below him he treated with disdain. This old gentleman, then, I thought to myself with a smile, was someone of consequence. He was elegantly dressed; but sparely, in clothes that made no concession to fashion. He had a natural dignity, and, under his beard, a stern mouth.

Just then he glanced at me and caught me smiling; and I was sure he returned my look of amusement.

Outside, back in the courtyard, I paused at the frozen fountain and considered my change in fortune. I had known immediately I should take Count Gratian's offer; I would return next day and tell the chamberlain. Hooves sounded on the cobbles and I glanced up. A stable-lad was leading a grey mare from the yard. As he walked he patted her side and whispered in her ear, and she, as if she understood his words of endearment, tossed her head, nodding contentedly, her breath pluming in the cold air. A group of uniformed young men passed by, talking and laughing. Soon, I thought with a smile, I should be one of them.

I found, to my surprise, that I was thinking of my father. I wished I could tell him, and see him proud and pleased. I pushed the thought away. He was gone, along with all my past life. What's done is done, as Gratian said. Easy words; I wondered if he had ever confronted the hard truth that lay behind them. Yet in his brusque way he was right: there is no return, for all man's longing, and a man must make the best of it.

I resolved to offer something to Diana the Huntress, whose deserted temple I had found during my wanderings about the city. Within, there was a faded wall-painting of the goddess set against the new moon, clutching her spear, young and proud and dark-eyed. Since my return from the country, I had taken to going there, and pausing alone in the silence.

But first, I thought, stirring myself to leave, I would see Balbus, and tell him my news.

I was just turning, when from across the stable-yard I heard a voice that made me stop and look.

He had his back to me. He was talking to the groom, with one broad hand resting on the neck of the grey mare. His hair, deprived of summer sun, had returned to its natural colour of old bronze. In his simple plain cloak he might almost have been another of the stable-boys. But even in beggar's rags I should have known him.

'Marcellus!' I cried.

He looked round startled, and seeing me he began to smile. But then he frowned.

'Hello, Drusus,' he said coolly.

I thought, 'He is angry with me, and who can blame him? I expect he waited half a day for me.' I stood staring like a fool. I wanted to tell him all that had happened; but the groom was watching, and I felt ashamed. So instead, as if it mattered to me, I nodded at the horse and said, 'A fine creature.'

'Yes, a beauty. She belongs to Gratian.'

I stroked its sleek neck, and spoke a few words to the groom. Marcellus asked what brought me here to the palace, and I told him I had had business with Gratian, and was on my way out.

'I am waiting for my grandfather,' he said. 'He is inside.'

I searched for something right to say; but no words came. An awkward silence fell between us. From the stable-house someone called for the groom. We both watched as he led the mare away. Marcellus shifted on his feet and glanced towards the portico. He was looking for a reason to be gone, and I think he would have left then, except that he was waiting for his grandfather.

'Marcellus, listen. I am sorry I didn't meet you; I—'

'No matter. I expect something came up and you had things to do.'

'No, no, I didn't; it wasn't that, not at all.'

And then, hesitantly, I began to explain – a hard thing to do at that age in life, when one does not like to admit one is not one's own master.

But he had that open quality which makes one want to talk, and in the end, I even showed him the scar under my ear where Lucretia's ring had caught me, adding vehemently that I longed to be away, and that today, at last, I had my chance.

He eased my head round with his hands to look at the scratch. His palms smelled of horse and leather, and felt warm on my cheek.

'What chance is that?' he asked, inspecting the tiny wound. And when I told him he said, 'Will you accept?'

'But yes, Marcellus, of course.'

He nodded slowly. 'Then I am happy for you. But for myself I wish you weren't going away.'

I almost cried out, 'Do you really?' But instead I frowned at the cobbles and kicked at them with my boot. 'I don't suppose I'll be going far,' I said, looking up. 'I think Gratian will keep me in London, with the others; at least for now.'

'Your friends will be glad of that.'

I thought of the drunks and gamblers and retired whores I wasted my empty hours with. 'It won't concern them overmuch,' I said with a shrug.

'No?' He pushed his hand through his hair, then turned and met my eye. 'That day, when you did not come, I almost went to your uncle's villa to find you. I guessed something or other was wrong. You didn't seem the sort who would change his mind on a whim. I'm glad it wasn't that.'

'Oh no, Marcellus!' I blurted out, 'not at all! If only you knew! I have thought of nothing else—' I broke off, reddening.

But the fine contours of his face moved in a smile. 'Is that so? You know, it's only by chance that I came here today, and now I find you waiting. I think some god had a hand in it.'

'Yes,' I said, looking at him seriously, 'I think so too.'

The low winter sun had shifted, leaving the courtyard in shadow. He took a deep breath and pulled up his cloak. His breath showed in the cold air. 'You must be proud. To be chosen as a Protector is quite an honour . . . Not,' he added with a grin, 'that they'll have much to teach you about fighting.'

I laughed. My spirits were lifting. There are times when the heart knows straightaway what it has been seeking. Mine knew it now. I said, 'You haven't seen my horse-riding, though. I think I have forgotten how.'

'You don't have a horse of your own then? But no, of course, I should have realized. When did you last ride?'

'Not since I was a boy, at my father's house.'

'It's not something you forget. We'll go riding one day if you like. At home we have a whole stable, and you can take your pick.' He glanced at me, adding, 'But maybe I am presuming too much? . . .'

'No,' I said, 'I'd like that.'

He smiled. 'Then good.' His head went up. 'But here's Grandfather at last.'

I looked round. Across the square the bearded white-haired man I had seen on the stairs had appeared under the portico. The chamberlain had waylaid him there. The old man's face wore an expression of bored courtesy while the chamberlain talked on. His eyes were fixed absently on the row of Corinthian capitals under the roof.

'I'd better go and rescue him,' said Marcellus. 'He loathes the chamberlain.' He paused and looked at me. 'When shall I see you?'

'Tomorrow?'

'Tomorrow – for sure. I'll be at the basilica in the forum, at the hour when the Council meets. I'll wait for you on the steps.'

'I will be there,' I said.

'I am glad to hear it,' said Balbus, glancing up from a shipping-account laid out in front of him on the desk. 'It is good news.'

'Yes, sir. I believe it is.'

'And it is what you want?'

'It is, sir.'

'Then you must go. Of course you must. Though I wonder how I shall manage without you.'

That year, he had ejected the neighbouring tenant in the Street of the Carpenters and expanded his offices. Even in winter he was busy. He had taken on new clerks; and just then everyone was working on a large consignment of supplies to the forts along the northern border, for which a small fleet of ships had been hired. The province was prospering, and so was he.

'Now where is that manifest?' he said, looking away. 'I had it a moment ago.' He began pushing at the clutter on his desk.

'Here,' I said. I lifted a folded wooden tablet and handed it to him. He gave the document a cursory glance and set it down, then looked at me sadly.

'You see? I shall miss you, my boy. Why not leave generalship and government to others? There is nothing to be gained from it, if I am any judge of such things — Yes? What is it?' One of the new brash young clerks had entered to say the shipping agent was waiting. Balbus waved him away. 'Still, Drusus, business will not wait, and I must press on and deal with Vibianus. I am expected at the docks.'

Lucretia sat basilisk-faced when I told her, as if even my leaving were a slight on her.

'There is no money, if that is what you want.'

'No,' I said.

There followed an unpleasant pause. Her fingers tapped on the damask cushion of her couch. Then she said, 'You always looked down on me. You think you are better. But you are nothing at all.'

'I looked at her pinched, mean face and said, 'No, madam.' Beyond her, from behind the gaudy hangings, where a new myrrhine vase stood on a fluted ornamental table, I saw the image of the simple, sad youth gazing out at me.

Like a squirrel preparing for winter, burying his acorns for the day he would have need of them, I had stored up over the months and years many ugly words I wanted to say in return for her slights and petty cruelty. But now I realized, as I looked at her hard face and modish clothes, that I had left her far behind. She no longer mattered. She had allowed envy and bitterness to mould her; she had succeeded in bending her son to her will, and had crushed the life out of him. Her husband, as she surely knew, absented himself from her whenever he could. Only the

177

slaves remained, and, though they could not leave, they were a torment to her as much as she to them. She was her own punishment, and I perceived that any words of mine would diminish me, not her. I was free. It was enough.

And then, for no reason that was clear to me, I found I was thinking of Marcellus.

Next day I washed and dressed and hurried out, not having thought to ask what time the Council met.

I arrived too early. The low winter sun was only now rising over the surrounding roofs, casting long shadows across the great porticoed expanse of the forum square.

The food merchants – always the first to market – were setting up their awnings and laying out their baskets and urns. I stopped at a baker's in the colonnade, bought a warm honeycake, and watched the activity around me – fish sellers with racks of oysters and casks of swimming fish; grain merchants unloading sacks of wheat and barley and pulses; greengrocers; herb sellers; spice importers and men with stacked amphoras of oil and wine and piquant sauces. As Balbus liked to say, the market was better than any soothsayer's scattered stones for telling the health of the province, and it was filling from one side of the colonnade to the other. Trade had been good since Gratian had driven out the Saxons.

I swallowed the last of my cake and made my way along the colonnade, past the offices of the lawyers and city officials, to the great basilica which fills the forum's northern edge. Groups of clerks and rich men's clients were already loitering among the tall granite columns, wrapped against the morning chill, clutching writing tablets or scrolls. I wandered among them. Marcellus was not there.

Litters began to arrive, carrying members of the Council. Decurions and magistrates stepped out and mounted the basilica steps; the waiting clerks and clients stepped forward. Then, turning away, I saw him, striding purposefully across the open area of the piazza, looking fine and handsome, dressed in a woollen cloak of dark green. His grandfather Aquinus was with him and they were deep in conversation, the old man making some point and gesturing as he spoke, and Marcellus nodding.

For a moment I wondered if he had forgotten me. But I need not have worried. As they approached he glanced up, scanning the steps. Seeing me his face brightened, like the break of dawn light. His grandfather turned to meet me.

'So this,' he said, 'is what all the fuss was about. I am glad to meet you at last, Drusus, though I perceive now that we have met before, even if we did not speak.'

Behind me someone said, 'Good day, Quintus Aquinus.' Aquinus inclined his head in acknowledgement. Around me I could see others ready to step forward, waiting to speak to him.

'Today,' he continued, ignoring them, 'the Council deliberates on the subvention for municipal works, so it will be a long and tedious morning of listening to decurion after decurion explaining why he cannot pay.' He nodded down the steps to where a rotund, balding man was climbing out of a sedan. 'There is one. They come in clothes borrowed from their slaves and tell us they are poor; yet they arrive in gilded litters with a retinue of bearers and suppose we do not notice. And quite apart from that, have you ever seen a poor man who is so fat?'

Beside him Marcellus coughed and shifted. 'However,' continued his grandfather, 'let us not dwell on such people; the world is full of them, and I shall not bore you with the city's woes.' He turned to Marcellus, raising his heavy white brows. 'He is a good-looking boy. I see now why you were up before the house-slaves.'

Marcellus reddened, and pushed his hand uncomfortably through his mane of hair. His grandfather turned back to me with a glint in his eye. 'I believe you are to join Gratian's staff. Then I congratulate you. Perhaps, when you have time from your duties, Marcellus might bring you to visit us in the country. You will be welcome.'

I thanked him. At the high bronze door of the meeting chamber a gong sounded. 'But now,' he said, 'the Council summons, and my clients here wish to address their petitions, so if you will excuse me . . .' He nodded to us both and moved off. The crowd closed around him, chattering and importuning.

'That,' said Marcellus, frowning after him, 'was my grandfather.'

'I like him.'

'Do you?' he said seriously. 'He is quite impressive really; he speaks his mind, and some people don't like that, especially in the Council.' He paused, and met my eye with a sheepish look. 'And I wasn't up before the slaves . . . well no, that's not true: I was. But not just for you; I had other things to do as well.'

I could not help but laugh. After the tension of waiting, wondering if he would come, and of meeting Aquinus, it suddenly seemed funny. I said, 'I've been here since before sunrise. I didn't think to find out what time the Council met. I was afraid I might miss you.'

'Really?' He looked at me with concern. 'But I thought you knew—' Then our eyes met and he laughed too. 'Still, it doesn't matter now. What are you doing this morning?'

'Nothing at all,' I said.

'Good. Then let us get away from all these people.'

I do not recall everywhere we walked, or everything we said to one another, for it seemed we ranged all over London and talked of everything. But I remember as if it were yesterday the intensity of that day. It was like a perfect note of music, like the clear voice of a flute breaking through the noise of my discordant life. We walked to the pleasant places in the city – up to the ramparts; out along the Walbrook, and west to the Fleet; through the open meadows around the hippodrome, and north beyond the wall to the high ground where we could look out from the grassy slopes at the city spread before us, with its walls and red-roofed houses, and archways and statues and painted columns. We talked of our lives, our pasts, something of our hopes, and delighted in finding what we had in common, as new friends do. Never in my life had I felt so easy in another's company. I sensed, even then, that behind our words there was a matching of our souls, as if I had found by chance some missing half of myself, wandering apart and waiting to be reunited.

Before I knew it the light was fading. We wandered

181

down to the bridge and leaning side by side on the balustrade watched the water ebb around the piers, and the orange sunset clouds billowing up in the west. On the riverside wall, the lamplighter was kindling the cressets in their tall standards. They flared up, one by one. Beside me Marcellus said, 'The day has gone so fast; I hardly know how.'

I said, 'Nor I.'

'Yet there will be other days, if we choose it. Do you choose it, Drusus?'

I turned to him. The last of the sun had caught his face, reflecting like flame in his eyes.

'Yes,' I said, speaking what my heart felt, 'more than anything.'

He smiled, and said, 'I too.'

After that, we walked together up the hill, pausing here and there; but at the crossroads by the forum arch, where our paths took us different ways, we fixed a place to meet next day. And then we parted.

It was one evening not long afterwards that I nearly died, and this brings me to the subject of the gods.

After the night on the hilltop, and the girl beneath the yew tree, and the old woman who spoke in meaning riddles, I had thought again about what I had assumed I understood. I sensed the pull of some deep undercurrent, like form within chaos, or the patterns of the myriad stars.

Though I possessed no clear words for what I felt, yet I found my mind returned there, as a creature turns to water, or a plant to light. And so, as I have told, I had taken to visiting the little temple of the Huntress, up by the northern gate; for she, it seemed, was my particular god.

One would scarcely notice the shrine, and perhaps, for this reason, the Christians had left it alone. The entrance lay behind the low spreading branches of an oak that filled the square outside. Above the lintel, hidden from view unless one craned one's neck to look, was carved in relief a scene of hunting dogs, their noses hugging the ground, running with the goddess. Within, the shrine was larger than it seemed, having been built between two houses, so that beyond the door one came into an atrium half open to the sky, and from there through a row of sturdy columns to an inner room with the fresco that so moved me.

Though I had never met another person there, I always found a lamp alight within the sanctuary, flickering in the draught behind the plinth, so that the statue itself seemed to shimmer and move. Here I would wait a while, sometimes leaving a small offering, sometimes merely standing in the presence of the god. It was my own private communion with a reality I could not name.

I had wondered at first who tended the lamp; for no one ever came, and in time I began to think of the place as my secret domain. So I started back with a cry when, that evening, a figure suddenly leapt out from the shadows.

'What are you doing here?' he demanded. He was a spindly, sharp-faced youth with aggression etched on his features like dirt. For a moment I wondered if he was the keeper of the lamp; but there was nothing priest-like about him, and I had seen his type before, loitering among the stalls and gambling dens, waiting for trouble, or looking for it.

'What business is it of yours, stranger?' I said.

He hawked and spat at my feet. 'Has no one told you not to worship devils?'

So that is it, I thought. If he did not care for the old gods he could have kept away; yet instead he had lain in wait. I had heard of such people.

Durano had taught me never in battle to allow anger to cloud my judgement. He had said that in an ambush one can tell by watching him whether a man has hidden accomplices. But feeling my very soul was being defiled my temper rose within me and I forgot. I said, 'If you do not like it here, then leave and mind your business.'

His thin mouth twisted in a sneer. 'But it is our business. People like you are vermin.' He snapped his fingers, and from the shadows behind the pillars stepped five grim accomplices. They looked gaunt and weak; but each was brandishing a weapon – an iron bar, a broken chisel; the one nearest held a rusted barber's blade.

'So, devil-lover,' he said, 'it seems you have forgotten that *pagans* are not wanted here. So we must teach you to remember.' He laughed at his eloquence. The others grinned and grunted.

I knew there was no point humiliating myself by try-ing to reason with them. Words they would take only as weakness. They intended to hurt me, probably kill me. That they were in the sanctuary of a god counted for nothing. So much for their outraged piety. Six to one, I

184

thought grimly; well, I shall make sure they pay a high price for it.

I forced myself to think, clearing my mind, pushing fear aside. This too I had learned from Durano. And I recalled another of his lessons: make sure, he had said, that you have an escape; but if you do not, then bark louder than your bite, for you have nothing to lose by it.

Forcing calm and menace into my voice I said, 'You are in a holy shrine. Get out now; this is your last chance before I kill you.'

The pallid accomplices looked at one another; so I added, for good measure, 'The god will pursue you. Do you not fear her? You will never sleep easy.'

The grins faded from their faces. But the ringleader merely laughed. 'Don't listen, idiots. He is trying to scare you.'

I could feel my sweat beneath my tunic, and my own heart beating. I had won a moment with this ruse, but the moment was passing. So before their attention returned I sprang, leaping forward and smashing my shoulder into the leader's midriff. His breath rushed out and he doubled over, grasping at my hair and pulling me down with him. I shoved him and wrenched free. Then something hard struck my thigh. It hurt, but it had not hit home: whoever had struck had been aiming for my head. I rounded and kicked out, and caught someone a heavy blow in the groin.

I backed and crouched, and took in my surroundings. The others were advancing in an uncertain line; the ringleader was still clutching his stomach and gasping for air. I grabbed the edge of his tunic and heaved him round, and sent him falling into the others; then, using a wrestling move I knew, I ducked down to the floor, seized the ankles of the nearest youth and snatched them from under him. He fell back with a cry, crashing between the pillars and striking his head on the stone torus of the column. It stunned him. He dropped his weapon – a long, turned mallet handle. I lunged in the shadows for it, then standing to my full height I brought it down on the head of another.

As we fought we had dropped back, out of the glow of the lamplight. The thick columns loomed about us. In the noise and confusion it was hard for my attackers to discern friend from foe, and it slowed them. As for me, I knew each one I struck was an enemy.

From the direction of the atrium a glimmer of moonlight showed between the columns. Beyond, some way off, was the door to the street. I considered making a run for it, but anticipating this they closed to block my exit. A movement flashed in the corner of my eye. I ducked; but even as I moved I knew it was too late. The youth with the iron bar had taken a swing at my head. I avoided the worst of it; the end of the bar went crashing into the pillar behind me. But on its way it caught me a heavy blow on the back of the neck.

I staggered. My sight went dark; my head swam. I tripped on something, and fell forward onto the flagstones. Then they were upon me, like hounds on a hare, beating and kicking. They pulled me to my feet, twisting my arms behind me, laughing as I cried out in pain.

The ringleader came swaggering up and planted his

hands on his hips. He tried a sneering grin, but winced instead, and I saw with cold satisfaction that he had taken a heavy blow on the forehead and was bleeding. I drew myself up, and waited for the death blow.

But before I died he wanted to crow his petty triumph, and see me suffer, and quake, and beg for my life. So when he was sure I was held fast and could not strike him, he stepped up and spat hard in my face.

'You spit bravely,' I said.

'Shut up!' he yelled, and I could tell from his voice that he was badly shaken. Then he launched into a tirade of commonplace insults mixed with threats. I hardly listened. My head was reeling. I closed my eyes.

Suddenly he ceased. I thought, 'So now I die; but at least I have given him something to remember me by.' Then I thought of Marcellus, whom I had arranged to meet. He would wait, and once more I should not come. I felt a wave of grief for what might have been, and wished it swiftly finished.

Yet it was not to be. I became aware that the pause was lengthening. I opened my eyes. The youth was still standing before me, but his face had gone vacant. Then I saw the long knife-blade pressed tight to his throat.

I blinked and stared, for an instant as confused as he. He moved, but it was not of his own volition. Someone had shoved him from behind; and I saw then who held the blade.

It was an old man. But old as he was, he held the youth in a grip of iron. Hard sinew showed in his lean forearm, like a ploughman's, or a soldier's. 'I should like,' he said slowly, 'to slit the throat of this dog and offer his blood to the god. But I will not insult her with such a worthless sacrifice, and so I shall kill him for myself.'

His grip tightened; the blade moved.

At this the youth began to whine and mewl, like some bitch's pup. Water sounded on the stone floor; he had pissed himself.

His accomplices stared, their appalled gaze moving from the gathering puddle to their leader's face. They looked away in disgust.

'Rah!' the old man shouted at them. They jumped and fled, stumbling and flailing in their haste to reach the door. Then he returned his attention to the ringleader. 'Where is your courage now, brave one?'

But the youth was too far gone to answer. He just carried on snivelling, snot and tears dribbling down his trembling face.

In disgust the old man cried, 'What sort of man is it who will take another's life, but lacks the courage to lose his own?' And then, with a sudden slap, 'Shut up! Or I'll cut your throat to silence you.'

The youth swallowed his whining and stared forward.

'Well?' said the man, glancing at me. 'Will you kill him or shall I?'

I shook my head. It hurt. I could smell my own sweat. I felt dazed and sick. 'Let him go,' I said. 'There has been enough defilement here.'

He looked at me, and I looked back. I saw a weariness in his old eyes. He took a long breath and slowly exhaled the air.

'As you wish,' he said.

He withdrew the knife, shoved the youth away, and gave him a clout. 'Remember,' he told him, 'that it is a *pagan* who spares you!'

The youth staggered, then found his feet and scrambled towards the exit. At the door, where he was out of reach, he paused and turned, and yelled back, vowing he would come and get the old man.

Then he ran off into the night.

The old man looked at me. 'See what you have spared?' He slid the knife back into its sheath, and began picking up the weapons scattered about on the floor.

I said, 'Was it you who lit the lamp, sir?'

'It was I. My father was the priest here, and his father before him. But I have no son, and soon I shall be too old to fight off these Christian dogs.'

I had been helping him pick up the debris. But now I paused and looking at him said, 'They claim they will destroy the old gods. But why? I cannot understand it.'

'So they claim, and so they wish. But if men are prevented from worshipping the gods in one way, they will find another. We may give them different names, but the gods do not change.'

His eyes moved to the statue flickering in the lamplight. 'The Christians may drive us from the temples, but they cannot drive the truth from men's souls. And perhaps, one day many years from now, when I am dust and this city is forgotten, some farmer with his plough will stumble upon the image of the goddess, lying here in the earth beneath his share, and he will know her.'

I stooped to pick up a vicious-looking cudgel. It had been lovingly sanded-down and wrapped with string about the handle – a labour of many hours. So much effort, I thought, for such ugliness. And as I bent down, there was a sudden stabbing pain in my side.

I winced and dropped the weapon on the floor. The old man came over and rapidly felt my side, asking where the pain was. A cry from me told him soon enough. He pulled up my tunic and probed at my ribs, muttering to himself. Then he nodded and grunted.

'It will bruise,' he said, 'but the bones are not broken.' He reached up and felt the back of my head. When he took his fingers away they were red with my blood. 'But this,' he said, frowning and naming a concoction of herbs, 'you must bathe; and afterwards you must rest.' He looked into my face. 'You have been here before, haven't you?'

And when I told him yes, he said, 'Then come in peace, my friend. But next time bring a dagger.'

Claritas washed my head, and the cook prepared the herbal salve. By the time Marcellus saw me, my side was blue as a storm sky.

'What were you thinking?' he cried. 'How long would you have lain there before someone found your body?'

'I had promised the god.'

He let out his breath and pushed his fingers through his hair. 'Everyone has heard of these Christian mobs – except you, it seems. Why do you think the temples are empty? It is because decent people dare not go. They do not want a battle each time they visit a shrine or make an offering to a god, and so they stay at home. The Christians know this. And then, when the temples are empty, they claim it is because the people have ceased to care.' He looked at me and shook his head. 'At least next time take me with you.' He gave me a gentle cuff on the ear.

'Ouch!'

'That's so you remember.'

I smiled, in spite of the pain. I treasured these signs of affection. They were like food to a starving man.

We had met every day since our first meeting, taking advantage of the time he was in London with his grandfather. Each day, with a mixture of nervousness and joy, I wondered what it was he saw in me, who in my own estimation was so flawed.

And though, without doubt, he was beautiful in form, powerful and sleek as a young stag, this was not all that moved me. There was a natural goodness and open simplicity to him. He talked with ease and knowledge, of things which up to then I had supposed were my private thoughts alone. There was nothing that was mean in him, nothing small.

During those first days I took each step carefully, expecting at any moment that he would see me for what I was and tire of me. At first I waited for it. But as the days passed and still he stayed, I began to trust what I found. I became aware of a change in me, a thawing within, like the shafts of dawn through morning mist. I had supposed, inasmuch as I had ever considered it, that my destiny was to find my way through the world alone. Solitude was what the Fates had allotted me. Yet each day with Marcellus brought me signs that after all this was not so. I hardly dared trust what my feelings told. I hardly dared reach for pleasure. I knew – though I lacked the courage to let him see – that my soul cried out for love. I was ardent, but I was wary.

I found I noticed the small, private things about him, and stored them in my secret heart: his well-formed hands, and how he ran his fingers through his hair when he was troubled or embarrassed; the way he paused in speaking and frowned to himself as he collected his thoughts; the blond down on his legs and wrists and forearms, which I should have liked to touch, just to feel it, if I dared; or how he stole quick glances at me when he was talking, to check I was not bored. I knew like some precious perfume the pine-scent of the wash he cleaned his hair with, and the deeper male smell of his body. I had never been so aware of another's physical presence before: I basked in his attention; I walked in sunlight.

Then at last, too soon, came the time to return to the country.

We parted with promises to meet, and I saw him and his grandfather Aquinus off, walking with them across the bridge, and alongside their carriage till it pulled away.

Returning I paused on the path on the south side of the river, and gazed across the water over the roofs of the city houses to where the columns of the governor's palace showed in the distance. It would soon be my home. The order had come for me to present myself at the barracks there.

Shortly after, I said my goodbyes at the house, such as they were, and packed up my few possessions in the old oak clothes-chest I had brought from home.

Only the slaves saw me off – Claritas and old Patricus and the cook. Balbus was taken up with business. Lucretia stayed within, in her private rooms. And Albinus, just as on the day I had first arrived, was at the bishop's.

Seven

A STURDY BROWN-HAIRED young Pannonian
received me at the barracks. His name was Leontius, and
he was head of the corps of Protectors.

He spoke a rough upcountry Latin and had a blunt
manner, but seeing I was unsure of myself he was pleasant
with me, when a worse man would have delighted in
being harsh. So right at the start I decided I liked him.

I was fitted out with a uniform: a kilt and tunic and
red woollen cloak, winter leggings, a sword-belt, sword
and dagger, and a pair of standard-issue military boots.
Then Leontius showed me my room, which I shared with
three others, in the barrack-house behind the palace
stables.

I had turned seventeen, and what with one thing and
another, I felt quite the man. But I soon discovered I
was the youngest in the corps; and being new as well,
I was the object of all the usual jokes and teasing and
curiosity.

Of the others, most had followed Gratian from posting to posting, and regarded themselves as old hands. There were a good many burly Pannonians – which he favoured, being Pannonian himself – but also Africans, Gauls, Spaniards, and a few more recent recruits from Britain.

Gratian, I was informed, expected his cadets to be good horsemen, which I was not. But his great passion, which he had kept since his days as a young recruit, was wrestling.

Anyone who has met a Pannonian will know that this is a sport they adore; and, being on the whole a stocky broad-shouldered race, they are well suited to it. I had not forgotten that it was Gratian's success in a bout, one day when a general happened to be watching, that led to his being singled out for advancement. Now, it seemed, wrestling was for him the key to all success – the test of a true man – and we were all expected to take part, whether we cared for it or not.

So I was not wholly surprised when, one day that early spring, a few weeks after my arrival, Leontius came to me in the mess and, slapping his hand down on the long rough-wood table, announced with a broad grin, 'Your turn next, Drusus. You'd better get some extra practice, and put some weight on.'

Along the bench there were some smirks and exchanged laughing glances. I knew what it meant: the new boy was going to get a thrashing. I went to the board in the corridor and checked the team-lists. I was pitted against a wiry Spaniard called Catius. I knew him. He was no great fighter; I could handle him.

But on the evening before the appointed day, as I lay

relaxing on my bed, one of my comrades said casually, 'Have you seen who you're fighting, Drusus?'

'Yes, Catius,' I answered.

'Not any more,' he said grinning. 'You'd better check again.'

I leapt up and hurried off to look.

Catius's name had been crossed off the list. In its place was written the name 'Meta' in an illiterate hand.

Everybody knew Meta. He was a youth from the wild inaccessible hills of Illyria, an ox-like brute with a broken nose and a taste for violence. I stood and stared, with a sinking feeling in my gut. This was their joke – a typical Pannonian joke. Well, I thought, I shall not let them see I care; and when I returned to my room to the curious gaze of my comrades, I merely shrugged and said, 'It was Catius; now it is Meta. Wish me luck.'

Next morning the corps assembled, crowding round the horse-paddock, buzzing with excited chatter. They cheered when I took up my position – everyone likes the underdog – but there was no doubt in any of their faces of the outcome, and I could see why.

I had some muscle on my body, but compared with the Illyrian beast in the far corner I was a milk-skinned weakling. It was not a fair fight, and I had already understood it was never intended to be. It was an offering, a sacrifice, a breaking-in. And I was the victim.

I watched him nodding and grinning his peg-toothed grin with his clique of thickset friends, grunting as they imparted advice, rocking from foot to foot like a wrought-up bull. In my mind I ran through my strategy one last time. He would crush me if I let him; it was no good taking him head-on. My only chance was speed, and whatever skill I possessed.

The signal drum sounded. I stepped forward onto the sand, naked but for my loincloth. Around the paddock my comrades raised a cheer. I pranced and shifted, getting the feel of the sand under my toes, moving my limbs to warm them, for it was a cold, clear morning.

On the far side my opponent began advancing, plodding forward in rigid splay-legged movements like an ox heaving a plough. I eyed him carefully. His thighs were like oak-trunks, so wide and knotted with muscle that they chafed as he moved. His bare feet, tiny in comparison, looked absurd beneath his great slab-like bulk. It seemed almost impious that he had turned himself into such a creature.

At the edge of the paddock the crowd shifted and drew apart, and through the corner of my eye I saw Gratian step forward to the rail. Another reason not to be humiliated, I thought bleakly. And then, as I looked back at my opponent, I knew that humiliation was the least of my worries. I wondered how many this Illyrian monster had killed, and whether Gratian would permit the fight to go so far. Gratian prided himself on being a hard man; he did not make concessions to weakness.

I pushed all these concerns from my mind. My opponent had halted; and now, in some fighting-ritual he had learned, he began slapping the flats of his hands on his muscle-twisted upper arms, and glancing back to grin at his friends. One might have supposed I was not there at all, so little attention did he pay me, and it was clear he did not expect to exert himself. He intended to make a spectacle of my defeat.

His friends guffawed at his antics and called encouragements. But someone else in the crowd shouted, 'Get on with it!'

Then, with a lolling shake of his head, he charged.

The ground under my feet thudded with his footfalls. I watched him carefully, gauged the speed and direction of his advance, and prepared to leap. I tensed; but at the last moment something made me hold back and I stilled myself, and thought again. His attack was too obvious: surely it was a decoy, to hide some cleverer trick. I paused, but he kept on coming, grunting as he loped forward, his bulging face set in concentration, as if movement alone took up every resource of his mind.

Remembering what I had learned from Durano, I searched his body with my eyes for the first telltale sign – a twitch of muscle, an involuntary sideways glance – anything that would show me he was about to swerve, or leap, or throw himself down to trip me. But none of these things happened, and at the last moment, when he was almost upon me, I threw myself to the left, rolled and straightened, and thrust out my right leg in his path.

His small feet skidded in the sand. But either his dull mind or his hulking body did not respond fast enough. His ankles struck my outstretched calf, and for good measure I used my other leg to give him a side-kick. He gave a furious bellow, then fell forward, slewing into the ground on his convex belly like some ungainly overweight flightless bird.

All around the paddock the audience broke into merry laughter. This was fun they had not expected. They called to me and whistled, but I had no time to acknowledge them. The Illyrian was already up again, wiping his face and spitting sand. The whole of his thick upper body had purpled with rage. He was not the kind that cared to be laughed at.

I thought quickly. So far, he had supposed I could be toyed with as a cat plays with a mouse. Now he knew different. His next attack would be more dangerous. I remembered Durano's lessons, and cleared my mind, and silently spoke my little private formula against fear.

This time he tried to trick me with a feint. It was one for which Durano would have slapped me, for being too obvious. I held my ground, undeceived. Then, with a sudden bellowing cry, he came at me like a wild thing, all flailing arms and piggish furious eyes. I crouched, balancing myself with my outstretched arms, and threw a deliberate, nervous glance leftwards; and this he read just as I hoped. I saw him compensating in his step, preparing to move in the direction of my glance; and when the moment came, I jumped not left but right.

I thought I had foiled him again; but this time he was prepared, knowing now I was a trickster. He swerved to cut me off; then lunged at me, snatching with his fingers.

I leapt back. I almost fell. But I righted myself, span round, and as he passed I slammed into his huge broad back with a force that would have felled any normal man. But I might as well have run into a barn wall. I merely bounced off him. I stood and stared, momentarily dazed and at a loss. And all the while he was turning, growling like a bear, and raising his arms to seize me.

I threw myself down before him. He blinked and stared. I think he supposed I was about to prostrate myself in supplication. But I was not beaten yet. He clubbed his fists and took a downward swing at me. It would have broken my ribs; but I rolled and avoided it, then grabbed his thigh with my arms, shoved his back, and pulled. The hold was poor, but he was half-turned and off his balance, and I was using his own force against him.

One moment it seemed nothing would shift him; the next he came crashing down beside me.

At once I scrambled onto his back. He heaved and bellowed and kicked; but I was on his neck with all my weight. I grabbed his wrist and forced his arm behind him, bending it upwards. 'Yield!' I cried.

Everywhere the crowd was yelling and whistling.

'Yield, you fool!' I shouted again in his ear, 'Must I break your arm?'

But the great writhing mass beneath me refused to give way.

He tried to get up. I smashed him down. All around me the voices were chanting, 'Yield! Yield! Yield!'

He cursed and bucked, trying to throw me off. I forced his arm hard up. He cried out. Even prone like this and held in a lock, he was hard to manage. He was too strong for me, and slippery with sweat.

I sensed a change in the crowd, like a false note in a concert. Some of them, their voices hoarse and thick with blood-lust, had begun urging me to break the Illyrian's arm. It was his sword arm. They knew it was. They did not care.

Then, with a sudden ringing shout, Gratian's voice broke out over all the rest. 'Give way, you idiot! Where is your honour?'

The Illyrian froze beneath me. I think, in his blind rage, he had forgotten Gratian was there. Beneath my thighs his great barrel-chest exhaled. Then slowly, grudgingly, he raised his palm from the sand and gave the sign of submission. And, all around me, the crowd broke into a deafening roar.

Later, when I was drying off in the bath-house, Leontius came and found me.

'Well you're a dark horse, young Drusus,' he said, clapping me on the shoulder. 'You didn't tell us you could fight like that. Gratian is talking of nothing else.'

'Good,' I said. 'I expect I surprised him.'

I threw the towel down on the bench, and rummaged among my clothes.

'What is it? You won.'

'I know, Leontius. It's just that I don't care for this kind of fighting. That's all.'

He laughed and said, 'Don't let Gratian hear you say that. Remember, this is the army.'

I turned and looked at him.

'Yes, it's the army, and I will kill when I need to. But did you not hear the cries? There were people baying for blood, calling for me to break his arm. He isn't my friend – even less so now, I daresay. But he isn't some barbarian either, come to burn our homes and kill our families. He is one of us, a comrade – even if he is as stupid as a peasant's ox.'

Leontius frowned at me. After a moment he said, 'I know. I heard them.'

He stood for a while in silence, watching me as I dressed. Then he said, 'Would you have done it – broken his arm?'

I paused and turned. It was a question I had been thinking about all the while I was in the baths.

'Yes,' I said. 'Those are the rules, if a man will not yield. But I don't have to enjoy it.'

He nodded slowly and drew a long breath. I saw him glance up and down the room before he spoke again. Then, dropping his voice, he said, 'I'll tell you something, Drusus, but don't you dare breathe it to another soul. I don't care for Gratian's accursed wrestling either, and that's far worse, because I'm a Pannonian like him, and it's supposed to run in my blood.'

He looked so grave and concerned that one might have supposed he had confessed his mother was hawking herself at the local tavern, and in spite of my heavy mood I could not help but laugh.

'Don't worry, Leontius,' I said smiling. 'Your secret's safe with me.'

He nodded grimly, and waited while I finished dressing. Then together we made our way to the mess, where the others were already celebrating my victory.

After that day, no one treated me as the baby of the corps. For some time, Meta the Illyrian avoided me. When, eventually, he realized I did not revel in his humiliation, he even managed to be civil. I doubt we should ever have been friends, even without the fight. But at least we had not become enemies.

I think, in the end, what shamed him most was not his defeat, but not having conceded honourably. He knew, in his own dull way, that the others thought less of him for it. I was never asked to fight him again.

As Marcellus had predicted, I found my horse-riding came back to me. Of course, I had never learned cavalry skills, and these my comrades taught me – how to wheel in close formation, or throw the lance at a gallop, or stay mounted when struck. I kept myself lean and fast and strong, and grew used to my new life.

I even supposed, with the ignorance of youth, that it would go on forever.

'I have received a letter from my friend Flavius Martinus,' said Aquinus, setting down his wine-cup.

'Oh?' said Marcellus. 'Is he in Italy still?'

'No; he has been summoned to Gaul by Constans. He is at Autun, with the rest of the court.'

'I thought he kept his distance from the imperial house.'

'So did I. But Martinus has always stayed close to power, and sailed with the prevailing wind where politics is concerned. And besides, Constans is not a man to be crossed or refused, by all accounts.'

It was the evening of my first day with Marcellus and his grandfather. It was high summer, and, having been granted a few days' leave, I had ridden out to visit them in the country. We were seated in the great summer dining-room, which opened out onto the loggia and the inner gardens. The lamps had just been kindled. Outside, through a row of columns, the last glow of daylight showed over the flowering shrubs.

'What does he say?' said Marcellus. 'Has Constans changed, now he has the whole of the West to govern?'

Aquinus delayed his answer while the servants took away the last of the dinner things. When they had gone and the door was closed he said, 'It takes great self-mastery to rule, and Constans came to power too young. His father Constantine would have served Rome better if he had passed the imperium to the man best able to wield it, rather than to his sons. But still. He placed ties of family above the advice of reason, and we must make the best of it. Since the victory over his foolish brother, the sycophants that surround our young emperor have been flattering him that he is master of the world, a man invincible, who may take what he wishes. That is strong wine for such an unformed mind. Power such as his needs restraint sitting at its right hand, not licence.'

He paused, frowning under his white beard. 'He lives for pleasure, and like all men who live for pleasure, he has become its slave. His self-seeking courtiers know this, and ensure his every whim is pandered to, thinking thereby to control him. He has conceived a passion for hunting, a pastime for which his advisers assure him he has great ability. He spends each day chasing deer and boar in the hills around Autun, and every night celebrating his good fortune with his friends, often until dawn. It is said the grooms take bets on whether he will be sober enough next morning to mount his horse.'

Marcellus laughed. 'Well it's no secret he is governed by his desires.'

'No, it is not. Yet I fear we underestimate them. There are some German princes at the court. They are "guests" of the emperor, as it is called, kept there to ensure the loyalty of their warlike barbarian fathers. It seems there has been an incident.'

'Oh? What happened? Has he insulted them?'

'Worse, both for them and for Constans's hard-won and delicate relationship with their royal fathers. He ravished them.'

I had been reaching forward for my wine-cup; but now I paused and looked first at Marcellus and then at Aquinus, thinking I had misheard.

Marcellus said, 'What, *all* of them?'

'Do not joke, Marcellus; it has caused a scandal such as you would not believe. No one dare say anything to Constans, of course; but behind his back the court is in uproar. Even the Bishop of Autun will scarcely speak to him, and he is a man who seldom scruples about morality. One dreads to think what the boys' fathers will do when they hear.'

'Perhaps Constans was drunk.'

'Let us hope he was not sober, or what can we expect when he loses his self-control?' He brushed a crumb from his fine woollen tunic, sighed, and glanced at the door to make sure the waiting slave had not returned. 'The truth is that the whole imperial family are nothing but ruffians and yokels; I wonder they do not just elevate some illiterate barbarian to the purple and have done with it. Arrogance coupled with ignorance; over-indulgence, sexual excess: hardly the virtues one looks for in a prince. How does Martinus put up with it all?'

That day, riding in from the east, I had properly seen the great house for the first time. The long approach was flanked by stately poplars, at the end of which a pillared gateway opened to the large enclosed demesne.

Within, there was an orchard, and elsewhere fishponds and well-tended lawns divided by paths edged with low box hedges. Further off, still inside the walls – for indeed the enclosure might have contained a small town – were barns and granaries, and a row of neat whitewashed houses where the farm-hands and servants lived.

The house itself was two and three storeys high, with vaulting arches, tall shuttered windows, and fluted pilasters, with a fountain of leaping bronze dolphins cascading water into a circular pool.

Marcellus had been waiting on the steps when I arrived, dressed simply in his working clothes and looking as fine as ever. The farm-hands had seen my approach, and had called him. We embraced, and then I turned and gazed in wonder at the marble columns and carved pediments, and the summer-ripe gardens that stretched out before me.

'What do you think?' said Marcellus, smiling.

'It's – well, it's beautiful.' And, strange as it sounded,

that was the word that came to me, for the house and grounds seemed the very embodiment of harmony and order, an image of perfection, fashioned by man's patient attention, year upon year.

Marcellus laughed, and put his hand on my shoulder. 'Yes, and it's a lot of work as well. Come on, let's go inside.'

The atrium within was the height of two houses, a great oblong space of inlaid marble panels and rose-pink columns, with sunlight shafting from high windows across a polished floor of dark-green serpentine. The warm summer air smelt of jasmine and resined wood, and through an arch on the far side, from a shaded inner court, came the sound of a trickling fountain.

A well-dressed elderly steward approached. 'I have had a room in the west wing made up, sir, if you will come this way.'

'Don't worry, Clemens,' said Marcellus. 'I'll take him.' And then to me, 'Come on, I'll show you round.'

Later, when I had washed and changed, and was lying on my bed, the steward came tapping at the door. He enquired if all was to my liking, then said that Quintus Aquinus was waiting in his library, if I would care to see him.

He led me back to the atrium, and through an inner garden court to a long room lined with books. The room was cool and still; the sharp fresh scent of cedar oil hung in the air. Under a sunlit window, Aquinus was seated on a fine carved chair beside a table.

He stood and greeted me, and asked after my journey.

Then, seeing me glance at the rows of stacked scrolls and books of bound parchment, he said, 'My library; I doubt there is a better one in the province.'

He took an open scroll from his desk, fine calligraphy held with a polished wood binding and a tie of scarlet ribbon. 'This,' he said, 'was sent to me recently by a friend in Constantinople. It is a copy of Aristotle on comedy. You would have to travel a long way before you found another.'

For a moment he gazed at it with absent affection, adding, half to himself, 'There is no education without Aristotle.' He set the book gently down. 'To build such a collection has taken years – generations even. Many of these volumes I got from my father, and he from his. I have friends who scout for books I do not have, and trained men whose only occupation is to copy and pre-serve. It is an endless task . . . But come,' he said, taking my arm, 'I am being tedious, talking on of my great passion so soon after you have arrived. Has Clemens seen to your room? Good. Then let us get some air, and sit for a while in the sunshine. I wanted to see you before Marcellus takes you off; he has been talking of nothing else for days.'

We passed through a door to a small courtyard gar-den. On a stone patio under the mottled shade of a lilac tree there were two chairs and a trestle table, and upon it a flask of chilled wine and a dish of sweet-cakes and fruit. We sat, and when he had poured the wine and invited me to eat he continued, 'All my life I have worked with one purpose, to see to it that good men rule in the province. Your father was such a man. It is a sign of the age that he was taken from us in the manner that he was. We used to lend each other books. He too had a library, I believe.'

'Yes sir,' I said, 'and now the bishop has it, I expect.'

He turned to me with raised brows. 'The bishop? Surely not.'

I explained how our estate had been confiscated, and who had benefited. He listened without comment. When I had finished he sat gazing across the garden at the trellis of climbing roses on the far wall, with his face set stern under his white beard.

I began to wonder if I had spoken out of turn, and was about to say I was sorry for bothering him with my own business, when he turned and spoke.

'That I had not known,' he said, his voice hardening. 'Then of course the library will have been destroyed – sold off for what it could fetch, if I know the bishop, though I doubt he would have been aware of its value.'

'You know him, sir?' I said, surprised. It seemed somehow contrary to nature that this austere, noble man could be acquainted with a creature like the bishop.

He sighed.

'Regretfully, yes. There is no one in the government who does not. Indeed it was only a few weeks ago that I myself had an unfortunate exchange with him. It appears he has run out of money to build that wretched cathedral of his, and so he came to the magistrates demanding a subvention. They told him to speak to the emperor, who has already seized the temple revenues and debauched the city finances. It was the emperor, after all, who provided him with the funds, and the bishop seems unable, or unwilling, to give a proper account of them. At any rate,' he went on, 'the city does not have the money for such a project. But then, the following day, if you can believe it, he came beating on the door of my London house to protest at the way he was treated, blaming me for it all.'

'What did you do, sir?'

'I had the slaves throw him out – him and that odious death's-head assistant of his, the deacon. Really, he is a charlatan of the worst kind, a false pretender to knowledge. He preys on the poor, and on the lazy of mind, and offers them the prospect of truth without thought, and the grossest kind of mindless intolerance, which he calls piety.'

He paused and looked at me. 'It is rare that I call a man my enemy, Drusus; surely such an extreme is not the way of philosophy. But I struggle to find any good in that man. Tell me, is it true, as I have heard, that your uncle Balbus is a friend of his?'

'He knows him, sir; and it is true my aunt Lucretia is a friend. But I am not.'

'No; of course. How could you be? Let us not dwell on it – and we are forgetting our refreshments.'

And after that we spoke of other things.

He was an imposing severe man, and though he was quiet, and listened far more than he spoke, his presence always dominated those around him. Nothing he said was pat or second-hand, and he was impatient of imprecision and laziness in others.

At first he made me nervous; but there was nothing harsh or cruel in him. He seldom smiled, and his manner was old-fashioned and exact. And yet, as I came to know him, I was sure I detected humour too beneath that white

210

beard and in those old grey eyes. He took for granted those things which are the ends to most men's striving – money, status, even power. For Balbus and Lucretia, wealth had been a thing to be coveted, hoarded, displayed, cooed over and nurtured. Aquinus, on the other hand, whose fortune was immeasurably greater, scarcely acknowledged it. He dressed simply; he ate without excess or greed; the house, large as it was, was sparely furnished with a few pieces in understated good taste.

At first I thought this mere affectation; but I came to see that for him wealth was but a tool, which allowed him to pursue those things he considered valuable in life: learning, the cultivation of friends, the good management of his estate, and the well-being of the province. These were his concerns; they represented for him the pillars of civilized life within which good men found their place.

What he made of me I could not tell. He could hardly have failed to perceive my ignorance. But I think he hoped to share a little of his wisdom, if only I cared to listen.

Marcellus I found attractive in ways I understood more easily.

Each day we rode, or walked, or swam, or basked beside the pool under the summer sun.

Mostly we were alone, but on the last evening of my leave we ate dinner with Aquinus in the walled inner-court with its fragrant trellises and gentle burbling fountain. The slaves had taken away the tables and left us with the wine, and we were quietly talking under a twilight sky streaked with pink and magenta. I glanced across at Marcellus. We had ridden that day to the ruined circular temple where we had met, and gone on after to look at Balbus's villa beyond the brook. The villa stood empty once again, and I had taken Marcellus up the hillside behind, showing him the clearing under the yew tree, and the pool in the dip below; though I did not say what had happened there.

In the flickering lamplight his face looked happy and peaceful. His hair fell curling on his brow; his tanned arm hung lazily over the end of the couch; and with his fingers he was idly touching at the lilies in the fountain basin. He looked, I thought, like some god at rest.

He must have sensed my eyes on him, for he looked round and smiled. I smiled back, wondering if my thoughts showed in my face. Suddenly, in the midst of this, I realized that Aquinus was talking to me.

He had been speaking, when I had last attended, of the city, and justice. Now he said, 'But tell me, Drusus, how do you suppose a man learns to know the Good?'

If I had answered at that moment truthfully from my heart, I should have said, 'By being with your grandson, who to me is beautiful and perfect.' But that would not do, and so I stirred my wine-clouded mind and answered, 'Why, I suppose, sir, by seeking out good men and trying to be as they are.'

'That is a beginning,' he said, fixing me with his eye. 'And yet, if one is to learn from good men, one must first recognize good when one sees it, don't you think?'

'Yes sir,' I answered, knitting my brow and trying to think.

'So which, then, would you say, comes first?'

'Grandfather!' cried Marcellus laughing. 'Will you give

poor Drusus no rest at all? We have been out riding all day, and he is half asleep with tiredness.'

But I had been thinking, and now I set down my cup and said, 'I cannot answer, sir, with a theory or a formula; but I believe one knows goodness when one sees it, as a budding shoot knows the light. The words come later, but the knowledge – well, the knowledge comes first.'

'A fine answer,' he said, giving me one of his rare smiles. 'You see, Marcellus, he is more awake than you think. A man must be what he wishes to seem, and in time the man becomes the mask. But Marcellus is right, and I have talked enough for one evening. I shall leave you in peace.'

Presently, when we were alone, Marcellus said, 'Don't mind Grandfather. He wouldn't quiz you like that unless he liked you.'

We were lying side by side on the couch, our bodies touching, looking up at the great sweep of the Milky Way. The day had been hot and close; but now a night breeze was rustling the poplars beyond the wall, bringing a welcome freshness to the air.

I said, 'I'm glad he asks. He makes me think. He makes me yearn to be more than I am.' I shook my head, thinking I was making no sense. 'For instance, yesterday, when you were with your mother, he said that good and beauty and truth are one, to be found in the same place, and that love and reason guide us there . . . He says such things so easily you would think he was making some observation about the weather. But, you know, I can't get it out of my head.'

213

He was so long silent that I turned. He was staring up at the dome of stars, his brow furrowed. I propped myself on my elbow and looked down into his face.

'Yes,' he said smiling, 'he always manages to say the right thing. I used to believe it was some kind of magic. Now I think it comes from hard work, and learning to see clearly. That is the hardest magic of all.'

He reached up, and rested his hand on my arm, at the place above my elbow where the muscles tightened. His touch ran through me like fire, and in the silent pause it seemed my mind was aware of every tiny thing – the nightjar chirping in the shrubs, the sound of the fountain, the stirring of the trees. I saw the contours of his face, his nose and lips and sun-bleached brow, and the gentle movement of his chest beneath his tunic. And suddenly there came over me a great wave of longing and love such as I had not known before. I gazed at him, feeling naked, unable to divine what thoughts lay behind the grey eyes that looked up into mine. And so I hesitated; and after a long moment I let out my pent-up breath, and lay back once more beside him, and stared up at the silent sky.

For a long while afterwards we were still, gazing at the vast mystery of the universe, and considering the mystery within us, until eventually the footfalls of a passing servant broke the silence and the moment was gone.

'Come,' said Marcellus, sitting up. 'You have a long ride tomorrow. You must get some sleep.'

*

I returned to London and my life at the governor's palace.

The corps of Protectors had been constituted a generation before, when Diocletian was emperor. It was a proving ground for officers, or, under lax generals, a favour to the sons of friends.

But there was nothing lax about Gratian. No officer, he used to say, should expect his men to perform any task he could not, or would not, do himself. And so, each morning, we were up before dawn, running on the parade-ground, or practising sword-work and javelin-throws, or marching and riding in the fields beyond the city walls. He ran us harder, and drove us further, than any regular trooper. For some it was too much: they broke, and left. But I stayed. I would die before I broke. I took whatever was thrown at me.

And when we were not out in the field, he set us to studying ancient battles, laying out the dispositions of opposing armies on the square table in his room, showing us the moves that had led to victory or defeat. We learned administration too: for no army, he told us, could survive without a well-managed supply line, and a good general should know how to organize such things, as much as he should know strategy and tactics.

The summer passed. Out in the fields the ewes were in season, and the farmers gathered the harvest. When I was not occupied with my duties, I was with Marcellus. At the end of the summer, business had brought his grandfather back to the city, and Marcellus came with him.

In the first months of our friendship it had seemed that

there was only he and I. But now, in those weeks of autumn when we were in the city, I began to see what I should have guessed at, that he had a life before he knew me.

He was popular – how could it be otherwise? – among the sons of Britain's well-born families. They kept houses in London, and once they knew he was resident in the city, invitations began to arrive.

To me his friends were always civil. They had been bred to it. The best among them disdained to notice that I was lessened by my father's death, and by the seizure of all he owned. But I was proud, and defensive, and sensitive to slights; and perhaps because of this I was not always easy with them. I felt I was being brought into a closed circle, a place where I was tolerated, but did not quite belong.

I perceived something else too, that it was not only among the well-born sons that Marcellus was popular, but the daughters too. With all the alertness of a hunting dog I began to notice significant looks, whispered messages, and all the discreet amatory embassies that, in such circles, make up the ritual of courtship. Afterwards Marcellus would show me some little scented note, or a gift brought by a slave, and say with a laugh, 'Look what Eutropia sent me.' Or Clodia; or Vinia; or any number of the eligible secluded daughters of the provincial gentry. I would smile and make some joke. I did not like to admit to myself that I was growing possessive.

The cadets at the barracks were always boasting, in their rowdy boisterous way, of this or that girl they had tumbled, of their conquests and their plans. At such times

I kept my own counsel; I had, I knew, my own reasons for reticence, and told myself my tastes lay elsewhere. I had not, until now, considered what Marcellus felt. At first it had seemed not to matter; now that it did, I could not bring myself to ask him, thinking it base and small-minded.

I had never given thought to questions of marriage, which simply had not featured in my world. As a boy, it had been part of the pattern of the future, like growing up. Later, at the house of my uncle, mere survival had taken all my strength, and I had thought of nothing beyond that.

Yet for Marcellus, now that I saw the lives of his friends, I realized marriage was an inevitable duty, one of the constraints and expectations he had always lived with. I tried to imagine what a wife of his would be like; whom he might choose, and how she might regard me. I asked myself what would become of our friendship, and tried to tell myself it did not matter, that I was being foolish.

But then, alone at night, lying in my bed at the barracks, my heart would tell me what my reason would not admit, that I did not want to share him. It made me ashamed, and secretive.

I daresay I should have got over such folly in time, and nothing would have come of it. But that autumn an old family friend of his, the son of a rich British aristocrat, returned from Gaul, where he had been at one of the expensive schools of rhetoric. His name was Scapula.

I disliked him from the start. He could not have been more different from Marcellus. He was gross from an excess of food and drink; he flaunted his wealth; he was coarse; and he possessed an unfailing talent for exploiting the weaknesses of others. With the lavish allowance he got from his doting father, he could afford whatever he wanted; and he denied himself nothing. Yet not all things were for sale, and it was these, which he could not possess, that he desired most.

He knew how to be charming, when there was something to be gained. Though money did not interest him – he had a surfeit of that – influence did, because influence was power. He liked to play the go-between, he liked to manage people – or, as I saw it, manipulate them. He reminded me of a certain type of pederast, which any youth who has exercised his body and has a modicum of looks will have noticed at the baths, lurking in the shadows, whose souls, through years of pandering to base desire, have grown gross and flabby, until no viciousness is beyond them. They brush up against one in the hot pool, seemingly by accident – until one sees their eyes and feels their searching fingers; or they lie in wait for the unexpected death of a father, or some other upset in the family that has left it short of funds. Then they come forward offering help – at a price.

Love cannot stay hidden for long. No doubt mine showed in a thousand small ways. And Scapula hated it.

When I first caught his scornful, appraising eye upon me I supposed he felt envy; but I was wrong. He had no conception of what I had. Friendship for him was not a meeting of minds or a common striving for the good, but a contest for advantage. He was a man whom any kind of goodness offends, because it holds up a mirror to his soul.

There were usually girls of one sort or another at the parties and dinners we went to; bright educated women who made me laugh and whose company I enjoyed. The girls Scapula invited were different. They attended his gatherings for a fee; they were paid to stimulate the flagging passions of the guests, like spices in a tired stew.

Even so, it took some time even for me to realize he was putting these girls in Marcellus's way deliberately. At first I could scarcely credit it. But I watched their rehearsed heavy-handed advances with growing under-standing, and growing anger. Marcellus, in his decency and innocence, did not see; but I, with a cynical eye, knew what they were about, and who was behind it.

I said nothing. I hid my thoughts even from him; out of shame, and contempt for the pettiness of it all. But Scapula, sensing my true feeling with the keenness of a dog snuffling around the midden, would sidle up to me, slap me on the back with false jollity, and ask with a mock-ing eye why I was so sullen when I should be enjoying myself like everyone else. He would point with his fat finger at one of his girls, ask my opinion, or speculate with a knowing leer whether Marcellus might be lucky tonight.

To these provocations I would give some short answer; and he, regarding me with the amused eye and dry sophisticated smirk he always wore, would move on.

He knew what he was doing. It amused him to see me suffer. And he knew I had no defence. He was confronting me with the darkness within my soul, where jealousy lived, and fear, and what I could face least of all, my own weakness.

But, worse than that, Scapula had found a fault-line in our friendship; and, like a mason hewing stone, he chipped away at it.

EIGHT

THE HARVEST WAS IN. The last of the heavy ocean
traders sailed for the mainland. The city prepared to celebrate the autumn festival – and Scapula announced he
was holding a party.

That night Marcellus and I had dined with friends. By
the time we arrived at the fashionable mansion of Scapula's father it was already overflowing with raucous
drunken guests.

As was usual with Scapula's parties, the room was
dark. The only light came from tiny shaded side-lamps,
glinting from the alcoves. The air was hot and heavy, and
reeked of incense mixed with expensive perfume – the
kind of scents from Egypt and Syria my uncle sold in his
shop in the forum. Up to then the evening had been
pleasant. Now, greeted by the press of people and the
sound of braying drunken laughter, I braced myself for
something different.

The doorman took our cloaks. I said frowning to

Marcellus, 'I think half the city must be here.' After the dinner we had left, it was like an uncouth tumult. I was about to suggest we called for our cloaks and left; but, before I could speak, Scapula's voice boomed out from among the dark expanse of braying heads, and a moment later he came pushing through the crowd, flushed and laughing, with a golden oak-spray in his hair.

He greeted Marcellus with fulsome warmth, turning his back on me, seemingly by accident. I was used to these slights. I left them talking and wandered off; then I ran into a friend, and next time I looked, both Marcellus and Scapula had gone.

I took a drink and edged through the crowd to the terrace. The guests were spilling out down the steps, onto the lawns and walkways of the garden. One of Scapula's flute-girls came sidling up and began some patter, complimenting me on my looks and feeling the muscles in my arm and such things. I sent her away. Then I saw someone I knew from the governor's palace, and went to talk to him and his friends.

Time passed. A slave came by with more wine and I took it. Marcellus was lost somewhere in the throng of people. I talked, and drank, and drank some more; and presently, when the group I was with broke up, I turned back into the hot, crowded room. By now it was almost impossible to move. Someone shoved me hard on the shoulder and I turned. It was Scapula.

'Looking for Marcellus?' he asked over the din.

'Not really.'

'No?' He gave a flick of his eyebrows to show he knew I was lying. 'Well he was looking for you. What do you make of the company tonight? There are some pretty girls, don't you think? Pretty and *available*. They ought to be; they cost enough.'

I gave some short answer and moved to get away from him. But he raised a blocking arm.

'Let me save you some time,' he went on. 'Marcellus went that way, into the garden.' He threw me an arch look, adding, 'Oh, but now I think of it, he may not want to see you; not quite yet. You see, he had company. Marcellus knows how to enjoy himself, even if you do not.'

He aimed his barbs well, but I would rather have died than let him see it. 'Good,' I said coolly. 'I daresay I'll see him later.' And before he could speak again I went pushing off in the other direction. One of the hired girls accosted me, and this time I paused and spoke to her, I forget of what. But, of course, curiosity soon got the better of me, and when I passed an open doorway to the garden I stepped outside.

Small covered lamps had been placed along the balustrade of the terrace. They glowed red and blue, but cast little light. Beyond, narrow paths extended into the shadows, leading off between the tall shrubs. I could not see Marcellus among the people gathered there.

I finished my wine and set down the cup. Not wishing to return inside, I made my way down the steps to a stone bench at an ornamental pool, thinking to sit alone for a while. In such little ways do we delude ourselves. I even paused at the pool and watched the dark shape of a swimming carp. Then, as though pulled by some unseen thread, I walked on.

223

There was no moon; away from the terrace it was hard to see. The path was lined with high bushing shrubs. I paused and considered. I knew I was being foolish; once again I had allowed Scapula to goad me. I drew a deep breath and looked up at the night sky. My vision swayed and I blinked. I had drunk more than usual; and at Scapula's the wine was always strong.

By now my eyes had grown accustomed to the gloom and I went on. Soon the path widened, opening into an arboured walkway. I glanced back; I was some way from the house. I could hear the laughter carried in waves, braying and ugly. Then, somewhere close, I heard a different sound.

I turned. A figure was seated under the arbour, in a recess in the high wall, half-concealed by climbing plants.

Even in the deep darkness I knew his form. 'Marcellus?' I whispered, and at this his head turned.

'Oh Drusus, it's you. Where were you?' His voice sounded thick and strange.

I took a step forward, saying, 'What are you doing out here, all on your own? I was—' But then a movement silenced me, and I perceived he was not alone after all.

'This is Lollia,' he said.

From the darkness beside him a tousled girl with crimped hair jutted her head forward and glared at me.

'Hello Lollia,' I said, too woodenly for manners. I had seen her earlier, with Scapula; she had been laughing a great hoarse laugh at some crude joke of his; but now she only flinched her face in a way that made it clear I was intruding.

My head cleared; my illusions fell away. I ought to have turned on my heels and strode off. But, fool that I was, I hesitated and peered through the darkness at him, sensing, though I could not tell what, that something was amiss. As I paused, the girl cried in her harsh voice, 'What! Can't you see we're busy?'

I looked at Marcellus in amazement, but he just fell back in her arms, and gazed at me with amused, unfocused eyes. Only then did it come to me that he was falling drunk. It took me aback more than you might suppose, for he was always restrained with wine.

'You're drunk,' I muttered, more out of surprise than anything else.

The girl snapped back, 'And what's it to you?'

There were many answers I might have given; but I was not going to let this creature of Scapula's trample on my pride. I turned to go, and in that instant, somewhere close behind me, I heard a movement, the scuff of a shoe on stone. I swung round, knowing even before I saw him what I should find.

Half-hidden in the shadow of a tall oleander, Scapula was cowering. I might have guessed he would not have missed this for the world. He grinned, looking sheepish. I suppose he had thought he could slink off into the bushes before I saw him.

My misery turned to anger then. 'Seen enough, have you?' I shouted, 'or do you need a little longer for your pleasure?' And to make my meaning clear I added a few barrack-terms, which I am reluctant to set down. I shoved past him; but as I strode away I heard his hurried steps behind.

I was halfway through the door to the street when he caught me. He grabbed me roughly by the shoulder, swinging me round.

'What now!' I shouted, rounding on him.

Heads turned; voices fell silent.

'Why so angry?' he mocked. 'There are plenty of others like Lollia, just take your pick.' He paused, pretending to think, then added slowly, 'Or perhaps it is not him you envy, but *her*?'

He said no more, because my fist had closed his mouth for him. He stumbled; his foot caught on an upturned tile beside the path; his arms went up; and he fell crashing backwards into a privet bush.

Two days later, at first light, I rode from the barracks with a troop of my comrades. We crossed the bridge over the Thames and took the road south, which leads through the Downs to the coast. Gratian had called for a snap inspection of the shore-forts before the winter set in. I was the first to volunteer.

We passed through remote hamlets. Children came running from simple earth-built huts to see the horses and the fine soldiers. On high ground, or beside water, or in the midst of ancient groves, we saw old country shrines, simple crude work of wood and thatch. Anywhere near the city such places would have been desecrated and smashed; but here they were swept clean, and planted with flowers, and adorned with harvest offerings.

One or two of my comrades sneered, and made jokes about rustic peasants, for there were Christians even in the Protectors. But they soon fell silent. We were far from the city: the Church counted for nothing here, and their clever words sounded empty and foolish.

On the afternoon of the third day the blue-grey sea showed on the horizon and we saw our destination, the towering walls of Pevensey fort, with its new stonework rising sheer and white, dwarfing the fishing settlement beside it.

Gratian had been wise to send out a chance inspection. The garrison, which according to the reports was at full complement and ready to ward off any invasion, turned out to be half empty. There were no lookouts posted, so that we were able to ride through the open gates and into the inner court unchallenged. Even then it was only a sleepy guard who stuck his head out of an upper window and called down, asking what we wanted.

The garrison captain was summoned. Leontius was severe; but, standing in the corner, I had my eye on the captain's face when he thought no one was looking. He was a burly black-bearded man from Gaul, and he scarcely troubled to hide his sneer of contempt. He was not going to be told his job by some over-promoted upstart come swanning down from London. The barbarians could be forgotten; Constans had driven them out, and the forts would keep it that way. Besides, his men had not gone far, only to their mothers and wives and children, and what was the harm in that? They would drift back in time.

Next day we took the coast road to Lympne. The navy had once been stationed here, till the imperial authorities diverted the funds elsewhere to meet some crisis or other.

227

Now the town was faded and half-empty. We saw to the fort, then rode on to Dover, with its twin lighthouses beckoning from the hilltop.

There is always chatter among soldiers on the road. But on this mission I was quiet. At one point, on the Dover road, Leontius pulled his horse up beside me and asked if I was ailing for something.

'No, nothing,' I answered, and said no more. He looked at me, then gave a shrug and urged his horse away, leaving me to brood in peace.

I was angry with myself for having let Scapula bait me. I had known what he was about; I told myself I should have steeled myself against his taunting. It had been a brief moment of pleasure to hit him and see him sprawling among the bushes, humiliated in front of his fashionable friends. But that pleasure had passed with the night. Now I felt foolish, and wretched. He had wanted to drive a wedge between me and Marcellus; and I had let him succeed.

Yet the voice of my injured pride spoke too, telling me to start anew and make the best of my soldier's life, relying on no one but myself, where no hurt could touch me but the sword of the enemy, which was as nothing.

That night, at Dover, in a tavern on the waterfront, we fell in with a group of Gallic sailors. They were rough men who, like all sailors, took the uncertain world as they found it, and snatched pleasure where they could. I envied them their unreflecting simplicity; there seemed sense in such a life.

When, later, the girls appeared from the back, I over-came my reluctance and beckoned one to sit with me, a pretty dark-skinned Italian with a bright smile and laughing eyes. Next morning she sang my compliments and waited for her money. I paid her, wanting her gone; and when I was alone I buried my head beneath the pillow.

But my troubled thoughts would not leave me. Soon I threw the pillow aside and got up. It was early still. Outside, the traders' wagons were rattling over the cobbles on their way to market. Through the thin wall I could hear a man snoring, and somewhere downstairs a woman's laughter. My body smelled of the girl's scented hair, and of sex. I splashed my face with water, pulled on my clothes, and went out.

Overnight the wind had strengthened. Flecks of spindrift gusted over the breakwater, and in the harbour the painted fishing boats, moored up one to another, bobbed and swayed, their rigging whistling and clattering in the gale. I stood for a while and watched the sea; then headed off to the bath-house.

The baths were closed. I walked on, coming presently to the steps that led up to the cliffs. I climbed. At the top a chalk path led across the green slopes towards the lighthouse. Up here, beyond the shelter of the town, the wind blew in strong sudden gusts, buffeting me and snapping at my tunic.

I noticed, as I drew close, that built up beside the lighthouse tower there was a small rectangular temple, half in ruins. I paused to look. The Christians had carved their crude defacing symbols on the walls under the porch. Within, a colony of pigeons had taken up residence; they cooed and fluttered in the rafters. The place was damp

229

and lifeless, a corpse from which the soul had gone. I left and walked on, following the path along the curve of the cliff top.

I halted where the track jutted out in a grassy head-land. The wind surged and eddied, buffeting in my ears and snatching at my hair and clothes, urging me forward into the empty air two paces ahead. And a voice within me spoke, saying, 'Step forward now, what could be easier? Or do you lack the courage even for this? Your name will be forgotten, and so will your father's, and your bloodline with it. What of it? All else is lost.'

I knew the voice: it bore the insinuating tones of Scapula. With whatever bleak skill he possessed, he had managed to prise open the dark place in my soul and lay it bare, and all I saw was ugliness, terror, jealousy and anger; and beyond that nothing. Virtue and goodness were vanity; only this was my true self: a naked, fear-filled, solitary creature, always alone, always afraid. It filled my being, and my instinct recoiled.

Yet still I stared, lashed by the wind, suspended between the sea and sky, transfixed by the lure of the vision. The scudding clouds fissured and parted; far above, in a gully of clear blue sky, the daytime moon appeared like a disc of silver. 'Still I am here,' she seemed to say. 'I too was real. But the choice is yours. Nothing is had for nothing.'

And suddenly my mind was clear, and I knew my pride and anger for what it was, and what the god required. I watched with my mind's eye as the child in me bled away, and in its place stood the man. And then I thought of Marcellus, with whom I had not spoken since the night at Scapula's. It was in my power to give him something, if I chose it.

It seemed I stood a long time still. I bled. Yet now, at last, I knew I should heal.

I was shaken from my thoughts by the sound of distant cries carried on the wind. I looked round. From the light-house tower a man was waving his arms and pointing out to sea. The westward-driven clouds coiled across the sky; the sun broke suddenly through, slanting across the water; and in the midst of this path of light, far out beyond the sea wall, I saw movement, a sail taut in the wind, black on ochre, and beneath it a sleek ship, its prow rising and falling in the swell.

I ran back along the path. When I was close enough I cupped my hands and called up to the watchman.

'It's an imperial cutter,' he shouted back. 'Are they mad?'

The ship was closer now, and on the sail I could make out the insignia, the black rampant eagle of the imperial fleet, and, behind the mast, two men clutching at the great stern-oar, fighting to hold their course.

By the time I had descended to the port a crowd was waiting on the quay. I saw Leontius and the others, standing at the front. I pushed through.

'Where were you?' he said. 'I came to wake you, but when no one answered I thought you were still busy.' He nudged me and winked, adding, 'And there was I thinking you weren't one for the girls.'

'I was out,' I said. I turned and looked across the har-bour to the breakwater. 'I was up at the lighthouse. It's a naval cutter; I saw it.'

He whistled slowly through his broad farm-boy teeth. 'In such a blow? Then it won't be a pleasure cruise, that's for sure. Did you see the mark?'

'An eagle; black on red on gold.'

'Then,' he said, 'it's from the emperor.'

Someone cried, 'Look there!' All along the front, heads turned as the vessel rounded the sea-wall. On the deck the master was running to and fro, seizing ropes and barking orders as the sail came down. And in the bow, rigid and ashen-faced, stood an imperial legate, his eyes fixed ahead of him at the point where they were to make landfall.

'Come on,' cried Leontius, tugging me. 'We had better find the captain of the fort.'

Gratian swept into the hall of the governor's palace. He mounted the step beneath the window, surveyed our faces, then paused. I could see a new calculation in his sharp hawk eyes.

'Protectors,' he began, 'you do not share the lot of the common soldier. You have been singled out for preferment, and so it is fitting that you should hear first what will soon be in everyone's mouths. You will understand, when you have heard, the dangers that we face. I trust we shall be able to face them together.'

He paused. There were murmurs of assent. Outside in the yard I could hear a groom calling and laughing, oblivious of the tension within. Gratian frowned at the sound, then continued.

'Yesterday an imperial legate arrived at Dover. Leontius and others of your comrades have ridden through the night to bring his news to me. I must tell you that the divine emperor Constans has been murdered, treacherously killed by an officer of his own household. That officer – that *traitor* – is called Magnentius – a name that will surely remain forever cursed. He has seized the purple, and already he is illegally styling himself emperor of the West.'

There were cries of anger and outrage. Someone, one of the Pannonians who was standing beside Leontius, called out that surely Constantius would march from the East and depose the traitor. Others assented to this, adding their own calls of warlike bravado. But Bretius, who was one of the three who shared my quarters, turned and answered that Constantius already had his hands full with the war against the Persians, and was many months' march away.

He had spoken no more than the truth, articulating the kind of lesson in strategy we had all been taught. But heads snapped round and glared at him as if he himself were part of the rebellion. He had been about to speak again; but seeing what he was confronted with he pressed his lips closed and said no more. I think it was then that I began to realize what was coming in the weeks ahead.

I had heard the news already, during the headlong ride from Dover. I knew what my own first thought had been: that my father's death had been avenged and at last his murderer had come to justice. I remembered what Marcellus's grandfather had said about Constans, that he was a drunkard and a fool, and it seemed to me no great loss that he was gone. I hoped, if the dead know anything, that my father's shade would know he was avenged, and would be glad.

For the rest of the day the barracks was like an upturned hive, all vaunting talk and pointless tense activity. But I had another task which pressed on my mind, and that evening, as soon as I could get away, I walked out through the palace gate and took the street that led up beside the Walbrook, to the suburb where Aquinus's town-house lay.

The doorman admitted me, and I stood waiting in the entrance hall. The first cold of autumn had come on. In the corner a brazier embossed with prancing horses glowed. Soon Clemens the steward appeared from within; he greeted me kindly, for he liked me, but when I asked for Marcellus he said that he was sorry, the young master was away in the country.

I nodded and frowned. I was about to take my leave when he coughed and went on, 'But Quintus Aquinus is at home. He asks if you can spare a moment with him.'

'I suppose,' said Aquinus, when I was admitted to his study, 'you have heard the news?'

I answered that I had been in Dover when it came, and had been among the first.

'Magnentius has a British mother; did you know? It would be better for Gratian if it were not so.'

Not having slept, my mind was slow. I asked him why.

'The people did not care for Constans, and they do not care for his Eastern brother either; there has been too much rotten fruit from that tree. But Magnentius is from the West; his home is here; people believe he will fight off

234

the barbarians, instead of carrying the legions away to distant wars that mean nothing to them.'

He saw my eyes move to the closed door.

'You need not fear; Constans had no friends in this house. Besides, he is dead. The question is: who is emperor now? Constantius, because he is his brother? Or Magnentius, by force of arms? We all know Gratian owes his loyalty to the House of Constantine: for him the choice is clear. But he will be hard pressed to carry the province with him.'

I looked at him. It seemed a whole new world of doubt was opening up beneath my feet. 'But sir—' I began; but before I could continue there was a tap on the door. It was Clemens, come to say that a deputation of city councillors had arrived.

'Tell them to wait,' said Aquinus. And, to me, 'They have heard; and now they have come to ask me what they should do.'

'And what will you tell them, sir?'

His eyes met mine, and I saw the glint of humour there. 'I shall tell them,' he said, 'that they must decide for themselves. That will stir them up. But if you ask my own view, then I choose the path of stability; for without that we shall have the barbarians once again at our gates, and no one to protect us.' He paused, then added, 'But which path is that? Which charioteer do we back? That, at the moment, I cannot tell you. Be prepared, young man. You are going to have to make hard choices. We all are ... But come, let us see what these councillors have to say.'

He stood, and we made our way towards the inner

courtyard, where they would be waiting. As we walked I asked after Marcellus.

'He has gone to the villa. He said there was estate business he wanted to attend to – though I cannot think what was so urgent – and that he had had enough of the city for a while. I think he missed you, while you were away. He has been sullen as a Pictish slave these past days, which is not like him at all.'

At dawn next day the palace courtyard rang with the hooves of horses – of couriers bearing urgent dispatches from Gratian to the captains of the outlying forts, from Brancaster and Richborough in the east to Pevensey in the west. He ordered the stable-master to lead out his fine grey mare, and wearing his finest dress armour with its gold-embossed cuirass and helmet of white and scarlet plumes, he rode in procession from the palace, through the streets and up the hill to the city fort.

Overnight a dense autumn mist had come rolling up the river from the sea. It lay over the city like a mantle, obscuring our view and muffling our marching footfalls. Within the wide square parade-ground of the fort the troops of the garrison stood waiting, line after line, standing to attention, their ranks receding into the mist.

Already, in one night, rumour had spread like a heath-fire in a gale. The centurions had reported that the men were nervous. They did not like political upheaval. One sensed unease everywhere.

I saw Gratian look about and scowl at the weather. He knew the power of a fine entrance and saw the day could not have been worse. But it could not wait. He said something to Leontius, then mounted the dais.

He liked to think he had the common touch, having come from peasant stock and risen through the ranks. When he was before the troops he adopted an easy bluff, swaggering manner. Many men do it, and it can be carried off well or badly: either way it is an art, a deception, a rhetoric; an attempt to convey what is not; or, at best, to create the illusion of what once was. I do not know what went wrong on this day – the weather, or his own mood, or something in the men – but from the start his address to the troops was ill-starred and faltering. His words, which he had intended to be booming and uplifting, were engulfed in the damp haze like pebbles tossed in mud. He recounted Constans's murder, going on at length about the foul injustice of it. Even as he spoke, as if to mock him, the mist swirled and thickened round the dais, and the men, whom he had intended to fire to anger, stared at him in stolid silence.

Not far from where I was standing, I saw a trooper lean over and whisper something to his neighbour. His neighbour smiled and nodded and whispered back. It was an unacceptable lapse in military discipline; but the centurion at the end of the line, though he must have noticed, looked resolutely ahead. They talked on, and discreetly I turned my head to hear. Their conversation was not in Latin, but British, and though I could not hear all their words, I could tell enough. What did they care for Antioch and the Persians, and for remote divine Constantius in his perfumed Eastern palaces? Magnentius would see them right; he was one of their own. Their words were close to treason; but even as I thought this, I recalled what Aquinus had told me.

In front, Gratian was talking on, indistinct, irrelevant. I glanced once more at the centurion. He was dark-haired and olive-skinned: no Kelt then; he would not understand the troopers' words; and, judging from the look on his face, he did not wish to. Just as well, I thought. He knew enough of army discipline to know that it was not the time to haul the men out of line, with the mist descending and the troops unsettled.

I gave a loud cough into my fist. At this, one of the whispering men glanced up and met my eyes through the haze. I glared at him, and made a gesture at my ear to show he could be heard. He closed his mouth and jabbed his neighbour in the ribs; and after that they stayed silent.

Meanwhile, Gratian was losing his stride, hesitating, departing from what he had planned to say. He was losing the men, and he was too old a hand not to sense it. He hurried on, bringing the address to a swift end. Then the tribunes raised their batons and called for an acclamation. I waited, scarcely daring to breathe, for silence then would have been open mutiny. But eventually a weak cheer rumbled along the line, dying to nothing even before Gratian was off the dais.

Back in the mess hall there was uproar. As soon as I walked in, Leontius called me over. 'Did you see Gratian's face? Whoever told him the garrison is loyal is in for a drubbing.'

The cadet beside him, a broad youth with lank brown hair who was in with the wrestling set, chimed in with,

'They may as well have had "Magnentius" written on their shields, the dogs. I say Gratian should ship them all off to the Persian frontier to teach them a lesson.'

Leontius gave him a shove and said, 'Shut up, Marius.' But I saw a fleeting veiled look pass between them – a look that was new to me, but which I should soon come to know.

I sat down with them on the bench. That morning, while we were up at the fort, another messenger had arrived from Gaul. I asked what news there was.

'Only this,' said Leontius frowning; and he went on to tell me what had happened the night Constans was deposed.

Magnentius, he said, had waited till his tour of duty brought him to Autun, where that year Constans was wintering. On an appointed night, he invited the foremost men of the court to a banquet; they feasted late, and Magnentius made sure the wine flowed freely. When the party was at its height, he withdrew on some pretext, changed his clothes, and returned clad in imperial purple and wearing the diadem.

'He must have had supporters there, waiting for the moment. It was all rehearsed. As soon as he appeared they all cried out, hailing him as Augustus and emperor.' The other guests, drunk, and bewildered at this spectacle, had gone along with the prevailing mood and added their own voices. Then the guards beyond the door were called in, and were asked to take the oath of loyalty; after that the city gates were sealed, and Magnentius spent the rest of the night securing the garrison, the treasury, and the imperial palace.

'But where was Constans all this while?' I asked.

'Away; out of the city, hunting.'

'Ah, hunting.' I raised my brow and nodded; and this was enough to draw down on me a grim line of Pannonian faces, glaring from along the length of the mess table.

After that, I returned my attention to my food and said no more. It was later, from Catius the Spaniard, that I heard how Constans had met his end.

When the news of Magnentius's coup had reached Constans, he had vowed to fight and regain what was his. But his courtiers, the same men who had fed his vanity and promised him he was invincible, now wrung their hands and said that all was lost: the Gallic legions had already declared for the usurper. No one dared tell him, even then, with what speed and enthusiasm they had done so. Upon hearing this, Constans flew into one of his rages. Why had they not warned him? Surely someone among them must have caught a rumour of what was afoot. For what other purpose had he kept an army of costly spies?

The courtiers stared at one another, and repeated what they had already said; and eventually, as realization dawned, Constans's rage turned to terror. He would go to Autun, he said, and throw himself at Magnentius's feet. He would ask for mercy. 'No!' retorted the courtiers, thinking of their own fate; better to make for the East and his brother Constantius, who would surely help.

And so Constans fled.

He had reached the town of Elne, at the foot of the Pyrenees, when Magnentius's horsemen overtook him. He ran to the church there, and sought sanctuary. The troops dragged him out, and on the steps they put him to death.

In London, Gratian summoned the Council to assembly. On the afternoon before it met, a deputation of Pannonians went to him, asking to attend him as his escort.

He thanked them, but declined. To take an armed guard into the Council chamber would be a clear sign of his distrust, just when his purpose was to persuade. The Pannonians protested. In the end, he agreed to take Leontius and one other – but unarmed.

No one said what was becoming clear to us all, that the corps, of which we were so proud, was beginning to fracture and divide. One saw it in the mess hall, or in the chance gatherings in corridors and courtyards: Pannonians with Pannonians, Gauls with Gauls, Britons with Britons. Old friendships frayed; whispered conversations were suddenly broken off as one passed, and resumed after.

But it is generosity in adversity that one remembers. Soon after mess there was a tap on my door; it was Leontius, asking me to be the one to accompany him to the Council. He could have chosen a Pannonian, and there were many whispered complaints later that he had not. But he chose me, to show he was above the faction.

We woke next day to low grey sky and steady rain; but at least the fog was gone. At the porch of the basilica a crowd was waiting – decurions, city officials, clerks and common citizens, all curious and afraid. The falling rain hissed on the wrought iron of the cressets; the torches flared and spluttered, sending smoke curling upwards under the coffered stone roof.

Leontius was tense. It would be an easy thing, among so many, for an assassin to strike Gratian down. From the corner of my eye I saw his hand move instinctively to his sword belt; then move away as he remembered we were unarmed. I scanned the crowd as it parted around us, looking for the telltale signs – a conspiratorial nod, an arm seeking under a cloak, an edging forward, a sudden step. But there was nothing; and moments later we were through them, passing over the threshold of the council chamber with its tall bronze doors and marble lintel.

A hush fell as we entered. From the tiered seats the assembled decurions stared. Eyes moved from Gratian to Leontius and me, and then to the place where our swords would have been. I saw their faces and understood that Gratian was right to refuse an armed guard: these men were no threat; an entourage with swords would have smacked of tyranny.

In the front row, I saw Aquinus sitting among the senior magistrates and other officers of the Council; behind them, from the rising tiers, the decurions looked down like birds on a wall. Voices resumed. There was a buzz of tension. The air smelled of incense and lamp-smoke. Leontius and I took up our places, out of the way beside the doors; the presiding magistrate spoke a few words; then Gratian stepped forward, his boots sounding on the black granite floor.

First he outlined the military situation in Gaul, speaking disparagingly of Magnentius, calling him traitor and usurper, predicting that soon Constantius would bring his mighty armies from the East and crush the rebellion. His voice boomed; he spoke too fast. He seemed oddly ill at ease. As I cast my eyes over the faces staring down at him, it came to me that he was used to addressing soldiers, men who listened and obeyed.

Eventually he paused. The only sound was the splutter of the hanging lamps suspended on their long chains. He had not invited questions; but now, breaking the brief silence, someone from high up in the tiered seats called out, asking which legions in the West were loyal to Constantius.

Gratian's head jerked up, searching for the speaker. For a moment, before his face set, his irritation showed. Who were these civic nobodies to question him on military matters?

'They have all declared for the usurper,' he answered.

'So Magnentius holds Gaul, Spain and Italy?'

'For now, that is true.' He turned his head away, indicating that the exchange was over.

But the speaker continued, 'There is a rumour that Illyricum has also declared.'

Gratian's mouth hardened.

'I did not tell you,' he answered slowly, 'that the emperor would not have to fight—'

'You mean Constantius?'

'I mean the emperor. There is no other.'

'But Constantius is at war with the Persians. He must be half a year away.'

'He will disengage, or make peace, or send another army.'

'How long,' someone else called from the back, 'will it take him to assemble such an army?'

Gratian turned. His colour had risen. 'A year,' he snapped. 'Perhaps longer. But he will come. In the meantime, we shall hold out against Magnentius. He will not dare move east with his flank unsecured.'

There was a pause and muttering after this. Then a retired magistrate, an old squire in from the country, rose to his feet.

'Do you mean to *fight* Magnentius then?'

'Of course.' Gratian looked at him as if he were a fool.

'And yet Magnentius claims he is now the rightful emperor in the West. Does that not make *us* the rebels, if we move against him?'

I stole a glance at Leontius. He was standing rigid, but at his side his fingers were tapping angrily. He did not care for all this quibbling talk. It was not how things were done in the hill stations of Pannonia.

'Constantius,' answered Gratian slowly, 'is the senior Augustus.'

'By whose authority except his own?' returned the squire. 'If we resist, Magnentius will strike against us even before Constantius is ready. We must consider the safety of the province, of our homes and families.'

'Let him strike. We shall repel him.' Gratian turned impatiently away. But the old man had not finished.

'It is forbidden for us citizens to bear arms. We cannot defend ourselves. And, even if we were armed, we have forgotten how to fight. The imperial government taxes us, and in return promises us safety, not civil strife. And yet,' he said, turning and surveying the rows behind him, 'three times my house has been razed by the Saxons, my livestock slaughtered or carried off, and my people murdered. Three times I have made good what I lost – but I cannot afford to start again. Let the emperors fight their own war! We have no need of it.'

The old man sat down, chewing on his gums in agitation. There were murmurs of agreement, quiet at first, and timid, but rising in confidence and volume. The presiding magistrate beat his rod of office on the floor, calling for order. Gratian frowned at the rows of men in front of him.

'I understand what you say. I cannot support such a policy.'

The presiding magistrate asked if he would like the Council to move to a vote.

'No!' he cried, his anger at last breaking forth, 'I have not come here for your vote. I shall consider what I have heard, and I will consult elsewhere. You shall have my decision when I have made it.'

In the days that followed, Gratian kept to his quarters. The palace twittered like a roost of starlings; everyone had heard that the meeting of the Council had been a disaster, that he had not received the support he wanted. In the barracks the air was tense, and among the Protectors the factions began in earnest.

Those who had been with Gratian longest, who had come with him from his command in Africa, sided with Constantius. So, of course, did all the Pannonians. The rest kept quiet, which was viewed by the others as support for Magnentius. Blood and tribal loyalty won out; and, though there was much talk, there was no place for reason.

While Gratian waited for his messengers to return from the cities and forts, we were confined to London. When I could, I called at Aquinus's town-house. Marcellus had not returned. I found I could think of little else.

Eventually I went to Leontius and told him I had a pressing matter I had to attend to.

'Take a horse,' he answered. 'I'll make sure you're not missed. Two days, mind. No longer.'

The shadows were lengthening by the time I reached the avenue of poplars that led to the gate. I found Marcellus behind the house, working in the low gully beside the entrance to the hypocaust. His hair and tunic were thick with mortar-dust; he was peering into the dark tunnelled space below the house, while behind him a slave stood waiting, holding a bucket and trowel. The brick-work arch, which formed the entrance, had collapsed. It lay in a heap on the ground. Marcellus had advanced half inside; he had not seen me.

The slave looked up and recognizing me smiled. Just then Marcellus called to him, 'See here, Cato, it's as I thought; the beam has collapsed. Come and help me lift it.'

I threw off my cloak and with a secret sign to the slave jumped down and crept in along the passage. Marcellus, up ahead, was saying, 'Now careful, it's heavy; you take that side, and I'll take this.' I coughed, and he swung round.

'Drusus!' he cried.

246

I could not but laugh at the look of surprise on his dust-smeared face. I stepped up and gripped the end of the timber beam, and together we heaved it back onto its brick post. It took some little while, and when it was done we were both out of breath.

We stopped and looked at each other.

'Now you've got plaster all over your uniform,' he said. He reached out with his hand, about to dust it off; but then he hesitated, and walked back outside, and sent the slave off on some errand. Turning he said, 'Why have you come?'

I drew my breath. My tongue felt like lead in my mouth. Eventually I said, 'I called for you in London. You were not there. I had to see you.'

'Oh?' he said coolly. His eyes surveyed the bricks that lay scattered on the grass slope. He stooped down and began arranging them, moving them pointlessly from one side of the fallen structure to the other.

'Marcellus, what are you doing? They're as much in the way there as they were before!'

At this he ceased. For a moment he stared at the bricks, then raised his hand to run it through his hair. Then he stopped himself, seeing it was covered with mortar.

He said, 'You shouldn't have left me like that.'

I spread my hands in a helpless gesture. I had been thinking all during my long ride from London what to say; but too much had depended on him.

'You were busy, or don't you remember? But it doesn't matter now. Scapula has been putting girls in your way for months. He wanted to see what I would do.'

247

'That's why you were angry.'

I thought of the girl in Dover and said, 'I had no cause. It's not my business.'

'No? I thought I was your business, and you were mine.'

Our eyes met. And then, at last, the words came tumbling out.

'I am sorry, Marcellus,' I cried. 'I had to face down my own weakness, or what use is my friendship, if I cannot for my own sake be good? I was jealous, and ashamed of it. I love you more than my own life, if you want to know; but no man can possess another. This one thing I had to find alone.'

He paused, frowning. Then he said, 'You know what Scapula is saying?'

'No; what?'

'He is saying that we are lovers.'

I kicked angrily at a fallen brick. 'To Hades with him! Let him say what he likes.'

'Are you ashamed of it?'

'No, Marcellus; never.' Then, looking at him, I said, 'I should be proud, if it were true.'

He gave a smile. There was a smear of dust across his forehead where he had wiped it. 'What else,' he asked, placing his hand on my shoulder, 'are we about? And I, for one, can think of no other whose love I should rather have.'

And then we embraced.

But not for long, for suddenly there was a scrambling in the gravel behind me and before I could turn I was struck by a great thump in my side. It sent us both reeling.

I jumped round with a shout; but Marcellus began to laugh.

'Ufa, you stupid beast!' he cried. The great clumsy dog had come bounding into the ditch, and was jumping and prancing at our feet.

'See,' he said smiling, 'we had better be careful; he's jealous already.' He knelt down and ruffled the dog's fur. Then, glancing up with a serious face, he said, 'You will stay tonight?'

'Yes,' I said, 'I'll stay.'

That evening we ate alone in the great dining-room with its damask couches, panelled walls, and ancient faded tapestries. A single lamp was burning on a standard of wrought Italian silver; it formed an island of light around the table and couches, enclosing and illuminating us, leaving the rest in shadow.

Marcellus had ordered up a flask of their best wine, a golden Moselle, and when the plates were cleared we sat over our cups and talked into the night, with Ufa sprawled contentedly at our feet.

He asked if I had seen his grandfather, saying, 'He wrote to me, telling me to lay in stores and see to the outer walls.'

'What, even here? But the Saxons have never come this far.'

'It is not the Saxons that concern him. He says that if it comes to war, everything may collapse. It has happened before, and we had best look to our own safety, if no one else will.'

For a while then we talked of the events in Gaul, and the corps of Protectors, and what the future held. A little later he said, 'You know, you gave Scapula quite a black eye. He told everyone he had tripped, but I knew it was you.'

'He deserved it. He wanted to see how far he could push me; now he has found out.'

'He bears grudges, and has a powerful family.'

'Then I shall watch out for myself. Besides, he won't be inviting me to any more of his parties.'

'No,' he said. 'I hated them anyway, and in truth I shouldn't have gone at all, except he came to me one day and said I was keeping you cooped up like a virgin bride, and couldn't I see you were yearning to get out.' He frowned at this, and I saw he was blushing. To hide it he went on, 'He said a lot of other things besides. I wonder sometimes where he gets it all from.'

I shook my head. I could imagine well enough. Scapula made vice and innuendo his business, as a rider knows his reins and saddle. But all I said was, 'I wish you'd told me. I hated them too; I only went because of you.'

'Really?' Our eyes met, and we laughed.

But presently he grew serious once more and said, 'You know, I have spent my whole life trying to get away from the likes of Scapula and his set; and sometimes I think my mother's only purpose is to force them on me.'

'How so?' I said, sitting up. 'What has your mother to do with it?'

'She sees them as noble, marrying stock. It's all she thinks about. As for me, I'd rather drown myself than marry into a family like that.'

250

'But surely that girl—'

'She has nothing to do with it; she was just one of Scapula's hired playmates. But he has a sister – not that he ever lets *her* loose at those parties of his. But it's her my mother had her eyes on . . . No longer though. I've told her. We argued.'

'But Marcellus, that's terrible. Why will she not leave you be?'

'Why?' He shrugged. 'She wants a grandson, that's why. All she thinks of is the bloodline, which ends with me.'

I frowned, wondering if this was in the nature of mothers. But then another thought came to me, and I set down my cup and looked at him. 'But she does not suppose, does she, that I stand in your way? I would never do that. You know, if that's what you want . . .'

'Oh, there is time enough for that.' He smiled into my eyes. 'But you are here now . . . let the bloodline wait.'

NINE

ONE BY ONE, Gratian's messengers returned from the cities.

Gratian, brisk and irritable, kept to his quarters. But one evening, just as we were finishing dinner, he appeared unannounced at the door of the mess hall. He always held himself straight. Inasmuch as he had learned deportment, it was to bear himself like a trooper on the parade-ground. But his face looked drawn, and the strain was showing about his eyes.

The chatter died away as he was noticed; and after a moment he came and sat among us at the long raw-wood table. Leontius poured a cup of wine and set it before him. 'What news, sir?' he asked.

Gratian paused, frowning at the dark wine. All across Britain, he said, the message was the same. Without the support of the cities he could not hold the province. This support, he now realized, he did not have.

Immediately the room broke into shouts of anger and

support, and wild suggestions for action. 'No,' he said, raising his voice for quiet. He did not intend to start his own civil war in Britain. 'Africa is still loyal to Constantius. I shall return there.' He would take with him those Protectors and troops who wished to join the cause of the East. But there would be no compulsion; each must make his own choice. We had been friends, and he hoped, somehow, that we could remain so, whatever the future held; for the present disruptions would surely pass.

This said, he got to his feet, and without looking round strode out, leaving his wine still untouched on the table. It was like watching some proud and aged wolf, beaten at last by a young rival, carry himself off defeated to lick his wounds alone.

When he had gone we stood about stunned, looking at one another like startled children, and for a short while forgetting our new-found animosities. We had messed together, bathed together; some, I knew, had even slept together. We remained members of the same elite corps. Now, at last, seeing clearly the day when we should have to step out and take sides in the approaching war, we treated one another with a wistful gentleness, remembering the good times.

I had long known what my own decision would be. When, soon after, Aquinus asked me, I answered, 'I will stay.'

He nodded slowly. We were walking side by side along the cloistered garden walk of his town-house, with its blue and white tiles, and carved pilasters, and urns of lavender and rosemary. At the end of the path, where there was a little bronze statue of Apollo holding a lyre, he paused, and with one of his inscrutable looks asked me why.

'Because, sir, Constans killed my father; and because I belong with Marcellus, and with you.'

He frowned under his beard and sighed. I suspect he did not quite approve of my reasoning, even if he had reached the same conclusion.

'You are giving up a future you have worked for. Are you sure you know what you are doing?'

'I know enough.'

He looked at me, then said, 'Yes, I suppose you do.' He walked on. 'Still, even now it may not come to war. Magnentius is proving more popular than Constantius would like. He will have a difficult fight if he decides to march west. There is still time for a settlement.'

Shortly after, as winter turned to spring and the crocuses and daffodils showed in the green places in the city, Marcellus returned from the villa. We were out walking one day on the street that leads down to the bridge, when from behind me someone called my name. I turned. A short, rather plump young man dressed in a showy cloak and fine ivory-buckled shoes raised his hand and began hurrying towards me.

'Who's that?' asked Marcellus, raising his brows.

I was about to say I had no idea. But then, under all his finery, I recognized him.

'Why, Ambitus!' I cried.

He came up grinning and laughing. His lean hungry look had gone; his hair, which had always been a close-cropped brush, was longer now, and he had oiled and curled it. Around his neck he wore a thick gold chain. He looked like any other rich merchant.

'But I thought you were away,' I said.

'I *was* away, in African Carthage, where I had business to attend to.'

I smiled to myself at his new important tone, which once he would have laughed at. But I could not dislike him. I introduced him to Marcellus and they exchanged a few polite words. Then, turning back to me, he broke into a happy smile and I glimpsed through the thickening features the old monkey-faced Ambitus I used to know. 'Guess what?' he cried. 'I am to be married. Yes, me! Would you ever have thought it?'

I congratulated him, and shook his hand; he asked us to drink a cup of wine with him, to celebrate.

He took us to a nearby tavern, in an alley beside the bridge. Marcellus called for a pitcher of their best wine. 'So when,' I said, after we were settled, 'do I meet the girl?'

'You won't, unless you come to Carthage.' He laughed happily. 'You see, she's the only daughter of a rich trading family there. Her name is Clarissa. She's Greek, you know, well half Greek and half Egyptian or something; I can't speak her language properly yet, but that doesn't matter. Her father wants me to open an office in Alexandria for him. So I'll be leaving Balbus at last.' He made a face, then added, 'I tell you, Drusus, the East is where the future is!'

We drank and talked. Presently he asked if I had seen anything of my uncle.

'I called once,' I told him. 'The servant said he was busy.'

Ambitus made a gesture with his arm. He was wearing a set of bangles on his wrist. They glinted in the light. 'Poor old Balbus,' he said, 'he never learns. He has made a fortune, but it has slipped away like water in a cracked jar. He thought the imperial contracts would go on forever, and now, with Gratian leaving, there is nothing. I warned him, when all this government business came his way, he should not have neglected his old clients. But he thought he didn't need them. As the ship-captains say, do not send the watch below when the ship is riding on one anchor. You'd think he might have remembered that.'

He said he had visited Balbus's offices the day before. Lucretia had been there, complaining of something or other. 'She has grown bitter as a sour berry,' he said. 'She tells everyone Balbus has failed her. She says the same of that spoilt-brat son of hers too.'

'What, Albinus? But she always doted on him.'

'Yes, well he hates her. I think he always did. He does whatever he wants, and she can no longer control him. She's gone all pious and pinch-faced, and claims the world has wronged her. Anyway, I expect you're glad you're out of that viper's nest.'

He drank his wine, commented on the quality like an expert, and returned to talking about his new wife. Later, Marcellus asked him if it was not too early still to find a ship for Africa.

'Not at all,' he replied. 'I'll find a ship as easy as this,' and he snapped his fingers in front of him. 'All the captains who can manage it are heading east – to Africa or Sicily or Asia, even if they carry only ballast. There is going to be trouble, and they don't intend to be here when it happens.'

Soon after, Gratian sailed away. It was only when he had gone that I discovered there had been a late secret move among some members of the Council to have him arrested, in order to curry favour with the usurper Magnentius.

I heard it from Marcellus. The conspirators had approached his grandfather, hoping to grace their attempt with the dignity and authority of his support. But Aquinus had condemned it for the cowardly act it was, reminding the councillors that Gratian had saved the province from the Saxons and, whatever they thought of him now, he was doing no more than remain loyal to the House of Constantine, which he had served all his life. Further-more, he told them, Gratian had not compelled anyone to follow his line, or persecuted them for not doing so. They would do well to learn a little honour and decency from him.

Thus he shamed them, and no more came of it. But after this he had made a point of coming to the dockside to see Gratian off. I was there too, along with those Protectors who had chosen to remain. Leontius, before he embarked, stepped forward and took my arm, saying with a laugh that he hoped we did not next meet at opposite ends of a sword. I made some easy answer and laughed back, to avert the omen.

That summer, delegates of all the cities of Britain

gathered in London for an extraordinary council. It was decided that each city would see to its own government, but that the Council in London, to which the other cities would send representatives, would decide matters that affected the province as a whole. Their first resolution was to reduce the ruinous imperial taxes, and restore the revenues of the temple lands, which the emperor had diverted to himself. Only the Christians objected.

That same month news came from Gaul. Magnentius had tried to settle, asking to keep only what he possessed, offering his daughter in marriage, and in return seeking the hand of Constantius's sister, to seal the alliance with ties of blood. This Constantius rejected out of hand, so Magnentius marched south in readiness for war, leaving his brother Decentius at Trier, to manage Gaul in his absence. He held the western provinces – Spain, Gaul, Italy, and, after a fashion, Britain. More important still, he had the loyalty of the battle-hardened western legions, who had never been defeated.

In London the corps of Protectors was disbanded. I said my goodbyes and packed, and considered what to do next.

I was sitting on my bed, my bag beside me, when a messenger arrived from the magistrates, requesting me to appear next day before them.

And so, at first light, I crossed the forum and mounted the steps of the basilica, and was admitted to a panelled room behind the council chamber. Behind a long table, a row of magistrates, ex-magistrates, and military men were seated. They asked what I intended to do, and when I told them I would do whatever was needed, they said that the army, partly disbanded by Gratian, was being re-formed from those units that remained. They wished to appoint me as liaison between the garrison and the Council; they felt it was a role I could perform well, knowing as I did both magistrates and officers.

There was a pause. Then the chief magistrate, an old landowner by the name of Gennadius, whom I had met before at the house of Aquinus, said, 'I have been told you may be looking for a place to live. If it is acceptable to you therefore, we propose that this position should carry with it the rank of tribune – a rank which brings with it rooms within the officers' quarters at the city fort.'

In my surprise I almost forgot to accept.

The officers' quarters lie within their own quadrangle inside the city fort, with a wall and archway on one side that leads to the parade-ground and the barrack-houses beyond. I had taken possession of my new rooms – a pleasant light-filled suite with a sanded pine floor and a view through a mullioned window onto the cobbled court – when I heard footsteps bounding up the wooden stair and Marcellus appeared at the open door. He was just back from the country.

He admired my new quarters, then threw himself down on the bed, propping himself up on his elbows as he watched me unpack my things. 'There is a new feeling in the city, have you noticed? Grandfather says it's that the citizens sense their fate lies in their own hands. He says such things change men; he says they have rediscovered their pride.'

I agreed; and though I did not tell him, I had also made a small private resolution of my own. Being youngest of the tribunes at the fort, I was determined I should give no man cause to say I had been promoted beyond my ability, or because of whom I knew.

And so, in the weeks that followed, I watched and learned from every man who possessed a skill or quality I lacked; and by degrees I made myself master of my role, as a man forges a sword at the anvil, beating and smoothing it until the blade is sharp and true.

In all this it never occurred to me that I might also be popular. But one evening during mess, when I was sitting alone eating my bowl of stew, the garrison commander, a broad-built fair young man called Trebius, set his bowl down next to mine and swung over the bench beside me.

Usually he was a man of few words, saying what was needed and no more. So when he began making small-talk I knew there was something else coming, and waited.

Presently he fell silent, and sat chewing thoughtfully on his bread. Then, as if it had only just come to him, he said, 'What do you know of Florus's company?'

'I have seen them on the parade-ground,' I answered, giving him a sidelong glance.

Everyone knew about Florus's company, because of Florus, and because his men hated him.

He had served with me in the Protectors, and everyone who has served in an army has come across such men. He was the only son of a well-off provincial family somewhere out west near Exeter; he was arrogant, dull-witted, and a bully. Though by nature he was weak and cowardly, he used his authority to put down men better than he. More than once, passing across the parade-ground, I had seen him out with his company, his ineffectual face purple with fury as he raged at some hardened trooper twice his age. He had managed to make himself a laughing-stock, which, dimly perceiving it, served only to heighten his anger.

'Well,' continued Trebius, 'it is Florus's company no longer. I have just relieved him of his command.'

I gave a nod. 'Too bad for Florus.'

'So now,' he said, 'I need a replacement . . . What do you think?'

I was just about to say I could think of no one who was not already assigned to some company or other, when I realized what he meant. 'What, me?' I cried, staring at him, 'But I'm only eighteen; I'm even younger than Florus.'

'Your age is not my concern. I've been watching you. Our forces are thin enough, and I need good morale and good leadership. I've seen how the men volunteer when you need a work party, and vie to be in your troop on exercises. I am not in the business of asking men to choose their commander, or we'd end up with a market-place rabble instead of a fighting force; but you are liked, and not for the wrong reasons either. They will work well with you.'

'But Trebius, do you think they will accept me?'

'I am not so many years older than you, Drusus, and I have a lot to learn still. But one thing I know: men will follow some men and not others, and the reason comes from within. If a man lacks that gift, or spark, or whatever you choose to call it, it cannot be trained into him,

261

no matter how long you work at it. You can carry on with your duties for the Council, of course. But I need you too.'

That evening I told Marcellus. He listened, sitting beside me in the bright of the summer evening on the step outside my room.

'Why are you surprised?' he said. 'You have told me yourself you will not punish the men unjustly, or favour one against another, or demand of them something you would not do yourself.'

'Of course not. How would they trust me otherwise?'

He laughed and threw some speck of nothing at me. 'Then you are better than most of the officers here, and Trebius has seen it. Come, you know you can do it; and besides, you owe it to the city.'

It is by our tasks that we come to know our powers. Trebius was right: I worked well with the men, and they with me. I began to notice, after that, the senseless punishments, the feuds, the overdone severity when leniency would have won the man. Once, when at the mess-table a tribune was complaining about his sullen company and asked my advice, I reminded him how, the day before, he had flogged a trooper with no cause. I got a short reply, and afterwards kept my own counsel. But I learned, and grew by learning.

That summer, Constantius moved westwards into the plains of Pannonia; and Magnentius, with the proud legions of Gaul and Spain, marched east through the passes to meet him.

We waited for news of the battle; but instead came word that Constantius had declined to meet Magnentius in the field.

No one could make sense of it; and it began to be said that Constantius had lost his nerve and knew he could not win. Then, when the barley was tall and golden, a trader put in from Gaul and hurried to the forum, bringing the news that Constantius had sued for peace.

We could scarcely believe it. He had offered to concede all the western provinces, and to accept Magnentius as fellow emperor. In return he required only that Magnentius should withdraw behind the Alps, which would stand thereafter as the border between them – the very terms Magnentius had sought only months before.

There was joy in the city. Magnentius, during his first months, had shown himself a moderate and effective ruler, free from the extremes and excesses of Constans. Now, without a fight, it seemed he had secured peace.

But it is a law of nature, or a law of man's nature, that hubris comes before nemesis. And so it was. I do not know what madness seized Magnentius then. To some men, success is as sure a poison as hemlock. Why, he demanded, should he be content with half, when he could have all? Ignoring the advice of his generals he despatched a haughty reply to Constantius, taunting him for his weakness, and offering him pardon if he would abdicate the purple.

People shook their heads and waited. As for me, I fought my own small battle at about this time. It seemed a victory of sorts. But it took me somewhere I did not want to go.

I had been out on manoeuvres with my men, and was returning through the city when I heard angry cries echoing down the street. Moments later, a group of aged men dressed formally in white togas came hurrying round the bend, their long unwieldy mantles hitched up and their headgear askew.

Seeing me with my troop they stumbled to a halt, and began to shout and point the way they had come. I recognized Gennadius the chief magistrate among them, and, quieting the others, asked him what was the matter.

He stepped forward, hitching his cloak back up on his shoulders, and, with it, trying to regain a little of his gravity. They had been offering at the temple of Concord, he said, and had just begun the libations and the sprinkling of incense, when a band of ruffians had come surging from the side-street and fell upon them. 'They were hiding, lying in wait. It was all planned.'

I knew the temple: it was a fine sand-coloured building that stood on a rise between the forum and the Walbrook. Like all the city temples it had fallen into decay, from neglect and lack of funds; but recently the Council, exercising its renewed power, and freed of the ruinous taxes to the imperial treasury, had moved to restore it.

I said, 'Calm yourself, sir. Where are they now?'

He pointed up the street, to where a plume of smoke was rising over the roofs.

'Stay back,' I said, and then to my men I gave the order to advance at the double.

The mob was still there, clustered around the temple like crows around carrion. Some heard us coming and ran; but most were too busy to notice. They were huddled within the temple porch, where they were trying to set light to a pile of timber stacked against the door. My men were in high spirits after the manoeuvres, and eager for a fight; they needed no encouragement from me. I let them loose, remembering the day I had stood with Ambitus and watched helpless as just such a mob had torn down the temple of Mercury.

Nor shall I pretend I was not pleased to see them get a beating. It was a taste of what, for too long, they had meted out to others with impunity.

The pleasure, such as it was, did not last. Next day, Gennadius, the chief magistrate, asked me to call at his offices. I found him with a small group of officials from the Council, sitting grim-faced on their heavy wooden chairs.

'Ah, Drusus, thank you for coming. And we must thank you for your help. If you had not arrived when you did, I fear we should have been done to death, and the temple burned. But please sit. Will you take a cup of wine?'

I sat, declined the wine, and waited. For it was clear from their faces that they had not summoned me only to give their thanks.

Shifting in his chair one said, 'It is striking, don't you think, that the bishop opposes Christians serving in the army, yet feels no compunction at having them make war upon unarmed men and women in the city streets, who are doing no more than mind their own business?'

'It is, sir,' I said, 'and I hope I have given them pause.'

Beside him Gennadius shook his head. 'Perhaps, for a time, you have. But I ask myself where it will all end.' He looked close to despair.

'Do not worry, sir,' I said, thinking to cheer him. 'They are nothing but an untrained rabble. We can stand up to them.'

He looked at me with a bleak, stricken face, as if I had said something that was not obvious. After a pause he went on, 'Tell me, Drusus, how many Christians are there among the troops of the garrison?'

'Christians, sir?' I frowned. I had never given the question any thought. I cast my mind over the men in my company, and those I had led on manoeuvres, whom by now I had come to know quite well. Not one of them was Christian, and I told him so, adding, 'It is not a cult that appeals to soldiers, sir. But why do you ask?'

'Since the time when Constantius's father was emperor, the Christian bishops have received a subsidy from the state. Recently Magnentius issued a proclamation putting an end to these payments.'

'Then good,' I said. 'Let them find their own money.'

'Quite. That is the view of us all. But a few days ago Bishop Pulcher came to us demanding money from the city treasury, which he required, he said, in order to make up the shortfall. We told him the city had no funds to finance his grandiose projects. We told him to make petition to Magnentius, who after all is emperor – at least for now. At that he flew into the most unseemly rage. He threatened, in his usual insinuating way, that if he did not get what he wanted he would unleash his mob of ruffians and spread chaos through the city. Since then, as you have seen yourself, the trouble has started. Really, he is a most vulgar, unpleasant man. But what can one expect? His father was a tanner.'

The magistrate beside him said, 'I heard he was a bath attendant, somewhere in Gaul.'

'What matters,' said Gennadius, dismissing this with a wave of his hand, 'is that he threatens us. It is clear he directs these wretched mobs, though he denies it, claiming the attacks are nothing but popular anger. His thugs are everywhere. It is extortion of the worst kind!'

'Then, sir,' I said, 'let me put your mind at rest. You need not doubt the garrison; and besides, if I am any judge, the bishop is not the sort of man any soldier would follow, Christian or not.' I paused and looked at their worried faces. 'But you are the government here. Why do you not have him arrested?'

'Indeed, and nothing would please me more. But these crimes can never be traced to him – not quite, not directly. And anyway the decurions and the committee will not have it.'

'But surely they don't support him!'

'A few do. Others he has bought. But most say Constantius may yet win the war – and Constantius is a Christian almost to the point of insanity, worse even than his late brother, who was bad enough. In short, they are afraid; there is no unity for action – of any sort. The Council governs only so long as it does nothing; the decurions set their gaze on the war in Pannonia, consult their soothsayers, and bury their silver plate in the garden.' He sighed. Then, fixing me with his old weathered farmer's face, he said, 'But we cannot permit this anarchy to continue, and you may be able to help us . . . I believe you are acquainted with the bishop?'

'Why scarcely, sir!' I cried, appalled that this information had spread even to the chief magistrate. 'And I have no liking for him at all, nor he for me—'

'Naturally not. But you can carry a message – which we, officially, cannot.'

I went, obedient to their bidding, alone and reluctant, to the bishop's sprawling residence on the hill.

Pausing in the scarred open space that had been the precinct of the temple of Diana, I felt the memory of my last visit like an icy gust on a warm day. The honey-coloured walls and roofless standing columns of the old temple were gone; in their place the frame of the new cathedral surged upwards, raw brick not yet faced, so that one could still make out the whorls and curves of pillaged stones and broken lintels. Scaffolding clung to the walls; buckets and builders' rubble lay on the ground beneath. But the site was deserted of workmen.

I was admitted to the long high-vaulted reception room. The bishop was waiting at the far end, behind his desk, beneath the embroidered tapestry. As I strode towards him – past sideboards of carved olivewood, gilt lampstands, and bronze statuettes on onyx plinths – he affected not to notice. But when the gaunt-faced deacon announced me, he turned in overplayed surprise and cried, 'Ah! The emissary from the Council. Have you come to arrest me?'

The air around him reeked of the same expensive

Asiatic scent I had smelled long before. The memory of it took me back to the child I had once been, whom he had wanted to deceive and use. I dispelled the first glimmerings of anger from my mind. I was not here on my own behalf. 'No, sir,' I replied, 'I have not come to arrest you.' To my relief he did not seem to remember me.

'Then why are you here?' he demanded.

I told him – following my instructions – that I had come merely to convey the personal request of the magistrates. They wished it to be known that they desired peace in the city and the province, which was threatened on all sides and needed least of all internal strife. 'They beg you to call off your supporters – for the common good.'

His small, suspicious eyes had been on my face. Now he relaxed, and took on an air of amused complacency. He strolled across to the ebony sideboard and filled a large silver goblet from a matching wine-flask. Though there were two cups, he poured only one. Then he raised it to his mouth and slowly drank, pausing between sips and considering the great tapestry on the wall – it was a river scene, with vineyards and meadows, and a rich embroidered border of Keltic spirals and dragons.

'Why ask me?' he said turning. 'I cannot control the acts of free men. It is the Council that causes offence.'

'Offence, sir?'

'They restore the temples; they permit the people to worship devils. They thwart me in everything.'

'But sir, these are matters that can be resolved with goodwill. They are nothing against the threats we all face. We have only a few troops left to defend ourselves; the empire is torn by civil strife and Gaul has been stripped of its legions. We must stand together, for surely, if we do not, our enemies will enslave us all.'

'But,' he said, raising a small fat quibbling forefinger, 'who are our enemies? Is the Council not my enemy? Are not you?'

Yes, I thought, I am your enemy, and you are just a fool who holds forth from this pirates' den of treasures because better men keep the borders safe. But I said, 'You know what the Saxons can do; compared with that, our differences are of little account. No Christian is prevented from worshipping as he chooses; yet you are not content to let others also choose for themselves. Why try to force men to believe what they will not? When the temples are all burned, what then? Will you burn the people too?'

'Force,' he said, 'is like medicine to the unwilling child. It is unwelcome, but necessary. It cures, though the taste is bitter. It is the true work of love.'

I stared at him; but he went on, like a man reading words from a book, 'Honest men will rejoice in the Lord. The Saviour says, "Go out into the highways and hedges, and compel them to come in, that my house may be filled." Do not think that I am come to bring peace on Earth; I come not to bring peace, but the sword; I come to set the son at odds with his father, and the daughter against her mother, and the daughter-in-law against her mother-in-law. A man's foes shall be the members of his own household, until *His* will be done.'

Suddenly he ceased and he peered at me, narrowing his eyes. 'But wait, do I not know you? . . . Ah, yes! You are Appius's son, who treated our dear sister Lucretia with such disrespect. You joined the army. Ha! What a fool you are, when you could have performed God's work. Christian prayers do more than soldiers' swords. You will find no salvation there.'

In a steady voice I said, 'I do not understand this salvation of yours, sir. But I understand knowledge and ignorance, and I believe I can tell a good man from a bad one. As for the rest, why did God give men reason, if not to discover the truth, and own it, each for himself? I do not know what salvation is without that, and I do not know how a man knows truth without hard mastery of the error in his soul.'

'Words!' he cried, with a sweep of his arm so close to my face that I thought at first he was about to strike me. 'The time for such questioning is past. Let me tell you something, my clever young friend, that once long ago I told your friend Aquinus. The people have no care for your reason and your complicated truths. They want certainty – simple, easy certainty – and I give it to them. That is why I shall triumph in the end, and that is why you and your chattering philosopher friends will fail. You can go and tell Aquinus and the magistrates this: their star is waning, their power is spent, along with the usurper Magnentius. I am the future now, and if Aquinus sets himself against me he will be swept away.'

He turned and strode to the carved sideboard, where the silver wine-flask stood. He did not hear me till the metal of my boot sounded on the floor behind him. He swung round startled, and for a moment, before his flushed round face set firm, I saw fear in his eyes. It was small consolation for the message I had been ordered to give.

'The magistrates instruct me, sir, to tell you this. In the interests of harmony they will leave the temples unrepaired. They request, in return, that you use your influence to restore calm to the streets. Peace among the citizens, they say, must come first. All else, they hope, may be resolved in time.'

'Well, well,' he said with a smile. He turned back to the wine-flask, slowly refilled the goblet, and raised it in his hand, fingering the delicate relief work of grapes and vine leaves and twisting tendrils.

I stood where I was, saying nothing, waiting while he savoured the moment. But my mind had been working; and now, as I watched him, it came to me with sudden clarity what he had become. He had toppled the old gods, and in their place he had set nothing but himself. He was a deceiver who had come eventually to believe his own lies, not seeing that what he served was nothing but his own vanity.

When at last he spoke he did not trouble to look at me. Even in victory there was no greatness of soul in him. 'Everything that happens is the will of God,' he declared. 'But perhaps we might have some little influence with the citizens, after all. You may tell your friends at the Council that we require funds. Then, perhaps, something can be done. And now, goodbye. I am a busy man.'

'I see from your face,' said Aquinus, 'that you have come to know the man.'

I nodded, and stared out across the summer garden. Wallflower and roses grew in a small raised bed under the wall. The air smelled of rosemary and lavender. It was later the same day, and I had gone to Aquinus and told him all that had been said, feeling he was the only one who would understand.

'There are depths of corruption,' he said, after a short pause, 'that it takes experience to perceive.'

'It is the unreason of it,' I said. 'It was like listening to a madman. What I can't understand is that people are taken in.'

'Well, Drusus, it is not so difficult, if one is dishonest enough. He uses an old sophistical trick, and his innocent followers are too simple to know what he is doing. What you said to him is true: there is no freedom without knowledge, nor is there what he likes to call salvation. But such questions are beyond him; he is no doctor of the soul. In place of what is true he purveys sugared sweets, casting them about like a confectioner at a carnival – the promise of eternal life, an end to doubt, and other pleasing stories. But there is no truth that does not begin with mastery of self, and that, most of all, he does not know.'

He sighed and looked out at the urns and flowers in the dappled sunlight.

Shaking my head I said, 'Yet he seems so sure; nothing shakes him.'

'It is an aspect of ignorance. But there is a certain structure to the world, whether he knows it or not, and he defies it at his peril, as all men do . . . Ah now, here is Clemens with some cakes and wine. Come and sit down, Drusus, and take some refreshment. You look as if you could do with it.'

The magistrates, when I reported what the bishop had

said, thanked me with glum, unhappy faces and shook their heads. They did not tell me what they intended to do about his demands, and it was not my place to question them.

The whole business sickened me, and I was glad to return to my own duties, and my troop of men. But whatever transpired between the magistrates and the bishop, there followed a stillness in the city in the weeks afterwards, which those who knew no better called peace. No more temples were set upon, and the bishop's mobs melted away.

'He despises the city government,' I said to Marcellus, one day when we were discussing it, ' – the magistrates, the decurions; all of them. He knew they would not dare oppose him, and he was right. He is shrewd as a stoat, but why do they fear him? He is not strong. I have seen the weakness in his eyes.'

We were walking along the street beside the theatre, with our cloaks pulled up. Autumn had arrived, blowy and unsettled and suddenly grey. From under the arches, the gamblers and hawkers eyed my uniform as we passed. Some of their faces I recognized; but none of them spoke to me, or gave any sign of knowing me. They saw the clothes, not the man; and, I reflected, the man too was different now.

We passed through the theatre entrance with its pediment of stone-carved masks and garlands. Inside we paused under the lee of the orchestra wall, where it was sheltered. Marcellus leant beside me, folded his arms and considered the high stage with its backdrop of arches and tiered red-granite columns.

'In truth,' he said, 'I despise them too. They have gone soft, like animals kept too long in a cage. They no longer believe in anything but their comforts. Once, long ago, there was nothing but marsh and scrub where this theatre and this city stand. But men came here with a vision of what could be, and made it real. They adorned the city out of pride, and love of honour, and because they saw that it was good. But our noble councillors are not such men. They have forgotten what it was that made us great.'

He kicked a pebble, and watched as it danced across the marble-tiled floor. It had rained that morning – a sharp cold squall – and the marble shone like glass. 'Have you seen Grandfather lately? He is starting to look old.'

I nodded. I too had noticed a change in him, a well-hidden weariness.

'He drives himself too hard,' I said.

'Little wonder, when the magistrates run to him for everything. They are supposed to govern, but cannot even decide what lamp-oil to buy unless someone tells them. But it is not only that. It is the simple people too. It breaks his heart to see them deceived, and incited to tear the city apart. They don't know what they are destroying, or what they would set in its place.'

Bitterly I said, 'The bishop knows well enough.'

'So he likes to think. But he is as much a part of the city as anyone. Grandfather says he is like a man who keeps a cub-wolf for a house-pet, believing he has tamed it. Then one day the beast grows powerful and turns on him.'

Across the theatre, halfway up the ascending rows of seats, an old attendant was sweeping leaves. I knew him from my life before, when the empty theatre had been one of my solitary haunts. He looked, then looked again, and raised a hand. I returned his greeting. I found I was thinking of Lucretia, and Albinus, and, for the first time in many months, of my father.

'I sometimes wonder,' I said presently, 'whether the bishop is right when he says that people prefer the lie. Does a dog dwell upon the nature of truth? No, he thinks only of his belly, and when he has eaten he sleeps.'

I felt Marcellus's hand on my arm. I had been looking elsewhere. But now I turned.

'He has affected you more than you know,' he said. 'Don't let him. It is a sickness of the soul. If you fix your eyes on the gutter, do not be surprised if you see only filth. Just because some men look wrongly, and see the good less clearly than others, does not mean the good is not. And even a dog can love, after his fashion.'

I frowned at the grey, cold sky.

'Yes, Marcellus,' I said eventually, 'I suppose you are right.'

I felt his hand seek mine, and close around it. 'Come, now. It is written all over you, it always has been. You are your own evidence that the bishop is wrong. He kills more than he knows, when he speaks thus.'

I nodded, and gave him a smile, and thought of his body beside me. The wind gusted. The leaves stirred and scattered.

Marcellus released my hand and walked a few paces off, and looked up at the shining red column, streaked with black. There was a small statue of Apollo in the niche beside it, naked, holding a lyre. I had not noticed it before.

'Soon,' he said turning, 'it will be the solstice. Come out to the country with me, and clear your head. There is little more you can do here.'

We rode out west over frost-hard paths under a sharp clear sky.

The farm-hands had hung the great stone entrance-gate with mistletoe and clusters of red-berried holly, and put candles in their windows to the gods of the night – observances that were as old as the land, and as integral as the sowing and the harvesting and the cycle of the seasons. For a time we forgot the city, and spent the days taken up with one another. We hunted deer and hare, riding out with our nets and spears, our breath steaming in the frozen dawn, and Ufa prancing along beside us.

On the morning of the solstice, when the sun was no more than a cold silver disc low in the sky, we gathered with the servants at the little carved shrine. Aquinus, his head covered like a priest's with the folds of his mantle, lit the flame and sprinkled incense, and whispered the ancient words.

I glanced across at Marcellus. He did not notice me. His eyes were fixed on the shrine, where the small clay figures of the household gods stood wreathed in wisps of fragrant smoke. His face was calm and intent, his mind dwelling upon some private place, beyond my reach. He could not have looked more beautiful.

Next day, having some estate business to attend to, he went off early with Tyronius the bailiff. I had intended to go out riding alone; but as I was dressing a servant tapped on the door and announced that Marcellus's mother wished to see me.

'What, are you sure?' I said, looking at him with surprise and some alarm. Always, when I had visited before, she had kept to her own suite of rooms in the far wing of that vast house. It had become a thing I noticed; for though Marcellus had said it was nothing, and that she was always so, I had supposed, as one does, that she had some objection to me.

Now I asked myself why it was she had waited until now, when Marcellus was absent, to summon me.

She was sitting on a white-cushioned couch beside a small bronze statue of a naked youth, a fine-faced woman with bound-up hair and clear eyes. She wore a long gathered dress of silk embroidered with blue twining roses, and on her breast a delicate necklace of antique silver. She looked like something precious and fragile and rare, like the elegant polished furniture around her.

'Please sit,' she said, indicating with a graceful move-ment a chair with turned legs and ivory inlay. 'How glad I am to meet you at last. Will you take wine? . . . No? Nor shall I.'

Her voice was measured and precise. She spoke quietly; but there was nothing weak about her. She enquired, in a studied yet desultory way, about my jour-ney and my life. She listened with distant courtesy. Then she said, 'Now tell me of Marcellus.' It was an easy question, yet I felt the muscles in my stomach tighten.

I said, 'He is well enough, madam. He has gone out with Tyronius; but he will be back in the afternoon.'

She gave me a look that said, 'Do not treat me like a

fool; I could ask him myself, if it were only his health and whereabouts that concerned me.' Then she said, 'He is last of the line.'

I nodded and said, 'Yes, madam.'

There was a silence.

'You see him more than any other. You know his friends in the city. Tell me, when do you suppose he will marry?'

Her eyes, so disconcertingly like his, fixed on me, waiting. I felt rough and crude beside her; I knew my cheeks were reddening and cursed inwardly, wondering what she would read into it.

'I cannot tell,' I said. 'I expect he will choose when he is ready.'

She was not to be fobbed off. With a voice like crystal she said, 'You are his closest friend. That is what he says. You can encourage him to do what is his duty, or' – and here she paused until I looked up into her face – 'or you can cause him to forget it. It would be a comfort to me to think I had your support.'

Our eyes locked then, like two men looking across their shields in battle. She had sprung her trap. I wondered how much she knew.

I said, 'It is for Marcellus to choose his wife, not me. Yes, I am his friend; and I shall support him whatever he decides, and whomever he chooses.'

She regarded me coolly, not with anger, but with a vague look of surprise, like a fastidious-mannered woman in whose presence some coarse utterance has been made. She let the awkward silence grow; and I sat in my chair, resisting the urge to look away.

I knew she had drawn me onto what was, for me, dangerous unsure ground, and though I had spoken truly, I had not spoken what lay within my heart, and I was sure my feelings were written on my face. I waited. I had wanted more than anything for her not to dislike me. But I saw she had planned this meeting, every word of it, intending, if I had given the answers she sought, to suborn me into whatever scheme she had in mind for her son. The price of her liking was too high. I held my tongue, and set my mouth firm.

'I see,' she said eventually. With a hint of a sigh – more a gesture than a sound – she looked away and allowed her eyes to dwell on the delicate epicene statue. I understood that the interview, or what mattered of it, was at an end. But she did not dismiss me there and then; her manners, which were faultless, would not have permitted it. And so, with a faint smile, she changed the subject, and talked for a while of I know not what – polite commonplaces: the servants; the winter weather; her friends in the city I had not met and, as she must surely have known, should never meet. But all I heard, in all these words, was the message she intended to convey, which was that I had failed her. It was subtle; expertly done. And brutal.

When, soon after, I had taken my leave, and was crossing the sea of shining floor to the door, her voice sounded behind me.

'Drusus.'

I turned. It was the first time she had used my name.

'Madam?'

'Time steals up upon us all.'

'Yes.'

'It carries what we love away when we least expect it. My son has his responsibilities, which are greater than you or me. I hope you will never forget that.'

'No, madam. I will not forget.'

I walked back along the gilded panelled corridor, angry at my own awkwardness, and angry too that she had tried to draw me into her schemes. Did she, coming from such a family, really have so little regard for my own honour that she thought she would succeed? She must have calculated that I would tell Marcellus. I tried to work out whether – and how – this could be part of her intention. But here I could not see clearly, and in the end I decided to say nothing.

But later that day, when he had returned and we were lounging in the baths (the only truly warm place in the house, for the hypocaust had never been properly repaired), Marcellus said after a period of silence, 'What did she want?'

I was lying naked on the wide ledge. He was sitting beside me, with one leg propped up. A shaft of diffused light, entering from a small misted window, illuminated his upper body.

I glanced up and our eyes met.

'No matter,' he said crossly. 'What does she ever want!'

He rose and went to where the water was trickling from a wrought bronze spout into the marble tank, and frowned down at the mobile surface of the pool.

I said, 'She seems in a hurry to marry you off.'

'Oh, you noticed. Since I was a boy she has talked of nothing else. Whenever she hears of some well-born eligible girl she questions me, and arranges visits, and goes through months of silent regret if it comes to nothing. Even before I knew what a wife was, she was telling me I should have one. You'd think there was nothing else in the world to do but marry.'

'And will you?' I asked, after a pause.

'I daresay, when I am ready.' And then, 'Girls one can take or leave, but a wife is another matter.'

'I suppose,' I said, 'it is what mothers think about.'

'Is that what you suppose?'

But then his face changed and he looked quickly up. 'Forgive me, Drusus; I did not mean it like that. I have no cause to be angry with you.'

He came padding back across the wet floor and pulled himself up onto the ledge, sitting close. I studied his body beside me – the contours of the muscles in his thigh, the arch of his broad well-formed foot, the little track of chestnut hair that ran down from his stomach to his groin. I felt the stirring of desire, and thought again of the meeting with his mother. Had she divined, with a mother's instinct, the feelings I kept buried in my private heart? It seemed to me she had. I wondered if she had guessed, too, that there was much more I wished for than I was getting.

But that was my business. In love, her son was never furtive, never ashamed; but it was as though other things were more important. This I accepted, because I had confronted him with my need, and because of the god, and because I must. Nothing comes for nothing. I had known that from the start. I could not tell what he sacrificed. If now an offering was demanded of me too, I gave it willingly.

Whatever I hoped, the time was not now; and, I knew with a pang of regret, that time might never come. I would live with it. In moments of clarity, I knew I needed some things more. What I had, even with its frustrations, was far more precious than what I missed; and I dimly perceived that these two parts – the gain and the loss – were elements of one whole, a contrary tension, like the prongs of a bow or a lyre.

Like a man who impales himself on his own sword I said, 'I told her I would support you, whatever wife you choose. You know that. But it is for you to choose, not me.'

He nodded to himself, and a frowning half-realized gratitude showed on his troubled face. He put his hand on my shoulder, and let it rest there.

'Yes,' he said. 'At least you understand.'

I said no more. I lay on the warm ledge, feeling his fingers absently tracing the lines of the muscles in my upper back, reflecting that in this one matter, perhaps, was the tender place in the armour of his pride, which even he did not see. I could exploit it if I chose. But that was not the way of friendship, or of love.

For a while after, we did not speak. The only sound was the water trickling from the spout, and the beating of my own heart, which I alone could hear.

Eventually, rousing himself from his thoughts, he shifted and said, 'She must not interfere between you and me. She must understand that. I shall decide for myself when I am ready.'

Overnight the snow came down, and we woke next day to high wisps of cirrus cloud and a covering of blue-white over the land. The farm-hands' children were out with the first light, throwing snowballs and sculpting statues out of the ice. The bailiff Tyronius shook his head and went off to inspect the vines, complaining that each winter was colder than the last, and one day Britain would not support vine-growing at all. But Marcellus and I ran out and slid about with the children, pelting one another and laughing and falling.

The gods bring us signs, and the ones that come unbidden are the truest. Once, in the midst of our horsing-about, when Marcellus had wrestled me to the ground and held me pinned, he stooped down and with sudden seriousness kissed me on the mouth. Then a snowball thrown by one of the children burst on his shoulder, scattering us both with snow. The moment passed, and he leapt up with a laughing cry and gave chase.

I climbed to my feet, dusting myself off, feeling the knowledge in my body even before it reached my mind. And then something, like the touch of an unseen hand on my shoulder, made me glance round, up at the high windows on the second storey behind the balustrade.

Even as I looked I knew already what I should find. I glimpsed her only for a moment, before she turned away.

I shivered and pulled my cloak around me, suddenly aware of the cold.

*

It was a trading ship from Gaul, an unremarkable old merchantman with some nondescript cargo, that brought the news of Mursa.

'Mursa?' people asked. But they learned the name soon enough. It was the place where Magnentius confronted the army of Constantius, and was defeated.

At first we heard no more than the bare fact, and there were many who refused to believe it. Everyone knew Constantius had lost his nerve, everyone knew he was suing for the most convenient treaty he could manage. He was a coward at heart, a Roman who had become corrupted by the beguiling luxuries of the East, a perfumed tyrant grown soft and timid.

But then the details began to arrive, and it could no longer be denied. Magnentius had been laying siege to the city of Mursa, in Pannonia. Early one morning Constantius's army had appeared over the hills, and Magnentius, seeing at last his chance for a decisive battle, abandoned the siege and lined up his troops across the plain.

The fighting raged all day. The line strained, then collapsed. There was a general slaughter, and by nightfall forty thousand men had died. Defeated, Magnentius fled with the remnants of his men, casting away his symbols of office in his haste, escaping west over the Alps. Only the onset of winter, which comes early in the high passes, protected him from pursuit.

But that winter Constantius did not sit idle. His diplomats plied the sea between Pannonia and Italy, making contacts, giving promises, greasing palms. The cities of Italy held their fingers to the wind, and, sensing its direction, one after another they closed their gates to Magnentius.

The weeks passed. Spring came. Aquinus spent all of his time in London, at the request of the magistrates, who needed his advice. I was at the London house with Marcellus one day when he returned from the basilica after one such meeting. He was not a man to make a show of his feelings, but even before he spoke I saw the set of his chin, and the hollow look in his eyes. Old attentive Clemens had seen it too. He was as much a friend as a servant; and now, without being asked, he hurried off to the kitchens and returned with a steaming posset in a covered earthenware bowl, fussing like a nursemaid, telling him to sit and rest and drink before it was cold.

'Yes, yes; in a moment,' said Aquinus, waving him away; and then, turning to me and Marcellus, 'Constantius has done the unthinkable. He has invited the barbarians into Gaul. Worse than that, he has *bribed* them to come. Think of it! An emperor of Rome paying his enemies to plunder his own people. The barbarians must think he has lost his mind.'

'Then they are right,' said Marcellus.

Decentius, Magnentius's younger brother, was still at the western capital of Trier on the German frontier. He had fought back the barbarians with whatever forces he could muster; but the main army was far off to the south with Magnentius, guarding the passes against Constantius's invasion, which everyone knew must soon come.

'Does he suppose,' said Aquinus, 'that the barbarians will return meekly across the Rhine when he bids them?

They will pick Gaul clean. They will leave nothing but a wasteland.'

The posset, I noticed, was trembling in his hand. He set it down on the table and frowned at it.

'What do Gennadius and the magistrates say?' asked Marcellus. 'What will they do now?'

Aquinus gave a shrug. 'They wait on events, as usual. In this case, though, they can do little else.'

'And Constantius's army? Is there still no news?'

'None. He proceeds with careful steps. But he will come.'

'Oh, sir!' cried Clemens, taking advantage of the pause. 'Will you drink, or must I spoon it to you?'

In the days that followed, each new ship brought bad news. Magnentius's troops, realizing their homes were threatened by the Germans, began to slip away, just as Constantius had intended. We even lost men from the city fort, whose families were in Gaul. Then came news that Magnentius had offered to resign the purple. It was Trebius at the fort who told me this, having got it from his own Gallic legate.

'It is a surrender,' he said, shaking his head.

But it was a surrender with terms; terms which Constantius rejected. Instead he issued a proclamation pardoning all those who had sided with Magnentius and guaranteeing their safety.

But for Magnentius himself there would be no pardon.

Soon after, Constantius landed an army in Spain. It marched north towards Lyons; at the same time, in a pincer movement, his legions swept down through the Alpine passes from Italy into Gaul. Magnentius marched up into the highlands to cut them off. The armies met at a place called Mount Seleucus.

Today everyone knows the name. It is the place where the pride of the western armies was annihilated. Deserted by his bodyguards, and guessing at the fearful tortures Constantius would inflict on him, Magnentius fell on his sword. Shortly after, when the news reached Trier, his brother Decentius hanged himself.

In London there was gloom. A prickling stillness settled upon the city. It was as if men trod quietly, hoping to avert the omens.

I had no time to dwell on it, for it was sailing season, and with Gaul in chaos the Saxons would know there could be no relief for Britain if they came. We doubled the watch on the shore-forts, and posted lookouts on the approaches. But that year we saw no Saxons on the grey, turbulent sea. The danger lay within, where we were not looking.

At the fort in London, it seemed everyone knew a family who had lost a father or a son at Mount Seleucus, or at Mursa. Wives came to the fort gates, tearing at their clothes and raising their children in their arms, crying out to know who would feed them with their husbands gone. In the end Trebius ordered the guards to keep them off. But they sat outside the walls, and their shrill laments echoed across the parade-ground, like some monstrous birdsong.

Constantius spent that winter in Arles – and his terrible revenge began. He had promised a pardon to Magnentius's supporters; now, with his victory secure, he broke his word and had them rounded up, tortured, and put to death. He behaved not as the liberator he claimed to be, but as a conqueror.

Only one man remained untouched amid the general sorrow: Bishop Pulcher. He strutted about the city like a peacock, accompanied by ruffian acolytes who pushed the citizens aside to let him pass. One might have supposed he had defeated Magnentius himself.

One morning a man came to me at the fort, bringing a note from Aquinus.

I went at once, and found him in his courtyard among the herb pots.

'I have just had word,' he said, 'Constantius is sending Flavius Martinus as governor. I knew him once, you may recall. He comes from a good family.'

'Yes sir,' I said. 'I remember. He served Constans.'

'Well, yes; that is true. But he is humane and decent; there is hope with such a man. I had feared worse, after what Constantius has done to Gaul.'

TEN

I STOOD ON THE QUAYSIDE, turned out in my
bronze cuirass and red-plumed helmet, standing in a line
with my fellow tribunes from the fort. Trebius, in his
commander's insignia, waited at the front, his eyes on the
cutter as it manoeuvred alongside. The black oars plashed
and paused as the pilot called out instructions. From the
masthead Constantius's purple and gold banner with its
dragon symbol curled in the breeze.

All along the waterfront the citizens had gathered, a
silent staring mass. The magistrates were at the front,
dressed in their formal striped robes, craning their necks
to see. They looked, I thought, like an assembly of curious,
nervous geese. Only Aquinus, standing a little apart – for
whatever his natural authority he was not one of the magistrates – kept his eyes ahead. He was looking down at the
landing-place, dignified and restrained, with a face under
his white beard that was giving nothing away.

On the cutter the pilot barked out the order to ship

oars. The vessel glided expertly to its place at the quay. A lanyard was tossed ashore and made fast. The gangboard was lowered; and Flavius Martinus stepped ashore.

He was clean-shaven, with a firm patrician face, not quite arrogant, but one that was long accustomed to authority and privilege. He came from ancient senatorial stock; his ancestors, as Aquinus told me, had been in government when the House of Constantine were still illiterate goatherds.

On the quay he paused, and with a single incurious sweep of his eyes he surveyed the assembled crowd. And we appraised him in return, knowing that the fate of the province lay in his hands. There was a tiny pause; then all the activity of ceremony and officialdom resumed. Gennadius, in his capacity as chief magistrate, stepped forward, and the other magistrates followed, obsequious and smiling.

Meanwhile, from the ship, there disembarked a retinue of civil servants, and I daresay I should not have paid these grey men any attention except that one, just as he was passing, caught his foot on a stray mooring line and stumbled. Thinking he was about to fall I stepped forward and caught him by the arm. His head jerked up and he stared at me, snatching his arm away. For a moment then his eyes dwelt on mine, and I felt a creeping in my hair. It was like the look of some night-time predatory creature, cold and unblinking.

He walked on without a word, but after that I kept my eye on him as he proceeded through the crowd. He scarcely acknowledged the magistrates and decurions, who in their eagerness to please were greeting everyone.

He returned their smiles with a look of cold appraisal, moving on even while they were speaking. He was tall, with black hair, not short-cropped like the others', but long and limp and oiled, so that it clung to his skull. His movements were careful and precise, like a stalking cat.

Presently, when the uneasy rituals were over and we had been dismissed, I went across to where Marcellus was standing and asked if he had noticed the man. I was all set to point him out, but Marcellus knew straightaway whom I meant.

'He is a notary,' he said, 'one of Constantius's personal agents. His name is Paulus. But they call him "the Chain".'

'The Chain?' I said. 'But why?'

'Because in his treason inquiries he manages to implicate anyone he chooses, one after the other, in a chain of conspiracy. Gennadius was telling Grandfather just now. Keep out of his way. He is dangerous.'

'Too late for that,' I said, and told him why.

'Well, he can hardly blame you for saving him from falling on his face.'

'No,' I said. But I shuddered all the same, remembering his eyes on me. 'But why is he here?' I asked. 'What has he to investigate? Magnentius did not set foot in Britain, and no one here declared for him.'

Marcellus shrugged. 'I expect we'll find out. Constantius trusts no one, and you've heard what he's doing in Gaul. We didn't declare for Magnentius, that's true enough; but don't forget, we didn't declare for Constantius either.'

After that Aquinus came up, accompanied by old

round-faced Gennadius, and we spoke of other things. But next morning early, while I was still dressing in my quarters, there was a tap on my door and Trebius entered. I took one look at his face and said, 'What has happened?'

'What do you know of the new governor?' he asked.

'Not much. Aquinus has met him before. He's old-school Italian, born to administration, not the kind of man to upset the apple-cart.'

'I hope so. I've just come from him. I went to present the new guard, but he has refused them. He says he'll use his own men.' He paused, and looked at me with his solemn, slightly shy expression. 'In short,' he said, 'he does not trust us.'

'Then let Martinus guard himself,' I said with a shrug. 'But what will he do with the rest of us? Dismiss us all?'

'That's what I asked him. He said no, we stay as we are . . . for now. Though we are to swear new allegiance, to Constantius.'

He turned and gazed out through the deep-set window that looked out over the cobbled court. In the silence I could hear the distant voice of a centurion, drilling men on the parade-ground, and the sound of boots on stone, moving in unison.

I said, 'To swear a new oath is no great surprise. There is something else, Trebius, isn't there?'

For a moment he did not answer. Then, with his eyes still on the empty court outside, he said, 'The notary wishes to see me.'

I was strapping on my belt, pushing the thick brown leather through the catch. He did not see my moment's hesitation.

'What of it?' I said lightly. 'No doubt he will want to speak to us all.'

'I expect you have not heard it yet, Drusus, but there are rumours about this notary . . .' He turned at last, and met my eyes. 'I can face the barbarians without a thought, or any battle you put me in. No man can call me a coward or weak. But these sly inquisitors with their subtle questions and double meanings scare me. They decide what they want, and then trick you into saying it . . . My son is not yet five years old, you know.'

I knew. I had seen the child – and Trebius's pretty, cheerful wife – going about the fort. He was a bright-eyed boy with a mop of curly light-brown hair like his father's. He stood to attention and called me 'sir' whenever I spoke to him.

'But Trebius,' I said, hurrying to reassure him, 'you have done no wrong; there is no need to fear.' But even as I spoke, I remembered what my father had said to me on the last day I saw him, and something within me shivered.

I talked on, lest he sense my doubt, and in the end he smiled and thanked me, and said he had better be getting on. I suppose he realized there was nothing more I could say.

That evening, after dark, I called at his private quarters. His wife opened the door and greeted me with a bright smile. I guessed that Trebius had not shared his fears with her.

He was sitting inside at the rough wood table. A single clay lamp burned, and by its light I could see the leathers of his uniform laid out, where his wife had been polishing them. We spoke of this and that, and then, with a touch of her hand, he sent her off. When she had gone he met my eye. He had been smiling at his wife; for a moment the smile still sat on his face, like something forgotten.

'What happened?' I said. 'Did he question you?'

He shook his head, then paused and listened. From somewhere I could hear his wife, talking to the child. She was too far off to hear us.

Trebius rubbed his face with his hand. Then he spoke. 'He took me to the cellars of the governor's palace,' he said. 'He has requisitioned one of them for himself. He showed me what were, he said, his tools of work, laid out neatly on a long table – tongs, spikes, pliers, hooks, curved blades like pruning knives; and in the centre of the room a chair with straps. By every infernal god, Drusus, I had not realized there were so many instruments of torture.'

I had been standing. I pulled up the stool and sat.

'Then what?' I murmured.

He looked me in the face. 'Nothing; nothing at all. He merely showed me the room, like a carpenter showing his workshop. He picked up the little metal instruments and set them down again, gently, as if they were precious fragile things, and when he had finished he told me I could go.'

Next day, the order went out for the Council to convene, and since no one had told me otherwise, I attended, as part of my old duties.

My mind was on Trebius. I had met Marcellus outside

and we had been speaking of him. But as I entered the chamber, I heard from among the press of formal robes and whitened tunics a high-pitched indignant voice that made me turn in surprise.

On the front bench – the seats reserved for the magistrates – a genteel commotion had broken out, and in the midst of it was Bishop Pulcher. His small bejewelled hand was snapping at the air as he remonstrated with Gennadius; and Gennadius, together with some of the other magistrates, was telling him he had no right to be there. But the bishop would not listen. He seemed to have decided he was going to sit on the magistrates' bench, and, the bench being already full, was attempting to push his way in.

Just then Gennadius caught sight of me and gave me a pleading look. But there was no procedure I knew for dealing with such a breach: such matters were left to tradition, and a general acceptance of good manners. Besides, I could scarcely eject the bishop onto the street, much as I should have liked to. I shrugged back at Gennadius and shook my head.

By now, through a mixture of shooing with his hands, and vulgar pushing, the bishop had managed to insert himself into a space too small for him, and was sitting with a look of triumph on his reddened face. And then Aquinus walked in. He paused at the door and greeted me. Then he turned, and I saw his white eyebrows rise. The bishop was wedged on the front bench, smoothing down the folds of his silk mantle, which had become creased and twisted in the unseemly struggle.

Aquinus hesitated; but only for an instant. Then he

walked across the polished floor and took his seat in one of the rows behind, inclining his head at the magistrates as he passed, ignoring the bishop who sat beaming up at him.

There was no more time to think on this. There was a stir at the tall double doors beside me, and then Martinus strode in, dressed in a long white robe with its senatorial band of purple, followed by his entourage of officials – and among them, dim and grey against the bright clothing of the others, moving with his gliding fastidious gait, was the notary.

The chamber fell silent. The session was declared open. Martinus stepped forward.

'I bring the emperor's words to you,' he began. 'His eternity the most noble Constantius has been' – and here he paused, affecting to find the appropriate word – 'disappointed . . . disappointed that Britain did not declare for him during the rebellion, and assist him in the conduct of the just war recently ended.' He looked round at the staring faces. No one made a sound. He spoke in a clear well-schooled patrician Latin, each cadence measured, each word perfectly formed and precise. 'But now,' he went on, 'the traitor Magnentius is dead, and the divine emperor considers his victory was ordained by the one God, in Whom he has unswerving faith. It is his pleasure and command, therefore, that laws hitherto enacted, but ignored, shall now be enforced with renewed rigour. Consequently all heathen temples shall be closed forthwith; all sacrifices shall be banned, and all worship of false images forbidden – upon pain of death.'

There was an appalled silence. Eyes strayed from

Martinus to the bishop, understanding now why he had been so eager to attend. This was his triumph; it was written all over his self-satisfied face.

Martinus turned to where, among the entourage, the notary was sitting on a wooden bench, his thin long-fingered hands resting oddly on his lap, his face as expressionless as a corpse. 'The emperor,' he continued, 'has sent to accompany me his personal agent, the notary Paulus, whose commission it is to investigate treason in the province. It is the emperor's belief that the roots of rebellion run deep. They will now be uncovered. The notary has full authority, upon the emperor's express instruction, and is to be given every assistance. I trust that is clear to all.'

There was a murmur like the flutter of birds, for by now word had got round of the notary's arrival, and his reputation. But no one spoke; there was nothing to say. Everyone knew that Martinus was not there to consult, but to instruct.

'I really cannot see,' said Gennadius later, 'why he does not dissolve the Council and have done with it.'

It was the evening of the same day. We were sitting in the study of Aquinus's town-house, with its plain chairs of polished wood, its lattice-doored book-cupboards, and shelves of neatly labelled scrolls. I had come to see Marcellus, and had encountered Gennadius walking up the street from his own house, accompanied by one of his house-slaves.

'Because,' answered Aquinus, 'it suits Constantius to

preserve the form of freedom, like all tyrants. But we are all guilty in his eyes.'

'He cannot execute us all!' cried Gennadius with a quick laugh.

But Aquinus did not laugh, and, seeing this, Gennadius broke off with an appalled look on his broad farmer's face. 'But he must know we did only what was best for the province,' he continued. 'Surely he must see that? Gaul is in ruins, and Britain prospers. What more evidence does he need?' He picked up his wine-cup from the little oak side-table beside his chair, then immediately set it down again as a new thought came to him. 'And what was the bishop doing? Did you see him smiling and nodding at that dreadful notary like some theatre clown?'

'It is rumoured they have become friends.'

'Well, like attracts like. Even so, surely he would not ally himself with such a creature.'

'The bishop is a man I find difficult to predict. But if one thinks the worst of him, one is seldom wrong. And as far as I can tell, he is a man who would set alight his house in order to bake a loaf.'

Clemens tapped at the door and announced that supper was ready. 'But come, Gennadius,' said Aquinus, 'will you not eat with us?'

'No, no. Thank you.' He got up to leave, adding with a frown, 'It is said Constantius trusts no one but his spies, and even they are spied upon.'

'Still, we have Martinus.'

'I did not see much evidence of moderation there. He made Constantius sound like an Asiatic despot.'

'I fear he portrayed him accurately.'

Gennadius shook his head. 'Oh dear, oh dear.'

Aquinus said, 'I knew Martinus once, long ago, when I was a student in Rome. No doubt he too is watched. But he is an honourable man.'

'I hope you are right. We live in a world where the cart leads the mule, and I confess I no longer understand it. It is time I returned to the country and left government to the young.'

But in the days following his address to the Council, Martinus invited the leading citizens to the governor's palace, and it was reported by those who attended that the notary was nowhere in evidence. Martinus, they said, was courteous, charming and urbane; he sought their opinions on minor affairs of state, and afterwards was praised for his good sense and humanity. When next I saw Gennadius he was in a better mood, saying he supposed his fears had been excessive.

The spring equinox passed. The whitethorn was in blossom, and the city air was scented with lime-flowers. One bright morning Marcellus walked into my room at the fort and asked me to come out riding. I agreed without questioning him. His face had told me enough.

We crossed the bridge and turned east, taking the tracks through reeds and marsh grass beside the river.

Marcellus drove his horse hard. After some time, when the city was far behind and the river had widened into the slow-flowing estuary, he turned off and walked his horse up a path that climbed a grassy knoll clustered with yellow-flowering gorse and heather tufts. He dismounted at the top, tethered his horse, and from his saddle-bag took the little pack of food he had brought. We sat on the grass. But instead of eating he gazed absently across the river plain and the glinting water beyond.

For a while I ate in silence, leaving him to his thoughts. His mother had been to visit; I had not seen him for some days. Presently I broke off a fistful of bread and held it out. 'Here,' I said, 'before I finish it all.'

He took the bread from my hand and looked at it.

'What happened?' I said. 'Or will you suffer in silence?'

He set the lump of bread down beside him and clasped his arms around his knees. 'We fought again. Remember last week, when she took me off to the country?'

I nodded. She had wanted him to visit an uncle.

'I knew she was up to something. Remember I told you? Well she took me to meet the daughter of some nobody she knows. I shouldn't have minded if only she had told me first; but I found out only when we were at the gates. It was humiliating, as if I were some child having a cure forced on it.'

'What then?'

'Oh, we sat on couches sipping drinks and picking at sweetmeats and trying not to look at each other, while my mother talked on and on, and the girl's father sized me up like a stallion at a horse fair . . . Here, you eat this; I'm not hungry. I tell you, Drusus, it makes me not want to marry at all.' He looked up. 'What's so funny?'

'So no luck for the squire's daughter then?'

He threw the lump of bread at me, but by then he too was smiling, in spite of himself. 'You'd think,' he said, 'that Mother was breeding hounds. In truth the girl was pleasant enough, in a dull, country sort of way. But with her father and my mother there, we scarcely spoke ten words.'

But after this his mood lifted a little. He ate some bread and olives, and drank the wine I had brought. Presently he said, 'You know, afterwards, she even went to Grandfather, to get him to speak to me. Can you believe it? It makes me angry.'

I asked him what Aquinus had said.

'He just laughed. He told her time was a wise counsellor – whatever he means by that. Anyway, she didn't like that either, and now she has gone back to the country to sulk.' He gave a deep frown and plucked at the grass. After a long pause he said, 'You're the only one I can tell these things to.'

I nodded. Sitting close, I could smell the weathered leather of his riding tunic, and the male scent that was all his own. He had fallen silent again, and was frowning out across the plain with its ash and hazel saplings and shining marsh-pools. The wind had dropped; high flat clouds were streaking in from the east, casting shadows beneath them.

'I suppose,' I said, 'she will blame me.'

'She has no reason.'

I remembered the day in the snow, and her look from the high window; and I thought, 'No? But what will she have me do? Walk away?'

I leant over and kissed him. 'There is her reason,' I said.

He looked at me with his grey troubled eyes, then looked down at the grass between his knees and nodded. 'Then let it be. I need you, Drusus.'

I drew a slow breath. In his proud male love he had never said such a thing before. I swallowed, and through my longing and desire saw that he was baring to me his naked soul, which it was in my power to nurture or to harm. Part of him was but a hand's touch away; and yet the greater part, I knew, was forever beyond my reach.

I said, 'I will be here always. You know that. I love you.'

He gazed out at the sky, as if considering. After a while he said, 'See, the clouds are passing; it will be clear tonight. We can build a fire, and make a bed from these blankets. Or must you be back in London?'

I turned my head and met his eyes, to make sure I had understood.

'Is it what you want?' I said.

He looked back smiling, then pushed me down in the soft grass.

'You know it is,' he said.

It was shortly thereafter that the first trouble in the city began.

It started, as such things often do, with something minor. Marcellus and I, having a day to ourselves, had decided to spend the afternoon at the great city baths near the forum. We were on the way to the dressing-rooms – passing through the entrance concourse with its vaulted arches, coffered painted ceilings and high criss-cross windows – when there arose a sudden violent shouting, and then a man's voice crying out for help.

People glanced round. There was another loud cry; the crowd parted, and in the gap three burly slab-faced men appeared, dragging a fourth from the direction of the warm-room, out across the marble floor towards the exit. The man in their hands – around whom a robe had hastily been thrown – was struggling like a snared rabbit, but one had taken his thin white legs, and the others his arms, and soon he was gone.

The people around us shook their heads and carried on with their business. It was a sorry sight, but every day at the baths there were spats of one sort or another; over a dice-game, or a boy, or some such matter.

We went off to undress, and I should have thought no more of it; but in the changing-room the man beside me said, 'Too bad for old Fabius, eh?' So I asked him what had happened.

Fabius, it turned out, was a carpenter who kept a small workshop not far from the docks. Earlier that day he had struck his thumb with a hammer; it was sore, and while he was relaxing in the warm-room he had mumbled a charm to himself to take away the pain. Within minutes men had come bursting in, accusing him of sorcery and of conjuring devils. The rest I had seen for myself.

I said, 'Don't the bath-slaves have anything better to do than bully old men?'

He paused, and I saw his eyes move to my soldier's clothes on the bench. Dropping his voice he said, 'Warned is protected, as men say. Those weren't bath-slaves; they were the bishop's people. I do not ask your beliefs, tribune, and you do not ask mine. But take my advice and mind you do not say a prayer before a temple, or wear a charm in the street. The city is full of spies. You saw what happened to poor Fabius, who is no more than a simple working man who hurt his thumb.'

We said no more.

Each person has his own tale to tell of those days, and what first alerted him to what was happening in the city. To begin with, people tried to ignore it and carry on with their lives, as a man will ignore the onset of some fatal sickness, which he has no power to avert.

Suspicion hung in the air. It crept around one like a cold chill. I began to take note of who was near me, and to mind my words; and, having begun to look, I noticed men with evasive eyes loitering on street corners, or the solitary person at a tavern table, nursing an undrunk cup of beer, bending his head to overhear the talk of those around him. I noticed the second glances and careful faces and speaking eyes.

Then the bishop, newly emboldened, turned his attention to the city schools.

There was a well-known teacher, a woman by the name of Heliodora. It was common knowledge that the bishop had a score to settle with her, for once, when he had objected to the teaching of logic and what he called pagan learning, and had challenged her to a public debate, she had bettered him in front of all the senior professors of the city. She had travelled widely, and had a reputation for outstanding wisdom; she had studied at the schools of Alexandria and Athens, and it was said that there was no one else in the whole province who could speak as knowledgeably as she about Plato and Plotinus. She did not charge more than a person could pay; she used to say, when others suggested that she could have made herself rich, that she preferred her students to possess good minds than rich fathers. Her school was always full, and people of all ages came to her for advice. It was even said that with the aid of music she had cured sicknesses of the mind.

All this the bishop resented. He called her learning sorcery and magic. He called her a corrupter. He mocked her for being a woman, and said she was strange and unnatural because she was unmarried. And now, seeing his opportunity, he moved against her.

I heard it first from Aquinus, one day when I had gone to call on Marcellus. Hearing my voice, he emerged from his study and asked whether by any chance I recalled the name of the bishop's deacon – 'that squalid-looking death's-head of a man.'

'His name is Faustus,' I said. 'But why, sir? Have you seen him?'

'He has paid a visit to Heliodora. He brought her a warning, saying that if she knew what was good for her, she would close her school and leave the city. I heard it only by chance, through a friend of Gennadius, who has a daughter there. She would not have mentioned it herself; she has no time for women who make a fuss.'

Marcellus said, 'We'll go and see her.'

'Yes; why don't you? See how she is.'

Her school lay just west of the forum, in the quarter where the copyists and bookshops are.

From the street one scarcely noticed it: there was only a faded wooden door beside a silversmith's shop. But beyond, a narrow brick passage opened to a courtyard paved with rose-coloured herringbone brickwork, and an enclosing colonnade decorated with frescoes and lined with pots of healing plants. The shuttered windows stood open. From within came the sound of a woman talking, firm and calm, and from elsewhere the plucking of a lyre.

We found Heliodora inside. A class had just finished; a small group of youths and girls were leaving as we entered. The room was simple and unadorned. On one wall a row of musical instruments hung from pegs. There was a cabinet of books, and a table of wooden geometrical shapes – cubes and cones and cylinders.

She was arranging them back in their places, and had her back to the door. Hearing us she turned. She was dressed in a plain workman's tunic; her hair was cropped short, and her face was fresh and boyish. She was, I guessed, about forty. Her large brown eyes were full of intelligence.

'Hello, Marcellus,' she said, 'I think I can guess why you have come.' And she gave him a humorous look.

'People are concerned,' he said, when he had introduced me.

She looked at the piece she was holding – a pyramid with symbols on its sides – then set it down. 'That is kind,' she said, 'but they must not worry on my account.'

'What did that deacon want?'

'He told me to clear out. Are you surprised? The bishop has been waiting a long time to close down the schools, and what better place to start than with me?'

'He is stronger now.'

She gave him a quick, businesslike smile. 'Then all the more reason to resist, wouldn't you say?'

'What did you tell him?'

'I asked if love of wisdom had been declared a crime, and when he answered that he had not heard so, I told him I would continue then. Besides, I have one or two promising pupils, who, given time, will bear the torch onwards; I could not leave them now, when they are in the middle of their studies.'

'I can't decide,' said Marcellus, frowning at her, 'whether you are brave or reckless.'

She laughed. 'Those who cannot face danger are the slaves of their attackers; we cannot unlearn the good that we know, merely to suit the whim of the bishop and his henchmen. It is not just the schools he wants to silence; he wants us to abandon the love of excellence, because the ignorant despise it, and that, surely, we cannot acquiesce to. Or do you have some other answer? Would you have me learn swordsmanship?'

He shook his head, and she continued, 'But it is a beautiful morning; let us go and sit in the sun, and leave others to dwell on ugliness and vice.'

She took us through to the bright courtyard, and brought a tray of refreshments – some pleasing herbal drink in an earthen jar. For a while we spoke of other things. But when we were taking our leave, Marcellus tried once more.

She heard him out, and smiled, and shook her head.

'We must bear ourselves as we would wish to be judged. Tell Aquinus we stay faithful to philosophy.'

A farmer, who had come to town to stock up for the winter, was caught with a votive lamp in the portico of the old shrine of Ceres. He was accused of offering sacrifice, and when he was dragged before the notary did not deny it, saying he came once each year to the city, and each year when he had completed his business he lit a flame and thanked the god for the harvest. He was never seen again.

One day, a train of mules appeared in the street in daytime, led by a band of the bishop's supporters. They took the creatures up to the temple of Concord by the Walbrook, tethered ropes around the slender columns, and brought the stone-roofed portico crashing down into the street. Then they set torches to what remained and danced all night around the fire. I could see the glow even from my window at the fort.

It was the morning after this, before dawn when I was still in bed, that I was woken by a knock on my door.

I leapt up naked, then hesitated and turned, and picked up my dagger from where it lay on the chair.

But it was only Marcellus. 'They have arrested Gennadius,' he said.

Before answering, I peered out onto the landing and down the stairwell. Then I pulled him into my room. 'When? What happened?'

'He went yesterday to Martinus, to protest about the burning of the temple. It was he who had seen to its restoration, and it angered him to see such a fine building destroyed. But Martinus was busy – or so he said – and the notary saw him instead. He told Gennadius he knew nothing about the matter and sent him away. Then, at dawn this morning, guards came banging on his door with a search warrant – you know his house, it's in the next street to ours. Gennadius admitted them, saying he had nothing to hide. But he had the good sense to send his slave out by the back door to Grandfather, to warn him.'

He poured himself a cup of water from the flask beside my bed and sat down, holding the cup in his hands and staring down at it.

'I went there straightaway; I ran, taking the alleyway at the back. But by the time I arrived, Gennadius was already gone . . . You should have seen the house, Drusus: it looked as if it had been looted. They had broken up the furniture, and smashed the vases and plate, and torn down the wall-hangings. I found his wife in the pantry, hiding with the maid. I calmed her, and eventually brought her back to the house, and she told us what had happened, once the terror of it had left her enough to get the words out.'

I sat down beside him. 'What did she say?' I asked.

'She said the captain of the guard had produced a letter written in Gennadius's hand, claiming it incrimi-nated him in treason. And it was his handwriting all right – it was a note he had sent to some merchant a few days before. But the incriminating part was at the bottom, where someone had added an extra line, cursing the emperor. It was in some crude hand, misspelt, clearly not Gennadius – even the colour of the ink was different.'

'But surely,' I cried, 'no one can take this seriously!'

He shrugged. 'They have already charged him with plotting to kill the emperor, and the sentence is death.'

I stared at him. 'Where is he now?'

'In the cells at the governor's palace.'

I knew the cells. I had seen them when I was still serving under Gratian. They were disused then, a store for discarded furniture and old pots, and anything else that could withstand the damp and the rats. I said, 'A week in that place will kill him.'

Marcellus drew his hand through his hair and looked at me. 'That's what Grandfather said. He has gone to see Martinus.'

'What?' I cried.

'I know . . . I know.' He shook his head. 'He says Gennadius is his friend: he will not leave him. I told him at least to take me with him, but he would not. He said it was better that he went alone and spoke to Martinus without an audience, and, if necessary, made claims on their old friendship, privately, one man to another.'

'But surely he cannot—' But before I could finish there was a heavy rap on the door. The words froze in my mouth. My eyes met Marcellus's.

'I was not followed,' he said in a low voice, 'I made sure of it.'

I strode to the door and snatched it open, and for a moment gaped like a fool. It was one of my troop, dressed in his full battle-armour with his marching-pack on his back. He had come to say the men were waiting in the parade-ground, and had I forgotten them? We had arranged for exercises that morning.

I stared at him, and he at me. I was naked still, with my dagger in my hand, like some Homeric image on a carving.

'You'd better see to your men,' said Marcellus. 'I'll be at the house.'

He moved to the door, but I caught his arm.

'No, wait. I'm coming with you.'

We ran through the streets to Aquinus's town-house. Just as Marcellus reached for the bronze lion-head door-knocker, the door swung open and Clemens appeared, with one of Gennadius's slaves standing behind him.

'Oh, sir, there you are! I was just coming to find you.'

'We are going to the palace,' said Marcellus.

'There is no need, they are here – the master, and Gennadius too.'

We found them in the formal sitting-room with its four painted panels of the seasons – spring, summer, autumn and winter – each season portrayed as a gar-landed nymph, set against a backdrop of fields and vine-yards and columned shrines. Gennadius was sitting on the couch, with his plump grey-haired wife beside him, and she was looking at him as if he had just climbed off his death-bier. He had not had time to shave; under the night-stubble his broad face was drawn and wan. One of the house-slaves had brought a cup of warmed wine and a dish of rusks. They stood forgotten on a little three-legged table beside him.

Aquinus said, 'I think, Gennadius, we had better begin again, now that Marcellus and Drusus are here.'

And so, between them, they told us what had happened.

Aquinus, when he arrived at the palace, had insisted on seeing the governor, and would take no denial. There followed some argument with the officials, but eventually he was admitted.

'Martinus was still in his night-robe. I had clearly woken him. He told me he knew nothing of the matter. So I asked him to summon the notary Paulus, and when, after a long delay, he finally appeared, I demanded to see the offending letter. The notary, if you can believe this, refused.'

'I imagine,' said Gennadius, 'he had not finished reworking it.'

'Perhaps so; but this was too much even for Martinus. He ordered the notary to fetch the letter forthwith, and, after an excessive wait and with a good deal of reluctance, it was finally produced. Really, I have never seen such a thing! Only a fool could give credence to such an illiterate scrawl – and that is what I told him.'

'You told the notary *that*?' I cried, shocked out of all civility.

Aquinus gave me a grave look. 'How not? The whole thing was a clear lie, a fabrication. I told the notary he must have been misled by one of his over-zealous subordinates, unless, perhaps, he could think of some other explanation.'

'What did he say?'

'He grew angry. I shall not dwell on all he said; but after some dispute he conceded that there might after all have been an error, and he would look into it.'

I shook my head, wondering at his coolness. But only when Gennadius and his wife had gone to another room

313

to rest did I say, 'You should not have gone alone, sir. You took a great risk.'

He frowned under his white beard. 'Yes, Drusus, and I am grateful for your concern; but as I have already said to Marcellus, there are laws of friendship which transcend any law the emperor may decree. Besides, I was guided by hard prudential reason, as well as decency. Gennadius was innocent. If we allow the bishop and his notary friend to move against him, then who will be next?'

After this, the last thing I expected was for Martinus to seek Aquinus out. Perhaps he felt shame. At all events, a few days later, Aquinus asked me if I was free next evening to dine, saying with an ironic sparkle in his eye, 'A guest has invited himself to dinner, and you may like to meet him. It is the governor.'

Martinus arrived next day at sunset, accompanied by an entourage of guards who waited in the street. He greeted us with easy, well-bred courtesy, the kind that comes to certain men without having to think. He was finely dressed in a woollen close-weave tunic with a simple border in green and gold; an inlaid belt; a small swan brooch of chased silver; a signet set with red cornelian. There was nothing forced, nothing showy, nothing out of place.

He complimented Aquinus on the banquet, adding that he prided himself on being a judge of good food; and in between the compliments he talked at length of his Italian estates, which were extensive, and of the schools of Rome where he and Aquinus had first known each other. He related minor political gossip – which friend of his was in the ascendancy and which had suffered a fall.

He spoke in affectionate detail about the alterations he was making to his villa near Arpinum, where he was adding a summer dining-room which opened onto a raised terrace.

It was all very civilized – or it would have been, if he had given any sign of awareness or concern for the barbarism on his doorstep.

It was only during dessert – stuffed figs and almond-cakes sweetened with honey – that Aquinus raised the question of the bishop and the notary. At this, Martinus's face took on the pained expression of a connoisseur of music who hears a false note at a concert, and with a sigh he set his glass bowl down on the table beside him.

'Of course the whole business with Gennadius was unfortunate. I have asked the notary Paulus to investigate, and indeed, since you have raised the matter, let me tell you that only this morning he assured me that the whole affair was a misunderstanding. You were right, my dear Aquinus, it was the fault of some underling, and I believe he will be reprimanded. I cannot understand how such a thing can happen; but . . . well, there it is, you know the wheels of government seldom turn as smoothly as one would wish.'

He held out his bowl to the slave, who had offered him a second helping. 'Still, let us not taint this pleasant evening with the matter. I need hardly tell you that the quality of officials nowadays is not what it was. One must accustom oneself to the realities, and we are not in Italy, alas.'

I was sitting diagonally opposite Aquinus. For a moment, while Martinus was talking, our eyes met, and I saw a flash of humour – or anger – there. I turned my attention to my food. It would not have done to smile.

When Martinus had finished, Aquinus said in a level voice, 'I am glad you have managed to resolve the whole unfortunate affair to your satisfaction. I must say, I regret it ever happened at all. Gennadius's house was turned over and ruined, quite needlessly.'

'Indeed, it is a sorry business. I am sure nothing like this will happen again. The notary assured me that only the guilty have anything to fear.' And then, raising his eyes from his food, which he had been prodding and exploring with a spoon, 'Even so, let us not forget that the notary Paulus enjoys the *full* confidence of Constantius.'

'No doubt he does.'

There was a slight pause. Then Martinus went on, 'We must bend with the wind, as my father used to tell me. It would have been better for all of us if the civil strife in Gaul had never taken place. I am sure you understand.'

After this he returned to the subject of his Italian estate, a seemingly limitless topic.

When we had seen him off with his armed guard, and had returned inside, Marcellus said, 'Do you think he actually *believes* any of that?'

'The man is a fount of platitude,' said Aquinus in response. 'He has spent too long with bureaucrats and politicians.'

He returned to his seat and sat down heavily. Now, among friends, his tiredness showed. He was slower on his feet of late, and I knew it irked him. He was not a man to let the demands of his body hinder the swiftness of his mind.

'I suspect,' he said, after a considering moment, 'that beneath all the bland urbanity Martinus is afraid.'

'Of the notary?'

'Yes, that too. But his fear encompasses more than that. He inhabits a world of abundant and fragile luxury. All he cares about is adorning his garden, and entertaining his friends. He has let his pleasures beguile him, and cannot do without them. He has allowed himself to forget proportion.'

A look of quiet, ancient sadness settled on his face, and for a moment he stared absently into the middle distance, at the burning lamp-standard, and the image of ivy-garlanded Winter beyond. Then, collecting himself with a sigh, he said, 'You know, when he was young he had great promise. Well, so it is. There is something tragic in seeing a good man wasted.'

But the arrests continued, slow at first, directed against those too weak to resist, unnoticed unless one looked, like a scrub-fire in woodland, which, unable to seize the tall trees, smoulders instead on the forest floor.

The bishop was everywhere about the city, often in the company of the notary. Base men, who lurk in the shadows of life, emerged full of confidence and found like minds. Disgruntled slaves were persuaded to betray their masters, and in the city the bishop's thugs set upon innocent men with impunity. Every rogue and villain who had ever held a grudge now sought vengeance, knowing that mere accusation was enough to condemn.

Astrologers and soothsayers were chased out of town; doctors dared not treat their patients lest their cures be condemned as sorcery; books were suspected by the illiterate of harbouring hidden spells, and priceless libraries were cast into the flames by their frightened owners. Old men who should have been sipping warm milk in their beds were dragged off and thrown into the cells, and when their sons or wives or servants came with food or blankets they were robbed and sent away, or were themselves arrested.

Against this growing madness Aquinus stood out, resisting, protesting, intervening with the governor. But he was only one man; and the madness was everywhere. It seemed to me that some dark force beyond reason had been unleashed.

It was Aquinus who showed me there was purpose in the madness. He said one day, after I had been complaining to him, 'You grew up on a farm, did you not? You must have seen the farm-hands burn the fields, to clear the old growth?'

'Yes, but—' I broke off, and looked at him amazed as understanding dawned.

He nodded, and gave me a thin smile. 'They are destroying the class of ruling men. They think they can start afresh, with beings fashioned in a mould of their choosing.'

I thought of the notary, and of the bishop's gaunt-faced, violent acolytes. 'A city is not a field,' I said bitterly, 'and free citizens are not merely chaff to be set alight in some holocaust.'

'No,' he said, 'though I doubt the bishop or the notary sees it that way. Each has his own purpose. Each thinks he is using the other to achieve his ends. They are both blind.'

But then two events occurred that gave them pause.

First the harvest failed – or so it was said. The truth was that Christian mobs rampaging over the countryside had so terrorized the farm-hands that they had fled, leaving the crops to rot in the fields.

The city poor were the first to suffer. They gathered outside the scaffold-clad shell of the bishop's half-built cathedral, and cried out for food.

'You see,' said Aquinus when I reported this to him. 'The beast has returned to its master, and the beast is hungry.'

The bishop reassured them, promising food for all. Then he hurried to the notary to ask how he was to deliver. No one heard what the notary said to him; but, shortly after, it began to be put about – no one could quite tell from what source – that the Council was to blame for the shortage.

The rumour was allowed to circulate unchallenged. Then the order went out from the governor's palace for the Council to assemble: the decurions themselves would be made to answer for the crisis.

It was hard to tell how much of all this was believed. By then men had grown close-lipped even among friends. Dinner invitations were declined, after a supper-party had been denounced as a conspiracy and the guests arrested. People ceased to visit the tombs of relatives, after one old woman had been found weeping over the grave of her husband and had been condemned for necromancy. No one wore a seal-ring, or a necklet, lest they be accused of carrying magic charms.

Those who could fled to their country estates, though even these were not safe from the itinerant mobs of acolytes and monks and priests, who went round smashing ancient shrines, burning sacred groves, and killing or arresting those who dared to resist. But through it all Aquinus stayed in the city, where, he said, he could do most good.

The poet says that those whom the gods wish to destroy they first make mad. And so it was. I was with Trebius in his quarters at the fort when the messenger came from the palace with news that the Pictish tribes had breached the Northern Wall.

'I have heard nothing of this, nothing from our people in the north,' said Trebius.

The messenger, one of the band of officials who had arrived with the notary, gave a shrug. 'That is not my concern,' he answered haughtily. 'You are to report to the governor's palace at noon, where you will be given your instructions.'

Later, when Trebius returned, he summoned the tribunes of the garrison to his quarters. There was a flush of anger on his lean, serious face. I did not realize, then, that it was on my account.

'We have been ordered north,' he announced.

There was an exchange of surprised glances.

The man beside me said, 'But I cannot understand it, sir. There has been no report of trouble. A coaster put in from York less than a week ago. He brought a report from the captain there. You saw the man yourself.'

Trebius had bent over the map on the table, though I had the sense that his mind was not on it. Without looking up he said, 'The governor must have other information.'

'Did he say where he got it?'

'No.'

Someone else said, 'Who will protect the city?'

Another said, 'The governor is a civilian. Does he realize how weak our forces are? I have lost half my men to desertion already. I doubt my company is fit to fight anyone.'

Others spoke up in agreement. I saw Trebius's body tense. Though he was always disciplined, he was never harsh. But now he looked up sharply and shouted over the din, 'What is this, a gathering of washerwomen? It is not for you – or me – to question orders. We are all below complement; we must manage with what we have.'

'Yes, sir,' said ten voices, ceasing in mid-flow. Eyes slewed to the faces of comrades, but no one else commented, not daring to say openly what was in each mind: that whatever the wild Picts might do, the real enemy lay close at hand, at the palace.

A dissatisfied silence fell; Trebius went on to talk of arrangements for decampment. He did not speak for long. In due course, when he had finished and we were filing out, he caught my sleeve and gave a sign for me to wait.

'Drusus, I am sorry,' he said, 'I did not want to say

321

this in front of the others. The notary has ordered that you are to remain here in London.'

Our eyes met.

I said, 'Did he give a reason?'

Instead of answering he tossed his head and gave me a look which at first I did not comprehend. Then, in a loud voice that carried to the wardroom behind, he said, 'So there! Those are our orders. Now come and walk with me across the parade-ground; I could do with some fresh air.'

He nodded, and took me by the elbow. Only when we were outside in the wide open of the marching-square did he speak again.

'I was instructed not to tell you this – the notary's direct order – and I am beginning to suspect he has spies even here among our comrades. Just now, in my quarters, when—' But he broke off, and with an angry sweep of his hand said, 'No, I will not play his game; there is enough of a stench in the air already. He says you are under investigation, for complicity in treason. That is why you must remain.'

I drew my breath and stared out at the line of the fort wall. A birch sapling had taken root in a wide gaping crack. In the midst of my own concerns I reflected, with a part of my mind, that yet again the city defences had been forgotten. Two sparrows were perched in the wavering branches, looking down at me, and it seemed to me that they looked with pity. I felt a sickness in my entrails: but it was not fear that seized me; it was disgust.

I shrugged. 'Well it was only a matter of time,' I said. 'I am a friend of Aquinus, after all.'

Trebius's pain was written on his face, like a man on the rack.

'I tell you, Drusus,' he said, dropping his voice even in the open, 'the governor counts for nothing here, whatever your friends at the Council think. It is the notary who plays the melody; the governor merely dances. Take my advice and get out while you still can. Tell Aquinus too.'

In the days that followed, the fortress was loud with the scrape of whetstones, and on the benches outside the long barrack-houses men sat burnishing their armour, oiling the leather straps, and preparing their knapsacks.

On the night before they left, I went out with my old company. We got drunk together. The wine dispelled the sadness, for a while. Then, next day at first light, I stood at the edge of the parade-ground as the centurions barked out the orders and the men moved into line. It was clear, seeing them all assembled, quite how depleted our forces were.

I watched, standing apart. But before the order to march Trebius beckoned me forward, and in front of all the men gave me a formal embrace. 'This,' he said in my ear, 'is for the spies and informers. Let them go and tell it to the notary. Farewell, Drusus; may the gods protect you.'

He stood back, and as he turned I saw his eyes were glistening. He mounted his horse, and with a drop of his hand gave the signal to advance. The trumpets blared, the drums resounded, and with the rhythmic beat of military boots on stone the men began to file out beneath the gate on their long journey north.

Three days later, Trebius was discovered in his tent, still in his bed. The sheets were soaked with blood. His throat had been cut.

As soon as I heard, I ran to his quarters. The door stood ajar. There was a half-eaten loaf on the table, and milk in the pitcher. I raced through the rooms, calling out the names of his wife and child. But no one answered.

Walking back round the building I almost stumbled into the quartermaster. He was, I knew, a Christian, and though we had always got on well enough, I was not minded to question him. But seeing where I had come from, and, I daresay, seeing my face as well, he took me aside and told me he had personally seen to it that Trebius's wife and child were safe. He had sent them off to the far west, out of harm's way, where her father's homestead was.

I thanked him and turned away, and returned across the empty silent parade-ground.

I thought, as I walked, of his young son with his brown mop of hair, who now would grow up never knowing his father. My throat tightened. And when I reached the flight of stone steps that led up to my room, I sat down in the silence on the bottom step, and buried my head in my hands, and wept.

In the days afterwards, black desolation seized me, and rage at the injustice of the world. I dared not go to Marcellus, which is what I yearned to do, out of fear that

I should draw down on him the same evil that lay in wait for me.

Days and nights merged into one. I sat about and waited in the silent wilderness of the barracks for the telltale scrape of footsteps on the stair, and the violent rap at the door. I was like a man who sickens, each day a little worse. But what ebbed in me was something in my spirit, a quenching of hope.

In the end, to hold myself together, I took to practising my old fighting moves, driving myself hard in the deserted sand-court behind the barrack-houses, rehearsing the motions and movements of old skills.

But I knew they would not save me from the rack, or the dagger in the night.

Then, in the midst of this, like the mote that breaks the axle, came news of Gennadius's death.

For a long time he had remained, out of loyalty to Aquinus, who had stood by him when others in the Council had turned their backs. But in the end he said he could bear the city no more. He could not sleep at night; his wife, who had never recovered from the shock of his arrest and the looting of their house, had become ill. He said he would return to his farm.

A few days later a hunting-party came across his burnt-out carriage, half hidden in woodland not far from the road. His servants, who had accompanied him, lay in the long grass, hacked to death. Inside the carriage, charred almost beyond recognition, were the bodies of Gennadius and his wife.

It was this news that made me break my self-imposed exile and go to Aquinus's house. It was a chill bright morning in November, early still, and I found Marcellus alone in the courtyard, swinging and thrusting with an antique bronze-handled sword, which had hung on the wall in the passageway.

Seeing me he laid it shyly aside, saying he had just thought to practise a little, to see how it felt.

'It seems to suit you,' I said, picking up the ancient blade and turning it in front of me. And indeed his sword-work had been fine, easily as good as mine, even though I had never seen him train at it.

I set the old weapon down on the garden table and gave him a careful look. 'Has it come to this?' I asked.

He shrugged.

'I shall not let them take Grandfather. Better to die fighting than rot in the notary's dungeons.'

I sat down beside him and gazed at the pots of herbs on the terrace. Our breath showed in the cold air, mingling in front of us.

'We must get him away,' I said.

Marcellus shook his head. He was looking down, with his elbows on his knees and his chin propped in the palms of his hands. In a bleak, quiet voice he said, 'He will not listen. He told me last night he intends to speak at the Council.'

'What?' I said, staring. 'Has the madness touched him too?' The Council meeting, long delayed because no decurion could be found to attend, was due in a few days' time.

'By God, I've tried to tell him, Drusus. He will not listen. He says it is time somebody had the courage to speak out.'

'But we must stop him. In truth, I wonder he has not been taken away already. Does he really think he can stand up to them?'

He made a small, helpless gesture, as if he had been through all these arguments many times before. I realized he was near to tears.

'He thinks he can shame Martinus. He says silence is complicity, and words are the only weapon he has left.'

I got up from the bench and stood, frowning at him. I took up the sword from where it lay on the cast-iron table and turned it, holding it up to the light, inspecting the old-style craftsmanship. The hilt had been fashioned into a twisting double-headed snake. I touched my finger to the polished blade. It was sharp still. I wondered if it had ever killed a man, or seen battle. I thought then of Gennadius. He had not spoken out; he had avoided trouble, or so he thought. Yet still they had murdered him.

I said, 'Let me speak to him.'

'Go ahead. We have all tried – Clemens; the groom boy; even the maids. But yes, go to him. He has been in his study since first light.'

Aquinus was sitting in a high-backed oak-wood chair beside the little charcoal-burning stove that warmed the room, wrapped in his thick winter cloak. He glanced round when I entered. Under his white beard his face looked gaunt and pale.

I greeted him, and in my clumsy way I tried to lead into what I had come for. I saw him regarding me with irony in his eyes, and after a while he said, 'I know why you are here, so let us dispense with all this talk about the weather and my health, and come to the matter.'

So I said what I had to say.

He listened without interruption. When I had finished he said, 'You are young; I do not know if you will understand. But I shall try to explain. All my life, I have striven to bring to government a co-incidence of power and wisdom. Without it there can be no good city, and no civilized life. But it is a constant struggle against ignorance and folly, for power is seldom wise, and wisdom seldom powerful. It is, you might say, a Sisyphean task. But if the city becomes destructive of what is best, then men will desert it and find some other, lesser place to fulfil their natures – their high-walled farms and gardens, or, as the Christians do, their monasteries. But these places are not an answer; they are not an alternative. No matter how remote the place or how high the walls, they cannot last if the city is corrupted. For such reasons as this I have served in public life, and I believe that my efforts, and the efforts of others such as your late father, have achieved some success: the province has prospered while Rome squabbled and Gaul was overrun. But now all we have built is torn apart by blind and evil men. My friends are murdered; farmers are chased off the land; the fields are barren and the people go hungry. It must be faced.'

I drew my breath to speak, but he raised his hand.

'Do you suppose, if I run away, they will not find me? Shall I hide in the forest, cowering in fear, and wait to be hunted like an animal? No, Drusus. This is my home, and there is no place to run. I grow old. I feel it. I shall face the end true to what I have lived for.'

He ceased, but when I tried to speak my voice broke and I choked on my words.

He smiled and, rising from his chair, came to me, and rested his hand on my shoulder.

Presently he said, 'Come then; the gods have spared us foreknowledge; but they have granted us reason enough to discern what is right, and where our duty lies. Let us not presume to know what tomorrow holds. Now call Clemens for me, and tell him to bring us some warmed wine, for the days are growing chill.'

ELEVEN

TWO DAYS LATER, on the day, as it happened, of my twentieth birthday, a youth came to the barracks with a message.

I looked from him to the sealed note. The note did not look official. Nor did the youth.

'Who sent you?' I asked.

He glanced at me nervously. I was dressed in my uniform. I suppose, to this slender boy, I must have seemed quite fearsome.

'My master Balbus,' he stuttered. 'Lucius Balbus the merchant. He says he knows you, that you are a friend of his.'

I opened the letter. It was the first time I had seen anything written in my uncle's hand that was not a shipping-list or tally of accounts.

'Balbus to his nephew Drusus, greetings,' it began, and after a long stilted preamble asked if I would call on him at his shop in the forum, ending diffidently with, 'The boy who brings this will direct you, if you have forgotten the place.'

Of course I had not forgotten. I sent the youth off, changed into civilian clothes, and set out across the city.

The shop was just as I remembered it – brightly painted walls done up to look like marble; here and there an expensive vase set into an alcove; costly perfumes ranged on silk-draped garlanded shelves in petite bottles of coloured glass; wines for tasting; expensive draperies.

The same dapper youth who had brought the note was there. Balbus came hurrying from behind. He was all smiles and civilities, as if I were one of his rich clients; but I could tell from his eyes that something was wrong. He dismissed the boy, and asked me to sit and drink a cup of wine with him.

He conducted me through to the lounge at the back, with its upholstered couches and fine furniture, the place where he entertained his most valued customers. He poured the wine himself, from a figured enamelled jar, fussing over it, avoiding my gaze. He had grown fatter, under his rich clothes. His heavy face had become florid. Only his hair, inexpertly dyed an absurd crow's-wing black, was the same as before.

For a while he talked aimlessly, fiddling with his wine-cup. But eventually he sighed, and setting down his cup with a hint of impatience, came to the point. 'I was wondering,' he said, 'with your connections, whether perhaps you might put a word in for me with Flavius Martinus the governor. Business has been bad, what with the recent troubles. I find I have overspent and am embarrassed.'

I looked at him in his plush clothes, in his lavish shop, and thought of Trebius and Gennadius and Aquinus. I paused before I answered. Even now, at the age of twenty, I was not always master of my anger.

'I am sorry, Uncle,' I said, 'but you have been misinformed. I have no connection with Martinus.'

'Ah; yes. Of course. But you see, I thought you might call on him, on my behalf. I need the business. I have suffered losses, and my expenses are high, and—'

'I do not think,' I said, gently interrupting him, 'they would even let me through the palace gates. And if they did, I should probably never leave. I am no friend of Martinus, sir; nor of that monster the notary either.'

His head swung round to the latticed partition behind. But I had checked before I spoke: the poison of fear had infected me too.

'You need not worry,' I said. 'There is no one here.'

He nodded to himself, a great lolling melancholy bull, dressed up in silks and gold chains; and as he did so I regarded him, reflecting on how, after these years of silence, he had sought me out only to further his own business, which through his folly and greed he had brought to ruin.

'What of Lucretia?' I said. 'Perhaps she could sell some of her jewels.'

'We have quarrelled; besides, I dare not. She was always a pious woman, Drusus, as you know, and she feels her husband and her son have been a disappointment and a trial. Nowadays she devotes her time to the bishop and to holy work.' He paused, and stared sadly at the dainty, gilded table. 'She tells me I have failed her, and I suppose I have. So you see, I could not ask her for help. Her jewels are important to her. She says they are all she has left.'

I nodded and looked down. I even felt sorry for him.

'Albinus too?' I asked, remembering how in her eyes he could do no wrong.

'Albinus has not grown up quite as we had hoped.'

He fell silent and looked at me helplessly. I reached across to the wine-jar and filled my cup, and filled his too, reflecting on the terrible consequences of what we cannot see. And for a while, before the shop-boy returned, we drank together, and remembered.

The sword-work I had caught Marcellus practising in the garden was no more than a private ritual of desperation. He knew as well as I that he could not fight off the guards if they came.

He knew, too, that it was forbidden for a citizen to carry weapons; though it seemed at that time that only the innocent lacked the means to defend themselves. I was reminded of this myself, one winter afternoon shortly before the Council was due to meet. Marcellus and I had gone to the basilica together, on some small business of Aquinus's.

The matter took longer than expected. By the time we emerged the night-time cressets had been kindled around the forum wall. We were talking of something or other when Marcellus suddenly paused on the steps. I looked round, following his gaze.

A misty rain had begun to fall. The forum square was

empty. Then, ahead, between us and the pillared archway to the street, I saw a group of youths, clustered under the light of a cresset.

'The bishop's men,' I said. 'Let's go back inside. We can ask to leave by the rear door.'

I turned. But Marcellus stood firm. 'No,' he said, glaring out across the square. 'Who are they to take away our freedom?'

I heard the steel in his voice and my stomach tightened. Seeing his mind was set I said, 'Come on then; but by the Dog stop staring at them.'

We descended the basilica steps and strode out across the wet flagstones.

After a moment Marcellus gestured and said, 'Who is that one, the one looking at you?'

I clenched my teeth and glanced up. At first they all looked the same: surly bitter faces pale in the gloom of evening, turning in on one another or glaring about with an air of menace. But then the night breeze blew and the cresset flickered, and I saw with a start that one of the dark-clad youths was looking directly at me.

Cold recognition dawned. It was a face I knew. Lines had formed there since I had last seen him, setting his sulky, pouting frown into a fixed expression of malice. His hair was hacked, in the style which just then was the fashion among a certain type of city youth. But the round shoulders and slovenly posture were just as I remembered them. Bitterly I said, 'It is my cousin Albinus.'

I averted my eyes and walked on, aware we were drawing their interest. But I had forgotten I was wearing my uniform; and now, as we drew closer, one of the youths began jeering and calling out mocking insults, as if to be a soldier were disgraceful.

Marcellus stiffened. 'No,' I muttered, taking his elbow and urging him on. 'Remember, we have no weapons. There are at least twenty of them.'

But it was too late. There was a shout, and the sound of running feet. I glanced ahead, gauging the distance to the gate. We could make it, if we ran. But even as this thought came to me, I saw others move out from the shadows under the colonnade, blocking our path.

Our pursuers were closing on us. I caught Marcellus's eye. He nodded, and then we swung round to face them.

They stumbled to a stop; but quickly they collected themselves and came swaggering closer, gathering round us, making a show of sizing us up. Eyes darted to my empty sword belt, and back to my face.

I thought fast, taking in my surroundings. Close by there was an empty market table; we might rush and upturn it, and break off the legs for weapons. I touched my arm against Marcellus and signalled with my eyes; he gave a slight nod, understanding.

The youths edged closer, nervously encircling us. None of them had drawn a dagger, not yet; but I could see their hands were poised under their cloaks. They were afraid of us, unsure what we intended, even though we were outnumbered ten to one.

I tensed and drew in my breath, ready to shout the signal to Marcellus and leap sideways. But then a voice cried, 'Wait!'

The youths parted; then from behind, Albinus stepped out.

I glared at him. It had not occurred to me that he could be the ringleader.

'Well, it's cousin Drusus, the soldier boy,' he drawled. 'Has no one told you it's dangerous these days to walk about the city after dark?'

The youths around him snuffled in amusement. But Marcellus said coldly, 'So why, then, are you here? You may find more than you seek.'

The laughter died. Albinus's head jerked round, and his face formed into a sneer. He stepped up until he was directly in front of Marcellus, then paused and stared at him. He had to pull himself up, I noticed, for though they were the same height, only Marcellus held himself straight. Then, insolently, taking the hem of Marcellus's cloak between his fingers he rubbed it, in the way my uncle did when he was buying cloth.

'So this,' he said, 'is the famous grandson of Quintus Aquinus, whom my little cousin thinks so much of.'

I have learned in life that there are different types of bravery. Mine comes hot, born of anger and fear. It has seen me through, up to now; but it is a kind of blindness. Marcellus's, however, like his grandfather's, came from some other place, cool and hard and full of self-knowledge, like a sword forged in a furnace and honed to a fine edge. In a slow but powerful movement he brought his hand up and locked his fingers around Albinus's thin wrist, paused, then prised his hand away.

'And who,' he said, with a voice of contempt, 'are you?'

Albinus glowered, rubbing his wrist. 'Hasn't the soldier-boy told you about his cousin Albinus, then?'

'He has,' said Marcellus. 'What of it? You are not he. His cousin is a merchant's son, not a common street-brawler.'

Albinus caught his breath. He pulled himself to his full height. He looked like some pi-dog who has strayed around a corner and encountered a lion in its path. But I was in no doubt of the danger. My eyes took in his every movement, waiting for what I was sure would come, when his hand would snatch within his cloak for the dagger. I stood ready to leap, even if it was the last thing I did.

Perhaps he sensed my thoughts. Something made him look at me. I locked my eyes on his and in a low voice said, 'Leave it, Albinus, do you hear me? If you harm him I shall kill you. I swear it.'

He stared at me, and I glared back at him, my heart full of anger and the knowledge of the truth of my words. I saw his weak chin begin to quiver, and then he flinched and looked away.

In the loud mocking voice I had heard so often he cried, 'Do you suppose I do not remember, brave soldier-boy, when you first came to our house, trailing around like a whelp, crying yourself to sleep. Ha! Did you think I did not know? I listened at the door to hear your snivelling.' He gave a braying laugh and jabbed his finger at my face. 'Do you think I did not see the need in your eyes? You would have done anything to be loved. Now you have a smart uniform and important friends, but beneath it all you are still the same snot-nosed orphan, crying for his mother.'

I heard Marcellus stir. 'No,' I said, 'it doesn't matter.'

And then, to Albinus, 'We fashion ourselves by the image of what we want to be. Is this where your philosophy has led you, Cousin?' And as I spoke I felt strange and detached, and there was a creeping in my hair, as I sometimes feel before a storm, or in the presence of a god. His words had cut deep, as he had intended; but it was not that which had left my mind taut and clear. It was as though I were looking down upon my life from some great height, seeing myself and all the world in true perspective, as a soaring eagle looks down on the land beneath, all as a whole, each part in its place.

The moment passed even before I had known it. Yet I felt changed. Around me the youths were staring, and Albinus was looking at me with a face that was ravaged and broken.

Then, with a lunge, he jerked his head and spat in my face.

'This time I spare you,' he cried, 'because it is in my power and I choose it. But you will not be so lucky again, little soldier.'

He broke into his harsh laugh, and went striding off, followed by the others.

But as he passed under the archway with its flickering torches he glanced back, darting a look at me; and once more, for a brief moment, I saw below the mask, to the wilderness that lay beneath.

Meanwhile, all around us, the madness surged and spread, destroying the natural bonds of man with man.

The bishop denounced his enemies, and one by one

they were arrested. At first they had been taken in the dead of night. Now, in broad day, men who had crossed him, or who possessed something he or his supporters wanted, were dragged off on some pretext, while the mob stood in the street like carrion-birds, waiting to loot whatever was of value from their homes.

And yet Aquinus, whom the bishop hated most of all, remained untouched. I asked Marcellus about it, saying, 'Is it his knowing Martinus that keeps them away?'

He shrugged. 'I know no more than you; he will not speak of it. Do you imagine the bishop and the notary fear Martinus? Somehow I doubt it.'

'No,' I conceded, remembering the man and his vain chatter.

And when I thought about it, it seemed to me these men of the bishop's were like the crowds who desecrated the temples, afraid to bring down what was best and highest, beginning instead with what was easy, as hunting dogs will snap at the heels of a noble stag, and yet hold back from the kill, until the creature has been felled by another and lies defenceless.

Almost daily, during those dark shortening days of late November, we called at Heliodora's school, fearing for her safety. One morning we arrived to find a group of her students gathered in the yard, speaking with the old silversmith who owned the shop outside. They turned in alarm when we entered, and relief showed on their faces when they saw who it was.

'What has happened?' said Marcellus.

One of the group – an intent, firm-featured girl from a poor family who was one of Heliodora's prize students –

said, 'The bishop has just left. He came with the deacon and some others.'

'They have taken her.'

'Oh no, Marcellus,' she replied. 'She is inside; she went to sit down for a moment . . . but here she is now.'

We turned, and there she was, in the doorway beside the column, looking as bright and boyish as ever.

'What did they want?' cried Marcellus, striding across the courtyard to her.

'The bishop had certain questions he wished to ask, and would I please accompany him.'

'But you are here!'

'I told him no. I told him I had a class to teach, and he was interrupting. I told him if he had anything serious to ask me – which I doubted – he could ask me here and now and be done with it, and I could get on with my work. But why are you staring? You look as though you had seen a ghost.'

'I almost think I have. What then?'

'Then he left. He is a coward at heart. He had no questions, of course – but I had one or two for him. I asked him whether he thought he was furthering the cause of truth by murdering everyone who disagreed with him.'

'By God!' whispered Marcellus, shaking his head.

'Yes, indeed. And what does our poor bishop know of God? He is shining on his outward side, but within is all corruption.' She gave a brief laugh. 'But now' – turning to her wide-eyed students – 'let us resume our study of Plato, who has something to say about such cases as this, I believe.'

It was, by all accounts, the last class she gave. That evening, when darkness had fallen, a band of monks paid her a visit and carried her off to a nearby church. What happened next we only discovered long after. For a while they questioned her in some sort of parody of a trial. Then they condemned her for being unnatural – a favourite accusation of the bishop's – and demanded that she recant the heresy of her teaching, though what that heresy was they could not say. In the end they stripped her and burned her with hot oil and cut her with knives, and when they were done with that they bore her almost lifeless body back to the school, set light to the building, and cast her into the flames.

No one witnessed it, or so they claimed. Even the old silversmith, who had seen the monks arrive as he was closing his shop, said, when we asked him, that he would not testify, for there was no point in bringing certain death down upon his own head too. As for the authorities, they said it was an accident – no doubt a spilled lamp, or a stray spark of an untended fire.

But everyone knew – everyone knew, and those who thought it was unjust merely shook their heads and said nothing.

'Do you think she expected it?' I asked Marcellus, when we had gone to inspect the ruins. 'Did she know they would come?'

'I believe so,' he said. 'She could have run; that was what they wanted. But she would not.' He looked away, and rubbed his face with his hand, and trudged off alone through the charred and smoking embers.

Something caught at my foot and I glanced down. It

was the blackened remains of a lyre. Gently I picked it up. The strings were gone; the carved wood was crisped to charcoal; the tortoiseshell box was cracked and black with soot.

For a moment I stared at it; then I cast it down in disgust and grief and anger. For it seemed, that day, there would never again be a place for music, or beauty, in the world.

The Council met at last. I put on my tribune's uniform and took my old position at the back of the chamber. On the front bench, at one end, was the place where Gennadius always sat. No one had taken it. In the rows behind, the ranks of decurions were much thinned. I wondered how many had stayed away, and how many were dead.

The notary entered, moving in his odd, fastidious way, drably dressed as if he were just another minor official, his pale, long face cold and immobile. At his side, like a preening peacock beside a raven, walked the bishop.

They paused. The bishop said something, and as he spoke he glanced behind him. We soon saw why. From outside came the sound of military boots on stone. The decurions turned and stared as a troop of about twenty guards marched in, armed with swords. At a sign from the notary they fanned out, taking up positions at the foot of each of the stairways that led up between the seats. A murmur rustled along the benches. I looked across to where Aquinus was sitting at the front. He had paused from talking to the man beside him and was frowning with disapproval. Further up, from his place high up on the tiered seats, Marcellus caught my eye and nodded grimly, as if to say, 'Are you surprised?'

The velvet glove was off the iron fist: this was tyranny pure and simple. Up on the benches I could see the minds of the decurions working in their faces, and as they digested what they saw, their outrage turned to fear.

I had almost forgotten the governor himself; but now Martinus entered. His old patrician poise had deserted him. His face looked flushed and anxious. Rather than take the floor, he moved off to one side and sat on a chair. It was the notary who stepped forward.

I had never heard him speak before, but now his voice cut through the fearful silence. It was thin and sharp and precise, like a surgeon's tool, or an instrument of torture. He repeated the same absurd charges concerning the harvest: that the decurions and their rich friends had caused it to fail; that they were storing grain secretly, to keep food from the people. It was, he said, a deliberate attempt to undermine the imperial authority. He could conclude only one thing: that another Magnentius was in their midst, fomenting rebellion. He suspected the traitors were in this very room; but wherever they were he would uncover them, even if every man in Britain had to be put to the rack.

The horrified decurions gaped down at him. I glanced across the chamber at Martinus. He was looking directly ahead, with a distracted, empty look on his face. I remembered what Trebius had said, that the real power lay with the notary. He had seen it well enough: had it only now dawned upon the governor himself?

My eyes passed to the slab-faced guards. I wondered

what order they had been given. Whatever it was, we should find out soon enough. Even Aquinus could not speak now, at the point of a sword. This was not a debate or a consultation; it was a trial; and, perhaps, an execution too. I thought of Martinus and his bland complacent inaction, and my heart filled with contempt. And then I thought of myself. Was I not also worthy of contempt? What else had I done but submit? And this, I reflected, was indeed the nature of tyranny, that even the tyrannized become complicit in the end, robbed of their humanity, sick of soul, party to their own enslavement.

The notary was talking on – carefully, smoothly, seemingly reasonable, and yet the whole content of his speech was insane. And then suddenly, in the midst of this, a loud thumping sound began.

The notary's head snapped up. His speech faltered. I had not imagined anything could have shocked him, who had presided over so much torture and death; but now his cold black eyes widened, and for a moment, before his pale face jerked round, I caught a glimpse of the hideous fury that burned condensed and controlled within, like the fire that rages behind a furnace door. In the midst of his address, without leave, without heed for the guards, and without any sign that an interruption would be permitted, Aquinus had risen to his feet, taken the rod of office from the magistrate, and was beating it loudly on the marble floor – thud! thud! thud! – reverberating about the high chamber in the signal that demanded silence.

Everyone stared appalled. Even the guards, who up to now had stood rigid, turned their heads and gaped. I heard an echoing in my ears, and realized it was my own heart straining in my breast. Then, in the dreadful silence, Aquinus spoke.

'I have heard enough of this madness,' he said, in a steady, thundering voice. 'Everyone knows who is the criminal here. He stands before us, the creature who has dragged innocent men to be tortured and murdered on no more evidence than the vague say-so of anonymous informers, men who are rewarded for their lies . . . And you!' he cried, rounding on the bishop, 'you dare to come among us and countenance this absurd tirade, when it is you, above all, who are the agent of this ruin.'

The bishop looked nervously about him, the rictus of a smile frozen on his lips.

'*You* are the guilty men!' cried Aquinus. 'You have reduced this province from plenty to want, so that men sit hungry beside burnt fields, and children die in their mothers' arms. Is this your imperial authority? A corrupt hypocritical bishop, an insane murderer of a notary, and an ineffectual governor. Shame on you all! Get out! We do not need you here.'

I think my mouth had fallen open. I wonder that I managed even to breathe. When at last I became aware of myself, my first thought was of Marcellus. I looked up. He was staring horror-struck from his place high on the benches. But Aquinus had not finished. He drew his breath and spoke on, his accusations crashing down on the heads of the notary and bishop and governor like storm-waves on the shore, beating and hammering, detailing each contravention of the law committed by the notary, demanding to know when the governor would take responsibility for the disaster his lackey had caused. 'Or perhaps,' he declared, turning suddenly to Martinus, 'you were not aware? Perhaps no one told you, though all the city and all the province has spoken of nothing else, when they dared to speak at all. It is hard to credit that a man at the centre of affairs, entrusted with the care of the province, could know nothing of the crimes he presided over. But better by far to believe in your ignorance, than to think a man who was once considered noble and good might countenance such evil and fail to act.'

He reached behind him and took up a scroll, and pulling it open began to read out, one by one, like the tolling of a bell, the list of men who had disappeared, or had been arrested, or put to the question, or knowing what was coming had chosen to open their veins in the comfort of their homes. I do not think anyone had heard them all before, or known there were so many. And when at last he finished he cast the document down, sending it clattering and unfurling on the floor, so that the rolling spindle came to rest at the governor's feet.

'Read it!' Aquinus cried, 'when next you are at leisure. Is this what your ancient lineage and long schooling in virtue have taught you? To stand by while a madman and a charlatan tear apart this province like jackals over a carcass? Remember your ancestors, Flavius Martinus! And, by all the gods, remember yourself!'

And then, at last, he sat down.

There was silence. It rang in my ears. The guards stood blinking, knowing that something terrible had occurred, but unable to fathom quite what it meant. On the front bench Aquinus sat with one leg crossed easily over the other, gazing up at the coffered ceiling with its filigree and gilding and high clerestory windows, seemingly calm, as if he had been doing no more than address a motion on the public works.

I became aware of a choking sound. It was the notary. His coolness had deserted him. For a moment he stared, his mouth struggling to form the words. Then he jerked round and screamed at the guards, 'Arrest him! Arrest this man! Take him away!'

The guards looked at one another. No one moved. And then every head turned, for Martinus had risen from his chair.

'No!' he said. 'There will be no more arrests.'

The notary whipped round and glared at him, his eyes like points of fire. 'What?' he said, in a low, dangerous voice.

But Martinus continued. 'You, Paulus, were charged by the emperor to search out conspirators and bring them to justice. That was your commission. You have arrested many men, but I have seen no evidence which would convince an honest judge. You have done enough. I relieve you of your duties, and I shall answer for it.'

From the benches came a low timid rumble of assent, cut short when the notary cried out, 'Oh no, Martinus! You are mistaken. My investigations are only just beginning, for I see now that it is you who stand at the head of this great conspiracy . . . Guards, I order you to arrest the governor.'

The guards looked from the notary to Martinus and

stayed where they were. For a moment nothing happened. Then the notary swung round and pointing his arm at me shouted, 'Tribune, arrest this traitor. Do it now!'

Our eyes locked. His slack hair had fallen over his brow. There were flecks of spittle on his chin. It seemed everything good that had ever touched me converged on this moment, so that I did not for one instant need to consider my answer.

I said, 'I will not.'

He looked at me, unable to believe what he had heard. Then, with a shout of rage, he ran to where the guards stood huddled about the stairway. 'You!' he cried, grabbing the first he came to by the sleeve of his red military tunic. 'Arrest him, or you will spend a week dying! The governor is a traitor. Do you hear me? In the name of the divine Constantius I dismiss him. I have the authority. Do as I tell you!'

The guard leapt as if bitten, startled into action by the sound of the emperor's name, and because he had been singled out. Uncertainly he advanced, and behind him the others began to follow.

Then I stepped forward.

'Halt!' I shouted in my loudest parade-ground voice. 'To attention, men!'

In moments of confusion, troopers, being what they are, will always follow a familiar order. They hesitated, then shuffled into line, and looked at me as a parched man looks at water, waiting for instructions. The tactic would have worked; but Martinus, after so many months of inaction, had determined he was going to finish what he had begun. Drawing his little ceremonial dagger he rushed flailing across the floor and lunged at the notary. There was a shout, and a confusion of clothing, and then the notary fell sprawling backwards.

I ran up. Being closest, I was first there. The notary was clutching his side, gasping. Blood showed red between his thin, white fingers. But Martinus was a civilian; whatever else he had learned, he had no skill in killing, and I could see at once that the wound was not fatal.

Often since, I have reflected on this moment. I ought to have drawn my dagger and finished him. The deed would have been done, the governor safe, and much evil averted.

But I hesitated at killing a man who lay helpless on the ground; and in that instant the notary sprang up with sudden force. He flew past me; a knife flashed. It must have been hidden within his cloak. I cried out and the governor turned. But it was too late.

He fell, and I caught him. The ivory haft lay buried in his chest, moving with his laboured breaths. Blood pulsed around the wound; he tried to speak; but instead he coughed and choked, and hot blood splashed over his white senator's robes and onto my hand.

Then he was still.

I became aware of a great roar rising all around me. I looked up. The decurions were on their feet, shouting. At first I thought they were calling out in righteous anger, asserting at last their ancient liberty which had been taken from them. But then I saw what they were at: they were scrambling in panic for the aisles, grappling and stumbling and falling over one another in their haste to reach the door. And at the next moment Marcellus was at my side, pulling me to my feet, shouting in my ear over the noise that we must get his grandfather away.

Somehow, amid the chaos, we reached Aquinus's town-house, through streets that had erupted into confusion and petty looting. I do not know what the notary and the bishop had intended that day; but whatever it was had been in some way thwarted, and everywhere sullen gangs were milling around the streets, like men waiting for an order.

Aquinus said little. He seemed dazed and troubled. He was mumbling over and over that we must find the good men of the city. But it was too late for that. The good men were scattered, or dead.

As soon as we reached the house, Clemens came running. Seeing his stricken master he gasped and clutched his hand to his mouth.

'Fetch the horses!' cried Marcellus. 'You must leave at once. Get the servants out too.'

'And you, sir?'

'I'll follow when I can. Now go, Clemens! There is no time. Set a guard at the farm. Close the gates. Admit no one you do not know.'

When they had hurried away and we were standing alone in the garden court, I said, 'Is your grandfather fit for such a journey?'

'He can ride in his sleep, he rides better than anyone I know—' He broke off as running footsteps echoed in the street beyond the wall. I held my breath, waiting for the sound of hammering at the door. But they ran on.

'We cannot stay here,' I said.

'I know. Where is your horse?'

'I have none. It went with the army.'

He pushed his hand through his hair and cursed up at the sky. Then he said, 'I know where we can find one.'

We waited for the cover of darkness, then left by the back gate, making our way along the narrow cobbled alley behind the house.

Somewhere, behind one of the high walls, an abandoned dog was howling. Elsewhere we heard the sound of drunken revelling, house-slaves who had broken open their master's wine cellar.

Marcellus knew this warren of backstreets from childhood; he darted this way and that through the narrow lightless alleys, and presently we stopped at a heavy, black-painted door set into a wall. On the far side were trees and dense overhanging shrubs.

He tried the latch. The door was bolted.

'Here, help me up,' he said. 'I can open it from within.'

I crouched down, locking my fingers together to make a step; he gripped my shoulder and pulled himself up onto the ledge, then dropped down on the other side. The bolts grated and the door opened.

Within was a paved yard with a row of stables, and, some distance beyond, half hidden by an expanse of shrubs and cypress trees, a rich man's mansion shuttered and in darkness.

I was just about to ask whose house it was, when

memory stirred and I looked again. I had been here before. The house was Scapula's.

'Great God, Marcellus!' I whispered, 'why here?'

His eyes flashed in the darkness. 'He has horses. He can spare us one for a while, don't you think? Come on.'

And indeed there were many more horses in the stable than any household could need. We selected a black mare and a young chestnut. Marcellus went off to the tack room. I waited at the door.

The clouds had parted; the freshening breeze rustled and stirred in the tall conifers, casting patterns of moonlight on the paving. Then, coming from the alley beyond the wall, I heard the approach of raucous drunken voices, bawling out to one another, laughing and joking.

I strained to listen, remembering the slaves we had heard, waiting for them to pass.

But instead the voices fell suddenly silent. A gust stirred the cypress branches. Then, with a sudden noise that made me start, the bolt rattled angrily and the door sounded on its hinges.

'Marcellus!' I whispered out, calling behind me as loud as I dared into the darkness of the stable.

The door in the wall half opened. Flickering torchlight showed behind it. I heard muted voices, talking urgently.

I called again.

'I'm here,' said Marcellus at my shoulder. 'What is it?'

Then he saw, and cursed under his breath. It was Scapula, with a crowd of his friends. Minutes later and we should have been gone; but they had chosen this moment to return, and had found the gate unbolted.

'Is there another way out?' I asked.

He paused. 'There may be. It's this way.'

We crept off behind the stables, along a narrow path between the high shrubs. Ahead in the distance the main house loomed; but then, before we reached it, our way was blocked by a second sheer brick wall and a gate. Marcellus pulled at the latch, then let out a sigh of frustration; it was secured with a heavy padlock. Voices sounded somewhere behind. Advancing shafts of light showed through the bushes. Then Scapula's voice cried out, shouting angrily for the night-guard. He had discovered the open stable-door.

Our eyes met. I said, 'We could try climbing over.'

He peered up at the dangerous-looking spikes at the top and shook his head. 'No, Drusus,' he said, 'it's better to face them.' He always had a hatred of being furtive.

So we turned, and stepped out into the torchlight.

Whatever troubles had beset the city, they had clearly not touched Scapula and his friends. He looked as if he had been to a party. There was a lily-garland on his head, and he had two women in tow. They squealed when they saw us, and scuttled back behind the others.

Marcellus, making the best of it, said, 'Scapula, forgive me, I need to borrow two horses. There was no time to find you. I am sorry if I have startled you.'

Scapula's eyes widened. He stared, first at Marcellus, then at me. His face was damp and flushed from wine. Then he let out a laugh that echoed round the yard, and behind him the two girls began to giggle and snort.

'Shut up!' he snapped at them. Then, in the snide

drawl I knew so well, 'Why, if it isn't my old friend Marcellus and his little bosom-buddy! Horse-thieving now, is it?'

'It's just for a few days,' said Marcellus patiently.

Scapula laughed unpleasantly, and his friends laughed with him. From the direction of the house running foot-steps sounded, and a clutch of slaves appeared with the watchman. 'Where were you?' cried Scapula, rounding on them. They would be in for a beating later. But now he returned his attention to us.

'Something tells me,' he said, frowning and putting a mocking finger to his brow, 'that your friend here is a wanted man. And who knows? Maybe you are too.'

Marcellus sighed. 'There is no need for this. It's only two horses, and you have a stable-full. You won't miss them, you know you won't.'

'I am sorry, Marcellus. There are no horses here.'

Marcellus glanced to the stables and started to reply, but stopped himself.

'I see,' he said flatly. 'In that case we shall not trouble you further.' He took a step forward.

'Oh, but wait. Where are you going? I don't think I can let you leave, not quite yet.'

'By heaven, Scapula, this is no time for games! They will kill us. Is that what you want?'

He folded his arms and considered, as if this were a question requiring careful thought. Even from where I stood I could smell the reek of wine on him.

'Very well,' he said eventually. '*You* may go ... but your violent friend stays. We shall see what the notary wants with him. He needs to be taught a lesson.'

I leapt forward, but the slaves grabbed me: they were not going to be caught napping a second time. They pinned my arms and legs; another gripped my neck; and the watchman stood over me with a dangerous iron club poised above my head.

'Well?' Scapula said to Marcellus. 'Are you going, or staying?'

Marcellus glared at him. 'I stay. I belong with my friend.'

Scapula laughed with delight. Then suddenly his face changed. Stepping up he raised his arm, and with a great side-swipe struck me hard across the face. I tasted blood in my mouth. He had used every ounce of his strength. Then he stood smiling at me, dusting off his hands one against the other, as if somehow he had regained his dignity, rather than lost it.

Presently the notary's guards came. We were taken to the governor's palace, to the ancient warren of underground cells, where countless others had been taken before us.

We were manhandled and shoved by barbarian German-speaking guards who forced us down a narrow brick-lined tunnel. The air reeked of acrid smoke from spluttering cressets, and of unwashed flesh, and human waste, and some underlying charnel-house smell I averted my mind from.

We went for some time, following the tunnel far under the palace. Eventually the guards jerked us to a halt beside a tiny low-roofed cell. They manacled us together, shoved us roughly forward, and slammed the gate shut behind us. Then they left, their footsteps receding up the passageway.

There was no room to stand. We sat awkwardly on the ground. Damp moss grew on the walls. Filthy grey straw lay about, and an old pile of human excrement, half consumed by rats.

For some time we hardly spoke, listening, waiting for the approach of the executioner, or, more likely, the assassin. I thought of dying and how it would be, held down in a stinking dungeon while some cowardly butcher wielded the knife. Would I be tortured first? The notary was capable of every kind of terror, of that I was sure. I recalled his eyes, staring at me across the Council chamber. He would remember me; and he would make me pay. I shivered, and felt the beginnings of terror like something cold and sharp, gnawing in my gut. I stole a glance at Marcellus, but he was taken up with his own thoughts.

Right up to the end I had pleaded with him to run, to leave me before the guards came. It had been a great amusement to Scapula to hear me begging him to go, and he had mocked and parodied my cries.

But Marcellus had refused, and in the end, when the guards' boots rang in the street outside and it was too late, I had fallen silent. Now I was glad he was with me, for without him I was not sure I could face such a death like a man.

Time passed. I must have dozed, for I awoke with a start, half slumped on Marcellus's shoulder. He was gently shaking me.

'Listen,' he whispered.

I strained to hear. From somewhere far along the passage came the tap of footsteps, uncertain and hesitant, picking their way through the gloom. I crept forward and pressed my face to the rusting bars. But I could see nothing except the opposite wall with its mouldering plaster, and beyond that darkness.

'Do you hear?' whispered Marcellus. 'It is just one person.'

An assassin then, I thought. Yet even an assassin would not come alone.

Marcellus edged up to the bars beside me. It was hard to tell how distant the footfalls were. They sounded, then stopped, advancing and pausing, as if the walker had lost his way. But each time they were closer. A shadow crossed the opposite wall; and then, silhouetted against the light of a torch, stooping in the passage, a figure appeared in a hooded winter cloak.

He paused and turned; then seeing me he jumped back startled. His hood was pulled tightly up, but his white hands showed, and his fingers bitten down to the quick. I cried out, 'Show your face, Albinus, for I know you!'

'Quiet! Be quiet!' He snatched down his hood and stared wildly back along the passageway. There was a growth of black stubble on his chin, and heavy blue lines beneath his eyes. 'Listen, will you: the city is in turmoil; the bishop and the notary cannot control the people. Martinus is dead, and there is a rumour that barbarians have overrun Gaul.' He paused and looked at me, and I saw his lip was trembling. Then, in a plaintive voice he asked, 'Is it true the notary killed the governor?'

'Yes. I was there.'

'He blames the Council.'

'It is a lie. It was the notary.'

He swallowed and looked helplessly at me.

Impatiently I said, 'Are you here to tell me this? They have handed the city over to the mob. Did they really think the mob would return it?'

He wiped his eyes on his sleeve and I saw he was crying.

'I did not want it like this,' he whined, 'he promised me all would be well. That's what the bishop said. He said he controlled everything, and I had nothing to fear. But now everything is broken.' He began snivelling, and in between his catching sobs he said, 'I will go away, far away; I shall find some desolate place, apart from other men, a monastery . . . There is a place across the sea, in Hibernia, a secret place where I shall be alone, alone with God.'

'You should stay and fix what you have destroyed,' said Marcellus with contempt.

Albinus sniffed and snorted, and a flash of his old anger returned. 'I have taken a great risk,' he snapped back. 'You have been condemned; you would not be alive even now, but for the confusion.' And then, returning to his plaintive tone, 'I have done many bad things, Drusus. I am ashamed. I want to show you I can do something good.'

He paused, looking at me with entreaty, as if by some magic word I could wipe clean the soiled slate of his memory. But it was Marcellus who answered him. 'Every man can do good,' he said, 'if he chooses.'

Albinus stared at him, as if such a thought had never before come to him.

'There is a ship sailing with the tide,' he said, pulling himself together. 'It is taking prisoners to Gaul. I can get you to the holding cell, it's not far. But you must hurry, and act the part of prisoners.'

'Why not just release us? You found your way in. Let us out the same way.'

'I can't. Listen, please. I cannot get you out of here; it cannot be done. The guards require a permit for everyone who leaves.'

'So you are sending us to Gaul to our deaths.'

He looked at me, biting his knuckles. Behind him a rat ambled across the faint pool of light, paused, and disappeared into the shadows. 'Truly I did not know it would end like this,' he pleaded.

I shook my head. Somewhere far off along the passage a voice sounded. Albinus leapt with fear, stared for a moment, then hurriedly poured out what we must do. When he had finished he paused.

I said, 'What now?'

'Remember, the guard knows none of this. When he comes, say nothing. Do not betray me, I beg you, or they will kill me.' He looked at us pathetically, pressing his hands one on the other, unable to trust. Then he turned and fled into the darkness.

There was a long wait. I began to suppose he had changed his mind and left us. But eventually he returned, leading two blunt-featured barbarian guards.

'This one,' he said, pointing at our cell.

The nearest guard lifted a ring of keys from his belt and squinted at them, his tongue lolling with concentration as he selected the right one. He unlocked the gate and ordered us out.

We were led away along the tunnel, and presently we descended a flight of slime-wet steps. As we walked the foul air began to freshen, replaced by the dank dead smell of river mud, which was perfume after the stench behind us. Finally we halted at a low grilled wooden door. The guard unbolted it.

'In there!' ordered Albinus, attempting to put authority into his shaking voice.

I gave him a quick private look; but he averted his face. Then the guards shoved us inside and slammed the door, and I saw no more of him.

I turned. The room was dark after the glare of the torchlight. I took a step forward. Something yielding caught my foot and I stumbled. I stopped and gazed down, thinking at first I had walked on a corpse. But then, as my eyes adjusted, I saw we were not alone, and I had stepped on a living man's leg. He raised his head for a moment, looked at me impassively, then looked down again.

Peering into the gloom, I saw there were others beside him, chained in a row against the wall. Beyond them, through a rusted gate, a landing pier showed in the grey dawn light; and moored there, shifting and creaking in the rising water, lay the prison-ship that was to take us to Gaul.

*

At sun-up the bolts sounded and the guards returned. They unchained us, talking heedlessly over our heads in their guttural barbarian tongue, as if we were no more than cattle. They opened the iron gate to the pier and herded us through, into the hold of the waiting barge.

We were bound once more – this time with mooring lanyard. When the guards had gone the bargemen came hurrying down from the deck, and felt us roughly for anything they could steal. But whatever was of value had already been taken by the guards. Finding nothing they kicked and cursed us, until the master shouted for them and they scurried back up the ladder to cast off.

I looked at the men around me. Their beards were growing, dark or grey or fair stubble on faces used to daily shaving; and though their clothes were soiled and torn, one could see they were of fine material and of a good cut. Such men as these had formed the backbone of the province: hard-working citizens who liked their comforts and wanted to build something for their own futures. But now not one of them spoke or met my gaze, nor had they resisted the guards or shown resentment at the violent bargemen who kicked and slapped them. They were broken men, waiting for death with bowed, accepting heads. I suppose the bargemen, who had been servile with the guards, had sensed this, and hurt them the worse for it. Marcellus and I, after an initial search of our clothes and a few careless kicks, they had left alone.

Outside I heard the rattle of the sail as it was hauled up. The barge began to move. There were no window-holes – the hold was not made for human cargo – but through the grilled hatch in the roof I could see a patch of leaden dawn sky. Marcellus questioned the others: who were they? What had happened to them? How long had they been held? But they merely cast their eyes down, shaking their heads, and did not answer.

In time the ship began to pitch, and I heard outside the screams of gulls. 'We are near the open sea,' I said to Marcellus, adding that no doubt the master had been paid a good fee to cross to Gaul, for the vessel was no more than a flat-bottomed coaster, good for little more than river work.

At this, the prisoner at my side, a middle-aged balding man in smart clothes, who looked as if he had been snatched from some well-heeled dinner party, looked nervously up at the hatch and mumbled, 'I cannot swim.'

'Hush!' said the man next to him, 'or they'll come and beat us.' And another said, 'What does it matter if you cannot swim? One way or another you are going to die.'

'But the notary Paulus said we were being sent for trial!'

'You believe that?' responded his neighbour. 'Then you're more of a fool than you look.'

'But they cannot just kill us! We have rights.'

'Wake up, you fool! They can, and they will. If you ask me, I doubt they'll even take us to Gaul. They will kill us here, and return for another load.'

The barge lurched. The man beside me looked wretchedly about him. He sneezed, and rubbed his nose. 'Wait!' I cried, 'why isn't your wrist bound?'

He gave a shrug. 'They forgot. They were too busy kicking me.'

'By God, then untie me!'

'Oh, no! It'll only make it worse for all of us.'

'Worse than what?' said Marcellus.

The man looked down and said nothing.

It took a lot of coaxing, but eventually he consented to use his free hand to unpick the knot that bound my arms. Once it was done the rest was easy, and I untied Marcellus and the others. Some even objected. I untied them anyway, calling them cowards and putting them to shame. I could almost have slapped them; but there had been enough violence, and soon there would be more.

Then we waited.

On deck, I could hear the voice of the master barking an order, and the feet of the crew pattering on the deck, and the creaking of lines.

'What now?' said the man next to me.

'We're turning towards the shore.'

I thought of what the other prisoner had said, that it was not worth our captors' while to take us to Gaul. That would explain the unseaworthy ship. The man was right: they intended to put in somewhere in the estuary and kill us. It would be easily done, and the tide would carry off the bodies.

I kept these thoughts to myself; already some of the men there were shivering with terror.

Presently the hatch opened and one of the bargemen came climbing down the ladder, feet first. Marcellus caught my eye and inclined his head at the man's belt. A knife was wedged into it. It had not been there before.

I nodded back. We understood each other. This was our only chance. I had told the men to conceal the strands of untied lanyard under the folds of their clothing;

but it was not beyond some of them to speak out and betray us, in the hope of buying their lives at the cost of ours.

The bargeman reached the foot of the ladder and turned. Marcellus, taking my cue, twisted up his face and said, 'You stink! With so much water around you, a man would think you'd find the time to wash.'

The man's eyes widened and he swung round. He was buck-toothed, with a deeply stupid face. He began to say something. Suddenly one of the prisoners cried out – he denied afterwards it was a warning to the guard – and at the same time I sprang up, snatched the knife from the man's belt, and cut his throat, silencing his death-cry with my hand over his mouth, then easing him down silently to the floor in a pool of blood.

'You killed him,' cried the prisoner who untied me, staring.

'What did you expect?' said another. 'A debate?'

'Now what?' asked a third.

I said, 'We wait.'

Soon another bargeman came, looking for the first, and I took him while he was still on the ladder. Then, armed with a second knife, Marcellus and I burst out onto the deck, and killed or overpowered the others. As I had already guessed, they were not brave, once it came to a fair fight.

When it was over the barge-master, a squat Sicilian with crimped hair and a gold neck-chain, grovelled on his belly, pleading for his life. We let him keep it, and ordered him to the helm.

I stood at the rail and looked inland. I knew the

territory – it was all tall marsh-grass and muddy inlets, not far from where my father's farm had been.

We beached the craft on an expanse of tidal mud-flat and waded ashore.

'Where is this place?' someone asked.

'Who cares?' said another. 'Would you rather wait on the ship?'

There were one or two muted laughs; it was a good sign. I told them I knew the place, saying there was a hamlet not far off where they could find help and food.

'And you, sirs? Will you not escape with us?'

'We are going back,' I replied. 'We have a job to do.'

TWELVE

ON THE RIDGE WE PAUSED. Ahead in the valley, behind its screen of poplars, the villa appeared as I remembered it, golden and rust-red against the winter sunset.

But Marcellus frowned and said, 'It is too quiet. Why has no one kindled the lights, and where is the smoke from the kitchen fires?'

We urged our horses on. As we drew near, a head appeared over the enclosure wall and a young voice called out a challenge.

'Open the gates, Tertius, it's me.'

The boy – one of the farm-hands – let out a cry of joy: he ducked down, there was the sound of heavy bolts shifting, and the great oak-and-iron gate swung open on its massive hinges.

'Is my grandfather here?'

'At the house, Marcellus sir. He has been waiting.'

We cantered our horses past the leafless orchard and

the lawns and fish-ponds, on through the second enclosure wall to where the great dolphin-fountain towered on its sculpted sandstone base in front of the house.

Someone had called Aquinus. He was waiting on the steps, a sombre, upright figure against the darkening sky, flanked by the vast Corinthian columns of the portico. Clemens stood beside him, and old Tyronius the bailiff.

'You are safe,' said Aquinus. His voice was flat and tired.

Briefly, quickly, Marcellus explained what had happened.

Aquinus listened grimly. When Marcellus had finished he said, 'You are here, at least. I was going to send a man to the city. I thought . . . well, no matter what I thought. Whose horses are those?'

'We took them from a horse-farm. We could not find the owner.'

By now the sun was no more than a blood-red afterglow in the west. A sharp, still coldness descended with the night. Clemens eased a cloak around Aquinus's shoulders. It was the kind of thing that, once, Aquinus would have told him not to fuss about; now he merely accepted it.

One of the servants emerged with a lamp, and by its flame, as I moved towards the door, I saw what up to now the failing day had hidden. I turned and stared. Aquinus glanced round.

'Ah, yes,' he said, 'I was going to tell you.' He frowned deeply at the crude ochre-painted Christian symbol daubed across the stonework. 'We have had visitors, and they have left their mark, as you can see.'

'You were not hurt?'

'I was not here. Tyronius and the hands took your mother to safety, concealing themselves below the house, in the hypocaust. Our visitors did not stay long.' He gave a slight smile, adding, 'The country makes them uneasy.'

Marcellus glared out into the darkness. 'Did they take anything?' he asked.

'Oh, a few items they could carry off, the kind that seemed to them of value. But mostly they just broke things for the pleasure of it, and daubed their foolish symbols.'

Within, in the atrium, the great floor of green serpentine still bore the marks of spilled paint. Against the wall, at the base of one of the rose-pink columns, an olivewood table lay on its side, two of its delicate legs torn off, the others protruding into the air like some felled animal. Shards of glass lay among the ruin. I remembered there had been a crystal vase upon it, engraved with a chariot and horses.

'You should go to your mother,' said Aquinus.

'Yes,' said Marcellus, frowning at the signs of violence that lay about. Something on the floor caught his eye. He picked it up. At first I thought it was a fragment of a painting; but then I saw it was an illuminated page, torn from its binding.

'Your library?' Marcellus said, looking round at his grandfather.

Aquinus gave a brief nod. 'They knew where to strike. The rest – the broken furniture, the slashed tapestries – was just done in passing.'

And so, with the heavy air of a man who returns to

the scene of great pain, he led us through the rooms to his library.

The shelves had been smashed with some blunt instrument. The stacks of books lay strewn across the floor. One by one, with systematic care, they had been trampled and torn apart; and in one corner charred remains lay on the ground.

We moved through the wreckage. After a short while Marcellus turned to where Aquinus was standing with Clemens at the threshold. 'I am sorry, Grandfather. What kind of man hates knowledge so much that he would do this?'

'The man who fears it. And there are many such men; do not deceive yourself. They lie in wait, until they sense their time is come. It is a mark of civilization that such men are kept in check – by what is higher, by what is better, by what is noble.'

He took the lamp from Clemens and advanced, pausing now and then to look around.

'I was too attached to it,' he said eventually, speaking in a low, remote voice. He shook his head. 'There were books here that will be lost forever. Is this what the bishop and his new world holds out for us; is this his promise for the future? Nothing good has ever come from ignorance.' And then he muttered once more, 'I was too attached to it.'

Under the high mullioned window, where the remains of his desk lay strewn about, he seemed to gather himself up. Turning to me he said, 'But enough of my own concerns; the questions we face are more pressing, and I have news.' The remnants of the garrison, he said, which had been sent north, had finally mutinied. They had found the man who had murdered Trebius. 'He was in the pay of the notary, and they will have no more of it. They are marching on London.'

'Then we must join them,' I cried.

'Yes, I supposed you would.'

In the flickering light of the single lamp I could not see his face across the room. But something in his tone made me ask, 'Do you disapprove, sir?'

For a few moments he remained still and did not answer. Then he said, 'Of course you must go. What else now is possible? But let us beware of what we break, and what we awaken. We have built something that was long in the making, and is not easily remade when it is gone.'

'We must trust in the gods, sir, who see further than men.'

He made a slight motion with his hand, I could not tell its meaning. Then, turning, he gazed out in silence at his darkened courtyard garden.

'And thus the young teach the old,' he said. 'Well, our fate lies in your hands now. Too many men have stood apart, hoping that some other would bear the burden.'

The garrison army had made camp three days' march north-west of London, on high defensive ground over-looking the road.

My men greeted me with all the warmth of old com-rades, and the enthusiasm of rebels. They recounted to Marcellus and me, with outrage and anger, the tale of the murder of Trebius.

The killer, it turned out, had been one of the garrison troops. 'One of our own,' they said in disgust – though not, they pointed out emphatically, a member of my old company. He was a sentry. He had bided his time, but eventually he had been posted to the night-time watch he wanted; and when all was quiet he had slipped round to Trebius's tent and entered unseen.

At first no one had suspected him. But he was a gambler, and a bad one at that – always broke – and it was not long before his new-found gold appeared at the dice-table. Someone had teased him about it, and meeting with an aggressive reply had grown suspicious enough to mention it to his superior. After that, the man's pack was searched. Hidden at the bottom were Trebius's signet-ring and his ceremonial dagger with its silver pommel.

The men, when the truth was known, had been in no mood for imperial justice. The killer was beheaded, and his body cast into a latrine-pit.

With Trebius gone, the other officers had chosen from among their number a new commander: a tall half-Greek from Phoenician Africa called Gauron. There had indeed been a minor disturbance in the north, Gauron explained, but it was nothing that called for the removal of the whole garrison from London. Perceiving this, and discovering too the truth of Trebius's death, the men realized they had been deceived. They put down the disturbance on the frontier, and afterwards, at about the time Martinus had died, they turned south, determined to rid the city and the province of the hated notary.

They had been joined on the way by volunteers – landowners and their tenants and workers, who had been harried and bullied by the bishop's mobs, whose farms had been burned and whose ancient rural shrines had been desecrated. There were, it seemed, good men still, who were prepared to stand up to tyranny.

On the third day after our arrival, on a cold, still, grey afternoon, we reached the outskirts of the city.

As we drew near, a ragtag band of the notary's guards and the bishop's roughs emerged, clad in ill-fitting armour and brandishing whatever they had been able to find in the garrison armoury.

We laughed at them; and they, having taken a careful look at our small determined force, retreated once more and closed the gates against us.

After that, feeling safe behind the walls, they discovered a courage of sorts. They jeered down at us, wasted a few javelins, and threw stones.

'Now what?' said Gauron, regarding them with distaste. 'We are too few to take the city by siege, and they know it. They will send to Gaul for reinforcements.'

But I said, 'I know a way.'

The tide was up. The piles of the old jetty loomed in the darkness.

'This is the place,' whispered Marcellus to the rowers behind.

The boat eased left, and from my place in the bow I stretched forward, grabbed the mooring-chain, and pulled us in. We paused and listened. Torches flickered from high up on the riverside wall, reflecting in the black still water around us.

I secured the boat and climbed out onto the wet planking of the jetty. The old wood creaked and I hesitated; but no light showed at the postern, and advancing I peered in at the iron grille.

The cell inside was dark. I made a sound like a bird-call. No one responded; there was no sound of sleeping bodies shifting. Then I tried the heavy door. It stirred, groaning on its rusted hinges. It was not locked.

I signalled; the others advanced behind me, and once again the foul stench seized my nostrils.

'By the Bull,' muttered the trooper beside Marcellus, 'what is this, a sewer?'

'It's the notary's prison,' said Marcellus. 'This is perfume, compared to what it's like inside. Come on; this way.'

The wall-torches had been left to die down and fail. But we found a clay lamp burning in an alcove, and took it to light our way.

Carefully, silently, we advanced along the reeking passage. Most of the cages on each side were empty; but every so often we passed a man lying in the muck and straw. Some were dead. Others shifted and stared, disturbed by the light.

'Where are the guards?' I said to one. But he just looked at me blankly.

'Why don't they speak?' said one of my comrades.

'They have lost their wits,' said another. He shook the door of the man's cell, rattling it on its chain. The man inside let out a whine of terror and curled up in the corner, covering his eyes with his hands, as if the evil could be averted if he could not see it.

'Be still,' I said to him. 'We are not here to harm you.'
But he seemed not to hear me.

Presently we came to a flight of stone steps, rising in a
spiral. At the top the air was cleaner. There was an air
shaft, and then, through a low brick arch, a wide hexag-
onal room with a bare-wood table, and, on one wall,
suspended on hooks, a collection of loose chains, and
irons, and sets of keys on rings.

'The guardhouse,' I said to Marcellus.

'And where are the guards?' he replied.

There was no sign of them. They had been called, we
guessed, to man the walls.

Further on we came to the cellars proper, white-
painted brickwork vaults where old furniture and storage
jars stood piled up. This part I remembered from my time
with the Protectors, and from here I knew the way up to
the governor's palace above. We followed old passages
and stairs, and emerged into a servants' corridor; and
then, passing through a door, we came into one of the
elegant rooms-of-state, a long chamber with arched windows, gilded furniture, and decorated panels.

Here we encountered a man – the first we had seen. It
was the chamberlain, the same self-important fussing
official who had conducted me to my first interview with
Count Gratian four years before.

'What are you doing?' he demanded, 'you are not
permitted here!' He had taken me for one of the palace
sentries, for whom the interior was out of bounds.

But then, from the doorway behind, the rest of my
company emerged with swords pointing. The chamberlain, whose only battles had been the intrigues of clerks

and the struggle for place in the imperial bureaucracy, raised his knuckle to his open mouth and stared.

'If you want to live,' I said, 'tell me where to find the notary.'

The chamberlain needed no persuading. 'He is in the private rooms,' he answered in a wavering voice. 'But he is not to be disturbed. Those were his orders.'

'This for his orders!' said one of the men, making a clear hand-gesture. The chamberlain goggled, appalled that anyone should dare to show such disrespect to a superior.

'Who is with him?' I demanded, showing him the point of my sword.

'He is alone. He always dines alone.'

'Well tonight,' I said, 'he will have company.'

We found him in the governor's private dining-room, with its green and gold painted walls, and expensive Italian couches upholstered in silk and crimson damask.

His head snapped round as I entered. A tall lamp of wrought bronze stood between him and the door, illuminating the couch where he sat, and the low table in front of him. He had not allowed the trouble in the city to disturb his dinner. The last of his meal sat there in silver dishes, and on the floor lay a mess of chewed bones, waiting for the slaves to clear away. No doubt he felt secure behind the walls, and knew our small army was no match for them.

He stared angrily, his eyes wide and unblinking, like a bird of prey disturbed at its meal. The light had dazzled him, so that, at first, he could not discern who was there. He began to speak – some sort of angry protest. But then my sword, and those of my comrades, flashed in the lamplight, and his mouth set into a hard thin line. He had been chewing. With a slight inclination of his head he spat whatever it was onto the floor.

'How did you enter?' he said quietly.

'No matter. We are here. The city is ours.'

Already a contingent of men had gone off to open the gates from within.

He gave a slight nod; I saw the calculation in his face. Whatever else he was, he was not a fool, and though he seemed unarmed, I did not allow my guard to fall, or permit myself to forget that he was dangerous.

And now, as he sat still and rigid, the notary made use of the weapon he had honed through years of expert practice: fear and insinuating terror, and the threat of the dark unknown.

In a smooth, reasonable voice he said, 'You have been resourceful in finding your way in, and I commend you for it. But now use your wits, and reflect for a moment that whatever you may do to me, you cannot win. The emperor is all-powerful, and I am his trusted servant. Let this matter end before it goes too far. Leave now, while I do not know your names, and have not seen your faces. You have taken a wrong turn in the corridors of the palace, that is all – an easy mistake, when it is dark. Go now, and no more will be said.'

There was a silence. He regarded us with a face of accommodating warmth – except for his eyes, which were deadly.

'I took no wrong turn,' I said.

His eyes moved to my face. I think, then, for the first time he knew me.

In a low, measured voice he said, 'This is treason.' He let the dread words hang in the air. Then he said, 'Think on it, all of you, and on what it means. Some of you have families – wives and children. So far you have done no wrong, just a simple error, no more. You stand on the threshold: do not cross it. You have been misled, deceived. You do not know what you are doing. Arrest this traitor, and all will be forgotten.'

There was a pause. My men were standing behind me. I could not see their faces.

Then one of them said, 'Go and tell it to Trebius's shade!'

The notary looked blank. The name meant nothing. One might as well have asked a butcher the names of the animals he had slaughtered. I knew the men had seen it too, and I knew that in that moment he had lost whatever hold he had on them.

I heard them shift, and felt their anger like heat from a fire. The notary let out a short sigh, as though he had lost some minor wager in a dice-game. He sat up straight, and smoothed his clothing with his pale long-fingered hand.

'Then let us have done with it,' he said. 'Which of you will kill me, or will it be all of you, so that the guilt attaches to no single one?'

I exchanged a look with Marcellus. We had talked about this, he and I and all the officers who had marched on London, and had made our decision. But still the words came hard, now that the man was in front of me, and my sword was in my hand.

'We are sending you back to the emperor,' I said eventually. 'Let him judge you.'

The notary's eyes snapped to mine, and for the first time I saw fear there – and this I had not predicted. He seemed to still himself; but then, in a flash of sudden movement, his hand darted to the table, and from one of the dishes, beside a sliced half-eaten apple, he snatched an ivory-handled fruit-knife. One of the men let out a snort of derision: did the notary suppose the tiny blade was a match for our swords? But my eyes had been on his face: I realized what he intended.

I threw myself forward, overturning the slender-legged table, sending the silver dishes sliding over the inlaid floor. The notary was fast; but I was faster. I caught his bony wrist just as the knife was at his throat. He struggled – he was strong, for all his emaciated look – and as I fought I felt the sting of the blade as it sliced my hand. But I had a firm hold of him. I prised his arm away, forcing it downwards until at last I heard the knife clatter on the ground.

Our eyes locked. I could feel his breath on my face. In a silken voice more menacing than any knife-blade he said, 'You fool! You should have let me do it.'

I understood, and for a brief moment we regarded one another in dreadful silence. The emperor's notaries worked in the shadows, performing what was shameful to be seen or known. And now this man had been exposed in all his crimes, and the emperor with him. Constantius would make him pay; and the notary knew it best of all. 'Take him down to the cells,' I said.

During the night the city was retaken, though it would be truer to say that resistance gave way without contest, as the rotten fruit collapses at the first touch. Only the barbarian German guards put up a fight. The urban mob, who had been so brave against ageing unarmed citizens, vanished from the streets.

Next day, we brought the notary from the cells and put him on a ship to Gaul.

Before he stepped on board he turned to me, fixing my eye. Even now, as a manacled prisoner, there was something terrifying about him, a reaching into one's soul. I forced myself not to look away.

Seeing this, and knowing his power, his gaunt face moved in a brief, cold smile. In a quiet voice he said, 'You had better hope we never meet again.'

I said, 'The emperor will see to that.'

For an instant he paused. My words had sounded brave and hollow, like a child's. I could tell it amused him; but I did not care. He had dwelt too long with the dark things. I did not want such knowledge as he possessed.

I thought he was going to speak again; but with a final chilling look he turned away, and the guard led him up the gangboard, and took him below.

The squat, iron-studded door of the bishop's residence stood open. Within, strewn about the courtyard, lay signs of destruction and hurried flight – a shattered wine-jar, its contents splashed across the old flagstones like blood; a single doeskin slipper with a silver clasp; the crumpled homespun of a monk's habit.

We walked on, through the deserted entry, into the bishop's grandiose audience-chamber.

The vast embroidered tapestry still filled the far wall. The heavy stag-footed gilded divan, where once I had sat, was still in its place before his marble-topped desk, and from the alcoves the heavy statues still stared impassively. But everything that was portable was gone – the gilded cups, the jewel-studded caskets, the filigree silverwork.

We stepped cautiously ahead. On one side of the divan a half-filled wooden chest stood. A goblet protruded from the straw packing, embossed with grapes and vine-leaves. I took it up and turned it in the grey winter light, and recalled the last time I had seen it, clutched in the bishop's hand.

Marcellus, who had not been here before, regarded the opulence and said dryly, 'I thought Christians chose to live in poverty.'

'Not this one,' I replied. I let the cup fall back onto its straw bed.

'It looks,' he said, 'as though the fat pigeon has flown.'

I frowned about the room. Even with his life in danger, the bishop had not been able to leave without his riches. The city gates had all been closed: he must have taken one of the small river-boats during the night, under cover of darkness.

At the great desk – sculpted white marble streaked

with cherry-red – I frowned and paused, then glanced up at Marcellus.

'What is it?' he said.

'Do you smell it?' The scent was fading; but still, in that great cold ornate chamber, the fragrance of sweet perfume hung in the air.

Marcellus sniffed and twisted up his face. 'Did he keep women here too?'

'No, not women. It's him. He's still here.'

We found him in his private chapel – a small room with a domed, painted ceiling and a carved altar like a sarcophagus. He was on his knees, bent forward, with his small thick fingers clutching the stone altar-top. A single silver lamp burned there, its flickering light glinting on the emerald and jasper and amethyst of his rings.

The door had been ajar; he had not noticed us. But then, as I stepped forward into the dim chamber, my boot sounded on the polished stone and he swung round.

'Get out!' he shouted. 'This is a holy place! Have you not taken enough?'

But then, seeing our military clothing, his eyes narrowed and he drew in his breath, and clutching his mantle around him he climbed to his feet.

'What do you want?' he said, and there was a wavering in his voice. 'Are you here to arrest me?' And when I did not answer he went on, 'I am the victim here, do you not see? I have been used, put upon by evil men, and now, in my hour of need, they have abandoned me . . . My friends' – he spat the word out, his round pink face suddenly twisting in bitter fury – 'my friends have deceived and robbed me. I am a good man – how not? I am a man of God – and I have been moved only by love. Damnation on all of them! They have deserted me.'

He turned back to the altar and began intoning a prayer, his voice sounding in hurried high-pitched gasps, like a keening woman. But in the midst of it he suddenly broke off and rounded on us.

'You cannot arrest me!' he cried, throwing up his glittering fingers. 'I am protected by the emperor. I am a bishop. Do you hear me? A bishop, and you have no authority.' And he went on to recount in tiny detail the complex legal exemptions to which his position entitled him, which the Christian emperors had enacted to privilege the Church and set it above the law, repeating them like some sort of charm against me. When at length he had finished he returned to the litany of the wrongs he had suffered – how his house had been looted; how those to whom he had devoted his life had turned against him; how he had lost everything and was destitute. And as he spoke he kept stretching his arms in supplication to the holy images on the walls, as if they would take pity on him.

Eventually, after some little while of this spectacle, Marcellus cut him off, raising his voice and saying, 'Not once, in all this, have you spoken of anyone but yourself. Where is your shame for all the men you have falsely accused, or for Heliodora, whom your monks dragged off and killed?'

'I am innocent, and what can you prove?' he retorted, eyeing us with a shrewd, calculating look. 'Leave me alone to pray. Do you not see how I suffer?'

Marcellus touched my arm and beckoned me back into the corridor.

'Has he lost his wits?' he whispered, when I had followed him out, 'or what is all this about?'

I shrugged and shook my head, and in the silence, from the little chapel behind us, the bishop resumed his mumbling chant.

'I don't know,' I said. I was feeling the same deep-seated nausea of my last encounter with him. 'He was lucid enough when he was telling us the rights granted to him by the emperor.'

I said it seemed to me his vanity and self-conceit had fully mastered him; and that, in itself, was an insanity of sorts. Perhaps, after all, the true implications of his crimes, which up to now had not touched him, were too much for his mind to bear, and he had retreated to his fantasies, so that he inhabited a twilight world with himself at the centre, and all else shadows and dreams.

Marcellus listened to my words with a stony frown, and as he listened he stared at the half-open door to the chapel, with the pale flickering lamplight showing through the opening, and the bishop's hurried breathless voice within.

'Then what shall we do with him?' he asked. 'Shall we arrest him?'

I folded my arms across my chest, and let out my breath, and looked away down the narrow unlit passage-way. From somewhere far within, a distant voice was singing, a rough drunken male voice, tunelessly rising and falling. It must have been a stray looter, left in the wine-store, drinking himself to oblivion.

Indeed, I thought, they had turned on their bishop in the end, the city poor and the disaffected feral youths who were his chief victims. They had descended upon him angry and afraid, and had wrought the only revenge they knew, returning a little of the chaos and destruction he had brought down upon their heads. It seemed unjust that they should suffer and he should not.

I found, as these thoughts passed through my mind, that my hand had moved to the dagger on my belt. As my palm touched the cold pommel, I felt my rage like a sudden fire within me. It would be the easiest thing of all to return to the chapel now and despatch the preening fool, and leave him as a sacrifice on his own altar. Easy for me: but, I reflected, easy for him too – a brief moment of surprise and terror, and all would be over; unless, as he claimed, there was some other underworld place where men such as he lived on, recollecting their misdeeds and paying for them. But I could not suppose it. Better, far better, to let him live, and face the consequences of what he had done.

Slowly I released my hand from my dagger and turned to Marcellus.

'Leave him,' I said. 'People will say we lock him up because we fear him, that we do to him what he has done to Heliodora. Let them hear him and see for themselves that he counts for nothing. He cannot continue; he must know that. His followers have deserted him. He has had his chance to rule, and he has brought nothing but ruin to the city. Everyone has seen it; the evidence is all around us. No one will follow him now.'

And so at last we left him, mumbling his prayers alone

in his gilded chapel beside his empty, unfinished cathedral, built from the looted ruins of what had stood before. We walked out through the open door, across the ravaged square, and away down the hill towards the river.

On the slope, beside an old smashed shrine, we paused and gazed out at the water, and the distant fields to the south and west, where finally the winter sun had broken through the clouds, casting diffused shafts of fading evening light.

I found I was thinking of Aquinus. My heart had been full of anger and revenge. But now I felt an emptiness, a stillness, a calm. He had been right, and I understood now his reluctance to meet violence with violence, when all about him there had been so much injustice. Nothing would be the same. The city remained – the fine buildings and open precincts, the gardens and baths and neglected temples. But its soul was retreating, ebbing away, dispersing like smoke into air.

Men had made the city because they believed in it, and in themselves, and what together they could achieve. They had filled it with their gods, and adorned it with objects of beauty. And now those men were gone, and the beautiful objects were looted and broken; and from the temples the gods had retreated back to the remote places of the countryside from whence they came – the secret streams, and dark forests, and mountaintops, and sacred groves.

All this Aquinus had seen, and resisted. What men had built, men had also undone, through their own folly, and ease, and complacency.

And, somewhere beyond the horizon of my vision, unseen enemies, who cared nothing for such precious things, were observing our self-inflicted weakness, and smiling as they waited, biding their time, and sharpening their swords against us.

AUTHOR'S NOTE

THE EVENTS OF THE STORY take place in the mid-fourth century AD (about AD 350), in the generation prior to the fall of the western Roman Empire. It was a time when people had grown used to a unified world of material plenty, where one could travel from York to Jerusalem speaking a common language, spending the same money, and dwelling in the same culture. People found it inconceivable that such a complex and powerful world could come to an end; they were simply unable to foresee the complete collapse that was the Dark Ages. My novel explores some of the reasons for that collapse.

The modern reader is likely to be familiar with the Roman world of Julius Caesar, but less familiar with late antiquity. For that reader, and for those who enjoy the details and feel like delving further, I provide a few pointers.

Since the reign of the emperor Constantine I (died

387

AD 337), the empire had been officially Christian. The
Church, growing in confidence, and bolstered by the
power of the state, was attempting to bring about by
force what it had been unable to achieve by persuasion.
This was a period of growing religious absolutism and
intolerance, alien to the accommodating polytheism of
the classical world.

The later Church liked to present the advance of
Christianity as inexorable; but in the mid-fourth century
its victory was not assured, and there is evidence during
this time of resistance and a general pagan revival, both
in Britain and elsewhere.

It is worth mentioning the terms 'Caesar' and 'Augustus'. Originally Caesar referred to Julius Caesar, and
Augustus was the honorific name assumed by Caesar's
nephew and adopted son Octavian when he became the
first emperor. By the late empire these terms had become
titles of office. An Augustus was an emperor; a Caesar
was an emperor's deputy and designated successor –
who was often, but not always, a family relation. Also,
at various times, it was thought expedient to divide the
vast empire between two or more emperors, each of
whom would rule a part (typically the West and the East).
So, during the late empire, there were often two or more
emperors, each ruling a different region.

For the purposes of the story I have simplified the more
complicated aspects of late Roman provincial administration. Provinces during this period were grouped together
into larger units called dioceses (a term later taken up
by the Church). Each diocese was administered by an
official known in Latin as a *vicarius*. These details, though

interesting, do not add to the drama of the tale I have told, and so I have left them out.

As far as place names are concerned, I have chosen the modern name where this is likely to be familiar to the reader. So, for example, I have preferred Britain to Britannia; London to Londinium; York to Eboracum; Autun to Augustodunum.